THE DEVIL'S MODE

ALSO BY ANTHONY BURGESS

NOVELS

The Long Day Wanes:
  Time for a Tiger
  The Enemy in the Blanket
  Beds in the East
The Right to an Answer
The Doctor Is Sick
The Worm and the Ring
Devil of a State
One Hand Clapping
A Clockwork Orange
The Wanting Seed
Honey for the Bears
Inside Mr Enderby
Nothing like the Sun: A Story of
  Shakespeare's Love-Life
The Eve of Saint Venus
A Vision of Battlements
Tremor of Intent
Enderby Outside
MF
Napoleon Symphony
The Clockwork Testament; or
  Enderby's End
Beard's Roman Women
Abba Abba
Man of Nazareth
1985
Earthly Powers
The End of the World News
Enderby's Dark Lady
The Kingdom of the Wicked
The Pianoplayers
Any Old Iron

NON FICTION

English Literature: A Survey for
  Students
They Wrote in English
Language Made Plain
Here Comes Everybody: An
  Introduction to James Joyce for the
  Ordinary Reader

The Novel Now: A Student's Guide
  to Contemporary Fiction
Urgent Copy: Literary Studies
Shakespeare
Joysprick: An Introduction to the
  Language of James Joyce
New York
Hemingway and His World
On Going to Bed
This Man and Music
Ninety-Nine Novels
Flame Into Being: the Life and Work
  of D. H. Lawrence
But Do Blondes Prefer Gentlemen

FOR CHILDREN

A Long Trip to Teatime
The Land Where the Ice Cream
  Grows

VERSE

Moses

TRANSLATIONS

The New Aristocrats
The Olive Trees of Justice
The Man Who Robbed Poor Boxes
Cyrano de Bergerac
Oedipus the King
Carmen

DRAMATIC WORKS

Oberon Old and New
Blooms of Dublin

EDITOR

A Shorter Finnegans Wake

ANTHONY BURGESS

BURGESS

THE DEVIL'S MODE

HUTCHINSON

London Sydney Auckland Johannesburg

© Anthony Burgess 1989

All rights reserved

This edition first published 1989 by
Hutchinson

Century Hutchinson Ltd, 20 Vauxhall Bridge Road,
London SW1V 2SA.

Century Hutchinson Australia (Pty) Ltd
20 Alfred Street, Milsons Point, Sydney NSW 2061, Australia

Century Hutchinson New Zealand Limited
PO Box 40–086, Glenfield, Auckland 10, New Zealand

Century Hutchinson South Africa (Pty) Ltd
PO Box 337, Bergvlei, 2012 South Africa

Set in Linotron Palatino by Input Typesetting Ltd, London
Printed and bound in Great Britain by
Butler & Tanner Ltd, Frome, Somerset

British Library Cataloguing in Publication Data

Burgess, Anthony 1917–
The devil's mode and other stories
I. Title
823'.914 (F)

ISBN 0–09–174194–7

To Leslie

CONTENTS

·— A MEETING IN VALLADOLID —·

The British delegation landed at Santander in filthy weather. They were to proceed thence to Valladolid on horseback and in hired coaches. They were met on the quay by a handful of emissaries from the Spanish court and an interpreter named Don Manuel de Pulgar Garganta. He was less interested in Milord This and the Earl of That than in a group of stage players very sorry for themselves as they uneasily watched their property cart brought to shore in a swilling boat rowed by swarthy roarers. They had to hire horses from a stable somewhere in the town, and they would send Robert Armin, a clown who was also the son of an ostler, to inspect, with Spanish assistance, what would undoubtedly be spavined nags. 'Rocinantes,' Don Manuel grinned. 'The better horses will already have been spoken for to convey Milord Thisness and the Earl of Otherness. But I will go with Master Armin, whom I well remember seeing at the Globe playhouse, hearing too, he sang very prettily, to ensure that he is not cheated excessively.'

'By God, you speak our British language, as we must now call it since the new naming of our kingdom, with a fine accent and fluminous smoothness,' Dick Burbage said. 'We shall be glad of it, I can tell you. There is not one of us here who speaks more than three words of your Castilian, those words being *si* and *no* and *mañana*. The times have been altogether against speaking the tongue of the enemy which we must no longer call you. Wait, *paz* is another word and a new one. It is to be a slow negotiation of *paz* at Valladolid, we are told. The King's Men are here to

5

spread a sort of honey on the dull bread of it. The daily grind of the flour of perpetual *paz*. Forgive me, señor—'

'Don Manuel, at your service.'

'As you say. Burbage, at yours. If I talk too much it is because these last weeks my mouth has been altogether occupied with retching and puking. There, see, by that bollard is one still puking. He has the weakest of all our stomachs.'

'That would be your Master Shakespeare.'

'You know us all, before God. A Spaniard in London, I say it without offence, could have been at no other work than spying. But it is all over now, or will be by the time we have played through our repertory.'

'I pretend not otherwise. It was a help to have an English mother loyal to Rome and hence necessarily disloyal to her country. Great matters of state are hard on the humble, as she so often said. Alas, she died of a fever in Avila and my poor father was not long after her. Your Master Shakespeare seems in some distress. Can I offer him and you a posset of sour goat's milk and the stiff wine of Jerez? It does wonders for sick stomachs.'

'Not him. But I will take your sherrisack without goatish accretions. You mean at that inn there?'

'The same. We will go and settle you till the matter of the horses is settled. Your noble lords and ours are getting on well enough, I seem to hear, in the Tuscan tongue.'

Burbage and Pope and Dicky Robinson and Will Shakespeare sat together over what they called sack while the rest of the troupe soaked in the sun (so many grey days at sea) at tables set under sycamores and ate. They ate fried *huevos* and *jamón* to which hog bristles adhered. Will shuddered. 'These young stomachs,' he said. 'I am too old for tossing in the Bay of Biscay. I am too old for anything. I have a mind to strip off the king's livery and tell him what to do with it. A man in his forties should mind his body and beach his soul in a calm harbour.'

'You are only just gone forty. It is no age.'

'All of forty-one. This sack bites. It knives. I would I knew the Spanish for barley water.'

'There speaks the man who did more for the farming of sack than the fierce sun of Jerez itself. Your Falstaff is a sham.'

'I never denied it.'

It was a wearisome clop over the Cantabrian Mountains, with a night in the midst of a round dance of fleas in a foul inn in Reinoso. Then on to Corrion where some had to sleep uncovered on a floor of scampering rats. Thence to Palencia and finally to Valladolid, a fine city on the Douro, where the British, whom the Spanish called *ingleses* and did not seem pleased to see, were greeted by a Latin sermon from a scowling bishop at the town cross. 'What did he say?' Burbage asked Will.

'He said, I think, that we smell of heresy and we need not think that the signing of a hypocritical peace denotes Hispanic tolerance for Calvinist perversions of the true faith. Words to that, or similar papist effect.'

'He should be told that we are as much against Calvin as his unholiness in the infernal city. Calvin equals puritan equals shutter of playhouses.'

'Wait. He said something then about filthy Harry Tudor and his ten wives and an *ecclesia diabolica* that was a *donum morganaticum*. A good phrase. A diabolic church as a morganatic gift. I must remember that. This is a filthy place and the sun shows it all up. Ragged urchins and beggars exposing their sores like medals. My horse adds, from the smell, a couple of smoking globes to the paving of uncleared dung. My stomach promises to heave.'

'It is always heaving. See, now he sourly blesseth the promise of a fair peace with dirty but doubtless holy water. It is done.'

'It begins, and my stomach will not stand it.'

The noble delegates were led to a sort of palace of peeling stucco, on whose walls slogans had been chalked or daubed to welcome the heretical British. VIVA LA PAZ – UNOS DÍAS and A BAJO LOS INGLESES. Don Manuel rode up to the King's Men smiling. 'I do not think you will have expected blaring trumpets of welcome,' he said. 'Our poet Góngora has been at his work already. He writes as if it is already all over.' He held a paper in his finely gloved hand. 'As you do not know our Castilian I will translate:

> We stage a pageant, rank stupidity,
> Also fiestas loud with lies
> For the legates and their spies

Who come in Lutheran cupidity.
Luther's rich but we are poor,
The peace I piss on – let that pass.
Here is comic matter for
The Don and Sancho and his ass.

Something like that. Forgive the doggerel English.'

'Who,' Will asked, 'are this Don and Sancho?'

'You do not know them yet? But I met a man in London named Shelton already at work on an English rendering. It is a long task. It is a very long novel.'

'What,' Burbage asked, 'is a novel?'

'Not the pretty little stories of a handful of pages that ladies in England beguile their too ample leisure withal. This is massivity and its building is not yet done. Its author is around somewhere. He has his house here. As for the Don and Sancho and his ass, you will see them in the bullring tomorrow.'

'You have bull-baiting here too?' Will said queasily.

'No baiting. An honest fight between bull and man. The bull does not always die. We have contrived a composite ritual of the Christian and Mithraic sacrifices. Sometimes the man is gored and disembowelled. He offers himself to God. Sometimes it is the bull. But the horses always suffer. No matter, they are always past their best, old nags, mere rocinantes.'

'You are always talking of rocinantes, whatever they be.'

'The Don shall ride one tomorrow. You will see all.'

'I like not horses to be mistreated,' Will said with passion. 'A horse is as it were an extension of a man, ergo part of him. We are all centaurs. I shall not be there.'

'You must, Will,' Burbage said. 'The Lord Chamberlain's deputy will count our numbers. We are Grooms of the Chamber and have our responsibilities.'

'I did not come to Spain to be witness to the torture of horses.'

'You can witness more terrible tortures,' Don Manuel said. 'The Inquisitions do things to heretics that make the disembowelling of horses seem a mere tickling of flies.'

'I need barley water for my stomach,' Will groaned.

'Come,' Don Manuel smiled sympathetically, 'the inn prepared for you has been swept if not scrubbed, and the bed linen is virtually flealess. Rest from your journey. I will arrange for a potion of red wine and crushed Valencia oranges. That works wonders for a sick stomach.'

While Will lay on the coverlet of the bed he was to share with Dick Burbage and the younger members of the King's Men sought out pretty Spanish boys or Moorish harlots, the servant of the Earl of Rutland came to announce the evening's entertainment. It was to be held in the Great Hall of the University and was to consist of a play by some nobody named Lope de Vega and followed by a comedy by Master Shakespaw there. They had best now make up their minds what and spend some little time cutting it lest it be too long.

'This is madness,' Burbage said. 'One portion of the audience knows no Spanish and the rest no English. It would have been best to prepare a masque of Anglo-Hispanic amity or some such thing. Ben had he been here could have knocked up some such thing. It is some such thing that was needful. What then do we do?'

'We do the Bottom bits from *A Midwinter Fright's Scream*. And if Ben Jonson had been here he would have started contriving a masque that would be ready in time for the resumption of war. Talk not of Ben to me. A man that is a versifying bricklayer and thinks Parnassus to be the top of his ladder.'

'That is witty. Who said that?'

'It has not been said yet. But it shall not be said to his rocky face. Mountain-bellied though he is, he is too quick with his little dagger. It is the only thing he is quick withal.'

'Look you, if we do the Bottom bits the Spaniards will say that we are mere rustic mountebanks. We need fair costumes, if the sea air and the bath they took in that bumboat have not ruined them. We need wit and eloquence. We need, in fine, *What You Will* or *As You Like It*. Though those titles are an affront, implying as they do that Will wills it not and the auditors may take it or leave it.'

'*Take It Or Leave It* is an apt title for all that I do these days. I do not think these Spaniards will understand any of our comedy. Let us give them the bloodier bits of *Titus Andronicus*. I am near to vomiting in this royal city. Let even the strongest Spanish stomach turn this night. Rape and mutilation and baking human flesh in a pie. At least they will not yawn.'

In the cool of the early evening, Don Manuel took on a walking tour of the city such members of the King's Men as were not wenching or boying or clearing their stomachs of the strong local wine. The rivers Pisuerga and Esgueva met here. The richness of the province flowed in by boat – grain and wine and oil and honey and beeswax. See the cathedral, shining new, no more than twenty years old, for all of Valladolid was destroyed by fire in 1561 and King Philip, who was born here, had all rebuilt. But ninety-nine years agone did Christopher Columbus die there. In that house, see, dwells Master Miguel de Cervantes Saavedra, father of the Don and Sancho and eke Sancho's ass. That is he now, look, leaving, looking neither forward nor backward nor to right nor to left, a man friendless and battered by the world who remakes the world in his skull. He is an old man, see, all of fifty-seven years, grey. There is a play of his to be performed some time during the peace celebrations, but he cares not. He has slaved in the theatre to no reward. I would not suggest that you seek to meet him. He knows nothing of your language and is laconic enough when he speaketh the Castilian. But sometimes he is voluble in the Moorish tongue he learned as a slave and a hostage.

'The Moorish tongue,' Will said. 'I was no slave or hostage but I learned somewhat of it. That was when I accompanied my lord of Southampton on the mission to Rabat, a failed mission to buy Arab horses for my lord Essex's campaign in Ireland. A failed campaign, I may add. I think now my stomach is quietened enough to take some supper.'

'Good,' Don Manuel said.

The King's Men kept away from the play by Lope de Vega Carpio, *La Boba para los Otros y Discreta para si*, or some such gibberish. They busied themselves in the chambers behind the Great Hall with shaking out costumes and searching for properties and having their faces painted by Dick Burbage. At the end of the performance of his play, presented by students of the University, the author himself came round to look on the King's Men, leering somewhat unpleasantly. 'Cap that,' he said, 'you barbarians.' He spoke acceptable English, having learned it when

10

secretary to the Duke of Alva and the Marquis of Malpica, both of whom believed in knowing the tongue of the enemy. He had also served in the Armada in 1588 and knew more than the tongue of the enemy: he knew their rapacity and bloodthirstiness, a race bloated with beef and pudding and ale and indifferent alike to the claims of the spirit and the intellect. Will chewed his nether lip doubtfully. These cultivated Spaniards were to see a girl ravished and her arms cut off and her tongue out, the rapists slain by the girl's father and baked in a pie to be eaten by their mother. There was also a Moor, Aaron, who was to be buried alive and die cursing. These Spanish knew all about Moors. It was too late to change now: the show must go on.

It was a truncated version of *Titus Andronicus* that both the British and their swarthy hosts saw. There was more blood (pig's, locally bought) then blank verse. Some of the Spaniards went through the motions of vomiting, a critical gesture, and those who had eaten largely and drunk deep went out to go through more than the motions. The British lounged comfortably and ate all the horrors up with relish, not excepting the pie. When, later, Will and Burbage lay together in their roomy bed, they both were aware that they had in some measure betrayed the aesthetic and intellectual pretensions of this new country called Britain, ruled by a king known as the wisest fool in Christendom. 'We must,' Will mused, 'cry off. We can no more. If we are not to weary with language uncomprehended, we must disgust with action all too comprehensible. It was an unwise notion of his majesty, God curse the Scotch sot and sodomite, to have us sent hither.'

'Have a care what you say, Will. Those black-cloaked accessory men who seem to have no function with the delegates may well prove to be King James's spies. Those rustlings outside the door are not, I think, the noise of rats at play. God bless King James Sixth and First,' he cried loudly before turning his back on Will to the end that he might sleep. He slept well but not silently, intermingling nonsense pentameters with raucous snores and dramatic gaspings. Will slept but little. Here he was wasting in Spain good time better to be spent in collecting debts in Stratford and negotiating for the purchase of arable land. His stomach growled and nipped. He had a brief nightmare about his daughter Judith giving birth unmarried to a monster fully-haired

11

and hump-backed. He had a briefer sweeter dream about swimming under the Clopton Bridge that spanned the Avon. Sweet air and wholesome country victuals. But the damned town was crawling with puritans who hated Master Shagspaw or Shogspore, any name but the right one. He awoke to strong Spanish sunlight and learned that today was the day of the bullfight.

The arena that afternoon was crammed with the common sort of Valladolid, who hooted at the British delegation in its fine clothes and cloaks. Will sat in the shade with his nut-chewing fellows of the King's Men, all got up for the occasion in their royal livery. The entertainment began with a tune on a high-pitched trumpet, and then there trotted into the ring a long lean elderly man with pasteboard armour, a helmet broken but mended with string, a broken lance dirtily bandaged together again, riding a deplorable nag whose bones showed through its mangy skin. He was followed by a little fat man astride a donkey, ever and anon raising to his shaggily bearded lips a dripping wineskin. These two acknowledged with waves the plaudits of the crowd, which clearly loved them. After them, at a fair distance, there appeared limping from the entrance-well a couple of men dressed as monks carrying, a pole apiece, a stretched banner on which was inscribed in red PAX ET PAUPERTAS. The crowd yelled approval and booed the British anew. Will said to Don Manuel:

'The thin mock knight and his fat squire – they come from a book?'

'Very much so. But they are too big for a book. They have escaped from it as from a prison.'

Will growled to himself. Hamlet and Falstaff were jailed in their respective plays. They would never emerge into a sunny arena to be cheered by a loving crowd. But why should he care? Land was the thing, and sacks of malt stored against the next bad harvest. Plays were but plays. Still, he growled and ground bad teeth. When the ill-made knight and his fat squire retired to a final burst of rapture, the real business of the afternoon began. Bullfighters came in procession with swords and had flowers thrown at them by ladies in black mantillas. Then a bull came out snorting. It was mercilessly teased by fat-rumped men with fancy spears. Then it gored a lean horse whose guts came tumbling out. The crowd roared as at high comedy. 'I am getting out of here,' Will growled to Burbage. 'I have seen more than enough. I find no mirth in spilled entrails.' He was derided by some of his own fellows as he climbed the ramp that led to the way out. At a stall in the plaza he bought some grapes with British silver and was permitted to wash them in a tub of wine in which grape-stalks floated. He chewed surlily. These were the people who considered *Titus Andronicus* an unacceptable bloodbath. Let Burbage and the rest do what they would tonight after the special supper to be graced by dukes and princes. He, Will, would not make himself a motley to pleasure the killers of horses. He loved horses. He had wept bitterly when old Brown Harry, his father's placid steed out of Suffolk with its mire-clotted leg feathers, had been sent to the knacker's yard for rendering into glue.

That night, while an unintelligible redaction of *Love's Labour's Lost* was convincing a high-born Spanish audience that British playmakers could either bore or shock but not delight or enlighten, a slain bull was being roasted in front of the cathedral and its flesh distributed to the clamorous poor. Sweaty plebeians scrambled for sinew and gristle and tore from other hands charred chunks of sirloin. How he hated the plebs, Will thought, as he took in with grudging pleasure the vitality of the scene – animated faces and spitting fire and the calm façade of the great cathedral. Don Manuel came up to him with a man whose face was vaguely familiar. The man sneered at Will and spoke unintelligible words. But the word *maida* was clear enough, and that was the Arabic word for stomach. This was confirmed when the man spoke what was evidently Castilian, sneering *Estómago*. Don Manuel said, regretfully:

'He saith that you have stomach enough for blood and guts in the playhouse, but you turn away from the reality. As this afternoon. He saw you leave. This, pardon the delay in introduction, is Miguel de Cervantes Saavedra. William Shakespeare.'

'Chequespirr?' The name meant nothing.

'I work,' Will said, 'in the *masrah* in Londres. I indeed have no *shahiya* for *dam*. I am a *mualif* who must *yuti* the people what they wish. *Limatza?* Because it is my *mihna*.'

Cervantes seemed hardly convinced. He was a hard-faced man, his beard grey and his hair fast receding from formidable temples.

The skin was tanned and lined. He stooped as though pulling a galley-oar and seemed ever ready to wince at the prospect of the swish of a whip on his shoulders. Will in his presence felt soft-palmed, spoiled, unsuffering. 'May I offer you somewhat to *yashrab?*' he said. To drink? Cervantes shruggd. Drink with a man who had no medium for talk? He said something else. Don Manuel said they were both invited to his house. There was wine there, better than the bellyaching ink or piss they sold in the bodegas. Cervantes would briefly show the hospitality due to a fellow-writer from a country no more, they were told, to be regarded as Spain's enemy and hence mankind's, but the visit must be brief. He, Cervantes, had a headache and must soon try to sleep it off. They walked away, Cervantes limping, from the dying fire and the depleted carcase. Man, Will was thinking as he walked, differed from the beasts of the field in his capacity for speech, but what did this avail him when he stepped out of his own narrow territory? The animals understood each other well enough. Babel was no myth.

> My lord, man differs from the brutish beast
> In one particular – the most, the least?
> Who can well say? He hath the gift of speech.
> Which is to boast but little. Has not each
> Tribe its own dialect, misunderstood
> Of other tribes? I ask: where is the good
> Of speech? Exiled – his careless kingly breath
> Pronounced it. But I gloss the word as –

Poor unpoetic Dick Burbage adding his own limping lines to Bolingbroke's speech in *Richard II*. Still, truth in it.

The house of Cervantes was small and pervaded by the smells of its kitchen – garlic, olive oil, spices that Will well remembered from Moorish *souks*. In the tiny living-room there were Moorish saddle-stools, an ink-stained round table, some eighty or so books. One of these books lay on the worn Moorish carpet at the feet of Cervantes, who had, with dry selfishness improper in a host, taken the one chair in the room. Will and Don Manuel sat somewhat lowly on the saddle-seats. Cervantes kicked the book towards Will, who humbly picked it up. *Guzmán de Alfarache* by a certain Alemán. A German would he be, with a name like that? It was one of these novels. Cervantes spoke. Don Manuel translated:

'That book has gone into twenty editions in the last year alone. It is about a rogue boy growing up in a rogue world. *Picaresco*, if you know the word, which I doubt. It answers some deep need in the Spanish soul, the need to be flayed and cauterised by a disgruntled God the Father who will not lift a divine finger to help what we are told is his dearest creation but rather puts stumbling blocks in his way. And at the end of a wretched life there is no rest, no peace, only eternal torment. That is the kind of story our nation loves. And that they expected from me when I left the wearying and rewardless world of the theatre for that of the leisurely narrative. A Don Quixote battered and bruised and broken in God's jape of blood and smashed teeth. But instead I give them comedy.' Will said:

'*Haya* is *sayyi* for all.' Cervantes exploded and Don Manuel unexplosively rendered the spitting consonants and wailing vowels as:

'Oh, do not play with ill-pronounced and ill-learnt Arabic in my presence. I have known Arabic as the speech of torture and oppression. Speak your own godless northern tongue, which at least I presume you have a minimal mastery over. I say this of you English – that you have not suffered. You do not know what torment is. You will never create a literature out of your devilish complacency. You need hell, which you have abandoned, and you need the climate of hell – harsh winds, fire, drought.'

'We have done our best,' Will meekly said. 'But I would ask, humbly, what can you know of our literature? You do not speak our tongue and our books and plays are not yet rendered into the Castilian. Perhaps with the coming of peace there will be a greater reciprocation of knowledge—'

'Peace, peace, how can there be peace?' Cervantes howled *paz* as if it were the name of some disease. 'You broke away from the true faith and opted out of the struggle with the heathen Musulman. That is the only war, the throwing of the Islamic heathen out of the holy places, the breaking of his power in the middle sea. He came here to defile our Latin. You he never invaded. You play with blood and cannibalism in your silly stage plays—'

'Only that once. I assure you, *Titus Andronicus* is far from typical. There is the problem of the language barrier—'

'The barrier is in the soul, not in the tongue and teeth. You are a decayed limb cut off from the tree of the living Christ.'

'Do not you talk to me of the soul,' Will said loudly. 'On your admission, you Spaniards see God as a foul father and man as an unredeemable beast. And the soul is committed to torturing priests who seek a confession of faith as the flames leap round the howling victim. Do not you speak to me of the soul.'

'Alemán's image of the world is not mine. A good God existeth somewhere, away from the fat bishops and the lean executioners. And how do we seek that good God? Not through the tragedy of spoiled lives but through the comedy of a mock-odyssey. It is a discovery that could be made only here, here, here.' The *aquí* was a left hand circling an imaginary map of Iberia, a right hand beating his own breast. 'It is through the ridiculous that the great spiritual truth must be confronted – that a good God exists. Your silly play of last night was ridiculous in another sense. You English are incapable of accepting God at all. You do not suffer and you cannot make comedy out of what does not exist in your green and temperate land—'

'Which you have never seen.'

'I see it in you, you of the mild eye and the unweathered skin. Bitterness is not in your cup.'

'We will hear this again,' Will said, with unabated boldness. 'We will go on hearing that we have not suffered like the whipped Muscovites and the cowed Bohemians and the swooning Spaniards. And that in consequence our art is as nothing. We shall be sick of it and we are sick of it now.'

'You will never produce a *Don Quixote.*'

'And why should I or we?' Will said hotly. 'I have produced other things and I will still.' But: Will I? he thought. Do I wish to? 'I have made good comedy and eke tragedy, which is the highest reach of the skill of the dramaturge.'

'It is not and will never be. God is a comedian. God does not suffer the tragic consequences of a flawed essence. Tragedy is all too human. Comedy is divine. My head is killing me.' His eyes seemed to beat in the light of the candle near his chair. He had offered no wine. If this was Spanish hospitality, railing and scorn, Will wanted no more of it. 'I must to bed.'

'You talk of comedy most uncomically,' Will said, and then: 'You have produced neither a Hamlet nor a Falstaff.' But the names meant nothing to the tortured man, former slave of the galleys, long awaiting ransom from his kingdom and, when it came at last, forced to the paying of it back at usurious interest. Don Manuel said:

'I have seen your plays. I have read his book. You will forgive me if I say that I know where the superiority lies. You lack his wholeness. He has seen more of life. He has the power to render both the flesh and the spirit at one and the same time. The flesh and the spirit walked today in the arena and the people recognised, hailed, loved. You will forgive me if I seem to disparage what you have done.'

'I have done no more than earn my bread. Art is nothing but a livelihood. He can be the greater for all I care. I make no pretension.'

'Ah, yes, you do.' Will looked bitterly at Don Manuel and then fearfully at Cervantes, who howled with pain. Cervantes said:

'Go, go. You should not have come.'

'I was invited. But I will go.'

'I must heave this cloven head to my dark bedroom. Finish your wine and go.'

'There was no wine to finish.'

'Communion under no kind,' Cervantes mumbled and then staggered from the room. Will and Don Manuel looked at each other. Will shrugged. Both men went out into a dark street with no moon, though the constellations flared. They walked towards Will's inn. Will said:

'Is it possible to read the book here?'

'If you will learn enough Spanish.'

'Much depends on how long this forging of perpetual peace will take.'

'I can translate some for you to give of its quality.'

'Can it be made into a play?'

'It cannot. Its length is its virtue. You cannot encompass so long a journey in your two hours' traffic.'

Will howled quietly. 'It is of the nature of a play to be short. Is there poetry in it?'

'He tells his tale plainly. He has not your gift of sharp and vivid compression. But he needs it not.'

Will invisibly brightened. 'He is no poet, then.'

'Not as you are.'

'That, then, is something. But poetry does not stalk an arena and draw loving cheers from the groundlings.'

'That irks you, I see. That they spring from the book and live in unrarefied air.'

'Somewhat.'

Will was asleep when Burbage came in. He did not wake Will to tell him that *The Comedy of Errors*, much shortened, had done well enough, confirming that the playwrights of England were dealers in small beer and easy laughs. But it was at dawn that Will did the waking. 'Eh? What? Eh? What in God's name o'clock is it?'

'Get up. There is much to do. All must be gathered together. I will go now and kick them out of their beds, together with what whores and ephebes they have garnered.'

Jack Hemmings, Gus Phillips, Tom Pope (his little holiness), George Bryan, Harry Condell, Will Sly, Dick Cowly, Jack Lowine, Sam Cross, Alex Cooke, Sam Gilburne, Robert Armin, Will Ostler (unhandy with horses) Jack Underwood, Nick Tooley, Will Ecclestone, Joseph Taylor, Rob Benfield, Rob Gough, Dicky Robinson, Jack Shank and Jack Rice sat bleared and in pain from the sharp Spanish light, displeased also at the enforced waking betimes, over possets and toasts to dip in them while they listened in disbelief to their poet. Dick Burbage had already heard it all: he had no gestures to make but shrugs and uprolled eyes. Will said:

'Tomorrow or the next day we play *Hamlet*. But we play it somewhat differently from heretofore. For in it we place Sir John Falstaff. Wonder not nor start so. It is all too easy of disposal. For *Hamlet* is what it already is up to the point of the prince's being sent to England, there to be murdered on the king's orders. In England, having read and destroyed the commission, he hears that the Danish force is to invade England for non-payment of tribute. At last he finds the name of action, and this holds off all thought of self-slaughter, as does the companionship of Falstaff and his crew. Falstaff may call Hamlet sweet Ham for Hal, it is but a letter's difference. The war is called off on the news of the death of King Claudius. Hamlet proceeds to Elsinore to succeed him. Falstaff and his crew follow but are, of course, cast off at the end. But Claudius is still alive and Laertes is to kill Hamlet in a fencing bout not in open assassination since the prince is loved of the distracted multitude. All ends as before except that Hamlet lives and Fortinbras upholds his claim to the throne. You will see that there is little to alter, though somewhat to add. You shall have a play of some seven hours' running time, and if they do not like it they may send us home. Preferably overland. I have a mind to see Roussillon.' There was the noise of loud protest, quietened by Burbage's bellow. Burbage said:

'There is much in what he proposeth. They cannot then accuse us of a lack of weightiness. And next day Hamlet and Falstaff shall ride through the bullring together. Nick Tooley here has understudied Hamlet. It is time he played it. He is also long and thin, so the line about his being fat and scant of breath, which once did well for me though not, thanked be God, now, may be cut. Alex Cooke that plays Queen Gertrude shall play also Mistress Quickly. Both are, in their different ways, bad women. We have deaths enow, including that of Hotspur, who is for the invading king. But Hamlet surviveth, so it is no tragedy.'

'It is then *The Comedy of Hamlet Prince of Denmark?*' Jack Underwood asked.

'Is it Engmark or Denland?' Jack Shank wittily enquired.

'Hotspur,' Burbage said, 'sounds more Danish than Claudius does. Enough of these impertinences. Will here is already inditing a running order of scenes. It may well be the best play we shall ever do.'

'The longest, no doubt,' Will Sly said.

The longest, certainly. 'Well,' said Will to Cervantes when the audience was tottering to its lodgings at four in the morning, 'do you now think us deficient in the comic?' Don Manuel translated. Cervantes, who seemed soothed by the presence of a small Moorish boy whom he clutched tightly to his left side, the boy drooping with fatigue, said:

'It was too long.'

'It shall to the barber with your beard.'

19

'*¿Como?*'

'It is by no manner of means as long as your accursed novel as you call it.'

'I do not call it accursed. The fat man and the thin man you stole from me.'

'Ah, no. They were already there in the London playhouse before ever I heard that you exist. What say you then now?'

'I understood not one word.'

'That is your tragedy.'

When the Hispano-British peace colloquies resumed the following afternoon, the morning having been consumed in needful sleep, one of the Spaniards, who had red hair and whose name was Guzman, asked of Sir Philip Spender in guttural Tuscan: 'Are there to be more of these interminable comedies?'

'It is proposed that the comedy of *Hamlet* be performed nightly so that its manifold and contradictory riches be the better understood.' Sir Philip was cheerful about it: he had slept very soundly throughout the performance. 'In which case it perhaps behoves us to be speedy with the drawing up of our terms of perpetual peace. I gain the impression that the people of Valladolid will be pleased to see our delegation depart. So it is to all our advantages that we hurry and make an end.'

'Amen,' Guzman said. 'I see no reason why the engrossing in two languages should not be completed by late tomorrow.'

'You mean true tomorrow or not so true *mañana*?'

'I mean the date that followeth the date of today. That may mean a midnight supper and, ah, no entertainment after.'

'These things always take long. We may set a healthful precedent of despatch. To work, my lords and gentlemen.'

'Amen.'

There was a mandatory *corrida* the afternoon before the departure of the British delegates. Will was not present, but a thin tall prince in black and a fat knight in buckram rode round the arena. They were taken to be a British tribute to a Spanish institution already well-founded and hence they drew cheers. A banner upheld by a Pistol and a Bardolph proclaimed VIVAN LAS MUCHACHAS Y EL VINO ESPAÑOLES. So all ended in amity. Will had already departed, being anxious to visit Roussillon on the way home. All's well that ends well.

20

He did not read *Don Quixote* until 1611, the year of the translation of the work by Shelton and also of the appearance of the
King James Bible. There are references to the lean knight and his
fat squire in the plays of Ben Jonson and Beaumont and Fletcher,
but none in the plays of Shakespeare. When he fell into his last
illness in 1616 he was still brooding about Cervantes's having
stolen a march on him in the domain of the creation of a universal
character. He died on the same day as Cervantes, but as the
Spanish calendar was ten days ahead of the British, it may be
said that even in dying Cervantes stole a march. Don Manuel de
Pulgar Garganta did not see Shakespeare again, but in 1613 he
was present at the destruction by fire of the Globe playhouse
during the first performance of *Henry VIII* (called at the time *All
Is True*), when the letting off of ceremonial ordnance started a
flame in the thatch. The relays of buckets of Thames water failed
to save the structure from dissolution. The great Globe itself, yea
all which it inherit shall dissolve. He spoke with Jack Hemmings
and Harry Condell in a tavern, where they were triumphant in
slaking their thirst, for they had rescued the greater part of their
poet's output from the fire. Only *Yet Think It May Be So, The
Comedy of Lambert Simnel* and *Love's Labour's Won* had perished.
Don Manuel said:

'For posterity. Put them in a book.'

'How? A book? Stage plays put into a book?'

'A folio. A great work. Only in the simultaneous presentation
of his entire production can he hope to match what I have in
mind.'

'And what is it you have in mind?'

Don Manuel thought it prudent to lie. 'Oh,' he said, 'if I may
risk blasphemy, your King James Bible.'

·—— THE MOST BEAUTIFIED ——·

/'T'he study of the beautiful,' their lecturer said, 'is anal-
ogous to the extraction of a precious ore from the baser
metals in which it is embedded. For there are so many
factors connected with the animal needs which must be cut away
before the pure object of what may be termed aesthetic contemplation may be revealed. The schoolmen, vestiges of whose teaching still cling to the philosophy of the children of the Reform,
who we must consider ourselves to be, saw beauty as an attribute
of the godhead yet could achieve no profounder definition than
"the beautiful is what pleases". But the predicate itself requires
definition. What is it that pleases? Mainly the satisfaction of an
appetite. Consider a game pie, a roast haunch of venison, a brace
of fowl turned on the spit, a cool jug of malmsey. These are
satisfying, therefore pleasing. Are they in consequence beautiful?
I do not refer to their appearance, of course, though considerations of colour and proportion may, as in the contemplation of
a picture, enter into our appraisal of a dish before appetite rav-
ages it. I refer to taste, the action of teeth and saliva, the consciousness of material satisfaction. Now this satisfaction is, of its
nature, animal. Hunger and the appeasing of hunger are in the
service of the life of the body. The problem of beauty becomes
more intense when it is applied to an object of sexual appetite.
When we speak of the beauty of a woman, what precisely do we
mean?'

The gowned students in the great hall betrayed their youth by
leering, shuffling, shifting their haunches, making covert manual
gestures at each other. The lecturer's assistant, seated towards

the back of the dais, pulled his pointed beard thrice then yawned. One of the two doors at the rear of the raked hall opened, and a university servant entered, raised his flat cap at the lecturer, bowed slightly, said, 'A message,' and ran down the long steps with their shallow risers to a mature-looking student in rich raiment under his gown. He bowed and handed over his message. The student read it rapidly and rose. To the lecturer he said:

'I ask permission to leave. A sudden summons home. It seems that my father is dead.'

The lecturer said: 'Regrettable. I condole. Death comes to all, and to some sooner than to others.' He looked solemn saying that and seemed to envisage his own death, the day and the hour, in a mullioned window that looked out on to the main square of Wittenberg. His assistant grinned. The mature student bowed and, with long strides, marched up and out. 'Shall we continue?' the lecturer said. It was a rhetorical question. 'We were about to consider the beauty of woman. How far can we separate the appetitive excitement associated with the female form from the austerer contemplation of that form as a structure of relations? As all women of childbearing age can be considered capable to a lesser or greater degree of arousing erotic desire, all women may be considered beautiful. This may or may not be so. But we would all accept a series of gradations rising from least beautiful – or most ugly – to most beautiful. Note that at that point of extremity even the vaguest concept of ugliness fails to apply. We are in the presence of a mystery, gentlemen.'

'Not for me,' muttered a loutish student from Bremen. 'I know what I want and tonight I'll get it.'

'My assistant,' the lecturer said, 'will now unroll a series of charts in illustration.' The assistant got up at leisure, fixed the muttering lout with a pair of black eyes whose pupils attenuated to needle-points and waited till the lout had collapsed into a dead faint. The lout came to in precisely five seconds, his face set in horror at the fiery eternity which had just unrolled in his head. The assistant rolled down a chart. There was a black and white drawing, some seven feet high, of a highly personable but quite anonymous girl of some seventeen or eighteen years, totally naked. 'Facial beauty,' the lecturer said. 'Exact symmetry of features. The eyes so set that a third eye could be placed between

23

them. The lips full, but not over-full. The forehead neither high nor low. We could apply the technic of exact mensuration, but that would not bring us closer to an aesthetic assessment.'

The rear door again opened and the same university servant entered, bowed, apologised. He bore a message for a less mature student seated near the back. The student rose and said:

'Master doctor, I regret the interruption. A sudden summons home.'

'Your father dead also?'

'Not mine. The father of my country. My mother believes I am needed.'

'Go, then, go. Is there to be no end to these distractions?'

'The breasts,' the assistant hissed, piercing first left then right nipple with a wooden pointer tipped with sharp metal.

'The breasts, yes. The firm, young, hardly formed. The mature and abundant. The ageing and lolling. All have their distinctive beauties but, again, what precisely does the term mean?'

The rear door opened yet again, and the lecturer cried: 'I will have no more of this.' It was the Rector standing there, grey, paunched, leaning on a stick of blackthorn. The Rector saw naked female beauty in black and white. He cried in his turn:

'It is the Senate that will have no more of this, sir. I have been hearing of your obscene discourses, the corruption of innocent minds. Clear the hall at once.' And he cracked loudly on the lintel with his stick. The lecturer's assistant pierced him with his eyes as lazily as he had pierced the black nipples. The Rector began coughing and did not cease until he coughed himself to the floor. From a near prone position he raised his right arm and coughed: '*Maledico.*' The lecturer said:

'Enough.'

The Rector entered and smiled benignly on all. 'The cupping of unripe breasts,' he gloated, 'the pleasures of youth. You men get good victuals here, and that breeds seed, and seed will out.' So saying, Dr Kessel left.

The prince rode to Magdeburg and there changed his horse. He rode to Brunswick and dined in an inn. Over his dinner he read from a thin book. He read: 'With the disintegration of the Church and its fragmentation into national sects we may expect in time the disintegration of the faith itself. For disunity, as has been observed in our own era, comes from asking questions, and, if enough questions be asked, there cometh a time when there will be no answers. It is enough to accept nature and incumbent on us to doubt the supernatural. For supernatural phenomena will not yield to enquiry, only to credulity, and hence must be struck from the programme of research into the nature of things.' The prince nodded. He agreed. He considered himself to be one of the new race of sceptics. Facts were facts and all facts verifiable. That his father the king was dead was a fact, nay a report, not yet a fact. He had no doubt that it would soon be presented to him as a fact: still body, the eyes shut, the beard sable-silvered as in life, no longer able to wag in discourse, in the expression of love or rebuke. Should he weep now? No, he had best eat his piece of roasted mutton seasoned with capers. He had best empty this tankard of Brunswick beer. He would mourn when it was proper to mourn, accept the succession of his uncle and the law that saw in the blood of a son a dilution of native royalty. For brothers were equal in blood, but the son had the blood of his mother. To each nation its laws.

At the Danish mission in Hamburg the royal coach awaited him with its four high-bred bays. He read till he crossed the border. He read: 'What do I know of anything? I must believe the evidence of my senses but how if my senses be cheated? The cheating may come from within, for often we see what we wish to see. We must take what is real to be an object of consensus, for what many see may reasonably be taken to exist of itself. And if a man sees what no others see, we may justly speak of a derangement of the senses. Some force within, once thought to be diabolic but now best explicated in terms of melancholy or hypochondria, may work on the senses of a man prone to it through some morbid alteration of the humours.' He pulled his heavy cloak about him. The northern spring was cold.

The less mature student made a slower journey. He was robbed and beaten by highway thugs near Sälzwedel. He arrived in time to see the committal of the body to the royal vaults and was, to his shock, then instructed to prepare fresh wedding garments. His mother pressed and aired them. He kept in the background at the ceremony and drank little of the strong brew. His nose was sensitive: there was an unlikeable odour about the new order.

In Wittenberg the learned doctor known variously as Vuist, Pesnica, Kulak, Pigmi and Qabda, for it was part of his humour to translate his name into the tongue of each land he visited, and he had visited many, sat with his three special students in a tavern midway between the houses of Luther and Melancthon. For Doctor Neve or Oköl or Egrof or Punho or Puma had, with his strangely recovered youth, taken to conducting his seminars in taverns, where, he said, the spirit of argument was quickened by Wittenberg beer and the throng of drinkers of the town rep-resented the world of quotidian enactments against which the most rarefied philosophy had to be tested. His assistant, whom none of the students liked, was away on business of his own. He had a poor head for drink and would start quarrels from which, with the speed and cunning of a fox, he would extricate himself when pots began to clang on heads.

'Master doctor,' said the student nicknamed Fussboden, for he was always too ready to be trodden upon in argument, 'I think we conclude that the height of female beauty is reached when erotic allure is, as it were, overborne by a kind of untouchable dignity.'

'By dignity you would mean some royal quality, the essence of the symbolic mother.'

'He means the Virgin Mary,' said Seide the smooth. 'To think of the mother of Christ, however young and beautiful, as a conceivable partner in the actions of the bed would, of course, be blasphemy.'

'Did the sainted carpenter who wed her then blaspheme?' said fat Matratze.

'She had not yet been exalted into the Virgin Mother and the First Lady of Heaven,' Seide said. 'Much apparently depends on history.'

'Or myth,' the learned doctor said. 'Let us not talk of—' The name stuck in his throat. 'If we speak of myth not history, which lady is accounted, in all the annals of Europe, the most beautiful?'

'Without doubt,' Fussboden said, 'Helen of the Iliad.'

'Her intrinsic qualities may well have been nothing,' Seide said. 'Her beauty is pure rumour. In besieged Troy I picture her as fat and pampered, bloated also with her own pride in being the argument of a ten-year war.'

'There is much in what Seide says,' the doctor said. 'An accretion of superstitious admiration unmerited by tresses inglorious and a wart on her left brow.' He drank deep and, with frothy lips, added: 'And yet we have the assurance to Paris of the goddess of youth and love and beauty herself that this was the most beautiful she of all the Greek islands. Hence, I would say, of the known world.'

'If she was Greek,' Fussboden said, 'she would be dark-haired, and I as a son of the north worship tresses golden and shining. Her eyebrows would meet and her nose be of an unbecoming largeness. Like the Jews,' he added.

'The Blessed Virgin was Jewish,' Matratze said.

'Alas that we cannot see her and all must be conjecture,' Seide sighed. The doctor stirred a little uneasily. Seide said: 'Our fellow-student, though mature, the departed prince, says there is no beauty in women. They are but machines for pleasure or for breeding and they are less beautiful than beautified.'

'A cynical prince,' Matratze said. 'A prince of the most profound scepticism whom few things delight. He denies the Christian tenets as incapable of demonstrative proof. There is no life after death, he says. I think from your nods and smiles, master doctor, that you share something of his negativism.'

'Very little,' the doctor said. 'That the soul exists, that there is eternal life, that God is just – these tenets must be accepted. That there is free will also, and that we may choose. We may, indeed, buy and sell.' The students did not well understand; they looked at him with curiosity. Seide at length said:

'Is it true what we hear? It would explain this remarkable recovery of youth and appetite in one who, if I may speak without offence, seemed likely to go the way of dust and drouth. In the manner, if I may so, of our revered Rector.'

'There are ways and means,' the doctor said vaguely. He seemed to make a decision. 'You say that Helen may not be seen. I suggest that we drain our tankards and then proceed to my rooms. If you are willing to intermit the pleasures of conjecture and confront the demonstrable, then you may conclude that academic studies are unprofitable. That, of course, is one of the dangers.' They looked at each other, doubtful, not sure if they understood, not sure if they wished – 'Come,' the doctor said, rising, throwing careless money on the table. 'Be bold.'

The students had not previously visited the chambers of the learned Poing or Yumruk or Pugno. They were very ordinary chambers in the University building, facing out on to a neglected garden and a wall on which fruit had once grown but no longer did. In the study, where had once been innumerable books, the shelves were filled with evidence of foreign travel – Chinese ceramics, Toledo brasswork, some exquisite figurines, parchments of erotic acts with explanatory texts in unknown alphabets or syllabaries. Academic studies no longer then profitable? A great portion of the study floor had been polished to an icy surface, on which Fussboden appropriately fell. The lecturer's assistant, who could not have seen this happen, nevertheless came in from the neighbouring room, perhaps the bedchamber, in high and cruel laughter. He was dressed as an Augustinian monk, as Luther had once been, and his hands were hidden in contrary sleeves. 'Anyone with a soul to sell?' he asked. 'No, no, I think not. There are few in the world worthy the purchase.' The students were uncomfortable and Fussboden rubbed his sore posterior. 'The circle is already there,' the assistant said. 'Fresh chalk, new chalk, and not one speck of dust to hinder a clean apparition.'

'The formula?' the learned doctor asked.

'I anticipated. You have only to call. But we need darkness.' He shut out the early spring evening with the shutters of the one window.

'And,' the doctor said, 'light. Keep to the walls, gentlemen. Do not approach.' They gasped as light came from nowhere within the chalk circle on the over-polished floor. 'And now.' A skeleton, upright of its own accord, no ceiling cords, no armatures, was washed in the light. 'Observe. Cervical vertebrae, first and second thoracic vertebrae, clavicles, sternum, humerus, radius, ulna, carpus, metacarpals, phalanges. I need not go on. Is there beauty here? You are reminded only of death, in which there is no beauty. You will now be disgusted as we fill this hollow structure with organs. See the heart beat, the lungs fill and empty, the liver at its silent and invisible work. Do not retch,

28

Fussboden – you are merely looking at your own inner self. Beauty comes with the laying of flesh over the patches of fat and muscle. Eyes, skin, hair. This, gentlemen, is Helen of Troy.'

'The hair is fair,' gasped Fussboden.

'The eyes blue,' the doctor said, pointing. 'The symmetry of features is perfect. Examine the flatness of the belly, the tapering of the ankles, the snowiness of the feet, above all the pertness yet fullness of the breasts. Is there beauty here?'

'It's a trick,' Seide said. 'I don't know how you do it, but it's no more than a trick.'

'Hurry,' the assistant said. 'We're due in Rome at dawn.'

'Beauty in women differs from that of art,' said the doctor, 'in that the organicity of art is pure metaphor. There is no blood in it, there is no motion. Watch.' And the creature came alive with visible breathing, the lowering of long lashes in apparent modesty, the raising of the lids for a frank gaze on the gazers. The weight rested on one hip, the feet gracefully moved and the splendour of the back and the inexpressible allure of the buttocks shone in the cold light. But the light became warm, became golden. 'This is the most beautiful woman who ever lived,' the doctor said. 'What do you wish, gentlemen? To take her in your arms, to smother that perfect face with kisses, to thrust a palpitant tongue between the lips?'

'But to this she must come and to this she came,' the assistant said. The creature was transformed at once into a mouldering corpse, still upright, the smell of decay and earth coming off it. 'Not yet. A mere reminder.' And the perfect body was not quite as it was before: it was lightly robed in green, zoned, sandalled, the pricked ear lobes tricked with hanging jewels.

'Beautiful,' Matratze breathed.

'Or beautified,' the doctor corrected. 'Art is always needful.'

'We must go,' the assistant said.

'Gentlemen,' the doctor said firmly. 'You will define a ghost as one who died and has been resurrected – opaque, translucent, transparent, a mere voice, the whole being. In that Helen is long dead, you have seen her ghost or resurrected essence. Do not speak of this, except among yourselves. You will be severely punished if you do. You may say goodbye to the paragon of the ancient world.' They gulped their farewell; the figure smiled and raised its right arm. Then it disappeared. The assistant, while the light faded, reopened the shutters and let in the darkening spring evening. 'Now go,' the doctor said.

They went rather quickly. They put some distance between themselves and the rooms of their instructor. Finally they rested under the great oak, just leafing, that stood ten yards or so from the house of Melancthon. Fussboden said:

'Oh my God.'

'Necromancy,' Matratze said. 'The black art. He need not be here on the faculty. He could have the whole world in his fist.' He tasted the word. 'Fist. Well-named.'

'He can't change his nature,' Seide said. 'Sold his soul but still teaches philosophy. So we have to believe in hell and the devil and eternal torment. In heaven too, I suppose. Also purgatory.'

'That's gone. No more purgatory,' Fussboden said. 'The impossibility of free thought. There's the horror. We have to believe.' He chuckled direly. 'A pity the student prince wasn't with us. He'd have to believe too. I don't suppose old Fist, but he's young now, would put on that show again. So the Dansker can go on not believing.'

'Personally,' Seide said, 'I was disappointed. I don't think she was all that beautiful.'

·— THE CAVALIER OF THE ROSE —·

(based on the opera libretto by Hugo von Hoffmansthal)

I

History is always the past. We never live through history. When we are old, we discover to our surprise that we have lived through it. When we die we join it. A sunlit morning in Vienna, two naked lovers waking in each other's arms – what has this to do with history? But outside the great bed, the silken chamber, the magnificent house on the edge of the city with the woodlarks crying, outside in the great world, history was preparing itself for the attention of the historians. Maria Theresa, a child of Vienna, daughter of the late Emperor Karl VI, reigned as Queen of Hungary and Bohemia and Arch-duchess of Austria. Her consort Francis Stephen, Grand Duke of Tuscany, was her equal partner in rule, and he had touched fashionable Vienna with the refinements of Tuscany and even the Tuscan language. Soon, though, France would be inciting Prussia and Bavaria and Saxony and Naples and Sardinia to bite at Maria Theresa's territories, shouting their justification in the extinction of the male line of the Hapsburgs. The War of the Austrian Succession was still to come, seven years of struggle to end with the Peace of Aix-la-Chapelle and Maria Theresa's confirmation as ruler of her realms and the election of her husband to the imperial throne. Of the movement of history the lovers knew nothing and cared less. The movements of their own bodies were of greater interest. They had put off their nominal roles in the hierarchy of Austrian rule along with their titles. The Princess and the Count had been reduced, or elevated, to the rank of mere adulterous lovers. Articulate, as befitted their titles, they had words as well as caresses. Octavian, the young Count, spoke of the beauty of his mistress, the refinement of her sensibilities as well as the treasures of her body. Ah, who could ever measure their perfections?

She, the Princess von Werdenberg, wife of Field Marshal Prince von Werdenberg, said, wittily: 'Mignon, don't grieve about the absence of a measuring rod. Do you want my perfections – your word, not mine – to be advertised in the daily courier or proclaimed in the streets?'

'Ah no, *tesoro*, angel, I'm happy enough to be the sole custodian of that knowledge.' He drew the white cambric shirt of the day before on to his spare white body. He was young, younger than she, and might be thought of as more beautiful than handsome. But there was nothing epicene there: he was brave, skilled with the sword, and would be ready to ride at the head of his squadron when the War of the Succession began. Only fools heard in the high clear voice and saw in the slim body the lineaments of the effeminate. There was nothing effeminate in his love-making. 'But when I say you,' he was saying as he dressed swiftly, 'and speak of your this and that, I'm just as foolish as when I say I. The words have no meaning. We lose our identities in love and become one being.'

'Which means,' said the Princess, 'that I may not say I love you. But I say it. I say it now.'

He was a little petulant as he squinted at the bright spring morning framed by the uncurtained window. 'I hate the day,' he said. 'When the day comes you belong to others. If I can't keep in the dark, at least let me shut out the bird-song. Voices of the world, ugh.' She smiled as he rushed over to close the half-open casement. In the distance bells began tinkling softly. He saw her smile and asked why she smiled. Love, her face said, I smile with love, with the pleasure of seeing you after a night of not seeing you. Angel. Beloved. He flew to her arms. The bells tinkled again. The bells approached.

'The couriers,' she said. 'The outside world.' She was already in the furred negligée of the morning. A woman of astounding beauty but a beauty that had already achieved its climax. She was older than her Mignon, the Count Octavian, and she knew it. She would not grow more beautiful.

'Letters,' Octavian said, 'from Saurau and Hartig and the Portuguese ambassador. I won't have it, I'll keep the world out, I'm master here.' There was a fumbling at the door. 'It's my morning chocolate,' she said. 'Quick. Hide behind that screen.' He did. A little black boy entered, all in yellow, with little silver bells ajangle on his shoulder-knots, sleeves and calves. He bore steaming chocolate and Viennese whipped cream on a silver salver.

'Your esteemed and beauteous highness,' someone had taught the boy to say, 'I bid you good morning. Here is your chocolate, hot. Here is Schlagobers, cold.'

And there was Octavian's sword with sheath and belt lying on the candy-striped couch. 'Thank you, Mahomed,' she said. 'On that table there.' So that the black boy, who was as much of a gossip as anybody in her household, should not see her grasp the sword and thrust it into the hands of its owner behind the screen. She frowned at Octavian, an earnest of words to come. Careless idiot. The black boy placed the tray on the little table, pushed a plush-seated chair beside it, bowed with his hands joined across his breast, then, in a kind of dance step that made his bells jingle, left the chamber backwards. Octavian came out, blowing with relief.

'Careless idiot. Featherbrain. Is it the done thing for a lady of rank and fashion to have a sword lying in her bedchamber? A certain lack of breeding shows in you sometimes.'

'If my lack of breeding upsets you,' he said, 'I could best express my love and devotion by removing my lack of breeding along with myself.'

A joke, of course, but she could not help hearing in it a kind of rehearsal of farewell. She smiled tenderly, however, and said:

'Bring a chair. Drink some chocolate. Share my cup.'

'No,' he said. He lifted the table with its aromatic burden over to the candy-striped couch. 'Here,' he said. So they shared the one cup and she stroked his hair and, when the chocolate was finished, he lay with his head in her lap. He spoke her name, which was also and primarily the name of their Archduchess: Maria Theres'. Octavian. Angel. Mignon. Beloved. My own boy.

Boy was right. She was in her thirties and he was a boy. Octavian said:

'Your husband the Field Marshal is hunting brown bear and black boar in the wilds of Croatia. And I lie here in the indolent flower of my youth. But what could be better? I'm so happy.'

It is always unwise, she thought, to say one is happy. Happiness is like history, something in the past. The mention of her husband cast a shadow. She said:

'Let him sleep, or hunt. I dreamed about him last night.'

His head started up from her lap. 'You dreamed of him – while you and I were—'

'I can't order my dreams as I order dinner. There's no need to look like that, Octavian. Be angry with the dream if you like, but not with me. I dreamed he was here, at home again.'

'Here.' He looked over at the bed and shuddered.

'There was a noise – horses clattering, the voices of men arriving. Then there he was – here. I can still hear it, that noise.'

'There is a noise,' he said, sitting up, then rising. 'Men and horses. It can't be your husband, though. He's at Esseg, isn't he – that's a hundred miles away—' Horses approached, men: he could hear them. Caught, the cuckolder caught? And any door out would lead to servants. The window? 'It can't be. It's someone else. Do you expect someone else?'

She seemed fearful, and this made him fearful too. No very honourable situation. 'It's amazing,' she said, 'how fast he can travel when he wishes. Why, there was one occasion—'

'What occasion? What do you mean?' he said jealously.

'Oh, nothing. I think the horsemen are passing. Nothing at all to bother you with.' She too was on her feet now.

'Despair! Despair.' He had the couch to himself. He threw himself upon it. 'Why do you do this to me?' It was very theatrical, a boy's behaviour. He had buried his head in a cushion. He could not hear what she now heard. She heard footsteps not in the antechamber, where strangers awaited the levée, but in the closet. Servants would not keep him out, would not even delay him. She grasped at Octavian's silken collar. She said:

'The dream was right. Up, out, he's coming.' Octavian had already drawn his sword. 'Don't be foolish, hide. No, not the

34

antechamber, it will be full of people. No, not there – hide – in the bed – close the curtains.'

He looked young and ridiculous, upright, sword brandished. 'I stay with you. We'll have it out. We love each other.'

'Oh, idiot. In there. Behind the curtains.'

'And if I'm caught here—' His sword-arm looked less sure of itself. 'What will happen to you, beloved?'

She stamped with impatience. 'Hide!' He was undecided where to hide. That screen again? No, the suspicious husband might push it aside. The bed, then. He crawled into the mess of pillows and tumbled sheets and drew fast the thick velvet curtains. She stood, waiting, turned to the door, trying to calm her breathing. She could hear servants trying to keep out a male with a loud and importunate voice. It did not sound like her husband. 'Our mistress is sleeping.' 'She is not well.' 'She has a profound migraine.' And then she recognised the voice. It was that of her cousin Baron Ochs of Lerchenau. Ochs coming here, and so early? Then she remembered something – a long letter from Ochs delivered to her when starting off in her coach for a drive through the Vienna Woods, her Mignon snuggling beside her, the first kiss as the wheels rolled, the letter forgotten. This was a kind of corruption. And if the letter had been from her husband, saying: Liebchen, I return at once, an urgent summons, business at court? Corruption, neglect, passion driving out reason as expressed in the cool business of the well-organised day, the letters carefully read and as carefully answered. Had they already gone too far? She heard the voices coming closer.

'Perhaps if your lordship would be good enough to wait a moment in the gallery—'

'Insolent nonsense, fellow. I am Baron Lerchenau. I wait for no one. Out of my path at once unless you prefer to be whipped out of it. Make way.'

'It's Ochs,' she told the hidden Octavian. 'He's battering the door down. Stay there, do not move.' And indeed a heavy fist, garnished with heavy rings, was already firmly rattattatting. But Octavian came out of hiding. He wore his mistress's nightcap, sufficiently like the mobcap of a servant, and his mistress's nightgown, which would serve as the daygown of a maid.

'Tell me my duties, highness,' said Octavian in the high voice of a girl, curtseying clumsily. 'Your highness knows that this is only my first day in your highness's service.'

'Out,' she said, and she ran over to kiss him. 'Go on, that way. If you wish to pretend, pretend properly. Mincing little steps, head shyly down. And watch that sword. It's sticking out at the back like a tail. And give me an hour, beloved. We'll meet by the fountain in the Italian garden—'

Octavian's hand was on the doorknob at the moment that the door was flung open. Ochs, and behind him footmen expressing their regret to their mistress with hands on hearts, hands held wide, wide eyes almost tearful. Octavian's head was lowered in a show of maid's modesty. Unseeing, he butted Ochs. Confused, he curtseyed and went to the wall. The open door was full of Ochs and footmen. No way out yet. But Ochs, with a ready eye for a wench of the lower orders, said: 'Pardon me, my dear, I trust I did not hurt you.' Octavian curtseyed his way back toward the bed. Change the sheets, a maid's chore. 'Pretty little thing,' Ochs said.

'Good morning, cousin,' the Princess said. 'How well you look.'

'There,' growled Ochs at the footmen. 'Welcome, you see? Expected. If you were in my employ you'd soon be out of it. Away, this is private.' And he himself slammed the door on them.

II

Baron Ochs of Lerchenau was sometimes called a Falstaff without the wit. His belly was more than Falstaffian: it denoted heavy dinners and heavy bevers before and after them. He would have looked more presentable with a Falstaffian beard, but this was an age of clean shaves and wigs. His nose was a maimed beacon: its red shine was marred by the lumps of good living and a wart on the left-hand slope, sporting three filaments which waved in the breeze of his passing. His eyes of a sharp blue were couched in fat. A high noble forehead might have counteracted the meanness of the mouth, with a pouting lower lip that flared crimson, the vast jowls and cheeks, the potman's nose and the swinish eyes, but his brow was narrow and low. It was a face that might have been more acceptable if nature had placed it on his no-neck upside down. The voice was hectoring and knew no variation of tone. He was dressed in flowered silk spotted from his early breakfast. He kicked off his buckled shoes, evidently tight, without permission as he sat on an over-dainty chair that grumbled quietly at its burden. He had thrown off his topcoat, and it lay like a dog on the carpet. His hat, which was panached like Cyrano's, he was slow in removing.

He sat and panted and looked around him. It was a noble room, though it was only a bedchamber. He nodded at its cream and gold and, as if deciding that it was worthy of his brief sojourn, he at last took off his hat and spun it in the direction of the couch. It did not reach the couch. 'Pick it up, my dear,' he told the back of the sheet-removing Octavian. 'Hang it somewhere.' And as Octavian obeyed he said: 'Pretty little thing. No more of that, though. Done with dallying. Settling down now.' And, to the Princess, 'I knew you wouldn't object to my coming early. They said out there that you had a bad headache or something. Lot of nonsense, of course. You look as fresh as a rose. Rose, yes. We'll come to that later. I like the early morning. Wake up hungry these days, good thing, gets me out of bed. No,' he said, in response to an invitation not given, 'don't bother to order me breakfast. I had a fine haunch of boar this morning. Hung five days, marinated in red wine, a bunch of herbs. A pint of sherry. A man has to look after himself. Those days of breakfast round the bathtub, Princess Whatshername, a regular invitation, where is she now? Not so young as I was, you can see that. Pretty little thing,' he said again, eyes on Octavian plumping a pillow. 'Not seen her here before.'

'She's just come up from the country,' the Princess said. 'She has a lot to learn, of course. You can go now, Mariandel,' she said to Octavian, wondering why she had chosen that name. Of course, her old schoolfellow, poor girl, made a terrible marriage.

'Let her stay,' Ochs said, 'charming little baggage.' And then: 'Well, what do you think of the news?'

'News?'

'Come now, the letter.'

'Oh, the letter. This headache drove it clean out of my mind.

37

Well,' she said cheerfully, 'it seemed to me to be very good news.'

'Glad you think so. Thought you might be a bit surprised, though. I mean, I never thought of myself as the marrying type.'

So that was what the letter was about. 'And who is the fortunate lady?'

'Come now,' and he barked as though at an impossibility, a letter from him, the Baron Ochs of Lerchenau, and unread, 'it was all in black and white, cousin. A peach and an unripe one, something to get these teeth into.' He showed his teeth, his only good feature. 'Barely fifteen, by God.'

'Of course. I was just saying the name to myself a minute since as you were coming in, cousin.'

'Ah, no. I didn't mention the name. A peach, I tell you. A waist I can get one hand round. Fresh as a violet. Thought I'd give you the important matters first – youth, beauty and so on. Wealth, and all the rest of it. Position – well, I have to admit to a bit of doubt. Not much of a family. Faninal. You wouldn't know it, of course. Faninal.' He tasted the sound of it, like some foreign dish he was not sure whether or not to like.

'A local family?'

'All too local. Viennese merchant class, that's the problem. Her Majesty's just put a von in his name. He was in charge of army victualling. Salt beef and flour for the troops in the Netherlands. I can see,' he said, 'from the set of your lips that you're not too happy about it.' But the slight pout had been intended for Octavian: take the tray and get out of here: your boots were visible when you bent over the bed then: nobody takes as long as that to change sheets. 'A misalliance, you may be thinking. But the girl – wait till you see her. Straight out of a convent, knows nothing of the world, voice like an angel. Such innocence.'

He said the word with a growl, as though innocence were for eating. 'And the old man – von Faninal, as we must call him now – owns half the bourgeois property in the city, got a fine mansion of his own, not long for this world, so his doctor told me. Heart. Heart.' He tapped the Princess on the knee boldly, grunting at the effort of leaning forward to do it. 'She's an only child.' And he winked horribly.

38

'Do take that tray out, Mariandel,' she said, 'and those dirty sheets.'

'Well,' said Ochs, leaning back. 'If she's taking the tray out she may as well bring another tray in. You're quite right, cousin, I am somewhat peckish,' finding, as he often did, an excuse for hoggishness in others' imagined exhortations to be hoggish. 'The morning air, it does indeed promote appetite, you are, as so often, perfectly correct. Not much, though. Some cold sirloin, underdone, and a new loaf perhaps. I have a passion for new bread. The bread at the inn was not fresh.' He glowered at her, as though it were her fault. 'But I've nothing against their marinated boarflesh, nothing at all.' He waited, as for a contradiction. And then, seeing Octavian going with soiled sheets and tray to the door, he levered himself up in his stockinged feet and padded toward him. 'Allow me to open it for you, my dear.' And then, in a breathy whisper, 'You and I could be very cosy together one evening. I'll arrange it, you just leave it to me, my love.' Octavian, as was expected, giggled. 'Here, let somebody else do the work, one of those bone-idle footmen out there.' He opened the door and cried: 'Come on, come on, help the girl, will you? And fetch me some breakfast – beef, ham, new bread, butter, beer – quick, quick, get on with it.' He, as it were absentmindedly, took the freed right hand of Octavian and padded back with him to the middle of the room. He said to the Princess:

'The real reason why I came was to ask you for an ambassador.'

'Ambassador?'

'Yes, you know the custom, somebody to hand over the silver rose to the bride-to-be. Damned silly custom perhaps, but it's expected. Marks the aristocracy off from the riff-raff of the bourgeoisie. I've brought it.'

'Brought it?'

'It's down below. One of my men has it. I came with a full retinue, never do things by halves is my motto,' and still he held on, as if absentmindedly, to the hand of Octavian, whose giggles were in danger of modulating to a more masculine guffaw.

'One of our kinsmen, you mean,' the Princess said. 'Who? Preysing? Lamberg?'

'I leave it all in your lily-white hands, dear cousin.'

'That shall be done, dear cousin. It's time for my levée. Is there anything else I'm to do for you?'

'Well,' he said, 'there's the matter of a marriage settlement. I'd like to see that attorney of yours, a good man, I remember. I don't retain one of my own, as you know, no use for them normally. I mean people of our rank are above the law, but this might be a bit of a tricky business, the bourgeoisie holds on to its money.' And still he held on to Octavian. The Princess said:

'Very well, cousin. Mariandel, go and see if my attorney is in the anteroom, will you?' But Ochs held on and said:

'No need, leave it to me. I'll yell for him.' And he opened the door with his free paw. His yell was forestalled by the entry of the Major-domo. Ochs had not expected that. He, a baron, had opened the door for a mere upper servant. The Major-domo bowed. He was a thin man and had the grey look of the ulcerated. He was ribboned and powdered and polished. The Princess said:

'Good morning, Struhan. Is my attorney there?'

'Yes, your highness, and also your steward, your *chef de cuisine*, and ah yes, his grace the Duke of Silva commends to your highness a singer and a flautist of high accomplishment.' A certain dryness entered his tone. 'And, of course, there are the usual petitioners.'

Ochs, meanwhile, was saying breathily to Octavian, who had yielded his burdens to another servant: 'A nice little supper, eh, just the two of us? Have you ever had a nice little tête-à-tête with a gentleman?'

'Let them wait, Struhan,' the Princess said. The Major-domo bowed and left. 'Taking your pleasure where you find it, cousin,' she said to Ochs. 'I thought I heard you say something about a new life, settling down.'

'Oh, your highness,' Ochs said formally, 'it's the atmosphere here, you know – relaxed, no Spanish affectation, friendly, I always feel I'm among friends here.' But he let go of Octavian's hand.

'A man of birth and honour, newly betrothed – come, my cousin, is this any way to behave?' Her tone was only mock-severe.

'Do I have to live like a monk just because I'm going to be married?' said Ochs, padding toward her. 'It's the hunting instinct in me, you know, always hot on the scent. You women, with respect, can never know the sensation. I mean, you're merely the quarry.'

'There's a season for hunting.'

'Ah no, this is a different kind of chase, no close season when love is involved. Seriously now, in all seriousness, I seek the acquaintance of your serving wench here to a different end. I ask permission to install her in my new household, a little gift, a well-bred attendant on my baroness. What do you say?'

'Your baroness will wish to make her own choice. Besides, this girl is my special jewel. High-bred, as you say, very.'

'Blue blood, I don't doubt,' Ochs said, 'it shines out of her. I always say a man of the blood should be surrounded by the blood, even when it flows on the wrong side of the blanket. I have a body-servant quite as well born as myself – a prince's son. He's downstairs at this moment, with the silver rose in his keeping. Whenever your highness shall deign to choose an ambassador, he'll receive the rose from the hands of a prince's son.'

'Mariandel,' said the Princess, 'will you be so good as to—'

'Let me have her,' pleaded Ochs with a low growl. 'I mean, let my baroness have her.'

'—bring me the miniature of the Count Octavian.'

Octavian stared at her. She smiled back. Octavian went to a small glass cupboard in the farthest corner of the chamber. Ochs drank in the mincing gait with admiration. He said:

'A prince's by-blow,' and then: 'Would it be a good thing to give the little Faninal an illuminated copy of my pedigree, just to keep her reminded, you know – or perhaps the lock of the hair of the first of the Lerchenaus, that's going back a bit, the first hereditary Grand Warden of the Domains of Carinthia?' The Princess said nothing; she took from Octavian's hands a portrait of Octavian, framed in silver, inset with small diamonds.

'Here, cousin,' she said. 'Here, I think, is your ambassador. What do you think of him?'

'As your highness wishes. That's settled then.'

'But look. This is my young cousin, Count Octavian.'

Ochs dutifully looked. He started. 'My God,' he said, his pig-eyes swivelling from the real to the pictured. 'No wonder I thought – I was right about the blue blood—' And Octavian

41

wondered uneasily whether his mistress was not perhaps going too far. Egad, it's the same, let's have that dress off her, by heaven, a young man in your room, the Prince shall know about this – But all Ochs said was: 'Knew I was right, always had a nose for blood.'

'Rofrano is the name,' said the Princess. 'Younger brother of the Marquis—'

'Ah, that explains this, then. I remember old Rofrano. By God, he had an eye and a hand and – Well, blood will always out. Who cares about the niceties?'

'So you see perhaps, cousin, why she's precious to me. Very well, Mariandel, you may go now.' Octavian curtseyed. Ochs accompanied her to the door, saying:

'Pretty child, leave everything to me. We'll have such an evening together,' very breathily. Octavian pitched his voice to the high limit:

'Naughty man,' and then was gone, slamming the door on Ochs's nose. The door opened, ah, she was coming back. But she was not coming back. A whole rabble started to come in.

III

A very ill-favoured old lady of the chamber came in first. The contrast with the supposed her who had gone out made Ochs retreat a couple of paces. Two footmen came in after her. They took the Princess's toilet table, placed it in the middle of the chamber, and concealed it from the entering mob with a three-faced screen. The Princess went behind it with the lady of the chamber. Then came the Princess's attorney, an old man in sour black with asthma, followed by the *chef de cuisine* and the *sous-chef*, who carried the leather-bound book of menus. A pert milliner was next, and then an evident scholar from the untidiness of his rusty black and the great tome under his arm. Small hairless dogs of a South American breed pranced in, followed by their keeper and would-be vendor, on whose left shoulder a marmoset gibbered. Then there was the Italian Valzacchi, a subtle but workless busybody, gossip, self-styled man of affairs, with a lady like a very gloomy Madonna, a great gossip-gatherer named Annina.

A widow, a military one left penniless, impoverished minor aristocracy clear in her gait and profile, led in three daughters in profound but tasteful mourning. She raised her finger at the girls and they broke into a scrannel song specially composed for them:

> High-born orphans we
> Who ask your charitee.

Then there came in Ochs's breakfast, on a tray borne by one of the Baron's own men, an ill-favoured starveling with a faint squint. The Baron had forgotten one appetite with the stimulation of another. He pointed to a low square stool: he would pick at it later when this mob had gone. He reckoned without the prancing dogs.

The milliner praised her new confection loudly: '*Le chapeau Paméla – la poudre à la reine de Golconde.*' The animal-vendor cried his wares. There was quite a din. An Italian tenor and a flautist were personally escorted in by the Major-domo, who would doubtless get his commission if patronage were secured. The tenor sang; the flautist provided a florid obbligato. Quite a din.

> Our father died in the war
> And left us very poor.
> Munificent Princess,
> Pray comfort our distress.

'*Le chapeau Paméla. C'est la merveille du monde!*'

The Princess's personal hairdresser, M. Hippolyte, waited with his assistant. The Princess scorned wigs, except on court occasions. She had the finest, silkiest, corn-yellow hair in abundance: to shear and hide it would be a deadly sin.

> Lap-dogs, monkeys, free from fleas,
> Accompanied by guarantees
> And really awesome pedigrees.

> *Di rigori armato il seno*
> *Contro amor mi ribellai*
> *Ma fui vinto in un baleno*

In mirar due vaghi rai . . .

The tenor showed off his high C flat; the flautist fluted in the breathy depths. The Princess appeared. The screen was removed. All bowed. She was ready to face the public morning, all except her coiffure. The Major-domo was by her side. He held a small purse. The Princess beckoned to the tallest of the three orphans, gave her the purse, kissed her gently on the brow. Such graciousness, such generosity, such condescension. The rusty-gowned scholar stepped in with his folio. A first edition Ariosto. Priceless, but it has a price, it would adorn your highness's library – But Valzacchi sneered and proffered a newssheet, a single black-edged page. He called himself its editor, but Annina did all the work. 'All the latest scandals,' he offered. 'Secret information. A dead body found in a certain count's town house. A rich merchant poisoned by his wife with the help of her lover. Very new news – happened only at three this morning – hot from my private press.'

'No,' said the Princess.

'*Tutti quanti* – the jealously guarded *segreti* of *le beau monde*.'

'No,' said the Princess. The orphans withdrew with their low-curtseying mother:

> Eternal bliss attend you,
> The holy heavens befriend you.

The hairdresser's coat-tails flew as he examined her highness from every angle. A courier in black, pink and silver entered with a deckle-edged note. The Major-domo had a silver salver ready. He handed her highness the note on its salver. She read the note. She did not like what she read. The assistant to the hairdresser handed him curling tongs. They were too hot. Some paper to cool them on. Her highness handed him the note. Bows and bows, that would do very well.

> *Ahi! Che resiste poco*
> *Cor di gelo a stral di fuoco. . . .*

The Princess introduced her attorney to the Baron. The Baron

44

led him to a gilded chair in the corner. The Baron sat; the attorney, panting asthmatically, remained standing.

'I'll put it simply to you, then you can dress it up in all the legal tomfoolery. I want a separate endowment, a gift if you like, nothing to do with the dowry, do you understand me? I'll tell you precisely what I want. I want the title-deeds of that demesne he owns, Gaunersdorf, see what I mean? No encumbrances, no claims, no entails—'

'With all due respect and in all dutiful submission, your lordship does not appear to realise that the husband may give a *donatio ante nuptias* to the wife, but not the wife to the husband. Such a contract would be quite without precedent.'

'But, damn it, man, this is a special case—'

'Law makes no recognition of special cases.'

'Oh, doesn't it? You listen to me. I, sir, am the living head of a family of ancient power and nobility. I am condescending – mark the word – to marry a certain nobody, a Mademoiselle or Miss Faninal, whose father has nothing except money – no pedigree, no patent of nobility. Now I doubt if our Archduchess would be pleased with such a union – I wonder sometimes if heaven itself doesn't frown upon it – and yet I'm going through with it. And I demand that you find something in the law that permits me adequate compensation for—'

Three more of the Baron's men came in – body-servant, almoner, chasseur. The chasseur's livery was too small for his yokel body. The face was that of the lowest village lout. The hands, square and horny, twitched as if wishing to strangle a chicken. The almoner had the cunning leer of a lay lawyer or village abortionist. He was stunted but beefy. The body-servant was lath-thin and had the idiot look of a long incestuous line. There was noble blood, there was no doubt about it. He held a stout leather jewel case.

'There it is,' Ochs said. 'The silver rose in its box, all cleaned and ready. You see how honourably I do everything? I demand some loophole in the law – see what I mean?' The attorney thought he saw that he would be strangled like a chicken if he did not find this loophole. The flautist started a new cadenza. The tenor began a new stanza:

Ma si caro è 'l mio tormento
Dolce è si la piaga mia,
Ch'il penare è mio contento
E' l sanarmi è tirannia . . .

'You could, of course, have a special clause put in the marriage settlement – *donatio inter vivos*, we call it—'

'No! Compensation, presented as such! Legal compensation!'

His bellow silenced singer and flautist at once.

'This won't do, Hippolyte,' said the Princess, twisting and turning before the mirror her tirewoman held. 'This won't do at all.'

In shock and horror the coiffeur flew round like a moth, his adjusting fingers like flames. Ochs looked for his breakfast, found bread, butter and beer but no beef. Small distended dogs lay around, innocently blinking. The Baron grunted, getting absentminded, looked for his shoes. The marmoset had curled up in one of them. He sent it scampering like a fly up the wall. It dropped like a feather into the arms of its cooing master. Ochs straightened the welsh-combed locks of his body-servant. The flames of the coiffeur's fingers sank. He surveyed. 'Better?'

'Much better,' said the Princess, and, to her Major-domo: 'Tell them all to leave.'

Valzacchi said to the Baron: 'Is your lordship looking for something? Can we be of any help?'

'My other shoe. Ah,' to the almoner, who had found it. 'Who the hell are you?' to the inclining Valzacchi.

'Discreet people ready to help, ready to be your lordship's most faithful servants. Discreet, silent—'

'*Come statua di Giove*,' said Annina.

'Useful,' said Valzacchi.

'Useful, eh? How useful?'

'We work as uncle and niece,' said Annina. 'We keep our eyes wide open. Supposing, now, your lordship were to marry a youthful bride—'

'How did you know about that?' Ochs was suspicious and impressed. Valzacchi was quick with:

'If your lordship had reason to be jealous, for example. *Dico per dire*. Who can ever tell? Human nature is frail, especially in

the young. Every step the lady takes, every *billet doux* she receives
– you understand? We are always around. It is our business.
Affare nostro. Your lordship follows me?' He dryly flicked thumb
against fingers. A little advance? A thaler or so? Ochs pretended
to be above understanding the gesture. He growled:
'Let's try you out, then. Do you know a lady named
Mariandel?'
'Mariandel?'
'Her highness's personal servant.'
'Sai tu cosa vuole?'
'Niente.'
'Information you wish?' said Valzacchi. 'No trouble. *Niente
problema.* We know what you want, I think. Trust us.'
Ochs grunted and turned to the Princess. 'And now, your
highness, there is nothing more to do than to leave with you this
– object.' He clicked his fingers impatiently. 'Come, Leopold, the
jewel case.' The body-servant awkwardly brought it forward.
'See,' opening it, 'the silver rose.' The sun caught it, frail,
exquisite.
'Leave it in its case,' said the Princess. 'Place it on that escri-
toire.' With ill-coordinated steps the body-servant did what was
asked.
'Or perhaps,' said Ochs, 'if you called your servant, Whatshername, she could take it to Count Whathisname. I could give her
a trip in my coach—'
'She has other things to do. Thank you. Leave everything to
me. And now, your lordship, I must ask you to go. I fear I shall
be late for church.'
He was all grunts and bows. The almoner had his plumed hat
ready, the chausseur his coat. 'The most gracious courtesy and
assistance your highness renders me – I am overwhelmed.' And
he leaned over as though it were he who was to do the overwhelming. He withdrew with his shuffling attendants. Valzacchi
and Annina joined the train, quietly, obsequiously, discreetly.
The last of the little dogs was scooped up. The tenor and flautist
bowed: they had been heard, they had given pleasure, the Major-
domo would get his cut. The Major-domo made sure the chamber
was clear of visitors. He bowed his way out. The Princess was
left alone.

IV

Alone. Great ill-smelling oaf, talking of honouring an innocent girl with his hot foul breath and his bone-cracking embraces. The holy state of wedlock. Straight out of a convent into the squalor of a grunting bed. Well, had it not been like that for her, Maria Theres'? Innocence defiled. Virginity, *les neiges d'antan*. The young Theres' who, soon enough, would be the Old Princess, the Old Field Marshal's Lady, there she goes, Old Princess Tess. We all grow old, and yet what devil permits us to remain young within? Throw away all our mirrors, let us decree a special mirror-smashing day in the courtyard. And yet we can't blind the rest of the world. The mystery of growing old. Is there some moment in time from which we date our growing old, as fixed as a birthday? The first wrinkle, the first thickening of the flesh beneath the chin? We wake up one morning and hear the cracked trumpets of the revelation: your highness has grown old. But her highness feels much as she did when she left the convent.

The door opened wide without ceremony. The servants had departed. Octavian strode in in his riding boots, his riding jacket tails bouncing to his stride, his arms open. They embraced.

'You were sad about something, angel. I saw.'

'Moody, if you wish. You know what I'm like – up, down, like a swing in the Prater.'

'I know what it was. It was fear, wasn't it? And it wasn't fear for yourself, beloved—'

'We imagine something happening and we feel – what can I call it? The appropriate emotions, I suppose. The feelings stay with us even when the vision has passed. Suppose it had been—'

'But it wasn't. It was only the buffoon, Ochs, well named. Nothing's changed. You're still mine and always mine.' He tightened his embrace.

'Don't. My old nurse used to say – what was it? he who grasps too much holds only air.'

'You're mine! Tell me that you're mine!'

'Oh, please—' She struggled, unwonted. Surprised, he freed her. 'Less strength, less wildness – be gentle, be tender. Don't be like the others.'

Suspicion froze him. 'The others – you speak as you spoke before – who are all these others?'

'I didn't say all. I was thinking of two – one came this morning – the other might have come.'

'You've changed, angel of light – changed in a single hour or two – I don't like it – it frightens me.' But he renewed his embrace.

'It will come even to you some day, Mignon – perhaps sooner than you think. The realisation that things pass, that life is a dream – all the rest of the worn-out coins that strew the boards of the theatres. And you know why writers still jingle those worn-out coins? Because they're the metal of truth. The truth is banal and can only be spoken in clichés. We're in a banal situation – something out of a play so bad it makes the spectators yawn. The lover and the erring wife and the husband's sudden return. Our love can't have permanency in it, and so I wonder if we can call it love. What do we do – run away, you a farmhand, me a milkmaid? This will all end. I see it. You refuse to see it.'

'I shall never leave you, never—'

'Oh yes. And sooner than you dream of. Oh, if only time could be reined like a horse. Sometimes, at night, while my husband snores and dreams of hunting, I get up and stop all the clocks in the house. They tick on to a future I dread. And then I wake in the morning and find that they've all been started again.'

'I don't believe in time,' he said. 'Love – that's the one reality, and love knows nothing of time. Love can't be measured by clocks or yardsticks or—'

'Like my perfections,' she said sadly. 'You remember, it's only an hour ago you were so eloquent about them. One of the gifts of youth – eloquence in the morning. Mignon,' she said, and she turned away from him, 'you'll leave me. You'll find somebody else. Innocent, young, pretty. You came to me as a pupil. This morning you spoke of being the master. You who learned will want to teach.'

He looked at her with a new coldness. 'I see. You're trying to drive me away. Too young, too awkward, too rough and callow and impulsive. Very well, I'll be tender, gentle, what you will. But you'll never drive me away.'

'Leave that to time,' she said quietly, 'to change. Nothing stands still.'

'You speak today like some ancient gloomy philosopher. But you're still my darling and always will be.' He embraced her gently. He kissed her eyelids as though bidding her bad dreams sleep.

'Mignon, you must go. I'm already late for church, and after that I must visit my poor uncle Greifenklau – he's very old and very ill – and lunch with him. I'll send a message to your house, Mignon, and let you know whether we can meet later. Perhaps I shall go for a drive in the Prater and, quite by accident of course, you will be riding there. Isn't that best?'

'All shall be as you command.' He bowed and left.

The door was scarcely closed when she realised that he had gone, or rather she had let him go, without one solitary token of – she had not kissed him, he had not kissed her. This was, really . . . She rang manically for a footman. The urgency of her ringing brought four running in. 'Run out,' she said. 'After the Count. Quick. There is something I have to tell him. Very urgent. Quick.'

It was too late. They came back breathless. Like the wind, they said, off like the wind. They called, but he did not seem to hear. Like the wind. 'Very well,' she said crossly. 'You may go.' But then she remembered something else. 'Send Mahomed to me.' She heard jingling bells approaching. The little black boy entered with profound obeisances. She pointed to the case, which contained the silver rose. 'Take it,' she said. He took it and started to leave, backwards, bowing. 'Wait, I didn't say where. Take it to the Count Octavian. You know where he lives. No message. He knows all about it. Off you go.' Bows, bows, backwards out. She sat there in a melancholy which birdsong and mounting spring sun did nothing to lighten.

V

Herr von Faninal was taking his leave of his daughter Sophia. He was old to have so young a daughter, but he had married late, at a point in his life when he felt he had accumulated enough wealth to qualify for marital alliance with the nobility. But none of the great houses of Austria seemed anxious to welcome a bourgeois son-in-law, despite the wealth. A bourgeois daughter-in-law was, of course, quite a different matter. So Faninal had decided not to abase himself further at soirées and in hunting lodges – to which, anyway, invitations were few and came only from younger sons to whom he had lent money – and to seek a bride in the higher reaches of the merchant class. After all, there was the question of an heir. The girl he married was delicate. Faninal mistook want of vitality, frailty, pallor for good breeding. She hardly survived the birth of their only child, Sophia. He did not wish to marry again. He looked for an aristocratic alliance through his daughter, with, beginning in a grandson, nobility, to which his own low blood had contributed, stretching till the crack of doom. So now, before going out, he said exultantly:

'This is a great day, child. A noble day, a holy day.' As if to confirm this, bells began ringing in the nearby church. Today the token of the noble alliance would be presented. Indeed, very soon. He gave his daughter his hand to kiss, a gesture he had learned from the nobility. Marianne, Sophie's duenna, a coarse woman easily impressed by the insolence of rank, which she confused with the attributes of nobility, was looking out of the window of the great salon, impressive mainly in its vulgarity. She said:

'Joseph's outside there, sir, with the new coach and four new horses, greys they are. All waiting for you, sir. Joseph looks lovely.' And then the Major-domo came in. Without deference he said to his master:

'By your leave, sir, if I may say so, it's time you were out and off. If I may remind you, it's an unpardonable breach of etiquette for the father of the bride to be present when the bridegroom's messenger arrives. The rose, I mean. He's due about now.'

'Very well.' Footmen opened the door.

'Even to meet him – on the stairs, in the driveway – bad luck as well, sir, apart from the unpardonable breach of—'

'Very well. When I return it will be with the bridegroom. Be ready for him, Sophia. Don't forget to behave like a lady.'

'Just think,' breathed Marianne reverently. 'The virtuous and noble Lord Lerchenau.' Faninal left. Marianne watched from the window. 'There they go. Francis and Anthony up behind, and Joseph cracking his new whip, and off they go, and everybody has a good look.' But Sophia was not listening. She was distraught and she felt guilty. She did not like her bridegroom. He was fat and coarse and his manners did not seem appropriate to the kind of nobility she had read about in books in bed, with a forbidden candle, in the convent. All she could do was pray. She thanked God for raising her above her class and she begged him not to allow her to be puffed up about it. But she did not feel in the least puffed up and she did not even think that thanks were in order. But that was sinful. She prayed to be allowed, in her sinfulness, to see the greatness and the sanctity of matrimony, to feel in her heart the conviction that she was entering an estate most pleasing to God. This meant that God approved of Baron Ochs, his pawing, gluttony, belching. Truly, the ways of God were very mysterious.

From without, approaching, she heard the cry, 'Rofrano! Rofrano!'

'They're all crying *Rofrano*,' cried Marianne. 'That's the name of the Count who's bringing the rose. The Rose Cavalier they call him. Can you hear? There it is – one carriage with the rose in it, and then another carriage, and a lot of servants bowing and scraping – and there he is. Awfully young he is, too. Can't be more than nineteen. Beautiful, all in silver, like the archangel Gabriel or whichever one it is that defends us in the day of battle. They're opening our front door. Get ready, child. Head up, smile, act like a lady.'

But Sophia prayed, and she did not quite know for what she was praying. The prayer did not get much farther than O God O God O God.

The footmen sprang to open the great double doors at the triple rap of the mace of the Count's Major-domo. The doors opened and a breathtaking procession filed in. Octavian, the Count Rofrano, came first, bareheaded, wigless, his hair like a flame, in white and silver, carrying in his right hand the delicate rose of silver. Then his household entire, footmen and Hungarian haiduks with their swords like scimitars, couriers in white leather with green ostrich plumes, then the more drably dressed household of Faninal. Marianne curtseyed joyfully: what a day this was. Sophia just stood, her lips parted. Octavian also just stood, his lips parted. There is always confusion and wonder and even fear in the heart when the eyes confront some new example of youth and beauty. Octavian, who had been bred at court and had as mistress the fine flower of imperial beauty and distinction, felt a kind of stage fright. He had formal words to utter and he stumbled over them. He was not used to the sight of innocence. He said stoutly:

'I am honoured, fair one, to be the ambassador of the most noble lord the Baron Lerchenau and to present to you on his behalf this token of his ever-living everlasting love and devotion, the silver rose of betrothal.' And he gave the rose to her. Sophia said, somewhat tonelessly:

'I thank your honour for his honourable condescension and am to your honour honourably, I mean eternally indebted.' So that was that. She held the rose delicately in her fingers. It was beautifully made, no doubt about it, petals hammered to a thinness most exquisite, and a scent came off it, or was that her imagination? She put it to her nostrils. 'It smells like a real rose,' she said.

'They do that,' said Octavian. 'I mean, they sprinkle a few drops of attar on it, Persian attar that is. It's what they usually do.' She gave it to him to sniff. 'Delightful, yes.' And he looked at her pert red lips and into her solemn grey eyes set wide but not too wide. Octavian did not like what was happening to him. A new door was opening, and he had not ordered the opening of the door. Innocence, that was what it was, freshness and youth and damnable, he meant blessed, innocence. He had forgotten all about innocence. As for her, she was like Miranda seeing her first man. Caliban she knew, and a father who was more prosperous than Prospero. O blessed Lord, she was going to marry Caliban. Her duenna came up and held out her hand. The ceremony was over. Sophia consigned the rose to Marianne, who put it back in its case. Now was the moment for a brief colloquy between rosegiver and rosegiven. This was, she knew, part of the procedure. Chairs were placed, the servants solemnly trooped out. The duenna signed to her mistress that the three of them should sit. They sat.

What Sophia said now was the truth. 'I know all about you,

dear *cousin*,' she said. She was to join the nobility; it was a fiction that the Austrian nobility was one great family: *cousin* was quite in order.

Octavian felt a tremor. Those innocent lips were to say something about a secret liaison that was no secret. 'What do you know, *ma cousine*?' he said, trying to smile.

'There's a book I read in the convent called *The Mirror of Austrian Nobility*. I still read it, I take it to bed with me every night. I know all about the nobility – that's only right since I have to join it. I know all about the princes and dukes and counts and barons. I know exactly how old you are – eighteen years six months three days – and I know all your baptismal names – Octavian, Maria, Ehrenreich, Bonaventura, Fernand, Hyacinth—'

'You know them better than I do.'

'And there's another thing I know—'

Oh my God here it came. 'What is it, *chère cousine*?'

'Your friends call you Mignon. Your best friends, I mean – the great beauties of the court. Mignon – that means darling or favourite or something. A kind of pet name.'

'That's right, a pet name.' But who had first used that pet name?

'Will you be coming to the wedding, cousin? It won't be long now. My fiancé was asked to wait till June, but he's very impatient.' Impatient, yes, he thought, and he drove away the ghastly image of that mound of blubber making the bed shake. Not merely obscene – truly sinful – and he, Octavian, the ambassador, was abetting that sin. But she was so innocent, she knew nothing, the nuns had taught her that marriage was a yoking of souls and they had failed to mention the yoking of bodies. She was saying something now about the sanctity of marriage and the duty of wifely submission and she was asking him . . .

'Do you think much of marriage, cousin? Or do you think yourself to be too young? Or do you want to remain a bachelor all your life? But no, you can't, can you, you have the responsibility of continuing the family line and – all the rest of it.'

She was too good, too beautiful. He was abetting the casting of this real pearl into the trough of a real . . . He found himself, to his surprise, saying the word aloud: 'Beautiful.' And then, seeing her blush, 'I beg your pardon.' But then: 'No, why should I beg pardon for speaking the truth? Your bridegroom is a lucky man.' He said it growling. She said, her eyes lowered, flames on her cheeks:

'You take liberties, sir, but I suppose a man of your rank is entitled to take liberties.' And then, with an innocence that nearly broke his heart: 'You are beautiful too. And good, I can see that. You are the nicest and most charming man I have ever met.'

'How many have you met?' he asked sadly.

'Only the Baron and his – er – friends.'

'Yes, that explains it.'

'Oh.' She rose, aflutter. The door was opening. Octavian rose; the duenna rose. Faninal, all bows, ushered in Ochs, and even gave Ochs's servants precedence over his own. There they were, the whey-blooded body-servant, the leering almoner, the village dog who was Ochs's chasseur, two others, country louts in livery that did not fit and bore the marks of napkinless meals, and a new acquisition – a dwarfish clown with a plaster on a battered snout, sadly waving a punchinello stick with bells on it. Faninal said:

'I have the honour to present to your lordship your lordship's bride.'

Baron Ochs bowed to his father-in-law elect. He went over to Sophia as though she were the wedding cake, not the bride. He said: 'Délicieuse. My compliments, sir,' as though Faninal were the chef. He kissed Sophia's hand and smacked his lips over it. 'A delicate hand. A hand of delicacy rarely found in the bourgeoisie.' He tasted it again. Octavian growled quietly.

Faninal introduced Sophia's duenna, who curtseyed low thrice. Ochs said: 'Yes yes yes,' and waved her away. Sophia moved as far away as she could from the one to whom she was condemned to be so close. Vulgar, she thought. More vulgar than ever. Like a horse dealer who's just bought a yearling colt. But Marianne, who had joined her, said, 'A real nobleman, very gracious, and very friendly with it. Your father's done well for you, dear. You should be the happiest girl alive.'

Ochs was talking to Faninal. 'This lad here,' he said, 'the one who brought the rose, he's the spitten image of a girl the Princess von Werdenberg has in her service. Charming little baggage.' He nudged Faninal and nearly made him fall. 'I may be engaged to be married, but that doesn't mean I have to wear blinkers, eh? No, I tell you this about him and this baggage just to remind you that aristocratic morality is a bit different from what you members of the bourgeoisie are used to. More free and, if you like, more generous. Seed spilt everywhere, regardless of class. You see that body-servant of mine, the long-legged one? Well, he's all royal blood. Interesting little case of dark secrets in a noble house, what? Forbidden relationships, do you understand me?' He nudged Faninal and nearly made him fall. 'You're one of us now, Faninal. Almost. Come here, Count,' he said to Octavian. 'I was just saying about aristocratic morality. I knew your father the Marquis – God, talk about wild oats—' He nudged Octavian, but Octavian did not even stagger. 'That little baggage the Princess has – but you wouldn't know, of course— Never mind, never mind.'

Sophia stood in the corner, ignored. Octavian flashed her a signal: sympathy, regret, vicarious apology, compassion, affection. His heart flashed him a danger signal of its own.

The Major-domo ushered in a pair of servants who bore a decanter and glasses (expensive but inelegant) and a tray of canapés. At the same time he ushered off the rest of the servants, including the Baron's. These limped and slouched and wiped noses on sleeves and commenced their country-bred guffaws before they were properly out of the great vulgar salon.

'Tokay, your lordship – a good vintage. I pray you, partake.'

'Well, you know what's what, I'll say that for you, Faninal.' He pinged with a horny thumbnail on one of the glasses. It rang sweet and clear. To Octavian he said, while the Tokay gurgled out, too loud, too vulgarly: 'You have to condescend a bit, you know. Friendly but not too much so. Let them know who's master. Let's have little Sophy over here.' He whistled like an ostler and laughed to show it was all in fun. 'Come, girl, come, filly.' Marianne pushed her towards the glass-clinking. 'Now, girl,' he said, his left arm fumbling for her waist, 'the time has come for you to learn what's what. There are two ways of going about things in society. There's the way of nonsense and flim-flam, *mille pardons* and by your ladyship's leave and all the rest of it, and there's the other way, the one I like – free and easy, nice and friendly, open and honest, to the devil with good manners, see what I mean?' And he tried to kiss her. She resisted. His overcharged glass spilt Tokay on the Turkey carpet. Octavian groaned in his very bowels.

But Faninal was thinking: 'What a prize, what a promotion! A real-life baron kissing my own daughter, and there's Count Rofrano, brother to the Lord High Steward – in my house, in my own drawing room! Bliss! Rapture!'

Octavian was thinking: Boor, lout. I'd like to poke under that blubber with my blade. I'd like to hear him squeak like the pig he is.

'I know what it is,' roared Ochs. 'You're shy, it's the Count here that's making you shy. Well, you'll have to learn, Sophy. The higher you go in rank the less shy you have to be. Why, I remember the time when I used to attend the Princess Whatshername in her bathroom, every morning. Steam and soap and coffee, and there she was, sponging away, not caring a fig for what your father here would call propriety. You can get away with anything. And why? It's because the aristocracy is the whatyoucall – I've forgotten the word, what's the phrase? You know it, Tavy my boy—'

'The arbiter of manners,' said Octavian icily.

And Faninal was thinking: Oh, if only these walls could change into glass and everybody see in. Seagreen with envy, the lot of them, that's what they'd be. Bliss! Rapture!

'Manners are what we make 'em. Get rid of your bourgeois airs and graces, Sophy girl. Give me a bit of a cuddle.' And he held her for a second or so. Tender young pullet. White and tender and I bet she's blushing all over. Ah, the luck of the Lerchenaus. Sophia tore herself away. Ochs waddled after her. Plucky little filly. He liked a bit of a fight. Her cheeks burning so you could warm your two thumbs on them, if she'd let you get close enough, damn her.

'Please,' pleaded Sophia. Octavian found he had crushed his Tokay glass in his hand. He let the pieces drip to the carpet. No blood, but there would be blood soon if the Baron did not . . . Marianne came running to pick up the shards. She said:

'Lovely to see them, isn't it, your grace? Like a little boy he is with his japes and tricks. Could laugh till I cry with his goings on.'

The door opened. The Major-domo came in with her highness's asthmatic attorney, accompanied by a sniffing clerk. The clerk handed to Faninal a bundle of documents. Something to do with that bend in the law that Ochs had commanded. Ochs meanwhile panted with the asthma of the chase. Sophia spoke ice and fire. She said:

'I have never in my life been so—'

'A short life, my love. Now you're starting to grow up. Come on, just one little peck.' He grabbed her. She pushed. Marianne looked on contentedly. Laugh till you cry. The ways of the aristocracy. Octavian found himself grinding his teeth, a thing he'd not done since childhood, and then only in sleep.

'Real spitfire,' panted Ochs. 'Oh well, that's the way I like 'em. Makes me feel young again. Talk about the luck of the Lerchenaus—' And then he saw her highness's attorney. He desisted from play, drew himself up, marched toward the law, or the bending of it. On his way he whispered loudly to Octavian:

'Business now. Don't be afraid to – you know, give her the odd sheep's eye, Tavy my boy. I don't mind your breaking her in. Makes it all the easier for, you know, the eventual rider.' He winked.

'If, my dear son-in-law,' said Faninal, trembling with the joy of the locution, 'you'd be good enough to withdraw into the ah withdrawing room – a little matter of legal business.'

'Certainly, hahaha father-in-law.' The door was opened. Ochs said: 'Matter of precedent, might as well get used to these things. Matter of rank. Three paces behind me, if it's not too much trouble.' And out he waddled, Faninal three steps behind, the agencies of the bending of the law going humbly after. Marianne curtseyed and curtseyed even after the door was closed.

'So, *ma cousine*,' trembled Octavian. 'That's the thing you propose to marry?'

'I don't propose. But I won't, father can put me in a nunnery if he wishes. Oh, if only she'd leave . . .' She meant her hovering duenna. 'If I could speak to you alone—'

'What would you tell me? What would you ask?'

'But it's no use. You're one of his own kind – oh, you know what I mean – I mean you aristocrats have to stick together.'

'Ah no. And besides, I don't know the lout. I never saw him before this morning. Stick together indeed—'

'You must help me, you must—'

At this moment the double doors flew open. One of Faninal's servant girls, a pretty little thing from Upper Austria, entered screaming, Lerchenau's body-servant followed in an ill-coordinated run. The clown with the plaster on his snout shambled after, his punchinello bells jangling with sad lust. The Major-domo entered, puffing, perturbed. He panted:

'They got at the wine. They're drunk, the lot of them. Come on,' to the duenna, 'help the girl, can't you?' And to Sophia and Octavian he bowed in embarrassment. He had never reckoned that this sort of thing would be part of the Major-domo's office . . .

The duenna rescued the girl, hitting out lustily. The Baron's servants they might be, but there were limits. Out, out. Octavian and Sophia were alone at last. It was most irregular.

And yet there was nothing to say. Nothing to do except take her hands and kiss them and then murmur: 'Dear Sophia, let me think. There must be something.' But, of course, there was only one thing. You protect a poor girl from her father's criminal folly, but what is the nature of the motive behind the desire to protect? You are not a substitute father. There is only one thing you can be. There was no such thing as love at first sight, but other emotions were permitted at first sight – pity, for example. Yet pity was never enough. Moreover, what false canon permitted pity for what was wholly admirable, indeed admirably holy – youth, grace, beauty? Only love gave one the right to brave fathers and legal contracts, and how could he utter the word? He was in love with a married lady, was he not? To her he owed the protection of his sword, the shedding of his own blood if need be. It dawned upon him that he was defiled, in no state of grace. He seemed to hear a heavy cathedral bell tolling the word *adulterer*. In a single tick of the ornate clock on the wall, writhing with gilt cherubim, he put himself in a state of grace. He took Sophia in his arms and he kissed her. He murmured the forbidden word that was not, after all, forbidden.

To the shock of both of them they found they were not, after all, alone.

VI

There were two great fireplaces in this salon, and both were covered with fire screens, and before the fire screens there were large vulgar vases filled with ferns and flowers of the season. From behind one fire screen Valzacchi appeared, from behind the other Annina. They were proving their worth to the nobleman they saw as a steady patron. They had entered early that morning as bearers of those flowers, an alleged gift from the Baron himself. In the crowd of servants they had soon been forgotten. They had hidden themselves in the empty chimneys. They both bore traces of soot, but not much: those chimneys had been well cleaned for the coming of summer. As they appeared Octavian and Sophia could do nothing but stare, but they did not loosen their embrace. But they broke the embrace when Valzacchi screamed:

'Baron Lerchenau, come quick, we found them at it!' And he tried to grasp the lithe Octavian, who was not willing to be grasped. Sophia began to make expiring noises. Annina had the door open and was yelling:

'Baron, your lordship, your wife-to-be is here with a gentleman, kissing and hugging. Come quick and see them doing it!' If she had had her way she would have had them thrust back into each other's arms, totally *in flagrante*.

The Baron was not long in coming in. He stood there, very calm, and he grinned at Octavian. After all, he had said something about breaking the girl in. Not too much of it, though – there were limits. Sophia came close to the protecting sword of Octavian. Octavian said:

'This lady has something to tell you.'

'I've nothing to tell him,' said Sophia. 'Whatever I said, he'd never understand.'

'Oh, you underestimate me, milady,' said Ochs genially.

'There have been certain changes in your arrangements,' Octavian said. 'That is what she wishes to tell you.'

'Well, then let her speak up.'

'This lady,' Octavian began.

'Dumb, is she? Or she's briefing you as her attorney, is that it?'

'This lady—' And Octavian looked to Sophia to say the word. But she said:

'I can't. You speak for me.'

'Yes, Mr Attorney?' grinned Ochs.

'This lady,' Octavian said firmly, 'refuses to fulfil an unacceptable contract. There will be no marriage.'

'Really?' said Ochs with large assumed interest. And then, with ferocity: 'Come on, milady, as the world will soon be calling you, since contracts have been mentioned, you may as well come and sign now. Everything else of a legal nature has been very satisfactorily resolved. So let's close the matter, milady.'

'No,' cried Sophia, hiding behind Octavian.

'Yes!' and he roughly tugged at her arm.

'You,' said Octavian, 'are an ill-mannered buffoon, a cheat, a dowry-hunter, a boor, a bore, a scoundrel, a lecher. Leave this lady and leave this house, or you'll feel the sharp end of my sword.'

'Orders, eh? Your house, is it? We'll see what the master of the house says about that. As for your offer of violence, you effeminate puppy—' He put two fingers in his mouth and whistled, as for a pack of dogs. The pack of dogs appeared promptly enough, and they all looked drunk. While they were shambling in Ochs said: 'You Viennese boys had better start learning where the true authority lies. The backbone of this country is the country barony. Her grace the Archduchess knows that if you don't, whippersnapper. Lay your fingers on me and you'll soon know all about it. Now get away from my affianced bride and out of my presence. One more whistle from me and you'll learn something else – what it's like to have your beauty spoiled by a couple of broken teeth. Now get out.' And he reached out a paw for Sophia. Octavian drew. He cried:

'Come on, let's have you, you lout. Draw!' Sophia cried on God and heaven.

The Baron stepped back. 'Showing a sword in a lady's presence?' he said feebly. 'Are you mad?'

61

'Yes,' said Octavian, and he lunged. Ochs drew too late. Octavian pinked him in the upper right arm. The sword's point ran deep enough under the fat to draw blood. The Baron yelled murder and dropped his sword. The rabble of servants growled and lurched toward their master's assailant. Octavian sent his sword whizzing among them. They growled their way to a wall, huddling. Ochs's almoner, assisted by Valzacchi and Annina, helped his lordship into a chair. His lordship cried:

'Look at the blood! Fetch a doctor! I'm dying! Put him under arrest! Call the police!'

His servants mumbled dirty words but kept their distance from that sword. The whole Faninal household streamed in, from Major-domo to third under-gardener. Valzacchi and Annina ripped the Baron's coat off. A thin trickle of dark red blood showed that a vein had been pierced. The Baron screamed that he was dying. One of Ochs's men made a drunken grab at the maid from Upper Austria. A free-for-all, all said and done. The maid hit back. The maid's sweetheart, the house carpenter and clockman, hit out. There was a lot of hitting out, but not at Octavian. The Baron groaned. Octavian put an arm round Sophia and said 'Dearest one.' And then Faninal walked in. Ochs was quick with his complaints.

'All these damned servants of yours, Faninal, and not one can fetch a surgeon or a basin or a bandage. Oh, the sight of blood – it makes me ill when it's my own.' The duenna wrung her hands and wept. 'Don't stand there whining,' yelled Ochs. 'Do something. Your mistress there is going to be married to a corpse if you don't – oh, the agony, look at the blood!'

Annina got in quickly with an explanation to Faninal: 'That gentleman there with the sword out, no, he's putting it in now, he was kissing and hugging your daughter here. We were watching, following his lordship's *istruzioni*. That *spiega tutto*.'

'Oh,' cried Faninal in terrible distress, 'oh, my dear son-in-law, to think such a thing should happen under my roof. You lot there, yes, you' – he meant his entire household – 'to horse, ride my thoroughbreds to death till you find a doctor. Wait,' he added. 'Let this be a lesson to all of you. Easy wages, eh? Easy pickings? No sense of responsibility. I feed the lot of you on the fat of the land, capons and cream, by God, and this is what happens. Go on, out, what are you waiting for?' Then he turned to Octavian. This was difficult: deference tugging at fury. 'You sir. I should have thought that a gentleman of your rank and breeding—'

'I beg forgiveness, sir,' said Octavian quietly. 'I cannot express my regret with sufficient humility or grief. But, believe me, it had to be. What was done was not done wantonly or frivolously. At a later time I would be glad to explain—'

'He acted like a gentleman of honour, father,' put in Sophia. 'And that man over there did not. He treated me like, like—'

'You are speaking of my future son-in-law?' said her father. 'You have the effrontery to suggest that my future son-in-law—'

'If you wish him to be your son-in-law,' said Sophia with unwonted boldness, 'then you must find another daughter.'

The father could not, of course, believe his somewhat hairy ears. He spluttered. Sophia said:

'Naturally, I must humbly beg your pardon.'

A doctor was brought in. He lived across the way. He had heard screams. He had no very large practice. He examined the patient. Faninal cried: 'She begs my pardon. She stands under the protective arm of this . . . this schoolboy here, if he will permit the expression.' In a burst of agony he howled: 'Ruined!' Meaning the scandal of his daughter's refusal to ennoble his house, the noble bridegroom dying for all he knew, the sneers and laughs of his bourgeois circle, the juicy story that would already be spreading about the neighbourhood. 'By God,' he cried, 'you will do as I say.' And to Octavian, 'You will leave instanter, sir. In all dutiful humility and deference to your rank. I order you never to darken—' He saw the melodramatic absurdity of the expression, he was no fool, he let it hang in the air uncompleted.

Octavian looked for his hat. It had been in the charge of one of his own servants, but he had previously arranged for those servants to go home after depositing him here, since it had been his intention to visit his mistress the Princess immediately after the brief ceremony he had envisaged. The ceremony had expanded itself into a brawl, and, almost casually, the whole world had changed. He would not now visit the Princess. He would write her a letter. A maidservant brought his hat, curtsey-ing. Profoundly cynical obeisances were exchanged between him-self and Faninal. The door was opened for him. But he could not go yet. His beloved was in distress. There was a distressing exchange going on between her and her father.

'I won't marry him! I'll die first!'

'You'll stay in your room till you learn right obedience and good behaviour.'

'I'll lock myself in. I'll starve to death rather than—'

'You'll be dragged out, miss, and be forced to do as I say.'

'I'll kill myself.'

'You'll do no such thing. You'll marry his lordship if I have to drag you to the altar myself.'

'You can't make me say yes. I'll say no no no no—'

'Take your choice – marriage or a nunnery. Locked up in a cell, penitence and bread and water for the rest of your days.'

At the sound of the word *water* the Baron cried: 'I'm dying of thirst. It's all the blood that I've lost.' The doctor indicated that the bleeding had stopped, the patient would live.

'My dear son-in-law, such a relief.' Faninal embraced him. The Baron howled with the pain of it: Faninal's fingers had gone straight to the throbbing wound. 'A convent, you hear?' Faninal thundered at Sophia. Octavian whispered words like: beloved, dearest, have no fear. Leave everything to me. He felt a plan stirring.

'What will you drink, dear son-in-law? Wine? Beer? Hippocras with ginger in it?'

'Wine, wine, gallons of it. I die of desiccation.'

Faninal clapped his hands as though applauding. Servants rushed to fetch wine. Octavian gave Sophia one last squeeze of the hand. Valzacchi and Annina hovered round their patron, not too sure now of his patronage. Things had not come quite as expected. Ochs glared at them. 'Made a delightful mess of things, haven't you? Out of my sight.'

'*Signore mio—*'

'*Non era la nostra colpa—*'

Octavian left. Valzacchi and Annina watched him leave, watched his discreet kissing of the fingertips toward Sophia as he left. They looked at each other. Transference of allegiance? If the young lord could be brought to understand that it was a mere trade, no hard feelings – Octavian had left.

Outside the salon Octavian saw the attorney and his assistant waiting. They were impassive. They had heard enough cries of agony in their time. Octavian approached them. He begged a sheet of paper and a pen.

'There is this small writing-room here, your lordship. A desk, ink, see – a newly sharpened quill . . .'

'For the signing of the marriage contract, I presume?'

'For that.'

Octavian wrote. Valzacchi and Annina hovered at the door of the little writing-room. 'Your esteemed lordship,' whined Valzacchi, 'I trust you will not hold it against us that we were merely practising our profession. We regret, both of us, that we chose the wrong – er – patron. We are not lacking in a sense of morality. After all, we are both Florentines. We are, if I may be permitted so to presume, always on the side of true love.' Annina nodded. Valzacchi had spoken in his native tongue. He took it for granted that his young lordship would understand. Octavian understood very well. He took some thalers from his purse. He explained very briefly what he wished them to do.

VII

Ochs lay on a sofa with a pint of wine in his fist. He was alone. He had requested solitude. He proposed to doze a little, quieten the beating of his heart. The bloodletting had, in fact, done him more good than harm. His wound had been bandaged and his arm rested in a silken sling. He'd got the better of the young puppy after all. Tail between his legs. A willing or an unwilling bride – where was the difference? Marriage was essentially a financial arrangement. Still, he anticipated with pleasure the struggles of the wedding night. In an hour or so he would eat something – something that combined daintiness with bulkiness. This Faninal, father-in-law hahaha, kept a good table.

He sniffed the scent of a woman. That Italian bitch was there behind his reposing head. 'We regret so much,' she said, 'my uncle and I. One last opportunity to show our worth. This we beg.'

'Out, out.'

'You remember you asked us to perform a particular service. It is to do with a young lady.'

'Lady?'

'I have here a note, see. Scented.'

'Give it me.' He was very alert now. He handed her his wine mug and tried to open the letter with his free hand. 'Damn. Need my spectacles. Read it out.'

'But perhaps it is very intimate, your lordship.'

'Read it out.'

'It says: "Most honourable sir. Tomorrow evening I am free of my duties to her highness—" '

'Her! She! What's her name now?'

' "—you were so gracious to find me pleasing to your lordship. But I was not able to respond because her highness kept looking at us. I am only young, you see, and not used to the ways of the great world. If your lordship would care to arrange what he suggested – *tête-à-tête* is, I think, the word you used – I should be pleased and honoured to accept. Pray grant me the pleasure of a note in your lordship's own hand and send it to me through the kind Italian lady who brings you this. Your devoted Mariandel." '

'Mariandel – that was the name. Remember her all right, sweet little baggage – couldn't recall her name. Well, well, talk about the luck of the Lerchenaus—'

'She wants a reply, your lordship.'

'I know she wants a reply. Can you write?'

'Of course, your lordship. Has your lordship forgiven us?'

'I'll think about it. Get pen, ink, paper. Quick, now.' As she hastened off, shaking a fist at him that he did not see, he picked up his wine mug, grinned, then drank to the luck of the Lerchenaus.

VIII

All was ready. Octavian's transvestite disguise was not, as before, a mere improvisation. He had taken trouble with it. He had procured a fine blond wig, had shaved with extra care, had made up his face with paint, powder, and eyeblack, and was clad in a demure evening gown of salmon-pink. Beneath the disguise, however, he was garbed like a man, even to the riding boots, though he had removed the spurs. When he entered the private room of the White Horse Inn, neither Valzacchi nor Annina recognised him – not, that was, till he lifted his skirt to get at his pocket. From the pocket he drew a purse, and this he threw with grace at Valzacchi. Valzacchi, past master at purse-catching, caught it deftly. Valzacchi and Annina ran to him and kissed his hands. 'Everything ready?' asked Octavian.

Yes, everything ready. Annina herself was in a kind of disguise. She was dressed in mourning, her eyes were outlined with kohl, she wore a veil. Valzacchi was as he usually was – discreetly dapper. He pointed out to Octavian the recess with the curtain before it that hid a bed. The trapdoor, see. The men? The . . . ? All was ready. Mariandel's duenna? The thing must be done properly. A decent old lady entered at Valzacchi's summons. A church clock struck the half-hour. Was that hoofs they heard, the rolling of the wheels of a coach? Valzacchi clapped his hands. They all left, except for Valzacchi.

When Ochs came in, arm still in its sling, he had Octavian with him. He beamed satisfaction. Valzacchi, who had opened the door, bowed and bowed. The landlord appeared, rubbing his hands dryly together. Waiters hovered. 'Is this as your lordship wishes?' asked the landlord. 'More candles? Or perhaps your lordship would prefer a more commodious apartment?'

'This will do,' Ochs said graciously. 'Too much light, though. This isn't a court ball. A little intimacy.' Candles were hastily snuffed. 'Where's that music coming from?'

'Oh, the musicians regularly play in the next room,' said the landlord. 'If your lordship would prefer that they come in here and provide whatever programme your lordship deigns to request . . .'

'I see, and pay for the privilege? No, let them stay where they are. What's that up there?' He pointed to a window.

'A window, your lordship.'

'I know it's a damned window, idiot. I don't want any fool looking in when I'm . . . eating. It puts me off my food. Privacy is what I'm paying for.'

'That's what they call a blind window, your lordship. It looks out on to a wall. May supper now be served?' The waiters stood to a kind of attention.

'What do those grinning apes there intend to do?'

'To wait on your lordship.'

'I don't want them. Shoo, shoo, off. Where's my man? Ah, there he is.' The whey-blooded spindly body-servant had stalked up to him. 'He'll do all the serving necessary. And you can leave it to me to pour the wine. All right, let's have the privacy I'm paying for. Sit down, my dear.' Valzacchi was the last to leave. 'See here, you,' Ochs said, 'do your best to keep the bill low. You know these places, they charge the earth if they can get away with it. I'll make it worth your while.' Valzacchi bowed and bowed and went out.

'Better, eh?' leered Ochs. 'Just you and me, sweetheart. A little of this wine, eh?' He started to pour.

Octavian adjusted his vocal cords. 'I don't drink,' he trilled.

'Oh, come now. Wine of the country, blood of the earth. It will put ink in your pen.' Got that wrong; it was himself he meant. He sat next to her and ventured a cuddle.

'Oh, sir,' cried Octavian.

'No, not sir. No ceremony. Forget that I'm aristocracy and you're only what you are. A man and a maid sitting down to a cosy supper – that's all we are. How about a kiss?' Octavian coquettishly turned his head away. With a great horny paw Ochs grasped Octavian's chin and jerked the sweet little face round to the kissing position. Then he saw not a sweet little face but the face of the dastardly young swine who had dared to . . . oh no. 'Haunts me,' he growled. 'Keep on seeing him – the vicious blackguardly young dog—'

At that moment the trapdoor by the table jerked open and the head of a man peered up. Octavian saw. Ochs was trying to kiss his ear and did not see. 'Not yet!' mouthed Octavian. Ochs now

68

thought he saw the face of a man down there on the floor. Then he saw that he did not see. Or did he?

'Did you,' he said somewhat tremulously, 'see something?'

'Something?'

'A man?'

'Is your honour feeling all right?'

Ochs filled himself more wine. 'Lost blood,' he said. 'Affects the brain.'

'What did your lordship say?'

'Never mind.' The door opened and let in a gush of music so loud it made Ochs gush sweat. 'Shut that blasted—' It was the body-servant serving soup. 'All right. Now get out. OUT. Better.'

'Your lordship is very fidgety. Does your honour feel not too well perhaps? Perhaps I had better go home. Some other evening perhaps?'

'No no no no no!' He took off his wig as though preparing for bed. He loosened his collar. 'Warm, that's all. A bit close in here.' And then he saw . . .

There was a face at the window the innkeeper had called blind. Blind or not, a couple of sad dark eyes looked at him from it. And then the upper half of somebody, some woman or other, filled the window, its arms stretched into the room. The figure was in mourning. A sepulchral voice filled the room:

'My husband! That's my long-lost husband!'

Ochs's dithering hand upset his soup plate. Soup all over his sleeve, he tremoloed: 'Who was that? Did you see that?'

'See what, your lordship?'

The window was blind again. 'Nothing, nothing. I lost blood, you know. See this sling on my arm? Attacked by a ruffian!'

'Blood, your honour?'

'Affects the—'

And then the door was flung open. Valzacchi, the innkeeper and three waiters were trying to hold somebody back. A woman, in deep mourning, the same one . . .

'I am his wife, I tell you. This is my long-lost husband. I swear before Almighty God. I demand justice. Restore him to my suffering arms—'

'Is this a madhouse?' wavered Ochs. He needed more light. Why was there not more light? Of course, it was he himself who had demanded the intimacy of darkness.. He put a soup-dripping hand to his brow. He waddled toward the group to see if it was really there. The woman cried his name:

'Leopold Anton of Lerchenau! Why did you desert me?'

'I know you,' said Ochs, peering. 'Seen you before. God, does everybody have a double?' He blinked at Octavian-Mariandel.

'Of course you know me! Your discarded wife! God is just, Leopold! He looks down on you now!'

At that moment four children came running in yelling: 'Papa!'

A bit too soon, Annina was thinking. She forgot her lines. Then she remembered them:

'Do you not see the fruits of our love? Your children and mine, Leopold!'

The children, their ages graduated from a lisping four to a yelling eleven, clutched at him, crying: 'Papa!' Ochs hit out at them with a napkin. Octavian whispered to Valzacchi:

'Did the messenger go to Faninal's house?'

'He'll be here, fear not.'

'Get all this lot out of here,' cried Ochs to the landlord.

'I don't have that kind of authority, your lordship. I have no right to interfere in family matters.'

'Family matters! Never saw them before in my life, never touched that hag there even with my walking-stick. These brats are not mine.'

'So your lordship says.'

'All right,' said Ochs. 'I'll have the police in. Get the police.'

'Is that wise, your lordship? A matter of desertion. Very heavy penalties —'

Ochs strode shakily over to the door. He noticed an open window near it. Not seen that before, who opened it? It gave on to the street. He bawled out to the street:

'Police! Fetch the police! A nobleman is being assaulted! A member of the aristocracy is in great danger!'

The cry of 'Police!' was being taken up out there. Good. A little entertainment. We villagers lead a dull life. 'Poliiiiice!'

Ochs ought to have been surprised by the prompt entry of a police inspector and a couple of constables. The inspector looked like a man who, like Ochs, had been interrupted at supper. He was buttoning his tunic as he frowned at everybody but particularly at Ochs.

'What's all this, then?'

'Ah,' said Ochs. 'Get this rabble out, will you, sergeant?' If a man of quality can't take his supper in peace—'

'The rank is Inspector,' the inspector said. 'Is this your house? No, evidently not. So you keep out of it. Now, who's lodging the complaint?'

'Well,' said the innkeeper, 'I'm the innkeeper here. There's been a bit of trouble, inspector. His lordship, that one over there—' And he jerked his shoulder at Ochs, who was looking for his wig.

'That fat man without a wig, yes. Calls himself a lord, does he? That's bad.'

'Look here,' Ochs spluttered. 'I'm not used to this sort of treatment—'

'No, sir? Well, there's time to learn. Who do you say you are?'

'SAY I am? Damn it, man I AM the Baron Lerchenau—'

'Can you prove it?'

'Prove it? PROVE IT?'

'Yes. Any witnesses?' The inspector sat down at the table. His two constables took up their positions behind him.

'Witnesses? I NEED WITNESSES?' And he looked around blazing for witnesses. 'You,' he said to Valzacchi, 'you know who I am, damn your eyes. Tell this policeman here.'

'*Non lo so*,' shrugged Valzacchi. 'He may be who he says he is, and he may not be. I know nothing about him.'

'You lying Italian scoundrel, you filthy foreign scum, tell the sergeant here—'

'Inspector. And keep a civil tongue in your head, sir. Hm. Things are beginning to look pretty bad, I'd say—'

Octavian let out a loud falsetto wail. 'Oh, I'm ruined – oh, my reputation—'

'And who's she, then?' the inspector asked.

'She? She – why, she's someone under my – er – personal protection. A kind of . . . a sort of . . .'

'Protection, eh? Looks to me as if you're the one in need of protection. Who is she? Come on, speak.'

'She, she,' spluttered Ochs, 'is young Mistress Faninal, Sophia

71

Anna Barbara, that is, daughter to – damn it all, you'll be hearing from me about this, Inspector as you call yourself— I'm not accustomed to this insolent interrogation. Her father's Faninal – he's well known around here—'

The room was crammed now like a court of law. The man who now entered had to push his way through. 'Yes, tolerably well known,' said Faninal. 'You sent for me, I gather. Why?' He sniffed: a strange sort of place for a man of Ochs's rank to be in. A common alehouse, he'd call it. 'I was in bed when your message came. Urgent I was told. Well, would you be good enough to—'

Ochs forgot for a moment that here was not only a prospective father-in-law but a man who admired, deferred, would help. He interrupted him coarsely. 'Who the hell told you to shove your interfering snout into my affairs?'

'Come,' Faninal said severely. 'Your messenger comes battering on my door, shouting about your being in grave danger – I see now what kind of danger. But, of course, we members of the merchant class are not, as you are, ABOVE THE LAW . . .'

'One moment,' the inspector said. 'I demand to know what all this is about. This is a friend of yours, is it?'

'I hardly know him,' Ochs said, still looking for his wig. 'Just seen him around, that's all.'

'Your name, sir?'

'Friedrich von Faninal. My address—'

'Never mind, sir. And you know this man?'

'Yes, my son-in-law – in a prospective sense, that is.'

'And this young lady is your daughter?'

Faninal squinted at Octavian. 'No, this is not my daughter.'

'This – er – gentleman here says she is.'

'I see. Well, as my daughter is waiting outside in a sedan chair, this problem of identity can soon be resolved. You sir,' he frowned at Ochs. 'I see now what you mean by the special morality reserved to the upper classes. You'll hear more of this.'

'Where's my damned wig? You, landlord, find the damned thing. For God's sake; to qualify as your son-in-law a man has to be a blasted eunuch. My wig, damn it.' He pushed the four children aside in his search for it. Automatically they started their 'Papa! Papa!' chorus.

72

Faninal recoiled in horror. 'Whose – are – these – chil – dren?'

'Nobody's. That woman there who says she's my wife, she's a damned liar. Never set eyes on her before now.'

'Oh, Leopold, how could you?' And Annina wept.

Sophia entered, hatted and cloaked. Ochs's first thought was of his unwigged bald pate. He found his feathered hat and shoved it on. Hatting himself on the appearance of a lady.

'I heard all this noise, Father – oh, Father . . .'

For Faninal, whose doctors had not lied to the inquiring Baron, was near to collapse. A chair, brandy – Ochs had found his wig. He doffed hat, donned it, felt slightly more in control of the . . . He said, jauntily:

'Well, so much for all that. I've eaten nothing so I pay nothing. Oh, the wine, yes—' He prepared to throw some small coin at the landlord. 'You,' he said to Octavian. 'Come with me, girl. We'll find somewhere select, really private. Damned madhouse.'

But Octavian ignored him and went over to the recess where the bed stood. Ochs watched with his mouth open as he closed the curtain. His mouth opened wider as he saw lady's clothes – gown, petticoat, false bosom – thrown through and onto the floor. The landlord rushed in to cry:

'Ladies and gentlemen – her highness the Princess of Werdenberg!'

And, to the surprise of everyone, the Princess's retinue filed in. Then the lady herself, a vision of beauty, formally dressed, with train. This last the little black boy, bells ajangle, carried. Ochs showed not only surprise but pleasure. He waddled toward her, bowing and bowing.

'Your highness – cousin – this is truly overwhelming. How did you . . . who told you?'

'This servant of the royal blood, as you call him—' She nodded toward the spindly whey-faced smirking scion of princely irregularities.

'This, your highness, cousin, is a token of true friendship. Now you can put this minion of the law in his place. For the Austrian aristocracy to have to submit to – well . . .'

But the inspector was at attention and saluting.

'Your highness, I am an officer of the commissariat for the district of—'

'I think,' said the Princess, 'we know each other.'

'Indeed, your highness. I had the privilege of serving as orderly to his highness the Field Marshal.' Octavian put his head through the curtain of the recess. Ochs saw the head and waved it away. Faninal had recovered from his faintness. He said:

'If your highness will permit . . .' He stood, bowed, tottered. 'A little unwell – if you, dear child . . .' And Sophia helped him out of the room. Who, wondered the Princess, was that almost excessively pretty girl? Then she knew. She showed no surprise though she felt it when Octavian, no longer Mariandel, came out from the curtained recess. He greeted her with a somewhat timid smile. A lot of explaining to do. Sophia came back. She curtseyed to the Princess. Then she addressed Ochs:

'My father is not well enough to tell you himself, but he charged me with the task of ordering you to keep away from our house. Keep away, he said. You will be hearing from him.' And she prepared to leave again.

'CORPO DI BACCO!' The Italian expletive was proper for the princessly presence and his own abated assertiveness. 'You, miss, you will not speak to me in that manner, do you hear?'

'Less than you deserve,' said Sophia. She left with dignity.

'And that young lady?' said the Princess to Octavian.

'The lady for whom I was made Cavalier of the Rose.'

'That I know now, idiot. I see your hand in all this. Well, not only yours. Didn't I tell you that – sooner than you expected . . .'

'I wrote you a letter. I wrote it many times. I couldn't find the right words.'

'Now then,' said Ochs, puffing toward Octavian. 'We've had enough nonsense for one evening. Put your proper clothes on . . .' And then: 'Oh. Yes. Your highness – I was trying to persuade Mariandel here to join . . . Yes, of course – that's all over. What I mean is . . .' He looked at Octavian more closely. 'By the living God, it's you – you young – it's you. Draw!' But he was not carrying his sword, and his sword arm was in a sling.

'WITHDRAW is the word,' said the Princess. 'Leave while you still have some dignity left.'

'Somebody has to suffer,' grumbled the Baron. 'It strikes me that there's been a sort of conspiracy going on.'

'The luck of the Lerchenaus,' suggested Octavian. He clicked his fingers. Annina took off her mourning veil. She said to the children:

'Say goodbye to your father.'

'Papa! Papa! Papa!'

Ochs hit at them with his hat. The innkeeper came in with a bill. Candles, food ordered though uneaten, hire of coach – it was a long one.

'The luck of the Lerchenaus,' said the Baron bitterly.

IX

Sophia saw her father, somewhat better, brandy and smelling salts had restored him, go off alone in his coach. The sedan chair she would no longer need. Her duenna, to whom it would have done good to be stripped of her illusions about the aristocracy, she instructed to wait. She would go back to that room alone. She knew that Octavian would be there.

But she had expected to find him there alone. She stood outside the door and listened. Another woman. The Princess.

'Now that the mob has departed,' the Princess was saying, 'at least grant us a little real privacy. Close the door.'

And it was coming to close the door that Octavian found his new beloved in the shadows. 'Sophia,' he said, more sternly than lovingly, 'you'd better come in.'

'She said she wanted to be private with you.'

'Come in.' And he led her in by the hand. She was shy, confused. 'You have not been formally presented to her highness,' he said. 'May I, your highness, beg leave to present—'

'I know. You're very pretty, my dear, and very young. And I congratulate you on your escape. Straight from the convent into the arms of – I know all about it, my dear. Not all girls are so lucky.'

'I owe my escape to, to . . .'

'To Mignon, yes. And now Mignon shall leave us for a little while. Go on, drink some wine with the roisterers in the trap-room, Count Octavian. Return in ten minutes.'

'But, your highness—'

'Fifteen minutes.'

Octavian left rather sulkily. At the door he turned back to give Sophia a glance fraught with various meanings – love, warning, dubiety, chiefly warning. The Princess was a strong-minded and clever woman. Sophia kept her face blank, but there was a little fear in it. The Princess saw the fear.

'Perhaps,' Sophia faltered, 'I ought to go and see how my father is.'

'Your father will be well enough. I know your father.'

'You know him?'

'My husband the Prince is a Field-Marshal. Your father has lately specialised in victualling the army. Your father is a man who knows his business. A feigned heart attack is a useful device of commerce.'

'Oh, but that's not true, that's not fair.'

'Soon, when we've had our talk, I'll fetch him back here. The night's business may as well end where it seems to have started. His heart will seem sound enough when he hears the news.'

'What news?'

The Princess heard the hope in her voice. 'Tell me, child, how long did it take you to fall in love with Mignon?'

'I see. It's you who christened him Mignon.'

'Yes. Darling of the court. Everybody's favourite. The name seemed appropriate. How long had you known him before you decided you were in love?'

She kept her head down. 'It was he who said it first. But when he said it – well, I knew . . .'

'My dear, Octavian's very young. This darling of the court has been more loved than loving. Don't think you've fallen in love with – well, a precocious libertine. You're better matched than you think. And he's more innocent than he believes.'

'You,' gulped Sophia, 'you're one of the ones who love him?'

'How could I fail? Youth is a fine thing. I grow old, child. There was a time when I thought I'd recover my youth by tasting his. A common illusion. In his presence I feel my age.'

'Then you don't – he doesn't—'

'Love me? Oh, he admires me, of course—' Sophia smiled a little at the *of course*: who could fail? 'But I'm a married woman, with duties, responsibilities – and a husband who, when he's not at war, is hunting inedible animals. I'm also a lady of rank and influence. I think it will take me about five minutes to persuade your father to give his blessing. I'll go now. I know the house. It belonged to the impoverished Duke of Sauerstadt. Have you a servant outside?'

'A duenna, as they call them —'

'She won't be happy at what's going to take place now. A boy and a girl alone together, and not even betrothed. Very well, come in, Octavian.' For she knew Octavian was waiting outside the door: she could almost hear his agitated breathing. So Octavian came in, and she left, saying: 'Be discreet. Soon you'll be free of the need for discretion. But not too soon. Things have been happening rather quickly.'

Sophia and Octavian stood a yard or so from each other. Octavian gulped. 'What did she tell you?'

'That once she thought she was in love with you, but then she decided she had better not be in love with you. She said also that I'm in love with you.'

'She knows everything. She's never wrong. Angel!'

'Did you call her angel?'

'Never!' He would be at confession first thing in the morning. He would cleanse his soul. 'You're my one angel, for ever and ever.'

But, being a woman, even if only fifteen, she knew better. That lady had taken something from him, and so she would never have him all. But what she had she loved. 'And you,' she said, 'are my . . .' She knew nothing of the language of love: she lacked his education. 'I love you,' she said.

'Angel!' And then they were in each other's arms.

They were not in each other's arms twenty minutes later. They sat at the table, hands clasped, talking eagerly about their future together: it was all roses and excluded the War of the Austrian Succession. They did not notice her father and his former love come in. They did not come in very far. It was enough for her father to see them. Enough for the Princess. But they stood, quickly, clumsily, bowed one, curtseyed the other.

'It's late,' her father said. 'The Princess's coach is outside. I'll be waiting there.'

The lovers kissed. And then, knowing how many tomorrows they had, they were willing to part. Dreams are part of young love, and dreams are best dreamed alone. They ran out together. Sophia dropped her handkerchief, a spotted one. In love as she was, she still had the makings of a thrifty housekeeper. Or so it seemed, for the Princess's own little black boy, Mahomed, came into the room, looking for it. He found it and ran out with a jubilant tinkling of his little bells.

In time, when he grew up, Mahomed left the old Princess's service and joined a troupe of actors. He specialised in the part of Othello, to whom the finding of a spotted handkerchief spells disaster not jubilation. Octavian lost a leg and an eye in the War of the Austrian Succession. Sophia died bearing her second child. The widowed Princess entered a nunnery. Baron Ochs married the richest heiress of all Austria and died at ninety-one in his bed. Or, if you wish, none of these things happened. The nature of a story is that it has no future in it. And there is no past in it either; we leave the past to history. So the young lovers are always young and live in eternal present. Mahomed's bells will always be jingling. You can tell the story again, and it will be the same as before.

'It would,' Sophia's father sometimes said, 'have made rather a good comic opera.'

·—1889 AND THE DEVIL'S MODE—·

Claude's ears buzzed. Buzzed with bonang and gambang, saron and gender, ketipung and kenong. A little Dutchman with the jaundiced skin and colonial egg of one long resident in the tropics had given him the names, even written them down on the back of an old envelope. Gong chimes, xylophone, metallophones, drums, inverted gongs. And then there were the three pesinden or girl singers and the gerong or male chorus howling away in the pentatonic scale: la do re fa sol. So, then, he had heard the Javanese gamelan. The black *touches* of the piano, putting the scale up a semitone. The white *touches* ignored, two especially, the si and fa that sounded the augmented fourth forbidden in the music of the Church. But that augmented fourth had been tamed into components of the dominant seventh. The great exhibition of 1889 proclaimed certain certainties of the future. What could be more certain, more sure of itself, than the final perfect cadence of Western music? Dominant seventh to tonic. Loud applause. Grinning Haydn, smirking Mozart. The damned banalities he, Claude, hammered out nightly at the *Chat Noir*. And yet that had to be all over. The voices of the Javanese brownskins said so. Claude said:

'You couldn't do it in music.' As he raised his eyes to the summit the smoke of the end of his caporal, already burning his lips, got into them. He lighted a fresh one from its spunk and coughed kashl kashl. He had picked up the habit of the heavy inhaling of rough tobacco in St Petersburg. He crumpled the empty packet and dropped it to join a great deal of crumpled rubbish: greasy wrappings of fried potatoes, cigar-butts, the twirled papers of caramels, bits of *Le Monde*. The crowd round the Eiffel Tower behaved as if no member of it had seen it growing. 'When the barriers are opened,' de Vogue had just written in *La Revue des Deux Mondes*, 'when the crowd can touch the monster, see it from all its angles, stroll about its limbs, even climb its flanks, the last resistance of its detractors will fade, even among the most recalcitrant.' Pompous, an academician. And who had written: '*Bergère ô tour Eiffel le troupeau des ponts bêle ce matin*'? It was the citizens who were the sheep, not the bridges. 'You could do it in notes, but notes aren't necessarily music. That isn't art, and it doesn't deserve art. Engineering, no more.' And yet and yet. It was the future, wasn't it? Austere, asserting the bones of its technique. No baroque, no rococo. No grinning Haydn or simpering Mozart. Bach was a different matter.

Gabrielle Dupont, twenty-two to his twenty-six, a mere child but with no infantine body, twirled her furled parasol and smiled faintly as an elderly man with a grey beard expressed admiration by wrinkling his eyes, beardily leering, fingering his moustache. She smiled more definitely and he tipped his top hat. 'Do you know that old ram?' Claude asked jealously.

'Do I have to know him?' Then she began to hum *Mon coeur s'ouvre à ta voix*. She liked *Samson et Dalila*, to which Claude had taken her, though they had had to sit in the cheaper seats. Claude, softened by the aria, sang in a baritone made harsh by harsh tobacco:

'*Ah! réponds à ma tendresse.*' Then he said: 'There's a tritone there, right for the *esse*. But you can't get away from that damned dominant seventh.'

'What's a tritone?'

'An augmented fourth.'

'What's a – whatever it is?' The crowd was all Manet, Dégas, Monet, Renoir. Did the human form and its coverings only come to life when converted into paint? Could any of those express the great skeletal tower in points of colour, the thing seen as it were with dewdrops on the eyelashes? No, it was mathematics. They would have to get their rulers out. 'Well,' he said, 'you have to know what a fourth is before you start augmenting it. Take the opening of the *Marseillaise*, which we've been hearing a little too much of lately. You climb from the *Allons en-* to the *fants*, and that's a fourth. And you climb again from the *la pa-* to the *trie*, and that's another fourth. An interesting succession of fourths, too good for a national anthem. You could imagine a symphonic poem starting with the phrase, deep down in the bass. A kind of awakening theme. Dawn over Paris. Dawn over the sea.' Gabrielle yawned, showing teeth as clean as a dog's. 'It bores you when I talk about music, doesn't it?'

'Music's for hearing.'

'Somebody has to compose it first. It doesn't grow on trees.'

'But it does. Birds, I mean.'

'That isn't music.'

They walked across the Champ de Mars, the tower behind them, she placing one delicate foot before the other as though treading a chalked line. She wore summer muslin of off-white sprigged with green and a wide round hat with scant feathers. Claude was in his heavy winter serge, sweating. She looked up at him with speckled hazel eyes widely set, saying: 'I got you some money.'

'God bless you, cabbage, I didn't like to ask. How much?'

'Enough to get you over there and back. And a night in a cheap hotel. But I thought those Italians might have been a bit more helpful.'

'They're not Italians, despite the name. At least they call themselves English. She's a poet and very poor. The brother writes prose but makes nothing out of it. A performance of the work in London – It's called the Philharmonic Society or something.'

'They don't want it for your benefit.'

'Perhaps not. But there'd be no music without those words.'

'And in English. They'll have you twisting the music about, you'll see. So that it fits the English.'

'It was written in English. Where did you get the money from?'

'That man. The old one you called the ram. Monsieur Cassou. He's paying court to my mother.'

'I see. One way of netting the daughter. Rich, is he?'

'He owns that cheese emporium on the rue Badouin. I'd rather meet him in the open air than in our drawing-room. Anyway, he's fond of music. He loves Mozart.'

'Tonic and dominant. We have to cleanse ourselves of that. It's gone on too long.' And then, fiercely: 'Why did he give you the money?'

'He didn't give it to me. I poured him some wine at dinner and spilled half of it over his sleeve. Then I took the coat away to sponge it. There was plenty of money in his inside pocket. He won't miss it, I'm sure.'

'You're a blessed damozel.'

'*La damoiselle élue*. Am I really that?'

Claude kissed her full on the lips in the crowded street. This was, after all, Paris. Robert Godet, crossing the street towards them, delicately avoiding horse-merds smoking in the sun, smiled in sympathy and doffed his straw hat. He was a Swiss without Swiss puritanism. 'Mademoiselle,' he greeted. '*Cher maître*.'

'Not yet.' Claude frowned minimally. At the moment of the engagement of lips he had heard in his head that theme of Saint-Saëns – *Ah! réponds à ma tendresse* – though on a somewhat breathy flute and with the missing note of the chromatic descent restored. A full chromatic glide from tonic to dominant on a pastoral flute heard inwardly in a street full of cabs and clatter. Then the glide back again, the theme recoiling on itself, getting nowhere, as was right for a shepherd lolling under an elm or alder in the shade of a Sicilian noon. Why Sicilian? Why should a shepherd possess a chromatic flute? Of course, it was no shepherd. Claude said:

'As for your notion of setting the Eiffel Tower to music, I was telling Gabrielle here that it could not be done. Perhaps a scale from bottom to top of the keyboard. The materials of music as that is only the materials of architecture. The bones, so to speak.'

Godet was a journalist, a sort of scholar, a kind of novelist, something of an amateur composer. He knew what Claude meant. 'It would have to be a scale in fourths or fifths,' he said, 'to emphasise the emptiness of the whole thing. The skeletal quality. None of the human warmth of a third, major or minor.'

'Organum,' Claude said. Gabrielle yawned, swinging her shut parasol from its wrist-hold thong. He explained eagerly to her. 'In old church music there was only monody, a single line to be chanted. But some voices could not reach high enough – the altos, I mean, could not reach the notes of the trebles, so they

82

sang the whole thing a fourth lower. You know what a fourth is?'

'Something to do with the *Marseillaise*,' she yawned.

'Like Chinese music. You heard that at the Exposition. Javanese too, to some extent. The fourth, the fourth. It's the basis of all harmony.'

'But,' Godet said, 'if you drew the Eiffel Tower as a scale in fourths, from bottom to top of the keyboard as you said, you'd have the trouble with the augmented fourth that they had at the dawn of real music, *musica ficta* I mean —'

'Oh my dear God,' Gabrielle exclaimed in real irritation, stamping her foot and poking Claude, not Godet, in the stomach with her parasol ferrule. 'Can't you leave all that alone?'

'Apologies.' Godet inclined towards her, touching the rim of his straw hat. 'Shall we go and lunch somewhere? I have a little money. An article I wrote on the great Eiffel himself for a Geneva periodical you will not even have heard of. A little money for a little lunch. What do you say?'

'I must go home,' Gabrielle said. 'I must help *maman*. We have a guest.'

'The old ram?' Claude said with brutal jealousy.

'An old ram that will butt you across the Channel and back. Here.' Gabrielle took an envelope from the little tasselled bag that hung on her arm. Claude received it humbly. 'No, not him. A certain Madame Texier. And probably her daughter.'

'Will you take a cab?' Claude humbly asked, pocketing.

'I'll walk.' She shook Godet's hand and accepted Claude's two humble pecks on her cool cheeks. 'You're playing tonight?'

'As ever. Though not tomorrow night nor the night after. Thanks to — I've forgotten his name already.' As they watched Gabrielle, parasol opened and variously inclined against sunshafts or leers as she walked, balancing with grace her lean haunches, admired, once whistled at by a delivering drayman, 'Not what you think,' Claude said.

'What do you think I think?'

'That we sleep one with the other. It's a kind of courtship, I suppose. Though how can I court with what I earn? You saw that she gave me money.'

'I heard something rattle inside that envelope.'

'That's to get to London to meet the Rossettis. Devoted to the memory of their dear dead brother. *La damoiselle élue*. The sister has some kind of connnection with somebody who runs the Philharmonic Society over there. But it has to be done in English.'

'They have the partition?'

'I sent them the vocal one, not the orchestral. The lady Christina says she can read music. Let's go and lunch.'

They lunched off cold roast beef and an onion and tomato salad with a jug of the house red at the *Triomphe de Bacchus*, a little bistro that stood at the corner of the rue Gluck and the rue Halévy. The name was ridiculous and pretentious and Claude permitted it to try to salt a now closed wound inflicted by that piano duet fantasy of his identically entitled. Claude had bought a packet of caporals on the way there and, over the coffee, let out in the bland Swiss face of Godet the thin strong exhaust of his deep inhalation. He said:

'You're right about the problem of relating a scale in fourths from bottom to top of the keyboard to the structure of that damnable tower: I mean, what happens when the tritone comes into it? You turn it into a perfect fourth either by sharpening the bottom note or flattening the top one. But that takes you into a new key. As you keep doing it it takes you into another new key—'

'Of course. *Musica ficta*.'

'And it impairs the image of unity.'

'Why not keep the forbidden interval? Nobody would notice.'

'But it stands for something faulty. Something shaky in the iron structure, a rivet missing or something. All our music's been based on avoiding the augmented fourth.'

'Wagner glories in it. Look at the opening of *Tristan*.'

'Yes, but his tritones aren't hollow. He puts one on top of the other. The French sixth. He's really trying to show breakdown, isn't he? Covering chaos in plush. The interval's a perfect image of the breakdown of the moral order.'

'That's why the Church called it the *modus diaboli*.'

'There was no sense of breakdown in that gamelan music. Fourths and fifths, perfect intervals. A stable society.'

'Isn't ours all too stable?'

'Tonic and dominant. We're past that. Beethoven wore it out.'

'Weren't the gamelan gongs chaotic?'

'Mere noise. A vinegar dressing.'

'And how would you get a gong effect on the piano?'

'Three white notes and three black, as low down as possible. Didn't Liszt do that? Yes, he did. Three tritones superposed, a full tone apart from each other. Oh my God, tritones again.'

'As,' Godet said, rummaging in the leather portfolio he always carried, a portfolio worn and scuffed, 'for the end of the tonic and dominant, here's another man who considers it finished. You won't have seen this.' He handed over a rather dirty half-sheet of pencilled music manuscript. Claude blew smoke at it and then choked.

'Jesus Christ, where did you get it?'

'A little man called Satie. Very dapper, but lives in the most appalling filth. *Les Fils des Etoiles*. That's what it will be called when it's finished, he says. What do you think?'

'It's impossible. Fourths on top of fourths on top of fourths. And, naturally, there's the salt and vinegar of the augmented one.'

'Diabolic? Horns on its head?'

Claude looked gravely at him, stubbing out his caporal in his coffee saucer. 'Is a faun diabolic?'

'Immoral, amoral. It depends on your point of view. Amoral, I'd say.'

'That damnable faun.' He lighted a new caporal and let the smoke walrus from his nostrils. 'That beautiful impossible faun. Definitive edition, he says. No more changes. In the *Revue Indé-pendante*. I gave a copy to Paul Dukas. Did you hear Lombardi's *glose*, as he calls it?'

'Which drawing-room did he play it in?'

'I forget. It sounded like Liszt. Illustrating every line, so he claimed. A disaster.'

'You'll do it.'

'I don't know.' He smiled, remembering how he and Godet had first become friends. The old poet in his rusty teaching suit, baggy with a sewn patch at the left elbow, scribbling away in a notebook at that concert, Godet and Claude leaning against a wall and then both inching forward to get a glimpse of what he was writing. Of course, it had been a Wagner concert, bleeding hunks of the *Ring*, the Tristan prelude, the Paris version of the Venusberg music. 'It sounds as if Saint-Saëns may have already done it without meaning to.' And he whistled *Ah! réponds à ma tendresse*, filling in the chromatic run from tonic to dominant.

'Put Satie's fourths under that and you might have faunal music,' Godet said. Claude said:

'No. Too acerbic. The faun wouldn't lie among thorns. I must meet this Satie. When I return, that is. What else has he written?'

'Three sarabandes. Based on consecutive dominant ninths.'

'That sounds more faunal.'

'Also mad.'

'Perhaps we'll reach the new sanity through dementia. Who knows?'

Not, however, through depression. Two days later Claude walked a grey Westminster, a Birdseye cigarette, blander than his caporals, between his pouting lips, his hands joined behind him. The sky wished to rain but, surprisingly in view of its long practice, did not seem to know how to. Vincent Street, Horseferry Road, Millbank, Great College Street, Westminster Abbey. On the train there had been sitting opposite him a pale redbearded man in knickerbockers who deplored the habit of smoking, drinking too, also meat-eating. He had the full orchestral score of *Tristan und Isolde* on his knees and sang:

> *Frisch weht der Wind*
> *Der Heimat zu*

Claude came in with:

> *Mein Irisch kind,*
> *Wo weilest du?*

Their German accents were much on a level. '*Français?*' the man had enquired and then, with a bad French tonality and with a vocabulary mostly learned, it seemed, from the scores of Gounod's operas, he had inveighed against the boastfulness of the words and the formlessness of the tune of the French national anthem. Claude had agreed with him, which put the man off. Neither had heard of the other. The redbearded one was coming back from Bayreuth. Claude had been to Bayreuth too that year, though somewhat earlier. And then the damned man had been on about the greatness of Wagner's orchestration, which Claude considered too heavy, and the brilliance of the chromaticism. Was this, then, the year of the *modus diaboli*? Not really singable, that man said, though eminently playable. Organ-builders, however, never had difficulty in braying out the interval, nor for that matter the scale of whole tones which provided the tuning basis of the organ. Claude did not know the organ nor really much care for it. Too churchy. César Franck's organ-playing had ruined his capacity to orchestrate. Still, he could sing a whole tone scale, which the redbearded man could not. It was a matter of giving out Bach's *Es ist genug* and then adding two full tones. Told that Claude was on his way to meet the two remaining Rossettis, the man had made a sour face. Never trust a poet, he said, and trust even less a lady poet. They think they enclose music, that music is the spume or *écume* of a well-turned poetic phrase and can present no sense unless lashed into being the slave of words. Neither of the Rossettis will be in the least concerned with promoting your musical career (what is the name again? I must make a note of it), only with reminding a forgetful public of the greatness of their defunct brother. And that brother – a bad and dirty man with a very minor talent in both arts – is best forgotten. His underwear was filthy, his love-making an unwholesome slobber. The blessed damozel indeed. The factitious purification of a Soho whore.

Well, it was prophetic enough. Christina Rossetti, smelling of gin and peppermint, speaking better Italian than French (Claude remembered enough Italian from his Rome sojourn), complaining that he, Claude, had set a translation of an early edition of the poem, later much emended, coughing while he breathed the opening chords on the untuned piano. If you want Pre-Raphaelitism in music, he had told her, here it is, though Berlioz had thought of it already in *L'Enfance du Christ*. Modes, not keys. Listen to the poignancy of these secondary sevenths. The brother, whose talent was journalistic, who had not one atom of poet or musician in his cheap, small soul, had shaken his head in canon

to the shaking of his sister's. Claude had stalked out, the copy
of the vocal score he had sent her under his arm, and gone to
his cheap hotel off the Tottenham Court Road. He fancied a
whore (spume or *écume* of his more rarefied love for Gabrielle)
but could not afford one. And now he wondered whether to
walk into Westminster Abbey.

But here was one walking out, a compatriot, the master himself. Claude gaped. Stéphane Mallarmé did not at first recognise
his fellow-Parisian. No reason why he should. Claude had paid
but one visit to Mallarmé's apartment, on one of the regular
Tuesday evenings when, his daughter Geneviève serving the
watery punch, his wife placidly knitting, the master had formu-
lated to his adorers, through a delicate weave of cigarette smoke,
the aesthetic of the future. Small men, poetlings, who perhaps
had no future – Valéry, Claudel, Gide, Mourey, the Jew with
asthma who coughed his way home early, Pierre Louÿs whose
future was not in doubt. 'Ah,' Mallarmé now said, gripping
Claude's arm, 'the young musician who stood in the shadows
with André-Something Hérold, saying not one word. The name
escapes me. I have seen their Poets' Corner, the atmosphere is
appropriately musty, and must prepare to open my lungs to the
green air of the sister island. You are staying here, living here
perhaps? I do not recommend it.'

'The night train from Victoria Station. A wasted visit.'

'We shall go to Dublin together. I am promised something
there, though how far the Irish can be trusted I do not know.
Edgar Allan the great – you're one of his admirers?'

'Indeed. I've thought of an opera on—'

'*La Chute de la Maison de* – I know. They all think of that. Even
Saint-Saëns mumbled something about it at some tedious soirée
we both attended. He envisaged a fall like the fall of his Philistine
temple in that banal biblical extravaganza of his.'

'But I rather admire—'

'It was Henri de Régnier – you know him? Of course you know
him – it was he who told me of the rumour of an unpublished
and indeed unknown manuscript of the master lying in the Irish
capital. In the hands of a Scotch priest, if you can imagine such a
being. Let's go together. I need a compatriot companion. Talking
English tires me.'

'And yet, *cher maître*, you—'

'Teach it, yes. I associate the speaking of the language with extreme fatigue. A train leaves from the station called Euston in just over an hour. Come.'

'I have no money. More, I have a commitment—'

'Our commitments, to the devil with them. The Poe family was Irish, you know, peasants from the County Cavan as it is called. The Scotch connection was purely adoptive. See, a cab lets down that gentleman at the corner. I will hail it.' Mallarmé carried an umbrella and now semaphored with it in the grey air of London summer. In the cab he said: 'Tell me, my young friend. Was it you who proposed a Wagnerian fantasy based upon my eclogue?'

'Nothing Wagnerian, no. Not Wagnerian, not by any means.'

'You do not like Wagner? Remember, you are speaking to the author of—'

'I know, *cher maître*, I know. *Richard Wagner, rêverie d'un poète français.* One could take nothing pastoral from Wagner.'

'Not the cor anglais solo in the third act of *Tristan*? Why, by the way, is it termed *anglais*? Did the English invent it?'

'It is a mistake for *anglé*. The instrument is bent or angled. Ah, this, I think, is Victoria Station. It was kind of you to take me here. We shall meet again, if I may so presume, in Paris.'

'Nonsense. I collect my bag from the left luggage office here and then we proceed together to the other station. You are coming with me to Dublin, I insist. You will offend me very notably if you say no.' The English cigarette between his lips wagged as he spoke. Claude's wagged back through a faint smile of deference.

'You transform your invitation into a command, *cher maître*?'

'You may put it that way.' He held out ridiculous British coins to the cab-driver. He took Claude's arm and dragged him towards the left luggage. Claude's luggage too was there. The station was very crowded. Steam hissed and there was an odour of rotten eggs. A stall sloppy with spilt tea sold sausage rolls and Claude wondered what they were. They fought their way through brawling British. 'There is,' Mallarmé said, 'an interesting restaurant round the corner. They serve the British dishes there, such as steak and kidney pudding. *Bifstek* and *rognons* stewed together in a heavy compost of *farine* and *suif*. A *boule de suif*, in effect. It is more appetising than it sounds. It is for Mr Pickwick and Sam Weller. See,' at the cabstand, 'it is a summer evening but fog is descending. Where would they be without their fog and mists? Vague shapes dimly descried. Their Turner is the father of *l'Impressionisme*. And yet they eat steak and kidney pudding.'

'What is a sausage roll?'

'I will tell you on the way to the other station.' He raised his umbrella at a cab.

The old man in an Italian suit, bulb-nosed and white-bearded, paid the cabman with care from a trembling handful, centesimi among the halfpence, then, helped by his stout stick, approached the college entrance. What he took to be a lay brother, though for all he knew it was a reincarnation of the Alphonsus Rodriguez who had watched the door in Mallorca, stopped biting what looked like a hangnail to enquire what his business was.

'I require to see a Father Hopkins.'

'Father Hopkins, is it? You've come to the wrong place then. He's in purgatory if ever any man was.'

'You mean that Father Hopkins is no longer alive? But I was assured on the best authority—'

'The poor man died of the cholera and wasn't the only one. Never looked after himself though, fasting when there was no call to. If it's a priest you're after there's plenty more.' The old man was now in the entrance hall. The college was empty of students since it was the summer vacation. But a priest swished down the stairs in a soutane to see something on a crowded notice board. Then he caught sight of the old man, seemed for a moment taken aback, swished towards him.

'Can I be of any help?' The accent was patrician British. A follower in the wake of Cardinal Newman no doubt, whose creation this college (*Idea of a University*) was.

'My name,' the old man said, 'is Robert Browning. I came to see your Father Hopkins but I'm told he's no longer with you. Has, in fact, departed this life for a better. In a word—'

'Indeed, dead. A considerable loss. A fine Greek scholar, you know. Robert Browning, you say? An honour and a most devastating surprise, though pleasant. I am Stephen Devereux, Father if you wish.' Bony in face, austere, undoubtedly aristocratic. 'Or Professor, of course. I teach the English Literature courses. Courses of course,' he then muttered, frowning. 'I apologise for the cacophonous concatenation.'

'As I have sometimes been asked to.'

'Naturally. "Irks care the cropful bird, frets doubt the maw-crammed beast?" A favourite line of mine. No matter. You are not taught here, we eschew the contemporary, but you are certainly read. I take it you came to visit poor Gerard in a literary capacity, no, impossible, he is not published, is indeed unpublishable. No. Something else then, I will not pry. May I offer you tea?'

'It is the hour. Yes, more than acceptable. I thank you.'

'We will not take it in the refectory. I will have a pot sent up to my room. The day is hot for Dublin. Have you just arrived?'

'Here, yes. I was in Cork. They have a Browning society there, of a sort. I was escorted over by three Corkmen who would not take no for an answer to their invitation to come over to read some poems. I read some – rather breathlessly.' He said no more, labouring up the stairs. The room into which he was half-bowed was book-lined, had a dead green plant in the window embrasure, and, on the walls, a bad picture of the Virgin Mary in sky-blue with stars floating above her and another of St Anthony with the infant Jesus, an impossible collocation. Above the fireplace the mature Christ writhed on his cross. The shut and dirty window looked out on to Stephen's Green. The narrow bed had its brown blanket tightly tucked in: strait, the word came to the poet. 'How long ago did he die?', sitting with old man's relief in a wretched chair meant to be of the easy variety.

'Dear Gerard? All of six weeks.' Father Devereux was still at the open door, arranging tea with a moronic-looking houseman in a green apron who went arrgh.

'How old?'

'Forty-four. A loss to the Order. A most delicate mind and, alas, physique. He was not meant to live long.'

'I met his close friend in London,' Browning said. 'A Dr Bridges. It was at a meeting of the Elizabeth Barrett Browning Society. All these societies,' he added.

'I know the work of Bridges. A most delicate poet.'

'But a robust physician. He sounded my bronchial tract. I told him I needed a priest who understood certain things. He showed me the manuscripts of some sonnets of this Hopkins. I did not understand them. They did not seem to scan.'

'They scan according to a system of his which I have never fully understood. It must be some time since you saw Bridges. I wrote him a letter informing him of our loss. The day after the funeral.'

'I have been visiting old friends in various parts of the country – England, that is. I meant also to take my blackthorn to an old enemy but I was too late. Edward Fitzgerald, if the name means anything to you.'

'Nothing.'

'There is not much time for adieux. I am all of seventy-seven.'

'So,' Father Devereux said, swinging a leg under his soutane, 'you come from Italy, which is all priests, to see a priest in Ireland whom you do not even know. I say no more. I bank my curiosity.'

The tea was brought in – grey sugar, milk with a swimming fly in it, big brown pot, slabs of fruitcake. The houseman made everything clink as he set it down on the table. He grumblingly seemed to admire Browning's beard before leaving, banging the tray like a drum. Browning said:

'I think I require confession and absolution.'

'I beg your pardon?'

'To confess a grave sin, to be forgiven, to do what penance is needful.' Father Devereux forbore to show surprise. He stirred his strong tea widdershins. Then he said:

'You are not of the faith?'

'I am a Christian.'

'But a Protestant?'

'Yes. I live in a country of Catholics and this perhaps ensures a steady maintenance of my Protestantism. You know Italian Catholics?'

'I have naturally visited Rome.'

'I admire the English hierarchy, of course—'

'Yes, yes, Bishop Blougram.'

'But I could never convert in Italy. That would make me one of an essentially pagan persuasion. If I were to stay in England the situation would be, might be, somewhat different. But I must end my days in Italy. You know Asolo?'

'Alas.'

'It is in the province of Veneto. The air is suitable and the heat comforts old bones. My brief wanderings round England have induced a bronchitic condition which, so Bridges says, harms my heart. I cannot easily support the cold and damp.' He munched fruitcake. Father Devereux remarked the crumbs in his beard. He said:

'I understand. If I may ask, why, if you require confession, do you not consult some minister of the Anglican Church who practises it? Some segments of your Church are very close to Rome. Indeed, I was an Anglican minister so close to Rome that I completed the brief journey. This is the great age of conversion.'

'I require forgiveness and an appropriate penance, if there is such a thing, at what might be termed the highest level. When I say I am a Protestant I mean it probably in a somewhat historical sense. An aspect of my nationalism. An Englishman in Italy, you understand. It would be unseemly to assimilate. If I do not speak the language with any great fluency, that may be considered volitional. We must remain what we are. I know little of the Anglican Church. I naturally know more of yours.'

'You know it cannot be done.'

'I think you are wrong. If I walked into the darkness of a confessional and sought to confess my sins, would I be interrogated as to my right to do so? A Jew or Mohammedan might do as much.'

'Yes, but the absolution would not be valid. You must accept the entire theological system which states what is a sin and what is not. If a Jew or Mohammedan confessed to eating pork, that would be of no interest to the priest. And yet he would not confess to eating meat on a Friday, since this to him would not be a sin. Do you now follow me?'

'Some sins are so vile that all faiths combine in their condemnation. Murder, for instance.'

'Have you committed murder, Mr Browning?' the priest smiled.

'And if I confessed that I had?'

'You would first have to settle the secular aspect of the matter, would you not? The police, witnesses, a trial, a verdict. Making your peace with God would be a different matter.'

'And if the murder took place so long ago that it was clear that the secular arm could not pursue it? If there were no witnesses?'

'How long ago?'

'Shall we say twenty-eight years? In 1861.'

'You are making it very exact for a mere hypothesis. Let me say another thing. A priest is bound to silence of what he hears in the confessional. Neither the objurgations of the police nor the torture of a tyrannical state can wrest its secrets from him. But a non-believer, a Protestant say, cannot approach the confessional in the expectation of that same silence. If, and we are still speaking, I trust, hypothetically, you confessed a crime to me in a non-sacramental capacity, then I should be bound to behave like any layman and consult the duty of an ordinary citizen. You follow me, I think. I would be under no obligation to maintain silence.'

'Oh yes, yes. Let us cling to our hypothesis and let me make it the more hypothetical by referring to a poem I wrote many years ago. It is about a man who loves a lady named Porphyria.'

'I know the poem. The man strangles her with her yellow hair. This is to ensure that her declared love for him cannot change. He commits murder and wonders that God has not said a word. A very disturbing poem.'

'It was meant to be. Good. Transfer the situation to real life, hypothetical however still, not poetical. A woman is dying in extreme distress. Her pain is considerable. Her husband is distraught by her agony and wishes that it be no further prolonged. He smothers her with a pillow. His motive is totally merciful. Does that count as murder?'

Father Devereux did not look at Browning. Instead he poured himself rather nervously another cupful of black tea and drank it down. Then he got up, a hand splayed across his chest, and walked to the window then back. 'Dyspepsia,' he said. 'An excess of tannin. The Irish make tea damnably strong. I am prone to dyspepsia. You,' and it was said with a ghost of viciousness, 'have always been eupeptic. A philosophy based on good digestion.'

'I have never had to worry over the state of my stomach.'

'Clearly from your poems. God's in his heaven, all's right with
the world. God may be in his heaven, Mr Browning, but all is
quite certainly *not* right with the world. Poor dead Hopkins saw
that all too clearly. Thoughts against thoughts in groans grind.
Our night whelms, whelms, and will end us. Of course it was,
would be, murder. Only God gives and takes life. I say no more.
Would you care to see the college library?'

'Books, books, I have done with books. Where would a man
go for forgiveness?'

'If he approved of his act he would not seek forgiveness.'

'The act was performed in horror. But it had to be performed.
Or, if you wish, the sin was committed in full awareness of its
sinfulness but other considerations prevailed. Tell me, is there a
hell?'

'Of course there is a hell. A hell not imposed by a tyrannical
God but freely elected by sinners. The non-believing sinner, the
non-Catholic sinner I would say, must do what he has been
brought up to do, make his peace in whatever way he can.
Pray directly for forgiveness but expect no forgiving voice. The
forgiving voice belongs to the true Church. He may beg for
forgiveness but never be sure that it is to be accorded him. You
see the grave state the heretic is in.'

'What must I expect on the other side?' Browning still had
cake-crumbs in his beard; they mitigated somewhat the horror
in his wide eyes.

'You have told the poetry-reading world, such as it is, what
to expect. God completes the work half-done. God rejects the
lukewarm but the manner of his rejection is not clarified. There
is no hell in your work.'

'It is only my work. True, not intended as mere diversion like
a cigar or a game of dominoes. But the work is not the life. To
call it the *epiphenomenon* of a sound digestion would be unjust,
but I recognise the frivolity. What right had I to sneer silently at
her work? The intention is all. She had good intentions.'

'I must read my office, Mr Browning. In which hotel are you
staying?'

'The one across the green. The nearest to you.'

'I will keep silent, of course. Out of deference to your greatness. If you sincerely wish to be instructed and received, there is no obstacle save time.'

'There is nothing to keep silent about. I have presented you with no more than a hypothesis. But I do not speak hypothetically when I say that any man of my age must be seriously disturbed about his future prospects. The Reformation,' he added, 'was a historical necessity.'

'So you Protestants are brought up to believe.' He extended his hand. The other hand beat his breast lightly: dyspepsia, not repentance. 'It was an honour to receive you here. If you wish further to talk, you know where to find me.'

In another room in the same college, Mallarmé and Claude sat with Father Allan SJ. 'The etymology of the name,' Father Allan said in good French with an Edinburgh tang, 'is not clear. Jokes were made on it in the poet's own lifetime. The father, David Poe, had it worse, being a notorious drunkard. In a magazine called *The Rambler* there was, in French, a scurrilous little verse called "Sur un POE de Chambre". It went like this:

> *Son père était pot,*
> *Sa mère était broc,*
> *Sa grande mère était pinte.*

Edgar never liked the name. The Allan was a mitigant.'

'And your own connection, *mon père*?'

'I'm descended from John Allan. As a schoolboy in London Edgar was always know as Master Allan. John sent him to a school in Sloane Street, Chelsea, to be instructed by two sisters named Dubourg. You'll recall that Edgar uses the name in his "Murders in the Rue Morgue".'

'I was not aware of the provenance of the name. Of Poe's adoption by the Allans I naturally know as much as the decrepit and dying Charles Baudelaire was able to tell me. Forgive my eagerness now to know of the manuscript unknown.'

Father Allan was a Lowland Scot of about fifty, hair very black and unparted, eyebrows bushy, teeth not good, with a nose and chin that Mallarmé described to himself, and in English, as *questing.* 'It's a poem,' he said, 'a schoolboy production. Written, without doubt, while he was still a pupil at the Manor House School at Stoke Newington, an establishment run by a certain John Bransby, Master of Arts. It describes the school. It was sent in a letter to John Allan's sister Mary, married to a certain Allan Fowlds and living in Kilmarnock. You sincerely wish to see it? It is a very amateur and immature piece of poetastry, if that word exists.' He turned his back on them and went to a desk strewn untidily with what looked like examination papers.

Claude took the opportunity to empty his cup of black undrinkable tea back into the brown pot, with scarcely a clink. *Ppp* – more, *ppppp.* He winced as what he had already sipped struck hard behind his breast-bone. It had been a rough crossing, waves and wind in violent dialogue: to the waves he had given much of a cardboard pork pie and pickled onions. Father Allan handed over to Mallarmé a browning sheet of paper with brown-inked prim print script on it, a schoolboy's proud fair copy. Claude's English was insufficient to understand, but he stood that he might see over Mallarmé's shoulder the work, albeit juvenile, of the undoubted master. The poem ran:

> The wall is solid, high and brick,
> Topped by a bed of broken glass
> In mortar set, a rampart thick
> Beyond which prisoners may not pass
> Save thrice a week. The escorting usher,
> Frigid as Russia, stern as Prussia,
> Walks us about the neighbouring fields,
> Weed and water, plough and tillage:
> That is on Saturday.
> Sunday yields
> Two visits to the squalid village
> Where, a troop of latterday
> Would-be saints, we hear and hear
> On the stillness of the atmosphere
> What the fretted Gothic steeple tells –
> Deep the hollow note
> Within the brazen throat:
> The clamour of the bells bells bells bells bells,

The clamour and the hammer of the bells.

'Hm,' Mallarmé said. 'A schoolboy's production, as you say, but he looks to the future. He describes the school and its routine in the story of William Wilson, I think.'

'There would be only one bell,' Father Allan said. 'I know the village. Indeed, in its church I heard the first whisper of my conversion. Why follow John Calvin, I seemed to be told, when I could follow Calvin's master Saint Augustine. It was a mainly intellectual conversion. But of that you will not wish to hear.'

'Well,' Mallarmé said, 'I am a little – inevitably, I suppose.'

'Disappointed? *Déçu*? You would not wish to translate it into French?'

'I think not. I had the romantic expectation of some lost master-piece. But we are grateful, *mon père*, and will take no more of your time.'

'Oh, you're welcome to it all, but I have my office to read.'

'Scotland,' Claude said. 'You come from Scotland. Is it a coun-try a Frenchman ought to visit?'

'It would depend what a Frenchman would be after. The ancient treaties, what in our language we call the Auld Alliance, the martyred Queen much of a Frenchwoman. In Scotland you will see much heather and flaxen-haired girls of rare beauty. But I am in Ireland now and must not grumble. It was a pleasure to meet you both. Let me add one thing – that the fear of hell was strong in Edgar Allan. From his stories I learnt a strong sense of the judgment. But that would not interest you.'

'It is as a poet—'

'Yes, as a poet. One of our fathers, recently dead and buried, alas, young too, young and brilliant, found some prosodic theory of his anticipated in the poems. But, he said, they are not good poems.'

'They have meant much to us of the new movement in France.'

'From the language doubtless you gain what we do not. The exotic.'

The exotic, Claude thought vaguely, hearing in his head the bonang, gambang, saron, gender, ketipung, kenong. It was always the exotic that primed the new. 'We will leave, then,' he said.

'My office,' Father Allan said, shaking their hands.

Claude and Mallarmé crossed Stephen's Green in somewhat watery sunlight. It was a sad sky of a misty blue; Celtic. 'I ought to lie down, I think,' Claude said.

'It is the stomach still? A glass of their whiskey might help.'

'Ugh.'

'Rest, then. Later we will eat some Irish stew and, after that, visit a brothel.'

Claude gaped. 'A brothel, *maître*?' He stopped walking among the sad greenery the better to gape. 'You must not go to brothels.'

'Oh, not for the purposes of lust. I wish to see an Irish girl naked, no more. There is, I understand, a quality in the texture of the skin of a special delicacy. I wish also to hear an Irish girl's voice in a state of intimacy hardly to be granted in a polite context. We must suffer for our art,' he said without irony. 'Who is that angry old man who beats the bushes with his stick? He mutters to himself. And what strange phenomenon is this?' Coming round the corner from Grafton Street was a small and ragged band, tin whistles and a *tambour militaire* only, playing what sounded like the *Marseillaise*. 'A compliment to the French, but how did they know we were here?'

'It is not for us,' Claude said. 'Those young men following seem to be Irish patriots. They carry a green flag, see. What they're singing does not go into good counterpoint with our anthem.' Mallarmé cocked his head the better to hear the words:

> The French are on the sea,
> Says the Shan Van Voght.
> They'll be here without delay
> And the Orange will decay,
> Says the Shan Van Voght.

Two policemen on horseback appeared. The old man with the stick, crossing the street, found himself caught up in a brief mêlée of scampering young men, whooping and laughing. The street soon cleared. One of the horses casually let drop a smoking globe or so, not from a full crupper. The old man stood panting, hand on heart, stick feebly raised. Claude and Mallarmé rushed, solicitous.

'You are not, by any chance, the poet Browning?' Mallarmé asked.

'You saw those ruffians? You saw the hoofs or hooves? The plural is in doubt.' A man of words, anyway, paling rather than browning. 'I thought myself not to be known in this city.'

'I heard you read in London many years ago. We are Frenchmen, by the way.'

'The French do not know me.' He was no longer panting.

'Here is one Frenchman who does. I have myself written a dramatic monologue.'

'I require brandy. Here is the hotel.'

'Our hotel too.' Claude, assured that this Englishman had recovered, bowed in the entrance hall and went up the stairs two at a time. 'Irish stew,' Mallarmé called. 'I will knock on your door at seven.'

In the salon of the hotel a rollicking priest took tea with two of his parishioners. The father of a family sang "Blarney Castle" to two sons and several daughters. One of the sons, a blue-eyed lad in sailor suit and spectacles, looked keenly at the two entrants. Browning sat heavily by one of the windows and banged his blackthorn on the low table to summon a waiter. 'The waiters are fools,' he said. 'You see they have two clocks here, each telling a different time. I pointed this out to one of them, and he said why should they waste money on two clocks that told the same time.'

'That is Celtic logic. There is some sense in it. Poetic sense, in a sense.' Mallarmé took out his little sack of caporal tobacco and deftly rolled himself a cigarette.

'What is a Frenchman doing in Dublin? Ah, I may know the answer. To escape from the centenary junketings in Paris perhaps. I passed through on my way here. I saw the ridiculous tower.'

'Childe Roland to the dark tower came.'

'True, I saw it at night.' He looked with some favour on Mallarmé. 'You are a teacher of English perhaps?'

'That, also a poet. I came to Ireland to pursue some researches into the work of Edgar Allan Poe. He has meant much to me.'

'A muckheap of a poet. An entertaining writer of horrific trivialities. My wife liked him for some reason. I will never understand you French.' A waiter came, announcing his coming with a tray rhythmically banged on his right kneecap. Brandy. Whiskey. 'That is the man,' Browning said, as the metallic drumming retreated. 'He is also the man who could not slide a message under the bedroom door because the message was on a tray.'

'Again, a kind of logic. He presumably saw the message and the tray as an indissoluble unit. As for not understanding us French, we are not hard to understand. We are our literature.'

'Which I no longer read. I am hard at Greek these days. The moral lessons of Aeschylus.'

'Literature,' Mallarmé said boldly, 'has nothing to do with moral lessons. Nor with ideas in general. Literature has to do with words.'

'Literature must have a subject.'

'Its subject must be itself. As with music.'

'Even music teaches its great moral lessons. I have written poems about music.'

'I know. Something about the dominant's persistance. Something about the *do majeur* of our life. It will not do for the future.'

Browning turned old wide eyes on him. 'I left it to my wife,' he said, 'to write for the present. The present accepts her as a great poet. What did I have, I often told her, but the future. The future in which all the subject-matter that is accruing in the world of railways and metal towers is available to the poet, not just buttercups and daisies. And the speech of poetry the speech of urban man. You talk of Edgar Allan Poe, a frowsty poetling stuck in the age of the Gothic. What has he to do with the future?' He drank off his brandy briskly. 'Better. Is there one poem written by any poet that deals with the revivifying power of brandy?'

'Gross. Gross. The mind is complex, our sensibilities are labyrinthine. We learnt that from Poe. Infinite delicacy of suggestion, as in music. Do not drag music into the realm of moral imperatives. Leave preaching to the priests.' He took from his inside pocket some sheets of violet-inked manuscript. 'I would value your opinion of this. It's an English translation of one of my poems.'

'Read it to me. My eyes are old. I trust it is not too long.'

'An eighteen-year-old Irishman in Paris brought me these few

101

lines. A beginning only. I know English but it is an acquired tongue. To have the opinion of Robert Browning—'
'Go on.'

> These nymphs – I would eternise them. So clear,
> Their luminous flesh, it rides the atmosphere
> Soothed by tufted slumbers. Was it a reverie
> I loved? My doubt, hoard of old night, in every
> Subtle tendril branching, among true trees,
> Proves, alas, that what I claimed to please
> Myself, alone, a trophy, was the lack
> Of roses in my thought. Think forward, back.
> What if these girls you ponder should dispense
> Wished fragments of your fable-making sense?
> Faun, your illusion slips out from those eyes
> Cold, blue, pure, a weeping spring. All sighs
> The other she – a contrast, would you say,
> Warm in your tousled fleece, a breeze of day?

'Enough, enough, for God's sake.'
'There is no more. But there is much more of the original.'
'It says nothing.'
'What does music say?'
'Music says that discords are evil, but they can be resolved into concords, which are good. And there is a final concord, an ultimate cadence, which is so good that it must be God.'
'You know this not to be so. Listen to the French.' And he began to recite with his eyes closed:

> Ces nymphes, je les veux perpétuer. Si clair
> Leur incarnat léger, qu'il voltige dans l'air
> Assoupi de sommeils touffus . . .

Browning, it seemed profoundly disturbed, bellowed:

> And pipe-sticks, rose, cherry-tree, jasmine,
> And the long whip, the tandem-lasher,
> And the cast from a fist ('not alas mine
> But my master's, the Tipton Slasher . . .')

102

The rollicking priest and his tea-drinking parishioners looked, and so did the family with the bespectacled boy in the sailor-suit. Browning mumbled a sidelong apology. Mallarmé said, rolling himself a fresh cigarette: 'You cannot evade reality by erecting a barricade of solid objects. The objects are not truly solid. You know where the solidity lies.'

Browning looked warily. 'What do you mean?'

'In irrational relations, irrational acts. Doubts, hoard of ancient night. The gods exist, but there is no God. There is no crime and there is no punishment. Velleities, unpurposed acts of the will, the surprises that spring wholly from within, not without. What the Church musicians called the *modus diaboli* is no more than an augmented fourth or a diminished fifth or a tritone.'

Browning worked that out. 'Fifth diminished. It cannot be sung.'

'Oh yes it can.' And he sang it – *fa si*. 'Our musician is lying down upstairs. He suffered from the crossing. He is worried about the tritone. You are horrified by it. You do not wish to think of the devil taking over the world. The point is that there is no devil. He is only a faun, and he is frightened of Venus. *Je tiens la reine! O sûr châtiment.* But there is no punishment.'

Browning deeply, first in jerks, then smoothly, breathed. 'You're saying no more than I've said all my life. Nothing to worry about.'

'Spoken like an Englishman. There is a great deal to worry about. Art is not easy. Art is excruciatingly difficult.'

'This I know.'

'This you have never known enough. None of you. You cannot rhyme *jasmine* and *alas mine*.'

'I will take a nap before dinner. What is your name again?'

'Why "again"? There was no first time. The name will mean nothing to you, Mr Browning.' Browning, rising with the aid of his blackthorn, nodded not unkindly. The little bespectacled boy in the sailor-suit was letting his tiny hands strike arbitrarily the keys of the upright piano in the far corner. Browning said, almost grinning:

'The music of the future?'

'At least there is no C major of this life.'

'So now I will try to sleep.' And Browning put one heavily-booted foot carefully before the other as he trod the Turkey carpet on his way out. On her way in was a Dublin lady, somewhat horsy in face, with a spaniel on a lead. Browning half-raised his stick at the dog, whether in greeting or menace was unclear, and left.

The cab slowed as they entered Mecklenburg Street. ' 'Tis terrible here,' the driver cried down from his perch, 'but the houses is better further up. I'll drop you at number ninety.' The worst slums in Europe, Mallarmé remembered having read somewhere. Claude retched.

'The Irish stew?' Mallarmé said kindly.

'The black beer. I think we ought to turn back.' It was filthy and full of filthy people crouching on doorsteps, taking in the cool of the summer night. A snotty child in unlaced man's boots bowled a hoop without vigour. Two louts without collars punched at each other one-handed. A woman with hair like a grey nest pulled up her skirt at the two Frenchmen and called raucously. 'Turn back,' Claude repeated.

' 'Tis better further up.'

Number ninety was a Georgian house in good repair. Mallarmé, fresh rolled cigarette between his lips, seemed unperturbed by his ambience. There were two girls at the open window; they made kissing noises. Mallarmé paid the cabman. The fine Georgian door, its new paint as yet undisfigured, was ajar. He led the way in. A girl clad only in a chemise said: 'This is a ten-shilling house. You know that, do you?'

'And the madame?'

'Mrs Mack's at number eighty-five. She'll be round later.' She took them into a fair-sized parlour to the right of a passage-way that smelt of ancient cabbage overlaid with a cheap but abundant perfume. Two other girls sat there in their chemises, lolled rather, smoking cigarettes and showing ample black-stockinged leg. There was a battered upright piano, there were pouffes and dolls. On the walls were the Virgin Mary with stars in her hair, St Anthony and the adolescent Jesus, the blessing Pope, the mature Christ writhing on his cross. 'La damoiselle élue,' Claude kept muttering. One of the girls said:

'Is there Irish on you?' Mallarmé said:

'We are Frenchmen from Paris. May we have the honour of knowing your names?'

'What's names to do with it at all?' said the girl who had shown them in. 'There was a priest here the other night that said you take off your name with your clothes.'

'A priest?'

'More of a minister. He said his wife had run away with the milkman. He had his collar in his pocket.'

'They call me Lady Betty,' the darkest and youngest said. 'This is Fleury Crawford and this is Becky Cooper.'

'*Fleurie*? A pretty name.'

' 'Tis not her real one. If you're from Paris give us some parley-voo.' Mallarmé recited, with wide gestures:

> *Que non! par l'immobile et lasse pâmoison*
> *Suffoquant de chaleurs le matin frais s'il lutte,*
> *Ne murmure point d'eau que ne verse ma flûte*
> *Au bosquet arrosé d'accords . . .*

Thickets sprinkled with concords, thought Claude, the flute pouring them in. The girl named Becky Cooper winked at him and drew the straps of her bodice down over her shoulders. Lady Betty said: 'I didn't understand one word of it, but it sounded lovely, sure.'

'It's the sound that counts,' Mallarmé said, nodding. 'My friend here is a musician and he will tell you all about sound.'

'Can he sing then?' Fleury Crawford asked.

'*Chanter*?' Claude said. He took out his cigarette and gave out in his harsh baritone:

> *Ah! réponds à ma tendresse,*
> *Verse-moi, verse-moi l'ivresse . . .*

'That,' Mallarmé said, 'is from the opera about Samson. We are not two Samsons, though we come for a little *tendresse* and, I suppose *ivresse*.'

'You've a flowery way of putting it,' Fleury Crawford said, 'but

105

if it's a couple of short times you're wanting put your money on the table there. A quid it'll be.'

Robert Browning woke refreshed and even hungry to the sad evening summer light. He had napped in his shirt and socks. His dream had been, surprisingly, erotic. Erotic though legitimate or even legal, since he had held the naked body of his long-dead wife in his arms. The spaniel had yapped viciously at first but later yawned and settled to sleep on the bedside rug. She had always had less pudeur than he, laughing at their first undressing for the act, since he had been shy of dismantling the bulky apparatus of his garments in her presence. Since when was genius found respectable? A line from that ghastly *Aurora Leigh*, which the world thought the greatest thing since Shakespeare. Love, whatever it was, was the great enemy of critical candour.

> First time he kissed me, he but only kissed
> The fingers of this hand wherewith I write;
> And, ever since, it grew more clean and white.

Naturally, since it was the ink he kissed off. And what was the other thing?

> Of all the thoughts of God that are
> Borne inward unto souls afar,
> Along the Psalmist's music deep,
> Now tell me if that any is,
> For gift or grace, surpassing this –
> 'He giveth His beloved sleep.'

Well, he had given her sleep, the eternal quietus, and, whatever God thought, her white body back from the shades had acquiesced in it, and surely he had not thrust words into her dead mouth when it said *Smother me, smother me with your love*. And, ah yes, the great god Pan had peered down from the flowery wallpaper (surely the wallpaper of the Wimpole Street house, not the Florentine?), half a beast, making a poet out of a man, though it should really be the other way round. The point was never the enactment but the motive, that was the trouble, and you had to have a God to judge of it. Very well, then, the motive had been altogether humane, and of the less conscious motive he had only become aware after the act. Could one be blamed for the delayed realisation of the true, or unconscious, motive? He had needed a poet-priest to explain, perhaps comfort. A poet who had written about a towery city and branchy between towers and then gone into mad galloping, destructive of metre, was a kind of Browning who had neglected to have himself drawn from the oven when overdone. Well, let it go. Her poetry had not been good, and it had been perhaps his true sin not to say so. Hell, he had read, had been a rubbish dump outside Jerusalem, grossly exaggerated into an eternal place of fiery suffering. Nonsense.

> My times be in Thy hand!
> Perfect the cup as planned!
> Let age approve of youth, and death
> complete the same!

Too much shouting there, overmuch assertion to disguise doubt. Was that Frenchman right, whoever he was? Keep ideas out of it? The great god Pan, hers, was the god of all, hence God, and could not play any tune called morality on his pipe. His bladder now pricked him, and he chuckled oldly. Pappa pisses. He had always left himself wide open to the jeers of the vulgar. He should have asked an East End cab-driver what a twat was. Well, British Public, ye who like me not (God love you!). He knelt, as in prayer, to the chamber pot from under the bed. The Edgar Allan some called it. It was a vulgar world, and he was ripe to leave it, he thought.

> One who never turned his back but marched breast forward,
> Never doubted clouds would break,
> Never dreamed, though right were worsted, wrong would triumph,
> Held we fall to rise, are baffled to fight better,
> Sleep to wake.

Let Pan put that in his pipe and smoke it.

Mallarmé was still in there, examining rose-moles on a whore's body doubtless, analysing the cadences of low Irish English. Claude, after his short time, padded in his socks into the empty parlour, *tristis post*, seeing the still virginal Gabrielle Dupont leaning out from the gold bar of heaven. And the souls mounting up to God went by her like thin flames. We two, she said, will seek the groves where the lady Betty is. And now the lady Betty entered in her corset and opened a cupboard where black bottles lay. She uncorked, foamed a yellow head into a murky tumbler and proffered. He shook his head sadly. She drank with thirst. He was standing by the open upright with its spotted keys. She said:

'Play us something then.'

'*Comment?*' She made spidery movements with the fingers of the hand unengaged by the glass. '*Ah. Tu veux que je te joue quelquechose?*' He sat in his as yet unbraced serge trousers on the moth-eaten velvet of the revolving stool. He played with his right hand only the descending chromatics of *Ah! réponds à ma tendresse*. The *la bémol* or A flat did not exist: it had flattened itself to *sol* or G. Oh my God.

'Out of tune, we know. The tuner's coming in next week. Blind he is. Plays lovely. You know, the real classical.' Claude did not understand. But the phrase he had played and now played again started on C sharp, or D flat if Saint Saëns preferred, and ended on G natural. A tritone, the *modus diaboli*. But the horned creature was not the devil. In a higher octave he tried it again. Hold the C sharp and miss the C natural and slide down chromatically to the G. It was it. The faun played it on his flute. His head span. He span round on the stool and called:

'*Maître! Je l'ai trouvé!*'

'*Un moment.*' The voice was breathy: he was approaching climax.

The tritone. It sneered at the Eiffel Tower. It sneered at all the laws and injunctions of mechanised and moralising society. Claude felt a terrible awe and fear. The major and minor scales slunk off. For you could travel from C sharp to G either chromatically or in full tones. There was a new scale, the whole tone. Three fingers on white *touches*, three on black, he played it from bottom to top of the keyboard. This was not the Eiffel Tower. Lady Betty said:

'That's not proper music.' He did not understand. If he had understood, what was the judgement of a whore? And a bass made of an alternating C sharp (or D flat) and G natural – what harmonies would it support? It was for the entry of Venus. Wrong to sneer at a whore, who was in the service of Venus. The world had changed, since there was a new way of looking at the world. Mallarmé appeared, fully dressed, dapper, even smoking a newly rolled cigarette. Claude said, wide-eyed:

'I've found the faun.' And he played. 'Hear it on the first flute. And here is Venus, I think.' A chord of D flat major alternating with – what could it be called? A secondary seventh on G, with E flat as a passing note? The textbook terms no longer applied.

'I think you have,' Mallarmé said. And then the front door opened and Madame Venus entered, Mrs Mack, brothel-mistress, fanning herself with an evening newspaper and saying she was all of a muck sweat. Lady Betty said:

'Paid and finished, ma.'

'On the contrary,' Mallarmé said. Claude triumphantly gave out, in octaves, the tritone. Mrs Mack said, fanning herself:

'Sounds like the very devil. If he wants to play, that young man there, let him play proper music.' Mallarmé translated and Claude happily swung into one of the inanities of *Le Chat Noir*. He would be back playing there tomorrow evening. Life had to go on.

·— WINE OF THE COUNTRY —·

'Thank you to Inche Abdul Rahman, to Captain Jack Ferguson, to Dr Ooi Boo Eng and, I mean no impoliteness in putting her last, rather the opposite, to Tungku Rahimah Noor, whose beauty and elegance only we in the studio have been lucky enough to be able to appreciate but whose wit and sagacity have contributed immeasurably, I don't doubt, to your enjoyment. The next edition of *Tanya Tanya*, or *Ask Ask*, as you please, will be in two weeks' time. Send your questions to Radio Brunei, Brunei Town.' Walter Sundralingam, sitting by him as silent assistant, gave George Adams a nudge. 'Oh, yes. Alas, I shall not be with you on that occasion, nor, indeed, on any other. My term of office has come to an end. I know you will accord a hearty welcome to my replacement, Mr Walter Sundralingam, formerly of Radio Singapore. And now – *selamat malam.*' And now, George said to himself, sod you and yours and thank Christ or somebody it's all over. Three years had been a long time. The Sultan and his advisers must have thought so too, for he had been offered no renewal of his contract. It had not been altogether his fault that Azahari, under the guise of an elementary talk in the local language on the anthropology of the great jungly island, had said harsh words about the inefficiency, ignorance and tyranny of the British Resident; it had not been at all his fault that Lim Seng Wa had recited filthy poems in demotic Hakka. He had arrived from Radio Singapore equipped with enough of the *bahasa* to scold the technical staff, all lazy, all remote cousins of the Sultan's number three wife; there had been nothing about polyglottism in his contract. It would be good to go back to the cool

110

and to the waiting job in the BBC World Service. Ferguson of the Security Forces was saying to Abdul Rahman the lawyer:

'I mean, if you're going to speak the bloody language, speak it properly. It took me a long time to figure out that a bullokah was a bullock cart.'

'We have not all had the good fortune,' Abdul Rahman said, 'to be born in what you call Austrylia.' Then he said: 'We know you. We know who our friends are.'

'What's that supposed to mean?'

'Irascibility,' Dr Ooi said. 'The tendency to become irritable or irate. It is dangerous in this climate.' To George he said: 'May we expect a cheque?'

'Alas, no. You did it for the love of disseminating knowledge.'

Dr Ooi smiled and bowed to Tungku Rahimah Noor before leaving. Inche Abdul Rahman made an ambiguous hand movement. Ferguson, adjusting his belt, said: 'A schooner?' George said alas again: too much to do: his packing cases were being transported to the docks at five. Walter Sundralingam said he had to see somebody but that he would be back in fifteen minutes and then he would drive George home. Tungku Rahimah Noor said that she would willingly do that, adding that his fifteen minutes would most likely prove an hour. To George she said:

'A drink at my place first?'

'A quick one. I was telling the truth about the truck coming at five.'

The princess, for that was what a female tungku was, drove with far more skill than George had ever learned. She had a white Porsche. Driving, she showed a delicious expanse of brown leg, for today she was dressed in a *cheongsam*. She showed patches of her brown body serially: some days she dressed as the Malay she was, with a low-cut *baju*; others, in a sari, she showed a great deal of her midriff. Always, with the Paris perfume that fought the varied smells of the town – buffalo dung, dung fires, turmeric, dried fish – she was alluring. She had been alluring to George for three years, but he had not fallen. He had been absurdly faithful to his wife Anne. Not absurdly, no. Why should fidelity be absurd? He had seen the dangers of infidelity in Singapore all of three years before. A man could not really get away with it, not with a woman like Anne.

111

Tungku Rahimah Noor, youngest daughter of the Sultan, did not live with the royal family in the *istana*. She had an apartment above the main branch of Grindlays Bank on Jalan Ibrahim. She did not need money, since the royal family was unbelievably rich from the oil that gushed up the coast in Seria, but she liked to work. She ran a dress shop which imported *haute couture* from Paris, Milan, Barcelona, Hong Kong and Bangkok. Her dresses were very expensive, and only the wives of the oilmen in Seria could afford them. Anne, George's wife, could not, that went without saying. The way up to her apartment was by a private elevator in which they stood dangerously close and her perfume was maddening. The apartment itself, with genuine Braques on the walls, with ponyskin furniture, air conditioning, a glistening metal bar, looked from a twenty-foot-wide window on to the mosque and the river. She served the drinks herself: her servants were off-duty. The ice shook in George's *stengah*. She said, her brown legs stretched, her shoes kicked off, in a frame of black-and-white ponyskin: 'Thank you for the beauty and elegance.'

'Well-known. Hence supererogatory.'

'You've been a good boy.'

'His royal highness doesn't seem to think so.'

'Father thinks what the British Resident tells him to think. Besides, I wasn't referring to your work as the head of Radio Brunei. I was referring to your morals.'

'Oh, that, those . . .' The ice clinked as he drank. 'A rectory upbringing.'

'Nothing to do with that, as you know. Nor a natural timidity, though that may come into it. It's just fear, isn't it? Sheer unadulterated funk.' She spoke like what she was, an alumna of Cheltenham Ladies' College.

'I've cause for it. Women get away with that sort of thing better than men. You, if I may say so, should know.'

'That sounds insolent.'

'I see. Perhaps I'd better call a taxi.'

'Oh, don't be stupid. Don't be so damned touchy.'

'It was you who were being touchy.'

'Perhaps you'd have done better here if you'd done the regular colonial thing,' she said. 'Flirted with the wives of the white

112

officials, made up to the BR's lady. Uxoriousness is taken as a kind of insult.'

'I'm not uxorious by nature. In Singapore I did precisely what you said I should have done here. I carried on a two-month affair with a Mrs Cartwright.'

'I don't know the lady. A good solid crafty name, very English.'

'You know the name. Melvin Cartwright is or was the Singapore agent for a parcel of British publishers. Fat, fiftyish. His wife was a good deal younger. Not fat, far from it. Asthenic. A hyacinth girl, sort of. Rain-washed. I believed we were being totally discreet. Morbidly so. After all, Singapore's a big city.'

'But a gossipy one.'

'Anne found out. How do they do it? Special antennae. She reacted hysterically.'

'White women should never come to the tropics.'

'I got salt and water to her. I threw the rest of the barbiturates away. I thought I'd told you about that.'

'Not so explicitly. Besides, it's not my business.'

'You've been a good friend. I hope you've admired my, well, self-restraint.'

'Wondered at it. It's after five. I'd better drop you.'

She did, but not at the door of his bungalow. She dropped him at the beginning of the dirt track that led to it, turned there and, waving, sped back to town. Discreet, as ever. George, jacket under his arm, sweated the hundred yards home. The truck from Boustead and Co. had not, of course, arrived yet. But Walter Sundralingam's Ford was there. Since selling his Oldsmobile to a group of Iban fisherman who could now cart their daily catch in it, independent of costly Chinese deep-freeze transportation, George had had to rely a good deal on Walter Sundralingam's car. At the window he now caught a glimpse of Anne in Walter Sundralingam's arms. Blonde British and Tamil deep purple. They seemed to hear his feet on the gravel; they disengaged. Well. He would not have thought. When he entered he found Walter Sundralingam picking up cigarettes from the floor: he had brushed the box on the PWD *pahit* table and made it fall. Anne was lighting a cigarette, not from the floor. She was thinner than she should be: he was taking her away from tropical anorexia just in time. Then the Boustead truck arrived and Walter Sundralingam, not George, supervised the loading of the packing cases. 'Thank you, Walter,' George said. 'Well, this is very much it.'

'I take you to the Rest House now?' The bungalow rang hollow. It had ceased to be a home. The Rest House tonight, the plane to Singapore tomorrow at dawn, the London flight the following day. As they lay in the twin beds under the joint mosquito net after dinner, George said:

'I saw, you know.'

'Saw what?'

'Walter Sundralingam's presumption. You know what Sundralingam means?'

'Lingam has a purely religious significance, so he told me.'

'Meaning that the earthier significance somehow came up in conversation?'

'How pedantic we're being.' She was a lovely woman still, though she had been eating too little and drinking and smoking too much. It would be good to get her back to England. 'Walter has done a lot for us,' she said, 'in the short time he's been here. He just brought his big but rather well-favoured purply black face near to mine and kissed me. He trembled rather. I don't think he can have kissed a white woman before. Now let me sleep. We have to be up at five.'

'He shouldn't have kissed you.'

'And you presumably shouldn't kiss the glamorous tungku or do worse. Not that it matters.'

'That's a thing I've not done. I've been faithful. Ever since Singapore. You made damned sure that I'd be faithful. I wasn't going to have that nonsense again. All right, sleep. Pleasant dreams.'

Before they boarded the plane at Brunei airport, Walter Sundralingam said quietly to George: 'Can you lend me a hundred dollars?'

'I don't think I – wait, I have travellers' cheques. I need cash for a taxi in Singapore. Will seventy do?'

'Thanks, George. I'll send you the amount in cash registered when I get paid. How long will you be at that address?'

'Till I find a flat in London.' He knew that Walter would not pay the debt nor even write to say why he was not paying it.

Tungku Rahimah Noor rushed in, just as they were responding to the final boarding call, with orchids for Anne. She said:

'George has been good.' And she kissed George in a sisterly manner on his left cheek. With Anne she shook hands.

'George has been good, has he?' Anne said, eyes closed, as they took off.

'Anne has been good too.'

'Some say that Anne is very good.' Then she dozed. When they got to Singapore they took a taxi to the Raffles Hotel and, in the bedroom as big as a dance-hall, she dozed further. George dozed too. Then she lunched with an old friend, Marjorie Morris of Radio Singapore, and shopped for trinkets. George sat on the bedroom verandah with a gin *pahit* in his hand, looking down at the Chinese bustle. They dined with Jack Fothergill and his wife and danced between courses. They went to bed early. It was only when they were seated in the first-class cabin of the BOAC Britannia that George said:

'What did you mean by that cryptic remark?'

'I don't make cryptic remarks.'

'About some saying that Anne is very good?'

'You're a fool, George. You never understand anything. What's a woman supposed to do in a hell-hole like Brunei?'

'You seemed to me to find plenty to do. Helping young Abdul Rahman with his English correspondence. Spare-time teaching at the Omar Yusof Ali Shaifuddin College, God what a mouthful.'

'Drinking the wine of the country.'

'What's that supposed to mean?'

'As I say, you never seem to understand anything. That stupid little affair of yours with Lydia Cartwright. Even now you don't seem to understand why it was wrong.'

'I've spent more than three years beating my breast because it was wrong. I don't want it brought up again.'

'If you'd carried on an affair with a Chinese or a Malay or a Tamil or a Eurasian it would have been totally different. That would have been sampling the wine of the country. One has a kind of duty to do that. You don't go to Burgundy to drink whisky.'

'You mean *you've* been sampling it?' Her eyes were closed, her hands primly folded, her seat thrust back to form almost a day-bed. 'That wasn't just Walter Sundralingam being forward and insolent? You've slept with the bastard?'

'It's all in the past now, isn't it? The past is behind us. Literally. We shan't be going east again.'

'Who else was there?'

'It was almost as if you knew, lining up Rahman and Boo Eng for the last of your futile little brains trusts. Not Ferguson, oh no. Never bloody Ferguson. I've done no playing away with an *orang puteh. Puteh's* a good word, isn't it? It means white but it sounds like putty. Putty-coloured bloody Ferguson.'

The curds-and-cream stewardess came up to ask if they wanted another gin and tonic. 'Not just now,' George said. 'Yes please,' from Anne. 'Not just now,' George said more firmly. The stewardess had gone before Anne could rescind his veto. 'We've both been drinking too much,' George said. And then: 'You slept with those two?'

'I've been through all the available colours except putty. I want another drink. Grab her.'

'Oh, all right. It doesn't matter. I'm bloody disgusted.'

'Why? It's not even what you'd call infidelity. They weren't real people. They were specimens of their races. I thought that was what foreign travel was all about. And now our foreign sojourns are all over. For the time being, anyway.' She took a fresh gin and tonic from the stewardess with a delightful smile.

'And I never knew,' George said sourly. 'I never suspected.'

'Men never do because they don't want to impair their image of themselves. The word cuckold is a word of fear, according to Shakespeare. You needn't fear any infidelity in the future – well, in as much of the future as I can see. I'll be a good little wife.'

'And I've been a good little husband,' bitterly.

'And also a fool. Any more Lydia Cartwright type escapades and I'll take a knife to you. You were a bloody fool even about those barbiturates. They were vitamin tablets. You made me sick, you bastard. But perhaps getting you scared out of your wits was worth it. Anyway, it's all over.'

All over, was it, is it? It was a long journey home, with a night's stop-over in Colombo and a couple of days in Rome. George watched Anne carefully in the little bar of the Albergo Tritone. How exotic did she consider that silver-haired Roman with charming manners and gold-headed cane? They reached London, where they put up in a bed-and-breakfast establishment run by an Italian lady born in Bermondsey and a much older husband born in Lausanne. The homeless stay in London might be long: flats in their price range were not easy to find. They could not really afford a hotel. Almost the first thing Anne did was to telephone her widower father in Nottingham. 'He's not well,' she told George. 'I didn't like the tone of his last letter. We're going to see him.'

'You are. I can't. I've got to do the rounds of the apartment agencies. I've got to see Clapton at Bush House.'

'You'll be all right here?'

'No mischief, if that's what you mean. There's no likelihood of any of that, is there?'

'I might be away a week. My bitch of a sister doesn't seem to be doing anything for him. I'll sort her out.' She was a very handsome woman, sitting there on the bed, stockinged for the first time in three years, showing a great deal of stockinged leg. They made love that night at her instigation. 'Oh, come on,' she said when he sulkily demurred. 'Autumn cool. No mosquitoes or flying beetles. It's supposed to be a pleasure.' In the morning he saw her off, lightly luggaged, on the train to Nottingham. She kissed him very warmly. Then he was alone in London. He had a feeble erection at the thought. Down, sir, down. London was a lonely place. He ate lonely luncheons in pubs, a sausage with much mustard and a pint of bitter. There were a great number of house and flat agencies, but there was a lot of head-shaking. He took dinner in chain restaurants where the beefsteaks carried much untrimmed fat. He took to eating especially hot curries in Soho. He telephoned Anne in Nottingham. 'Lonely,' she said, 'more than anything else. The doctor's not too happy about his blood pressure. I had a hell of a row with Hazel. I told the cleaning woman to go, no damned good at all, and got another one. I'll be back next Thursday. The train gets in at four something. In the afternoon, idiot. Meet it.' And then: 'I do love you, you know, fool as you are.' She seemed to kiss the mouthpiece. Then she rang off.

In an agency on Baker Street he had great luck. There was a three-room flat on Chiswick High Road within his price range.

The tenant just departed had had the place specially refurbished for his invalid wife. He had even bought undistinguished furniture in Hammersmith. The wife had thrown herself from the window in a fit of depression. The widower had gone back, depressed though not suicidally, to Leicester. The furniture was for sale. George liked what he saw, even the bustling shoppers (not at all like the view from the verandah of the Raffles) from the suicidal window. He had better not tell Anne about that; though, being a woman, she would take one look at it and say: 'Somebody fell out of that, or was pushed.' He signed a contract with the agent and then a cheque on Grindlays Bank for the deposit. Next door to the agency there was a tobacconist's shop run by Pakistanis, Muslims anyway, and in its doorway a number of plain postcards in a high glass frame, ill-lettered all of them, advertising services and commodities. Vacuum cleaner almost new. Massage. Models. His heart nearly failed him when he read: 'Rahimah charming coffee-coloured model 34 21 34 Tel. CHI 7894.' Of course, there were plenty of Rahimahs around the Muslim world, which now included the United Kingdom. It was, as it were, the basal exotic female nomenclature – belly-dancers at Port Said, gaidarophily in Cairo. He was not quick to telephone, though there was so little time. He had many pints of bitter in pubs on Marylebone Road before trembling out his coins in a public call-box. He was glad to get the engaged tone. When he tried again, just after 'let's-have-them-glasses' had been called, she, or somebody, was there.

'*Chakap Melayu*?' he asked. Yes, she did, but she had got used to speaking a variety of East End English. To model? Well, he took that to be a euphemism for – a what? Three o'clock Wednesday.

She was in a third-floor flat on Burford Road, not far from Brentford Football Ground. She had, rather pathetically he thought, decorated in what could only be termed a style of eclectic exoticism both the little sitting-room and the adjoining bedroom. There was Benares brassware and a chipped soapstone Buddha as well as a torn poster, sellotape-mended, advertising a film with P. Ramlee in the lead. The perfume was of some British variety he associated with the spraying of cinemas in his youth. He was, of course, no longer even in his late youth. He was as middle-aged as any man could be expected to be, though haired, flat-bellied and with the beginnings of a certain varicosity hardly visible. She was not wholly Malay, he could see that. There was Chinese blood there and something not quite placeable – Buginese? She was not one for chatter about her origins. The clothes she took off were Western and included stockings of the colour of gun-metal. George gulped. They danced near-naked to a record from which, through the barbed wire of many scratches, the song *Rukun Islam* was recognisable. It was more than three years' old; it went back to his time in Singapore. She rubbed her splay nose in his cheek; her teeth were, in the Malay manner, too prominent for easy kissing, not that she wanted kissing. She wanted, in her hard acquired Western style, the job done and the money on the mantelpiece safely stowed. When the job was done she resisted his gestures of tenderness. The social side of the act was reserved to a brief harsh catechism.

'You married?'

'Well, yes.'

'She no good in bed?'

'Very good really, I suppose.'

'You wanted a change, yes?'

'Yes, and I've had it. *Terima kaseh.*'

'*Sama sama.* A pig's language.'

'You eat pig?'

'I eat anything. You come again?'

'Now, you mean?'

'No, not now. You come once, is enough. Now. I mean again.'

'I doubt if I'll have the opportunity.'

'What is that long word?'

'Never mind.'

Anne was quick to note his buoyancy when he gave her his hand as she left the train. 'How is he?' he asked.

'Not too good but he'll survive. What news this end?'

'News you'll like. I've got us a decent flat, not too expensive. In Chiswick. No, not by the river. Ten minutes walk from Turnham Green tube. And there's another thing.'

'Well?'

'We're quits now. At least, call it quits. A certain generosity goes into the scale-pan. Exactly balanced.'

'Talking balderdash as usual. I could do with a drink. Of course, the pubs aren't open yet. This bloody country.'

'Would you like to be back in Brunei?'

'That's even bloodier. What do you mean, quits?'

'A little joke. Nothing. Forget it. Not important, anyway. I'll tell you later.' They were in a taxi now, making for Russell Square. In the breakfast-room of their lodging-house, Madame or Mrs Pécriaux was teaching her poodle to dance. Budgerigars twittered in their cages. 'You back then?' Mme Pécriaux said to Anne in an accent not unlike, it occurred to George, that of Rahimah of Burford Road. Tungku Rahimah's accent was altogether different, that of the educated East. Anne and he went up to their room. Mme Pécriaux called up the stairs: 'Your hubby been a good boy.' Little did she know.

Anne sat on the bed and opened her travelling bag. Nightdress, a frock or two, a cosmetic case. 'Now.'

'Make love you mean?' He grinned and soon ungrinned, for she looked up at him stonily. She said:

'Quits. What did you mean by that?'

'The wine of the country.'

'Explain.' He explained. He said:

'A bit belated, I know, and perhaps in the wrong location. Perhaps I was a bit stupidly slow in seeing your point. But I did see it. And so we're quits. Everything cancelled out. We can get on with repatriated living.'

'Oh my God,' she said and seemed to retch. 'Oh my God. I don't know which is worse, the sheer bloody stupidity or the filthy abominable piggishness. You go with a prostitute and then expect me to – My head spins. Get out of my sight.'

George looked at her in genuine bewilderment. Then he said: 'Your bloody Tamil lover Walter Beautifulprick owes me seventy dollars, do you know that? If you're going to bring bloody money into it.'

'Oh my dear God. To go with a prostitute. God knows what diseases you've picked up.'

'She was very clean and I was – well, well-protected. The point's not that she was a prostitute but that she was from Malaysia. From Johore Baru. Wine of the country. So we're quits.'

'I'll hit you with this bloody bag if you say quits again. Can't

120

you see, you filthy stupid pig, that it's not the same? It was all right there but it's not at all all right here. That wine doesn't travel, you piggish idiot. You're covered in filth and the first thing you want to do is to pass your filth on to me. Get out of this room. I can smell her from here.'

'Oh no you can't. I've had a bath since then. Two baths.'

'You'll never understand, will you? You're either so stupid it'll never pierce your thick stupid skull or so piggishly *evil* that you don't want it to. It's not the same thing at all. *It's not the same thing at—*' Then she began to weep rather loudly.

'She was very clean,' George mumbled. Anne threw a shoe at him and he slunk, bewildered, out of the room.

·— SNOW —·

A tour in the East is three years long.
After a year of unabating heat
We held a Christmas party, fans spinning strong,
Anchor and Tiger. Ted got to his feet,
I to the mess piano. He began to sing.
I'd always known he could sing. He sang his
Soused version of Walther's first act song:
Am Stillen Herd, in Winterzeit,
Mit Burg und Dorf all' aufgeschneit.
Mohamed Ali, Mat, drying
The slopped bar, while Redzwan mopped the concrete
    under,
Said, in wonder: *'Tuan ini tanggis'*
(This gentleman is crying).

That was the poem, if you can call it a poem, that I wrote
on the feast of St Stephen. It was the monsoon season and
the rain beat, it seemed to my fancy, with hate. I could not
hear the first act of *Die Meistersinger* on the record-player because
of its fury. My *amah*, Mat's wife Maimunah, had to clean the
mould off the books every morning, and brush it off my clothes
in the wardrobe, despite the lamp that burned there. If the rain
could not enter my bungalow as rain, it sneaked in as mould. I
sweated, but not with heat. The fans had not been spinning in
the Malay Regiment officers' mess: that had merely been a bit of
Maughamesque local colour. Ted was Ted Cooper, the head of
the State Anthropological Department. Redzwan was his servant,

122

and Mat, or Mohamed Ali, was mine. We had loaned them to the Malay Regiment mess for the evening, since the two regular stewards needed help.

My job at that time was exquisitely specialised. The British were soon to leave Malaya, and there were tasks to be performed which could not yet be entrusted to the sons of the soil, or *bumiputra*, who were already at work forming their independent government. One of these tasks was a phonetic description of the national language, or *bahasa negara*, and it was I who worked on this in a language laboratory in the *Makhtab Persekutuan* or National College not far from Kota Bharu's national airport. The politicians did not see the point of it, but the *Tungku Makhota*, or Crown Prince of the State of Kelantan, did. He had heard of linguistics in London, and he saw that the proposal to devise a new Roman alphabet for the national language depended on an exact appraisal of its phonemes.

Ted's work was more difficult than mine. He saw it as his duty to protect the aboriginal tribes of the State of Kelantan from the crackpot proposal of central government that they should be dragged out of the jungle, placed in reservations, and there forcibly converted to Islam. The Temiars of the Kelantan jungle were admirable people, very small, totally animistic, courteous, gentle, humane. They could count only up to three and they had quaint and harmless superstitions. To comb your hair in a thunderstorm brought bad luck to the whole tribe; if you laughed when a butterfly sailed by you were inviting death to your eldest son. They kept jungle pigs as pets and, when the time came for the senior pigs to be slaughtered for food, there was always a farewell ceremony with much weeping, followed by the blowpipe injection of a soporific, and then the regretful cutting of the throat. The Malays said that the Temiars were not civilised and demanded that they be taught the Koran and assemble at the mosque on Fridays. But, Ted knew, Islamicisation would kill them. He wept for the Temiars, whom he deeply loved. But, weeping while singing Walther's song, he had wept for something far removed from the Malayan jungle. He wept for the North.

And, after his song and another bottle of cold Anchor or Tiger, he had drunkenly orated about the North. 'All right,' he said, 'we miss the superficial things – snow falling while we peel a tangerine, though I've never once in my life seen snow at Christmas. The Queen's speech after the turkey, though we get that here crackling on the midnight radio. The fairy lights on the fir tree, the presents, Santa Claus.'

'That's just your childhood,' Lieutenant Reynolds said, near-shouted rather, since the monsoon rain beat heavily. 'I could bloody near cry myself.'

'But here in the tropics,' Ted said, 'I'm made aware of a civilisation built on the cold. It's stupid for an anthropologist to go all weepy when he thinks of the battle between the gods of winter and spring. But a specialisation perhaps presupposes an emotional attachment. I can't reduce the poetry of the northern seasons to cold science. The great achievements of man belong to the North.'

'Does that include the Mediterranean?' Captain Latiff bin Hussein asked, then repeated his question twice because of the pounding monsoon. He had visited Spain and North Africa. Islam linked them to South-East Asia.

'The Mediterranean went soft,' Ted said. His spectacles steamed; he took them off to wipe them with a humid handkerchief. 'It produced everything and then it went all soft. It left the continuation of the values of civilisation to the North.'

'You mean Germany?' Lieutenant Abrahams said. He had been near the piano and had heard Wagner's words as well as my version of his music.

'Why not Germany? Kant and Hegel and Beethoven. And above all Wagner.'

'Wagner begot Hitler,' Abrahams said.

'Ah, bloody nonsense. Germany went mad and forgot its culture. It rejected its Mediterranean heritage. It perverted its Nordic heritage for that matter. I'm ashamed of Germany.'

'That makes you sound like a German,' Abrahams said.

'My wife was German. German Jewish. A refugee. Is still, I suppose. I mean still alive. She ran off with a Polish refugee.'

That was the end of the conversation. We sang carols to my accompaniment, turning the infant Christ into a snow-king. *Schneekönig* sounded better. Ted led us in *Stille Nacht* and did not weep. Then the Singapore Cold Storage cold turkey was brought in.

124

It was at breakfast on the Feast of Stephen that Mat disclosed a hardly noticeable insolence, or perhaps an unwonted near-familiarity would better describe it. He cleared my papaya plate and put down thawed and fried eggs and bacon and said: '*Fasal apa tuan itu sudah tanggis?*' Why did that gentleman cry?

'Well, Mat,' I said, in my West Coast Malay, 'he cried for something you never see here. He cried for snow.'

'*Salji?*' I had said *thalji*, the correct form, but it was a loan word. Persian? Sanskrit? My linguistic training was narrow. The Arabic for snow was, I thought, *galid*. The Malay phonemic inventory contains no linguodental.

'*Salji*, if you wish. It is a kind of frozen water that falls from the sky in the cold season. It covers the earth and can sometimes be very deep.' Mat grinned, and the grin approached insolence. He had two gold teeth. He was serving me in an undervest not a shirt. Had I had him too long, encouraged his slackness by my own (especially as concerned mealtimes: dinner at two in the morning was perhaps going too far), overpaid him? 'You see snow in the refrigerator,' I said, 'especially when, as so often, you neglect to defrost it. The ice, or stone water, *ayer batu*, you have not put enough of in this glass of orange juice, you will meet in England on the ground in winter. You slip on it and break your hip or leg. You don't know how lucky you are to live in a climate like this.'

'You also,' he said, and then went out. He had not used *tuan*, obligatory for *hajis* and white employers, but *enche*, which serves for any member of the middle class. Still, the eggs and bacon were well-cooked, the tea was strong, and the toast he now brought in was hot and crisp. I let it pass. After breakfast I drove in my second-hand Austin Princess to the laboratory, where I listened to several tapes of up-river Kedah Malay and notated some of the phrases in the narrowest possible version of the International Phonetic Alphabet. It was the neutral link vowel, or vowel murmur, that caused trouble. It was hard to place in the section of the vowel chart which accommodates the English *schwa*. After lunch the rain stopped. In the monsoon season it often intermitted, permitting a partial clearing of the sky and even some weak sunlight. The green was greener in my *kebun*, the peppers on their bush gleamed as if polished, the pomelos had visibly swollen. The rain would start again after dinner.

In the afternoon Rosemary Dunning arrived in her little Ford from Pasir Mas, or Goldensand, where she taught in the little school. Her name will give the reader an impression of pink and white Englishry, but Rosemary was very black, a Christian half-Tamil in whom the Dravidian colouring had long swamped the white of the surname. She was a girl of twenty-five, of extreme beauty, the features totally Aryan, the naked body superb. Her view of love was strange. She considered herself engaged to be married to a Scotch propaganda officer who had been dismissed for peculation and gone home to sell cars. She wore his ring. He swore, in his rare letters, that he would soon be sending for her. She had slept with him and now she slept with me, making use of a body not dissimilar to his, but, eyes tight shut, imagining a face not mine at the upper end of it. I was more amused than offended.

It was while she was riding me and approaching the goal of her gallop that Maimunah came into the bedroom with her armful of laundered linen. Fool, I had failed to lock the door. Maimunah saw the *tuan* as succubus to a shining naked black body, looked both shocked and fascinated, said *'Minta ma'af'* and hurriedly left with her bundle. Rosemary, who soon lay panting by my side, did not care what the Malays saw. They were inferior animals, dogs. She settled to doze in my arms and, eyes drowsily shut, I stroked her velvet skin, murmuring: *'Thalji.* Or, if you like, *salji.'* I opened my eyes then sharply, seeing the absurdity of the comparison and also realising why the word existed at all in Malay. It existed in love poetry. The skin of the beloved was likened to snow, signifying the lightest possible colour of a Malay complexion. I knew a Malay married woman called 'Teh' or 'Puteh', meaning white. She was very far from white. But colours in the Malay spectrum seemed to be wholly comparative. The Malay assistant State Education Officer, Yusof Tajuddin, was an *orang pekan*, a half-Tamil Muslim from Penang, and he was popularly known as Raja Hitam, meaning black. There was, I gathered, a false belief abroad among the white promoters of negritude to the effect that, among dark races, our European colour symbolism was turned upside down, so that black signified good and white bad. This, I knew, was nonsence. To all the races of the world black was the colour of night, and night was a time of danger. What would shock Maimunah, and Mat when she told him, was the sight of my white body lying with a black one, letting not merely the white man's side down but the Malay one too. What they did not see they did not bother to imagine. Rosemary Dunning came often to my bungalow and went with me frequently through the pair of swing doors that gave off from the living-room. At the end of the corridor was my bedroom, but first came my study with its books. She often borrowed my books.

Mat grew a little more familiar and Maimunah slightly more pert, rolling her saronged hips as she took the laundered linen into the bedroom, giving me a woman-to-man smile as she emerged unburdened. She was about eighteen and was the youngest daughter of the head of a gang of axemen in the nearest *kampong*. The axemen, or *orang kapak kechil*, would kill your enemy outright for ten dollars and, on a sliding scale of payment, variously and unlethally wound him. This was not a full-time trade: the little axes usually came out only after dark, and the rest of the day was filled up with leading a buffalo on a string, thrashing *padi*, ordering a *berok* to throw down coconuts, or smoking the *rokok* called Rough Rider in the shade. The Malays named Rough Rider cigarettes *kuda*, or horse, in allusion to the picture on the packet. Mat, padding in to open the morning shutters, grinned '*kuda*' at me, and I wondered what he meant. Then finally I guessed what he meant: something to do with the sexual posture Maimunah had seen.

When the rains cleared, Ted Cooper paid me a visit, accompanied by a gentle little Temiar whom he was taking to the town hospital for treatment for *tahi panas* or prickly heat. The little Temiar was dressed in a pair of Ted's trousers, cut short in the leg and bound with string at the waist, also a child's tee-shirt with the printed legend BE KIND TO A KID TODAY. His strong splayed feet were bare. He crooned at the Chinese ornaments in my living-room, accepted a glass of orange crush from my hands, wandered into the kitchen and then emerged whimpering: Mat had probably delivered him a slap. Ted said: 'They've already sent in a Koran instructor to the poor little buggers. I had to interpret, but none of this Allah nonsense made any sense to them. One God – the concept just doesn't exist. None of the concepts exist. I feel like packing it all in, but somebody's got to try to look after them. It looks as if we'll have to protect the territory with open war, but blowpipes aren't enough. I wish sometimes I was bloody dead.' Then he began to cry. At that moment Mat came in with ice for our whisky. He saw Ted's tears and grinned, saying:

'Salji.'

'Or *thalji*,' I said. 'Look, Mat, he's not crying for snow. He's crying because the militant forces of your religion are trying to kill these gentle little people he's trying to protect.' Mat said:

'*Sakai*.' Talk about Western racism; *sakai* was worse than nigger. *Sakai* meant all the little people of the jungle, it also meant slave. Mat sneered at the Temiar, who cowered into a corner. I could see that Mat would have to go.

I saw this more clearly when he returned from Kota Bharu on his bicycle one night just having been to the cinema. The old film *Holiday Inn* tended to reappear at the Cathay at Christmas or just after and was often retained for a week or so at popular request. It was the song 'White Christmas' that appealed, especially to the young. Allah alone knew what they thought the song was about, but they loved to sing it. The various dialectal perversions of the English were well represented on my tapes. Mat had the insolence to enter my bedroom without knocking to announce that all white men were fools for wishing to believe that *salji* fell from the sky. He had seen this film, with its American earth covered with *salji* but then the filming of a film had been shown, and it was clearly demonstrated how this *salji* was made. It was made with machines: it seemed to be a matter of blowing a lot of *garam* or salt around. Why were we such fools as to be taken in? Why was that *tuan* who had brought the *sakai* to the house such a fool as to weep at what clearly did not in nature exist? I got mad, put down my copy of *Bhowani Junction*, and said:

'You can take it from me that *salji* or *thalji* is sent down by God or Allah in the northern countries during the cold season. I have seen it myself, walked under it, played games with it, built human effigies with it. If I though travel was capable of broadening your narrow mind, I would expend money on a return air ticket so that you could see for yourself, in Norway or Sweden or North Germany, that *thalji* falls from the sky and lies thick upon the ground. But you do not believe in *thalji*, except as a vague poetical expression, any more than I believe in Allah, so let's leave it, shall we? Switch off the light as you go.' We looked at each other through the snowy mist of the mosquito net, and he went out, crushing the light from the one bulb that sprouted from the ceiling, muttering something about *salji tid' ada*, there is no snow.

The next morning breakfast was late. This was because of a hell of a quarrel proceeding between Mat and Maimunah in their quarters. I could not understand much of what was shouted and screamed, for it was in the Kelantan dialect, and I had learned only the dialect of Johore, but I caught the words *perempuan jahat*, which literally means bad woman but, by extension, whore. I wanted my breakfast and walked to the kitchen, where no breakfast preparations were in evidence. I walked through the kitchen to the servants' quarters, where Maimunah seemed to be protecting herself against Mat's possible violence by clutching one of the five cats to her bosom. The other four cats had wide eyes and horrent fur as they witnessed this breakdown of human order. Mat turned to me and said things I did not well understand, but the name Mohamed Noor was an intelligible *leitmotif*. Mohamed Noor was a single man employed as houseboy by the Sandersons, who lived in the next bungalow but two. Mat seemed to allege that, while he, the lawful husband, had been absent at the cinema seeing pseudo-*salji*, she, the lawful wife, had been copulating with this Mohamed Noor. The evidence? The fat white *tuan* in Drainage and Irrigation had called in on his way to early work and informed him, Mat, that he would do well to keep his wife in order: he had repeatedly called Mohamed Noor to bring ice, and Mohamed Noor did not seem to be around. But he was around all right, and he had been exchanging *chium-chium* or nose-kisses with a girl who had no right to be there. Maimunah wailed to heaven, or the discoloured ceiling of the servants' quarters, that the girl had not been she. Let her be struck down dead instanter if it were so. I said:

'Tuan Sanderson has short sight and cannot see clearly. He is also a liar and a trouble-maker. Maimunah was in this house last night. She washed the dinner things. She played your radio very loud. There was a programme of *joget* music. I heard her singing to it. All right, you do not wish to believe me any more than you wish to believe that *thalji* or *salji* falls from the heavens. But what I say is the truth. Now would you be good enough to boil me two eggs, since I am already late for my work.'

That morning, after an hour of unprofitable labour on Malay plosives, I drove in to the Hong Kong and Shanghai Bank in Kota Bharu. I drew out four hundred dollars, of which three hundred and sixty would be for Mat and Maimunah – two months' salary, one of the months being in lieu of notice. There was a sulking kind of quiet in the bungalow at lunchtime, and the meal of cold tongue and canned potato salad was roughly served and in sullen silence. I would wait till the following day before announcing dismissal. And I knew that, the following day, I would wait till the following day. No, I would wait till the end of the month, less than a week off. There was a Chinese who cooked at the police canteen tired of the postures of uniformed Malay superiority: he, I knew, would jump at the chance of a change.

But it was the morning after the morning of the drawing of the money that I discovered that the situation was taken out of my hands. Maimunah came tearfully into my bedroom at dawn to say that Mat had left during the night, very quietly, not even disturbing her sleep. I had had a vague dream about a vague presence moving about the bungalow in the dark, but I often had such dreams. Now I guessed it was no dream. A couple of rather valuable Chinese figurines had disappeared; the four hundred dollars in my desk drawer were no longer there. Even a small bag of rice had gone from the store cupboard. Mat said nothing? Maimunah, her sleeping sarong knotted at the level of her armpits, so that her brown shoulders glowed in the *mata hari*, or eye of the day, said: 'Nothing, *tuan*.' But he had left a note for her, useless since she could not read; here was the note. The note was brief and in the Arabic script Mat had learnt from his brief schooling. It said: *Saya chari thalji*. I go to seek the snow. It was *thalji* and not *salji*. The curve on its back with a trio of dots above certainly stood for *tha*. The grapheme stood for a purely theoretical phoneme. Maimunah said:

130

'*Tuan* will look after me? *Tuan* will let me stay? I will be good to *tuan*.' As an earnest of this she unknotted her sarong and let it fall to the floor. The slim golden body was a possession any Malay husband would be jealous about. The breasts were high and pert. 'I,' she said, 'can do for you anything the black woman can do.' She no longer said *tuan*, though *tuan* was in order in a *pantun* wherein a lover addressed a loved one. The word she used was *yu*, meaning you, indeed indentical with it. There was such a bewildering selection of second person terms in the Malay language that *yu* was proving a useful neutrality. I said breathily:

'Dress. You can make tea? You can slice papaya? Get me my breakfast.' And I wondered what the hell Mat meant by seeking the snow.

After lunch, which was a can of dressed pork unopened and a loaf of Chinese bread unsliced, the inevitable happened. I lay in bed with a naked Malay girl not more than eighteen with, on my engorged phallus, a product of Malayan latex for which the Malay language had no name save for the periphrastic *pekakas untok tidak buat anak*, device for not making children. She had learnt one lesson from the black Rosemary and, a brown mare, she rode me. Then she lay in my arms panting, and said: 'You will look after me?' I stroked her brown skin, the Malay for brown was *hitam manis*, sweet black, and said it was like *thalji*. What the devil did he mean by saying he was seeking the snow? Then I thought of the men of the little axes in Maimunah's *kampong*, a mile away. Mat had done well to leave quietly in the night. He might well have cycled in the dark to the railway station at Kota Bharu and waited for the train that would take him across the Thailand border. The Mentri Besar had christened the train the *Sumpitan Mas*, or Golden Blowpipe. The blowpipes of the Temiar would be of no avail against the weapons of Islam. The little axes – oh my God. The afternoon sun, piercing the slats of the shutter, enflamed my scarlet pyjama-bag. I saw that I myself, and long before my tour was over, might have to start seeking the snow.

·—— THE ENDLESS VOYAGER ——·

I knew that the man in front of me was named Paxton, for the girl who processed his ticket called him that. Mr Paxton, an erect man with a full head of snowy hair, disclosing the trenched face of eighty or so years when he gave place to me and wheeled his two pieces of luggage away. We were both bound for New York, first class. (I travelled the world in those days as an accountant for Single Buoy Mooring.) Paxton had consigned no luggage to the belt that oozed to the baggage-handlers; I had my own heavy bag ticketed and launched on its journey. The bronze-haired agent checked my passport for an American visa, as she had checked his, and she smiled me off with an embarkation card marked Smoking. I saw Paxton precede me at the security check and then show his passport to the bored passport officials. I heard him say: 'Last time, my friend,' saw him receive the response of a half-smile uncaring and uncomprehending, then followed him into the departure lounge. Paxton grinned clean dentures at me, said, 'Watch this,' and then placed his passport in one of the deep rubbish bins, burying it under an accumulation of discarded duty-free bags, chocolate wrappers and cigarette packets. I said:

'You can't.'

'Can't I just. That's the end of that.'

'You'll need it at the other end. You can't travel without a passport.'

'Oh yes I can and will. I'm fed up with all that rubbish. Free as a bird, that's me.'

'Nobody's all that free. They'll want to see your passport at

132

Kennedy. They won't let you in without it. There's the question of the visa and checking in the big black book to see if you're an undesirable alien.'

'Undesirable, eh? I'm desirable to myself, and that's all that matters. Good riddance to it.'

'It'll get back to you. It'll be salvaged and taken to Petty France or somewhere and sent to you in a registered envelope.'

'Where to? I don't have any address.'

'Excuse me,' I said, and went to buy a duty-free bottle of Claymore and double pack of Rothmans. I met a good number of eccentrics on my travels, but this was the first I had encountered who had gleefully put himself in the situation of a migrant bird. But he would fly over no frontier. It was a closed world to a traveller who did not carry a little book telling him what he knew already: that he had this name, this colour of eyes, this weight of years, this citizenship. He had his embarkation card, however: he was behind me in the check-out line with a small bottle of Cointreau and a pack of Dunhill cigarettes. 'Broadens the mind,' he said to me, 'travel. Or so they say.'

'First trip to America?'

'First trip anywhere. By air, that is. Seen a fair part of the world by ship, but ships don't seem to exist any more. I'm quite looking forward to it.'

I got away from him and strode to the bar, where I ordered a large brandy. But he was soon with me, ordering a glass of London bitter. Those bags of his, I thought, must be a great burden. He couldn't wheel them on a trolley for ever. I looked at the bags and so did he. He bent down to open one of them. 'Look at this,' he said.

'God almighty,' I said. What he showed me was a large yellow plastic folder crammed with air tickets. He said, riffling through them:

'Going everywhere. Rio de Janeiro, Valparaiso, wherever that is, Mozambique, Sydney, Christchurch, Honolulu, Moscow.'

'If there's one place where you'll need a visa, it's certainly Moscow,' I said. 'But, damn it, how do you propose to go *anywhere* without a passport?'

'There's going and going,' he said. 'When I get to one place then I start off right away for another. Well, in some cases not

133

right away. There's a fair amount of waiting in some of the places. But they have what they call transit lounges. Get a wash and brush up. Perhaps a bath. Throw a dirty shirt away and buy a new one. Ditto for socks and underpants. No trouble, really.'

'In effect,' I said, astonished, 'you'll be travelling without arriving.'

'You could put it that way.' It sounded like a Hounslow accent. 'I've nobody left. Wife dead, kids off and married. I got a quarter of a million for the house, a joke, a bloody scandal, whichever way you want to look at it, considering what I paid for it at the end of the war. So what do I do with the money? Go to a travel agency where they gawp and bring in everybody to look at me. Open tickets, as they call them, most of them. No rush. If I miss one plane I wait for another. Then I've got those travellers' cheques, great convenience they are. The bit left in the bank is for Jamie, he's the eldest, the only one with any guts. Of course, a lot depends on how long I can keep up this caper. I may live longer than I expect, in which case I shall have to draw, won't I? But I'm pretty sure it's all going to end in the air. Stands to reason, how do the damned things keep up? One's bound to fall down one of these days, and I'll be in it with a bit of luck. So nobody's worrying.' He drank some of his bitter and listened, with the attentiveness appropriate to a sudden strain of music, to a voice calling a flight. I said:

'That seems to be us.'

I was thankful that we had not been allotted adjoining seats. There were not many in first class that day, and I needed an extra seat for spreading my papers. Paxton was across the aisle with nothing to do except, with the joy of a tyro air traveller, revel in the amenities of a luxury flight. He called the stewardess my dear and my little darling, grew tipsy on three gins but recovered over lunch. He smacked his lips, saying: 'This is the life and no error.' He watched some of the film, an indiscreet one about an air crash, listened open-mouthed to a concert presided over by a voice called Carmen Dragon, and rejoiced in the hot towels. He even went to the toilet to have an unnecessary shave with his electric razor and returned smelling of all the perfumes of Araby or somewhere. Eventually one of the stewardesses came round with immigration and customs declaration forms. She said:

'British passport, sir, naturally?'

'I don't have one any more. Chucked it away at Heathrow.' She gaped; she even sat down next to him.

'I beg your pardon, sir?'

'I'm not going to New York. I'm going to – let me see now, yes, here it is,' (consulting a typed itinerary headed SPEEDBIRD TRAVEL) 'next stop Trinidad. That'd be in the West Indies, am I right?'

'But you have to land at New York and go through immigration and customs. Everybody does that.'

'But I don't want to go to New York. I've seen New York till I'm sick of seeing it on the television. I want to go to this other place, that's right, Trinidad. And then I go to Miami and pick up a plane for, let me see, right, Rio de Janeiro.'

'But you can't land at any American airport without a passport.'

'What will they do? Send me back home? Well, it's just as easy to send me on to the next port of call. I don't see what all the fuss is about.' She left him, baffled. I, dutifully filling in the forms, felt a minimal prick at the sense of not being a free man. Abider by the rules, submitter to the white line in the immigration queue, to the customs official who handled my indigestion tablets as if they were an illicit drug. 'Lot of bloody nonsense,' Mr Paxton said to me. Well, yes, I suppose it was. I remembered old Ernie Bevin, foreign minister under the post-war Labour government, saying that any man ought to be able to go to Victoria and book a ticket for any place in the world. It was man's world, wasn't it? We all owned the planet together. A nation was defined as an agglomeration of people equipped for making war, and everybody said that wars were a thing of the past. Therefore there were no nations. Perhaps a nation was an abstraction whose one solidity was customs and immigration.

At Kennedy young black girls in uniform told Paxton that he had to do what the other folks did, so he hefted his heavy luggage to the immigration line-ups, grumbling about the bloody liberty, meaning the lack of it. I let him get in front of me at the desk, hearing clearly what was proceeding though I had to toe the white line a discreet yard or so away. He was told he couldn't enter the United States without a passport and a valid visa, hadn't all that been explained to him? Yes, but he didn't want to enter the United States, he saw too much of it on the nightly box, he wanted to go straight to Jamaica. That meant, the official said, proceeding to another Kennedy terminal, which meant entering one of the boroughs of New York City. Ah, got you there, said Paxton, this is British Airways and it's a British Airways flight I'm getting. Then Paxton and his bags were taken away by one of the black girls in uniform. Unable to wave because of his burdens, he gave me a cheery nod. It was my turn to be processed, and the official shook his head at the folly of mankind, meaning passportless Paxton. I said, unwisely perhaps: 'We're all sick of passports and visas. It doesn't keep the criminals out, does it? There's too much red tape all round. The world belongs to its inhabitants.' He did not argue but he looked at me balefully. I was implying that he was doing a useless job. He did some stamping and let me proceed to the chaos of the luggage carousels.

The next time I saw Paxton was about four months later. This was in the airport at Karachi, an ugly structure full of unhelpful brown functionaries who were doing as little work as possible because this was Ramadan and the sunset gun had not yet gone off. Paxton looked well enough but he was very hot. 'Air conditioning's bust or something, or perhaps these wogs don't have it. I'll be glad to get home to some cool and a drink with ice in it.' He wiped his neck with a towel.

'Home?'

'Well, that's what I call it. All the planes are the same, aren't they? When I get into a new one I feel as if I'm just going back to an old one. After all, it's the only home I've got.'

'How's it been going?'

'Well, I've had my meals irregular and sleep's gone a bit wrong. I've given my wristwatch away – an Arab kid it was in Abu Dhabi – because there's no point in thinking about what time it is. It's a different sort of time up there. Stomach's played me up a bit, but I take these.' He took one now, a Stums or something. 'I can't grumble, I'm seeing the world, and it's nearly all sea. Not much land about at all. I crossed the date line going from Auckland to Hawaii and lost or gained a day, can't remember which.

The stewardesses are very nice, and it's the ones furthest east that are the nicest. Felt like settling down with one of these Jap girls in a kimono. Felt like a nice little nap on land.'

'That's what you need. A week in a hotel somewhere. There's a very good one in Bangkok.'

'I know, I heard about that, travelled with a Yank party that were all going on there. Very loud laughers. When I want a couple of days ashore so to speak I go to Rome. In the airport there there's a little hotel, more like a hostel, very small, but it's this side of the barrier and there's no passport nonsense. I get a good kip, though I keep waking up at the nightmares, and a bath and I even wash my socks, saves keeping on buying new pairs, and then I just wander round the airport having a cup of that coffee with froth on and a bite to eat. Not much to see really, so I've taken to buying books. Paperbacks I can throw away. Travelling light now. Only one bag, as you can see. Threw the other one away at Heathrow.'

'Went back there, did you?'

'Had to, didn't I, going from Rio to Rome.' He then looked with a certain gloom at the huge plane marked AIRWORK sitting on the runway. 'And now it's Bombay. You too?'

'No, I'm going further east. You said something about nightmares.'

'Yes. Not had them since I was a kid. Very startling, some of them are. My old missis, dead these seven years, played hell in one of them because I'd turned the gas on the stove off. This isn't cooked, she said, and pulls a bloody big snake out of the saucepan.' He shuddered.

'The circadian rhythm has been upset,' I said.

'That's the word. That's the word this doctor used I met on the plane from Paris to Washington. Nice young fellow, cancer expert. He said the body goes its own way regardless of what happens outside it. And it gets a bit riled when it's sunset and ought to be midday. And your sleep gets buggered about, he said.'

'Yes,' I said, and then I spoke rather weightily. 'Strange that the great seeming absolutes are really all relative. Dawn, noon, night. They come at different times for different people.'

'And these poor girls on the planes, the stewardesses, have a lot of trouble with their monthlies. I wonder what kind of night-mares *they* have. I must ask.' And then: 'Birds don't get night-mares, do they?'

'Collective nightmares,' I said. 'Take those ravens outside the Mount Lavinia Hotel in Colombo. They all scream together in the middle of the night.'

'Nice place, is it, Colombo? In what country is it?'

'What they call Sri Lanka and used to call Ceylon. The hotel's nice, except for the ravens' nightmares.'

I met Paxton again six weeks later, and it was in the departure lounge at Heathrow. Inevitably, I suppose, he had become pretty well known on the air routes of the world, a subject of gossip where air crews drank. I found him at a little white table with an earnest young woman who was taking notes. He saw me and waved, rather shakily. 'I can't remember that word,' he said. 'The one about circuses or arcades or something.'

I sat down and introduced myself to the young lady, who said she was Gloria Tippett, a public relations officer of British Airways. 'If you'd just come to the office with me, Mr Paxton,' she said, 'you'll find a little surprise waiting for you.'

'I don't want any surprises,' he said fiercely. 'I've had enough. It's my rhythms all being upset.'

'Circadian,' I said. The word seemed new to the young lady. She had been christened Gloria, and this was unfortunate, for she was in no way glorious. She was an Ethel or an Edith, mousy and with a mouth full of south-of-the-Thames impure vowels. She said:

'I'll go and fetch it if you like. It's your passport. It was handed in months ago, and when your name came up on the computer it was just a matter of contacting Immigration.'

Paxton's response was manic. 'I don't want the bloody thing,' he cried. 'Take it away.' And he made frightful dismissive ges-tures as though it was already there. 'I'm a free man, aren't I? Free as the bloody ravens.' He remembered Colombo, then. On the great black indicator the name Istanbul clicked into place and a little red light started to flash. 'That's where I'm going,' he said. 'It used to be called Constantinople, there's even a song about it.' He did not show any of the expected crumple of his long and eccentric travels. He wore what looked like a Hong Kong suit and his snowy hair had been well cut. But the rhythm of his walk to the departure gate was ill-coordinated, and his one bag seemed too heavy for him.

'What were you trying to get out of him?' I asked.

'Well, it's a queer story, isn't it? Comparisons, really. How we compare with the other airlines of the world. And perhaps something for the in-flight magazine. He seems a bit touched. He used to be an ironmonger,' as though that explained it.

'You shouldn't say that about one of your best customers. Touched, I mean. He's spending the last years of his life doing what he wants to do. His only mistake is thinking he's a free man. Nobody's free these days. He's abandoned a structure and now the demons of chaos are getting at him. Quote me, if you like.' But she didn't understand and probably thought I was touched too. She took her little notebook away. Her legs, I saw, as she walked off, were, and I supposed I could use the term in the context of her name, glorious, shapely anyway, unmatching of the vowels and the mousiness. Nature was an arbitrary bestower.

In the first class club at Zürich airport, some two months after, I found Paxton stretched and snoring among prim business men reading the *Züricher Zeitung*. They gave him, as they say, a wide berth. I mixed myself a gin and tonic and glanced at the front page of the *Corriere Ticinese*. No news except summits and terrorism. A flight was called, to Berne I think, and many of the prim business men left. Paxton, whose unconscious had probably responded to the call, woke smacking. His upper set had dropped and he reaffixed it with two thumbs. He saw me without surprise. 'You do a lot of travelling,' he said. 'But then you're a young man.'

'I also have a wife and kids to go home to.'

'Know where I'm going to now? I'm going to Teheran.'

'That's a good place to keep out of. Where do you go from there?'

'I think it's to – I'll have to have a look – I think it's—' He made as to open his one suitcase but was too tired for the effort. 'Some Arab place, anyway. I keep wishing it could be all over. The Yanks have been shooting down civilian planes in the Persian Gulf. I ought to stick around there. And then we keep reading about these hi-jackers, but no such bloody luck. If they started threatening me with their guns I'd hit out and then get shot, and that'd be the end of it. You can't live for ever and shouldn't want to. I had my eighty-first birthday going to Tokyo. A birthday in the air. I told them and they gave me champagne, but they give everybody champagne, birthday or not.'

'Well, you've done something to be proud of. You've done something absolutely unique.'

'In Rome they have the Colosseum and in Paris there's the Eiffel Tower and I've not seen either. There's also the Taj Mahal at some place or other in India and I've heard a lot about that. But it's not for me. All that's for me is the same seat and the same thing you pull out to put your tray on when it's dinner-time, and it's dinner-time at all bloody hours. Breakfast at three in the morning. It's not natural. I suppose it's by way of being what they used to call a sin really. Racing round the earth both ways and not letting the sun do its proper bloody job, which is to rise at a reasonable hour. So I don't know how it's going to end up.'

'You'll stop it. There's no need to go on. You've made your point. Pick up your passport at Heathrow and go into a private hotel somewhere. Eastbourne, Bournemouth, somewhere like that. You'll have plenty to talk about.'

'About the inside of a plane and the places that were just names? Do me a favour.'

'Well, it was your idea.'

'And not such a bloody good one. Anyway, I'm stuck with it now. It's become a way of life, as they call it. A life-style or something. Where would you be going now, then?'

'Düsseldorf.'

'To do a job?'

'Not for a holiday, that's certain. I think I'll stroll to the gate now. We'll be seeing each other.'

'Oh, we will, God help me. We'll be doing that all right.'

True, very true. We met again in (why should I say of all places?) Stockholm airport. But this time he was not alone. He was with a man of about his own age though haler, as hale as Mr Paxton had been at the start of his pointless odyssey. Unhale Paxton hailed me at the bar. He was drinking thin Swedish beer to chase down an aquavit. 'An old pal,' he said. 'We were in the army together. Eighth Army. You didn't need a passport in those days to see foreign parts. I don't know your name,' he said to me, 'and I keep forgetting his.'

'Alfie,' the other said. 'Alfie Meldrum. Glad to meet you,' he said to me, taking my hand in a strong grip. 'This one here's being a bit of a bloody fool. He's shut himself up in a flying prison. He chucked his passport away so as to make sure he stays in it. He doesn't get the idea at all that it's a key for opening things up. He thinks it's for locking in.'

'I'll tell you,' Paxton said. 'It all happened at the end of the war when we got these ration books and identity cards and the rest of the government nonsense. They'd spelt my name wrong. They'd got me down as Pixton. I thought it was bloody funny at first, turning me into a sort of pixy. But when I changed my ration book and pointed out what they'd done, the bloody snot-nosed little clerk in Wolverhampton, I was working there at the time, he said Pixton was my real name now and I'd have to change it to that by deed poll. That was to turn somebody's stupid bloody mistake into an act of God so to speak. So some day, I said to myself, I'll bloody show them about their stuff and nonsense about bloody documents.' His agitation was, I thought, excessive. The disruption of his circadian rhythms had driven him into neurosis. 'When they want you to fight their bloody wars they don't talk about passports then, oh no. Build a free world, that was what it was supposed to be all about, and look at the bloody free world with its red tape. I had enough of that when I was trying to earn an honest living, what with income tax and VAT and the headaches I got with form-filling. Well, it's all over now. No more forms. A free man.' And, a free man, he dithered as though being punched up against the ropes.

'So,' said Alfie Meldrum, 'he can't come with me to Oslo, where my daughter got married to one of these Norsemen. Where are you off to now, then, Norbert?' Norbert, Norbert. That was no sort of name to carry about on an official document.

'Copenhagen. Then down to the Coat de bloody Zure, then Christ knows where. I've got it all written down here.' And he pointed a tremulous finger at his one piece of baggage.

I saw that the danger point was arriving three weeks later,

141

when Paxton and I were on the same aircraft. We were both going to Jakarta on a jumbo jet of the new ANSWER line (Air New South Wales Eastern Runs; there was an apparent paradox in our flying north-west: the mysterious East would never be east of Australia). The first-class cabin was full, and Paxton complained very loudly to the stocky Sydney stewardess about having to be stuck next to a Jap: fought the buggers in the last lot, I didn't but a lot did, including your dad for all I know, and there he is with his computers and transistors and honking away with his nose all bunged up and they haven't got round to inventing handkerchiefs yet for all their bloody cleverness. The Japanese merely smiled at Western folly, not understanding a word. Paxton's seat was changed, but he didn't seem to like the beefy cattleman, his new companion, either. When dinner was served he said the soup was bad, having gone off when waiting in its canister on the boiling aircraft parking lot, but the stewardess assured him that the bad taste was only the taste of a drop of sherry put in the soup to give it flavour. Then, when a film was shown, he said he'd seen the bloody thing already, and the stewardess brought in the second pilot to give him fair warning. Throw me off in mid-air, is that the idea? Well, get on with it, sport or cobber, or whatever you like to be called and stick it up your didgeridoo. I hid myself behind a copy of *The Australian*, though there seemed every likelihood of his not knowing who the hell I was.

The miserable story came to an end at West Berlin. I was ready to fly to Vienna, but Paxton was just arriving from Munich International at the moment when I was ordered to proceed to the departure gate. He was in a wheelchair and apparently strapped to it. He had two white-coated attendants and a couple of uniformed officials of Lufthansa to accompany him. He was shrieking something about always knowing it would come to this, the bleeding Nazis had got him at last and he was a free British citizen, got a passport to prove it but the bastards have taken it away. He was gently wheeled towards the exit, with no nonsense about immigration formalities. For his presumed destination no passport was required.

·— HUN —·

The town was called Oasis, small but clean and even luxurious, though its streets were thronged by dirty Egyptians. Some of the Egyptians who were not dirty but were still resisting the Roman modes of cleanliness brooded on a past when there had been no Romans. There had been a royal house that kept itself clean through incest and converted the mud of the Nile into a sort of washed wealth. Those kings had known Greeks and Hebrews, but no Romans. Here was an upstart race from an obscure province, bred of the milk of wolves, morbidly active and dedicated to greed. They procured wealth from subject peoples and called their procurators governors, or it may have been the other way about. The point about the Romans was that they would not last. No empire could last, as had been proved by Egypt's own history. They were soft at the centre. They had once had an opportunity to find a reasonable strength through the marriage of Roman obduracy and Egyptian wisdom, but they had missed that chance. They had submitted to the teaching of their Greek slaves and to a cynical faith of love and humility taught by a Jewish rabbi they had themselves crucified. No such confused people could hold out for long against the new barbarism, whose brutality was disguised by no sophisticated code, and whose unwritten languages had no word for hypocrisy.

Palm trees waved among Roman columns. Beggars begged loudly in the oriental manner for alms from Roman officials borne on litters. Maniples trotted from one scene of minor disturbance to another, their decurions whipping the way clear of its mobs with oak truncheons. The civilian functionaries more languidly

143

hit out with flywhisks. It was a typical Roman Egyptian colony. It had an elegant patrician bathhouse.

In this bathhouse a crotchety old man named Nestorius frowned at a fatter and balder old man named Proscius as slaves wrapped their wet hot nakedness in towels. 'I'm not at all satisfied,' he said, 'with your views of the personality of Jesus our Saviour.'

'Oh come, the bath is hardly the place for theology.'

'God is everywhere, even in this steaming water. And heresy is everywhere, though nowadays they call it orthodoxy.'

'Whatever His Holiness says is orthodox cannot be heterodox.'

'The Pope's a heretic. He won't accept the truth, the truth that God imparted to me to impart to others—'

'Nestorius, you may have been patriarch of Constantinople, but that hardly makes you the voice of God.'

'Bah. Anathematised for speaking the truth.'

'Yes, Nestorius,' Proscius said soothingly. 'God the Son is human and the divine is not to be found in his fleshly nature. I know. We all know.'

'That was *not* my doctrine,' Nestorius cried through the steam. 'I will drum the true doctrine into your thick ears till you're deaf to everything else.'

'No, Nestorius, please. May not a man enjoy a bath and a sunset cup of wine after without having the nature of Jesus Christ thrown into it?'

'Let us,' said a younger and stringier bather named Tibullus, 'go and have that cup of wine. And Nestorius can spit his theological pearl into his own.'

'Swallow a pearl,' Proscius said, 'and you know what happens to it.' Nestorius cried:

'That is obscene.'

It was easier for Nestorius to indoctrinate the patrician boys he taught in his little garden, he sitting under his solitary datepalm, they squatting and squinting at him in the sun, boys of various colours. He began one lesson by asking, 'How many years have passed since the death and resurrection of our Lord Jesus Christ?'

'Three hundred.'

'Six hundred.'

144

'A thousand.'

'You, boy, are stupid. It is five hundred and fifty years. Remember that, all of you. He said, did he not, that he had come to bring not peace but a sword. Yes? In that time, fulfilling his holy word, the Empire has let itself be hacked to pieces with swords of barbarians.'

'Why did you say *Empire*, master?' asked the boy he called stupid. 'You ought to say *Empires*.'

'One Empire,' Nestorius affirmed, 'but split into two. The Empire of Rome and the Empire of Constantinople. Disunity, boy. Two Emperors. Corruption within and the barbarians triumphant without.'

'But the barbarians are within, sir,' said young Audax. 'Franks and Alemanni and Lombards and Ostragoths and Visigoths.'

'That's true, boy. But when they serve the Empire and speak Greek or Latin they're no longer barbarians. To be a barbarian is to go bar bar bar. You see the Roman troops in our streets. They used to be bluebottomed Britons and bearded chewers of raw meat from the banks of the Danube. Blackamoors, even. Decent rations, a secure life, regular pay – that's what debarbarised them. Some of you come from barbarian stock. But barbarian is not a permanent name, like apple or sword. A sword is always a sword, but a barbarian can become civilised. And civilisation has to be protected from the incursions of Gog and Magog.'

'Who are God and Mygod?' asked young Hilarius.

'Watch out for blasphemy, boy. Gog and Magog, two giants in the Old Testament. It was prophesied that they'd come some day to smash our civilisation. God, I mean Gog – he's the Goths. Magog is the Huns. Back in, yes, the year of our Lord 440, the Huns were masters and the Romans seemed likely to become their slaves – a terrible time. All because of the true doctrine and the rejection of it. Mark my words, when God's people refuse to see the light, God sends a whip to them. God found his whip, very brutal and nasty, covered with spikes, and he put it into the big hairy fist of Attila.'

'Tell us about Attila, sir, master.'

'It's a long story,' said Nestorius, 'but perhaps you'd better hear it. It shows what happens to a people that rejects the true

145

doctrine taught by the patriarch of Constantinople and his holy predecessors.'

'Who,' asked an ill-advised boy, 'is the patria or whatever it is?'

Nestorius exploded at that and hit out. He roared and dismissed the class, hitting out with his old mottled gnarled niefs. On their way out of the garden Audax told the ignorant: 'It's him.'

'Who?'

'Him. The patriot of Constanti – that place that Constantine had built.'

'Then what's he doing here in Egypt?'

'Thrown out by the Emperor. For preaching something about God that other people didn't like. He used to be a great man.'

'He's certainly an *old* man. I wonder if he ever met Attila.'

Nestorius was calm enough at their next lesson. He said: 'As I've already told you, some of the barbarians were tamed. The Visigoths even became Christians, although it was the wrong sort of Christians, Arians, condemned by the Church, just as I was, but we won't go into that now. But it was the Persians who were the real danger, for a time anyway. Civilised clever people, even though they weren't Christians, still aren't Christians. Rome needed big fighting forces. Under the Emperor Diocletian Rome had a standing army and navy half a million strong. And then there were fortifications everywhere, towers and walls and ramparts. The Romans needed the barbarians to build them. In particular, they needed the Huns. At one time they needed the Huns to help push out the Goths. Always trouble, always. Not peace but a sword. The year you have to remember is 395. That was the year the Emperor Theodosius died.'

'The first, sir?'

'Yes, Theodosius the First. It was in that year that we had two emperors for the first time. Honorius in the West—'

'At Rome, sir?'

'Not very much at Rome. Rome wasn't what it had been in the times of the great Caesars. No, that's when the emperors of the West began to be at Trèves on the river Moselle, or at Milan or at Ravenna. Honorius was ruling the West and Arcadius was ruling the East. The year of our Lord and Master 395. And you know who was born in that year?'

'You, sir?' Nestorius hit out at everybody. In his accessions of calm the boys got the story of Attila.

Whose uncle Roas was saying goodbye to him before he set out on a lengthy journey. *'Go ranya tonoperfalas ga taka, Attilinya.'* To which Attila made dutiful reply: *'Sodoka, kragra Roaskya.'* The old man was wrapped in skins and his cheeks were scarred with the knife cuts of adolescent initiation. Into the scars the hairs of his beard had entered. Attila was not so disfigured, though he had just passed his fifteenth birthday. He had on a decent knee-length garment of white wool, leather boots softened by systematic caresses from hands slippery with warm horsefat, and a thick woollen cloak dyed scarlet. His tar hair was long but clean and combed. He rode a bay gelding and his secretary companion Demetrios rode, alongside him, a piebald mare. Demetrios was, of course, Greek but he was no slave; he was free and salaried. In front of the pair rode two Hun standard bearers, who each bore aloft a wooden pole on which three human skulls were affixed: these drily rattled in the jolt of passage. Behind cantered a Hun cohort. All these Huns were flat of face and barbaric of hair and dress. Attila was, though flatter of face than was strictly acceptable in the lands of the Middle Sea, handsome in Greco-Roman terms. He was also muscular. He rode, then, with his Hun train and his Greek companion, along the banks of the great silver river. Horns brayed their progress south. Startled birds rose from the wooded banks of the Danube. When night fell they made camp, and the Huns roughly roasted their horseflesh hunks, swigged fermented mare's milk, sang songs of the homeland. Demetrios said:

'You'll have some difficulty in reconciling two things, prince of princes. They worship a god and they believe this god had a son.'

'A king and a prince of princes. I know.'

'Not quite. The son is the father and the father the son. The father allowed the son to come down to earth and be cruelly murdered.'

'This I knew of. Aetius tried to explain it to me. But I still don't understand.'

'Well, you'll be seeing Aetius again. He can explain it better than I.'

'Does it matter?'

'You're going to stay at court where it seems to matter.'

'They worship a god who was murdered by the Romans, somebody told me. And yet they're Romans themselves.'

'Christian Romans. The others were pagan Romans. Now the thing you will notice is that they *behave* like pagan Romans, worshipping the gods of pleasure, money and cruelty.'

'A hypocritical people? Aetius wasn't like that. He always spoke the truth.'

'Aetius was young when he came to your uncle's court – the age you are now. He may have changed. Don't, if I may say this, trust him. Don't trust any of them. As a Greek I know how far to trust the Romans . . .'

Empty countryside relieved only by dead trees from which dried skeletons hung. A corpse, not yet pure bone, gnawed by carrion crows. The horns brayed. The horns brayed at last along the street of a town of northern Italy, where citizens stared at the uncouth cantering warriors. There was even laughter, and children made faces. The warriors shook their spears and then there was no more laughter. The Huns were coming. At length the Huns were gaping at a vision that glittered like mica across the plains: Rome set on her hills, her sturdy walls, abask in her Roman sun. 'History alone,' Demetrios said, 'makes her an Amazonian mother. She no longer has power to terrify. Do not be afraid of Rome.'

Attila was not afraid, but, as he waited alone in a vast cool room with floor of travertine, embracing with his left arm a column while his right hand held a ripe fig for his chewing, looking out on a garden set with cypress, pines beyond it, he felt a large unease. This was not his world. He yearned for woodsmoke and the smell of charred horse-meat. But then his name was called, and he spat chewed figflesh onto the travertine. 'Little father!' added Aetius, strong, young, but not so young as when they had been formerly together, entering the room with arms wide for an embrace. 'Isn't that what Attila means? Not yet a father, though, and no longer little. Have you chosen a wife or is it too soon, little father?'

'Time enough for that.'

'You accent's abominable. You mouth Latin worse than an Ostrogoth. But lessons have been arranged. Greek too. You're here,' and he smiled, 'to be civilised.'

'I thought,' said Attila, not smiling, 'I was here as a hostage.'

'Just as I was. Hostage is a bad word. Let's call it an exchange of guests between two nations at peace.'

'So,' said Attila, 'Rome could strike at my uncle and my uncle couldn't strike back. Because I'm a *guest* likely to be – what's the word – *crucifixus*?'

'We don't crucify people any more,' Aetius said cheerfully. 'And we'd never dream of even thinking of driving a nail into a prince of the blood. How is your uncle, by the way?'

'Eating. Drinking. Squinting at the east. Suspicious of the west and the south.'

'We're friends,' Aetius said heartily. 'The Romans and the Huns are brothers in amity *per saecula saeculorum*. And now we have to get you properly dressed for dinner.'

The dinner was a Roman banquet in the old style, with larks' tongues in Sicilian pastry, peacocks' stomachs stuffed with minced ostrich brains, sturgeons' milts in honey. 'But,' Aetius said to Attila, 'try this – more like what you're used to: raw beef with egg yolk and onion.'

The Emperor Honorius was on one of his rare visits to what was still the official capital of the Empire. He beamed somewhat sillily at his Hun guest and said: 'Little appetite, I see. Perhaps some mare's milk and pemmican?'

'What,' a lady, with a castellated purple coiffure asked Atilla, confusing him with the sudden intimacy of her exposed bosom and powerful perfume, 'what *do* you Huns eat?'

'Well,' shyly, 'we're a race that lives on horseback and sleeps in tents. Forgive my bad Latin . . .'

'Oh, I can speak Greek, if you prefer. I'm afraid the Hun language isn't taught in our schools. There seems to be no way of writing it down.'

'And,' an exquisite old patrician bleated, 'there seems to be no literature either. No time for that, I suppose. Raiding and killing all the time, what?'

'We're a young nation,' Attila said. 'We're ready to learn.' He did not say what.

Taken at his word, he was provided with what the imperial court considered to be the requisite what. A teacher named Philologos droned at him in one of the palace schoolrooms: '*Et dixit mihi: haec verba fidelissima sunt et vera. Et Dominus Deus spiritus prophetatum misit angelum suum ostendere servis suis quae oportet fieri cito*. Now we compare the Greek: *kai eiren moi: outoi hoi logoi pistoi kai alithinoi, kai ho Theos*—'

'That's Christian,' Attila interrupted rudely. 'I've no intention of becoming a Christian.'

'Dear me. You wish to remain a heathen?'

'I'll learn your languages, but I won't worship this man stuck up on a cross. I stay true to the traditions of my people.'

'And those traditions are what?'

'Whatever they are, they're not Christian.'

Philologos shook his grey head and selected another scroll from his scroll pigeonholes. 'We'll try some Ovid. Publius Ovidius Naso. Would you accept our language when it deals with *love*? Not Christian love – the other kind.'

As for love, boys, we will say little about it, meaning the other kind. What Attila did with the lady Galla Placidia is none of our concern. But she said to him:

'Tomorrow we go to Ravenna.'

'Is it beautiful, Ravenna?'

'Beautiful within, but without it is surrounded by marshes. The marshes afford natural protection, you know.'

'All you think of is protection. Walls and ramparts and marshes. There was a time when the Roman Empire was, well . . .'

'Aggressive? Oh, we're still aggressive, but only among ourselves. Watch Aetius.'

'Aetius is my friend.'

'He's also ambitious. He wants to stay friendly with you for very ambitious reasons. You'll see.'

'You mean – he wants to be Emperor?'

'No. He wants to be a maker and unmaker of emperors. Aetius the great general, able to call on half a million Huns because of his friendship with the young prince Attila. Watch him.'

'But I like him. Love him.'

150

'Oh, I love him too. Or did. That's something you have to learn. Love always generates its opposite. And hate can mean love. Human life is very difficult.'

'It seems simple enough to me.'

'That's because you're very young, Attila. Charmingly so. Have you been reading your Ovid? The *Ars Amatoria*?'

'It's difficult. I mean, the Latin's difficult.'

'But the content is very very simple.' And then – I say no more. There are some things that are best not even imagined.

Soon the entire imperial suite took horse and carriage to Ravenna. There was a splashing through very wet marshland. Aetius and Attila shared an ornate coach. Aetius said: 'I expected that. She takes you to her bed to corrupt you – she, a Christian lady. Oh, not corrupt your morals – you don't have any, dear Attila. Turn you against me.'

'Is it true what she says?'

'Have you ever thought of – what you'll become – when your uncle Roas dies?'

'A chief, like him. But I have an elder brother to contend with.'

'You elder brother was always a fool. And now you tell me he's turned into a drunkard. You'll be chief. But not just of the Huns on the Danube. There are other Huns – the Mongol Huns in the east. One thing you'll learn from the Roman Empire is the need to expand. It isn't enough to rule a tribe. You'll want to rule a nation.'

'She said that was your ambition too.'

'It is. But not as Emperor.'

'She was right, then.'

'Look, I'm not an Italian, I'm a Pannonian, but I'm still a Roman. I believe in the Empire. But the Empire can be sustained only by the army. The Empire's split in two, and under incompetent rulers. You've seen Honorius. Soon we'll go to Constantinople and you'll see Theodosius. Men of straw, both of them. Your friend Galla Placidia is the really ambitious one. She wants her son on the Western throne and she wants to be regent. Her son's a boy still, but he'll never be more than a nonentity.'

'A what?'

'A nothing, a weakling. Without a strong army we'll see both Rome and Constantinople fall to the Goths and the Visigoths.

That would be a ghastly waste. Centuries of skill – in law, literature, architecture, military organisation, engineering – all wasted.
I won't let that happen. Rome needs a strong army. Rome needs
strong allies.'

'Meaning my people?'

'Yes, Attila. Your people. And perhaps your people need us
as much as we need you.'

'So all this ceremony – welcome, prince, I have fine gifts for
you to take back to your esteemed uncle Roas – no respect, no
liking – just – what's the word? – policy.'

'I liked you when we first met at your uncle's court. Whatever
the situation, we'd still be friends.'

'But you want to turn me into a kind of Roman. For the sake
of . . . policy.'

'You'll never be a Roman. But I hoped you'd see – well, what
the historians mean when they talk of the glory of Rome. I will
not see that glory trampled to dust by vicious Teutons and Slavs
who don't know what civilisation means. The Empire,' Aetius
pronounced, 'is in danger.'

'The Empire,' Atilla pronounced, 'has put itself in danger. The
countryside – it's full of brigands, and the sea teems with pirates.
And you've forgotten how to breed soldiers and statesmen. I
smell – corruption and weakness. The people pay too many taxes.
The value of money goes down every day.'

'You've kept your eyes open,' Aetius said admiringly.

'And my ears. But I'd like to close my nostrils to the stink of
decay. You've had your time. You let Christianity in, the faith of
slaves. You've ceased to be warriors.'

'Not when I'm around, Attila. And not when you're around.
We need each other.

The great cavalcade had reached the southern gates of the city.
The trumpets sounded from the battlements, the guard presented
arms. The Emperor of the West and his train entered the imperial
fastness of Ravenna. There Attila was no more at home than in
the ancient city whence he had departed. Aetius went about
business unspecified, Attila made the acquaintance of young and
haughty Roman Ravennans. Like any despised and derided
stranger he nursed his sense of superiority. He attended a party
in the sun, on the wide sward behind the imperial palace. There

was a contest in archery, and the young Ravennans flexed muscles and shot arrows to the admiration of their female friends. There was one female of about Attila's age, golden, giggling behind her fan at the sour young Hun, her name Domitia. Attila desired Domitia. 'Come on, let's see how the Huns do it,' cried a boy whose name was something like Lepidulus. Attila showed them with three insolent golds. Domitia still giggled.

She giggled behind her fan even in the great basilica where Mass was said. Aetius went through the motions of devoutness and Attila followed him, eyes on Domitia. The censers clanged and clouds of incense caught the wind and were buffeted back to the golden solar monstrance. The Emperor Honorius beat his breast as he knelt on his silken cushions. Domitia giggled, though with no noise. A couple of aristocrats near Attila and Aetius played at covert knucklebones. It was a hypocritical empire.

She did not giggle when she came through the opening of the thick velvet curtains which enclosed a banquet to find Attila waiting for her, the nails of his left hand bitten to the quick. She pouted. 'The servant said there was an urgent message, and all I find is you.'

'With an urgent message. I . . . love you, Domitia. I can't sleep, I can't eat, I grow thin, look at me. I'd heard of love, but I never thought it would, it could—'

'But you're only a boy, and you're a – a – '

'Foreigner, barbarian, Hun.'

'Hun. What a silly thing for anybody to be called. It sounds like clearing your throat. You want to marry me, is that it?'

'Yes. I hadn't thought of that. All I thought of was that I—'

'Well, you'd better not. Besides, I love Sulpicius. And I'm going to marry Sulpicius. It's all arranged.'

'And who is this Sulp – whatever it is?'

'You wouldn't know, would you? A Roman and a Christian and a nice boy. To think I'd go riding off with you to some tent where everything smells of mutton fat and nobody ever takes a bath and – ugh. Urgent message, they said. Yah. I'm going back in.' And she went back in, leaving Attila to rage. Love as they call it, is no more than a dangerous diabolic fire: it led young Attila to the smashing of amphorae in a base tavern and the

153

vicious tearing of curtains and flesh in the brothel district of Ravenna. Love gave him a bad name: *rightly is he termed a Hun. We want no more of this Hunnish behaviour here.* Ravenna was glad to see the last óf him. He and Aetius and a suitable watchful escort took ship for Constantinople. Attila, very much a landsman, was violently sick for much of the voyage.

'There,' Aetius said at length, 'is the city Constantine built on the site of ancient Byzantium. Impressive, yes?'

'Aaaaaargh.'

'Do you ever dream, my poor seasick friend, of building Attilople, or whatever the Hun name would be?'

'I dream of taking cities, not building them.' Cities full of giggling blond Domitiae to be paraded naked and then lashed: that would stop their giggling. 'Leave the building to the little men.'

'Constantine *little? Constantine?*'

The great golden city rayed out light at them, riding secure on the Bosphorus. Officers of the imperial court awaited them on the quay with ornate litters and burly Ethiopians to lift them. This city was not like Rome; it lacked Rome's occidental sobriety; it was golden stone and tortured ironwork, and there were stiff robes of cloth of gold on the haughty functionaries who irritably waved staffs of office of most elaborate carving. It was all Greek here; the Emperor Theodosius II addressed Atilla, after a week of awaiting an audience, in very haughty Greek.

'Your uncle, yes. King – I'm bad at names.' He was a thin neck and a dissolute powdered and painted mask over gold that creaked.

'Roas, sir.'

'Roas, yes. Of course, he's one of my generals, officially. Roas the Eastern Emperor's Hun general. On salary. Yes. Well, I trust our admirable relations continue. It must be – ah – something of an experience for you, prince—'

'Attila is my name, *kyrie.*'

'Quite so. The achievements of Rome and Byzantium as I still sometimes like to call it. Yes?'

'Among my people an egg with twin yolks is regarded as uneatable. A thing of ill omen. But you're a sophisticated people, *kyrie.* If you can believe that three gods are one you can more easily believe that there's a unity in two empires.'

'One empire, one. We are still Rome. An old Rome and a new one. And it is not three gods we believe in. This boy, lord Aetius, has not been well instructed.'

'My people,' Attila responded with youth's arrogance, 'regard religion as a waste of time. There is too much to be done on earth to concern ourselves with what may or may not exist beyond the clouds.'

'Well,' Theodosius said with a semblance of good humour, 'you're safe from the charge of heresy or atheism, unlike most of my subjects. What my patriarch would call invincible ignorance. We meet at dinner, I believe. Make good use of your time with us. I bid you good day.' He gave Attila a pale hand with a blinding constellation of jewelled rings on it to kiss. Attila took the hand and blew on the rings to dim their brightness. He did not like this imperial insolence.

He did not understand the theological wrangles to which he was forced to listen. He was, after all, only a Hun. 'I do not believe,' said Augustinus, 'that we are expected to believe that all the bodies that were ever buried or burned will arise again on the day of judgment. The truth of the reality of the physical resurrection lies in the distance that obtains between the angels and the saints. We shall not be angels in heaven, since angels belong to a primordial and unchangeable order of spirits. Our spiritual nature shall partake of the physical.'

'How,' Celinus asked, 'can the spiritual partake of the physical? That is a contradiction of the logic of substances.'

'But God,' Othonius said, 'reconciles such disparities. It is possible to conceive of a spiritualised sensorium or of a sensorialised spirit. That has to be of the nature of a sanctified humanity . . .'

Attila wandered off from the academic grove and gladly joined the naked wrestling in the gymnasium (I apologise for that tautology: a gymnasium must necessarily be for the naked). He could, in his Hunnish fashion, appreciate this physical reality of a humanity unsanctified. There was a young man with long wavy hair like that of the sun-god who was too proud of his wrestling prowess, grinning at the onlookers and raising his arms in self-salute after each final throw. Attila stripped and took him on, grasping his legs after the first grounding then swirling him and throwing him – to the spectators' plaudits – into the midst of the spectators. Aetius, who found him there, was not well pleased. Later, as they walked a golden street, he said to him:

'Sick of this place, are you? Sick of the glory of the capital of the Eastern Empire? Here you have everything to delight the mind and senses, and all you can find to do is to *wrestle*.'

'You'll never make me an imperial citizen, Aetius. I've a strong desire to be back with half-raw meat and Hun beer. The smell of the grass and the wind from the river. My own language, which no one here speaks. And if they were taught to speak it they'd despise it.'

'It lacks subtlety, dear Attila. I speak enough of it to know. The future, remember, lies with the subtle and civilised.'

'Meaning the weak and the devious. I don't like either of your Emperors. They're devious, they're—'

'They can afford to be weak. The strength of the Empire lies not in the Emperor, a mere head on a coin. You know where the strength lies.'

'Can your God reconcile that contradiction – that you, the brilliant Christian Empire, should call on the heathen Huns for support?'

'Mutual need, dear Attila. As simple as that.'

'Not so simple, dear Aetius. Some day you'll see. We'll both see.' And he stared unseeing at the blue Bosphorus and its shipping, as though he had a vision in his head. Aetius saw him seeing the vision and he wondered what it was.

So Attila, boys, was very glad to be handed over by his Roman escort to his Hun escort just north of Ravenna. The two escorts looked at each other, turned about and were off. At length the silver Danube welcomed the young prince and the young prince continued his growing up in the wooden court of his uncle. It was not long before his uncle selected a bride for him, Enga, beautiful though too dark for a civilised taste, with cheeks somewhat leathery and heavy wedded brows, her unwashed condition masked by the distillation of flowers and a profusion of heavy metal ornaments. Naturally, Attila did not love her: the marriage had been arranged to quieten down her ambitious father, leader of an outlying tribe who felt he had been too long overlooked in the centre of Hun rule. The wedding was lavish and, as the bridal night approached, the celebrations mounted to barbaric madness, what with wild displays of horsemanship, stamped dances, howled songs and the waving of torches. Attila's brother Bleda grew quickly drunk and collapsed in his vomit. Roas beamed at everything but ate too much. At the moment when the bride was removed to the bridal chamber to the accompaniment of a nasal bridal chant from her handmaidens, the old chief coughed desperately, gasped for air which seemed all to have been consumed by the fires and torches, and fell heavily. He was borne swiftly to his bed. Attila, greatly concerned, went to him. He lay on a couch of stuffed cushions, covered with skins and furs, pale but no longer gasping. An overtaxed heart had issued a warning. Roas said:

'Go to your bride. I shall be well enough. Excess, excess – there is a limit to what an old man's body can take. But now you know you must be ready.'

'I'll be ready when Bleda dies – not before.'

'Bleda is useless. If only he were your *younger* brother. But things can be arranged. Bleda will drown himself in a beer-cask one of these days . . . go to your bride.'

'Enga will not run away. Or if she does I'll soon carry her back kicking and screaming. You said you had something to tell me, uncle. We're not often alone.'

'Not now. Fill your bride with your first son. Watch the line, think of posterity. Your son will have much to do.'

'I have much to do first.'

'Yes. And much to teach. You've seen something of the Romans. You have to teach them.'

'They seemed to think they had to teach *me*.'

'Alaric and his Visigoths – they pillaged the city of Rome, and what did the Emperor Honorius do? He didn't call on us. The Huns were not worthy of his attention. We're not big enough, Attila. Not yet. My own brother Ebarse, your other uncle – he knows we're not big enough, but he doesn't care. Stuck there in the Caucasus, a little king and very incompetent. Fill Enga with your son. Go to the Caucasus and teach Ebarse . . .' He ceased then, being very weak. Attila considered that he knew what had to be done, but first he went to a bedroom in which fertility dolls had been set around the bed by the shamans, there to fulfil an act, boys, which you are too young to be legitimately interested in. Enough to say that he heard a voice in his head saying *You'd take me to a tent somewhere reeking of mutton fat*, and that he said to himself, 'Roma uxor est, uxor captanda.'

It was early spring, a time for fighting. While his elder brother drank and his uncle recovered, Attila led four hundred horsemen armed with spears towards the Caucasus. Opposed horsemen watched from the hills and then came hurtling down into the plain. The fight was brief and very bloody, and none except Attila seemed to know why it was being waged. When the opposed leader called for permission to carry off the dead for burning, Attila identified himself, saying:

'Attila, son of the late King Mundzuk, nephew of King Roas and his appointed successor. I come to greet my other uncle, Ebarse. Your manners are atrocious. A prince is entitled to a more courteous welcome. You attacked my force without preliminary parley. You failed to recognise that I was come on a friendly visit.'

'You speak like a Danube man. You are in another country now. We have orders to repel all intruders.'

'The Caucasian Huns have lessons to learn. A friendly visit is not an intrusion.'

'You behaved in no friendly manner. And I do not understand all your words.'

'You will address me as prince. *Prince*. Do you know the word?'

'We address no man as anything. We are free people here.'

'Not all that free. I could take you back to the Danube as a prisoner and then exhibit your head on a pole, having first washed your lousy and clotted locks. You seems to me to be a soft nation, unused to war.'

'We do not seek war. We seek only to be left alone.'

'And repel intruders, I see. You did not repel me very success-fully. Now lead me to my uncle Ebarse.'

This colloquy had been held, in the Hun manner, dismounted. When Attila started to remount, the leader of the squadron of the Huns of the Caucasus spat and made a Hun howl indicative of contempt. Attila was sharp in his response. He left his horse and took five strides to strike the insolent ribald down with his gloved fist, saying: 'You are a bad man and an incompetent. My uncle will be given orders as to your disposal. *Orders*. Now lead me to him.'

Ebarse's headquarters was a mere agglomeration of tents. Attila's nose twitched at the dirt and disorder. Ebarse greeted his nephew while chewing the gristle from a mutton bone. He was slack and fat and his furs were filthy.

'Attila, your nephew. Greetings from your royal brother.'

'Royal? What is this royal?'

'I think,' Attila said, 'you had better call your council together.'

'You give me orders? From my *royal brother*?'

'I give no orders. I merely make a suggestion.'

A coarse meal was served in a large patched communal dining tent, its rough plank floor littered with scraps from other coarse meals. The council was of ten, and its chief members besides Ebarse were men past their best as warriors, if they had ever achieved their best – Foek, Maas and Telabre. Foek said: 'I do not consider any of what our uninvited visitor says as at all seemly. We are what we are. We have lived long in peace and contentment. We do not ask to enter the big world of the sunset. We are the children of the sunrise.'

Attila said: 'A poetical way of saying that you wish to be cut off from the great river that is called history.'

'Do not use these Roman words when speaking to us,' Maas said, blinking his one eye. 'We want nothing of Rome or of anyone. Leave us as we are.'

'The little cry of little people,' Attila said. 'You are to be dragged out of this littleness. You are to be made great.'

'Under the wings,' said Ebarse, 'of my *great* brother the king Roas as he calls himself?'

'I could not put it better,' Attila said. 'The Huns are to be one people. They are not to be people living in the stink of horse fat and verminous horsehides. They are to be a people with a capital city.'

'We know what happens to capital cities,' Telabre said. 'We are not ignorant men. We know what the Goths did to Rome.'

'But not,' Attila said, 'what the Huns could do to Rome. And to its sister city of the east.'

'We don't want loot and plunder,' Foek said. 'We wish only to be left alone.'

'As has already been said, and far too often. Very well. I speak hard words from King Roas. Submit voluntarily to his rule as paramount chief of the Huns or – well, he does not wish to talk of a fratricidal war.'

'These big Roman words.'

'Brother killing brother,' Attila explained. 'Hun killing Hun. Your forces are nothing. They're ill-disciplined. You live like swine guzzling in the trough. Your women are filthy and wear no ornaments.'

'So,' Ebarse said, 'my *royal* brother wants to turn us into Roman ladies and gentlemen.'

'No. Only to awaken pride in the race. In the power of the Hun confederacy.'

'Big Roman words again.'

'Communications,' Attila said patiently. 'That is the important thing. A system of posting stages. Stables and living quarters for fast messengers. Thus we draw together two territories too long sundered. We shall need a force of police, not warriors, a new thing, wardens of the peace, men to keep discipline and stop the breaking of the laws. From our river the Danube as far as your mountains. And our river empties into a great sea whose water is black.'

'This you have seen?' Ebarse asked.

'I looked out on it from Constantinople. To control the territories on the shore of that sea is to control, in time, in time, that imperial city.'

There was, in the imperial city of Ravenna, a man not sent from God whose name was John. He had, like Attila, great ambitions, but these were unsupported by royal blood. He stood in the imperial bedchamber at Ravenna in the shadows, well back from Aetius and Galla Placidia and the officiating priests who clanged incense and moaned prayers over the corpse of Honorius: 'Lord God, look down on him who was the father of his people, ruler of many, a diffuser of light and justice. Look down on his empire and have mercy on it. Lord God, receive his soul in the blaze of the light of the eternal morning. Glory be to the Father . . .'

After a quiet dinner head to head, whose delicate opulence carried no odour of mourning, John said to Aetius: 'You know I do not speak for myself—'

'Of course, not for yourself—'

'But consider – to have a woman ruling the Empire of the West . . .'

'There is no rule of nature which says that women are incompetent in that sphere.'

'Be honest, Aetius. You admire her, don't you?'

'John, there was a time when I more than admired her. She was a shining example of her sex. She has fine blood in her arteries. The daughter of Theodosius, the sister of Arcadius and the late lamented Honorius. Tough enough to control that Visigoth she married – the one who was killed at Barcelona—'

'The hairy Ataulphe, yes. Three times the man that Honorius was. And this son of hers will only be a second rate Honorius.'

'But she'll be regent, remember that.'

'Look, you know how it's going to be done – if she has her way. She's closeted now with Theodosius. She knows she won't get that brat Valentinian wrapped in the purple without a struggle. That means we have Theodosius's mercenaries on Italian soil. And they'll stay, so long as they're paid.'

'And Theodosius will stay too. Well, it's every man's dream – the East and the West united under one Emperor.'

'And what an emperor.'

'Theodosius will think about it. But he'll waver.'

'I wish,' John said, 'to talk about my own claim.'

'John,' Aetius said with great deliberation, 'you have no claim. You're mad even to think of the possibility of your having a claim. There's not one drop of imperial blood in your body.'

'All right,' John said. 'But how about Galba, Vitellius, Otho, Vespasian? None of them had the blood of the Caesars. But they lived to be called Caesar.'

'Not for long. Except Vespasian. And he's not remembered as a great Caesar. Only as the man who put a tax on public urinals. Why are you telling me about your non-existent claim?'

'Not non-existent. If I have you behind me. And you know what that means.'

'What will you give me, John?'

'Rule of the entire army. Commander in chief.'

'In other words, put me in a splendid situation for deposing you. Dangerous, wouldn't you say?'

'You don't want the imperium. You're a soldier. Soldiers don't become emperors any more. Listen, you know I can rule Rome. Only the weaklings get assassinated by jealous general officers. I have double strength – my own ability and your professionalism. Call it a kind of partnership.'

'It means,' Aetius said, looking somewhat dreamily at a jewelled crucifix on the wall, 'calling on my old friend Attila. The combined Hun armies of the Danube and the Caucasus. Are you prepared to risk that?'

'There's enough money in the imperial exchequer. All they want is our gold. They don't want our territory.' He added: 'Roas looks east.'

'Roas,' Aetius said, 'looks nowhere – only in the direction of his grave. Attila's army, not Roas's. And what do you propose be done with the princess Galla Placidia?'

'Send her into exile. With her darling son. Spain. She knows Spain. She likes the smell of the Visigoths.'

'Well, then,' Aetius said. 'Dispatches to the Danube . . .'

He met Attila and his staff near Trieste. The two generals embraced.

'Your uncle?'

'Not long for this world. Moribund, to use a Romanism.'

They sat together over elaborate glass pocula blown in Cologne; the wine too was Rhenish. Outside the tent Hun and Roman troops sniffed cautiously at each other. 'You know Galla Placidia?' Aetius said.

'She gave me a course of instruction,' Attila said primly. 'The textbook was Ovid's *Art of Love*. Look, Aetius,' he said, his jaw thrust forward, 'I don't want to hear about your imperial intrigues. My army is here because you asked for it. It's here to help the only Roman I trust. Why I'm helping him, apart from friendship and money, is not my concern. I don't like your politics.'

'Trust,' Aetius repeated. 'Trust to pay you, you mean?'

'That's unworthy. I'm one thing, my army's another. They have very primitive ideas of honour and glory. They don't understand what is meant by a *cause*. God they don't understand, but gold they do. Gold they will get, otherwise they about turn.'

'They will get gold. And your uncle will continue to receive his salary as an adoptive Roman general. Though I take it that the office has fallen to you. The task is simple enough. John proclaims himself emperor in Ravenna. That proclamation will be resisted at once by the legions loyal to the boy Valentinian. Meaning to his mother the lady Galla Placidia. The Emperor of the East has his mercenaries already on the way. He seems to have a remarkable intelligence service.'

'It's the Emperor of the East who pays my salary.'

'Forget about that. A mere formality. Only one thing concerns you. Be ready to march on Ravenna.'

'How soon? There's dysentery in my army.'

'John expects you in three days. My force marches with yours.'

'Three days is too soon.'

'Time is the main weapon, Attila. You ought to know that by now.'

But they were slow in arriving at Ravenna. Neither Aetius nor Attila was present to see John in his stiff purple imperial robes, golden *orbis terrarum* in his hands, smirking before the palace while the herald cried: 'Be it known throughout the Empire of the West that the most excellent and puissant Johannes is hereby proclaimed ruler of this realm, to whom all men shall show fealty and earthly worship under the Lord God.' The Emperor of the East Theodosius was a day's march away from the city when, according to the intelligence received by the general officer Septimius, the combined force of Aetius and Attila still had a day and a half's journey ahead of it. Theodosius and Septimius lashed their troops to a smart pace and joined up with loyalist forces outside the gates of Ravenna. They battered those gates apart and marched on the palace. The palace guards wavered when they saw the banners of the twin empires flapping in the wind. It was a lone and shivering John that Theodosius confronted in the palace yard. 'Traitor, ingrate, usurper, you are hereby placed under arrest. The rightful successor to the throne is proclaimed.

Do homage, all, to his imperial majesty Valentinian.' So a young boy shyly bowed from a balcony, and his mother, a most intricate crown of Byzantine workmanship upon her dark locks, smiled beside him. The boy was considered too young to witness John's dawn execution. He slept on, but Galla Placidia was up early.

Aetius, having received news of the disastrous ending to a brief imperial career some miles north of Ravenna, halted his troops and, regret duly expressed, informed Attila of a failed mission. He waited in his tent until himself informed that Theodosius had paid off his mercenaries and was on the sea back to Constantinople. Then he brazenly rode into Ravenna with a substantial escort and requested an interview with the princess Galla Placidia. He got it quickly. She said, her colour high:

'What prevents my ordering your immediate execution for treason?'

'I committed no treason. I warned John of his presumption. My league with the Huns was in the interest of restoring order after a disorder which was inevitable. I did not trust Theodosius to do what he did. I was surprised.'

'There are letters between you and John.'

'Forgeries. Look, princess, don't talk of treason and don't talk of arrest. I have a whole army of Huns behind me.'

'They have been sent back.'

'Not very far back. They await their pay.'

'They'll receive no pay. They'll tear you to pieces.'

'I think not,' Aetius said calmly. 'They want gold. They will receive gold from the imperial treasury. I recommend that you arrange for its disbursement instanter. If they do not get gold, they will burn, pillage and sack. It is in their nature to do so. Rome is only a treasure house to them. They have no interest in imperial claims and counterclaims. Pay them, and they will go home. Act at once.'

'You're insolent sir. You forget who you are.'

'But not what I shall be. Count Aetius, I think. Commander in chief of the imperial forces of the West.'

'I think not.'

'The Huns may think differently. Come, princess regent of this realm, you need me. You need me to forge a treaty of everlasting friendship with the Huns. And I think you need me in Gaul.

Whatever you think of me, princess regent, you cannot well do without me.'

He said no more but, with no gesture of obeisance, turned his back and left. He rode north, still with his substantial escort, to the Hun camp outside Trieste. He was, he told Attila, content to be considered a hostage until the gold arrived. It would not, he said, be long in arriving. Gold stamped with the image of a new Emperor. An Emperor to whom, Aetius stated without shame, he was now loyal.

'I don't understand,' Attila said, 'I will never understand. You wanted the young Emperor killed.'

'Not killed. Merely sent into exile.'

'Killing I understand. The other thing I don't.'

'It's all a matter of politics, Attila. If you fail with one candidate you succeed with another. I accept the young Emperor. I will even get myself appointed tutor to the young Emperor, so that he will tread the right path. The Emperor will see things my way, naturally. He'll be delighted with the new pact I propose.'

'A pact,' Attila said, 'which makes no sense. You don't attack us and we don't attack you. It means nothing. It's all too easy to attack you.'

'Or be rewarded for not attacking. The pact – a mere gesture of friendship, Attila. The important thing is our new cooperation in the province of Pannonia.'

Attila had a new secretary named Orestes, a sharp-eared young man who sidled closer when he heard that name. 'Ah, Pannonia,' he murmured.

'My homeland too,' Aetius grinned. 'I was born under the Auster.'

'The what?' Attila scowled.

'The south wind. Some of the Pannonians call themselves Austrians. The position as regards Pannonia, Attila, is that we share it.'

'Most of it is Hun territory already.'

'Some of it. And so we confirm it to be.'

'We don't need your confirmation,' adding: 'With respect.'

'With respect, old friend, we're entering an era of cooperation. We both have enemies – unwashed tribes that have to be put down.'

'So the Romans consider the Huns.'

'Ah no,' Aetius beamed, 'not that. Not any more. Never again.'
Attila did not beam back.

Attila put on a face of sorrow for the funeral speech. Ebarse's
camp looked more like a primitive town now than a muddy
agglomeration of tents: there was an attempt at a stonelaid street,
there were some huts of warped wood. Primitive still, these
people, and primitive the rites of the consigning of the body of
Ebarse to the pyre. The head had been cut off and, from a pole
held by a shaman, it looked down with little interest at the
sizzling of the fat and the charring of the flesh of the body. Attila
cried to Ebarse's bereft people:

'My own flesh and blood, brother of my father. It is a time of
mourning, but it should also be a time of rejoicing. For now we
truly become one nation. Now we may talk of the beginning of
our empire, an empire stretching from the Danube to the Caucasus. And it will grow as the grass grows, though it will never
yield to the scythe. From brother to brother the rule passes. I
bring words of mourning from Roas your king. I bring words of
rejoicing from Roas your king. At last we are one. We mourn as
one. We rejoice as one.'

It was Orestes who, at a brief nod from his master, signalled
to the musicians that they strike up a rhythm of joy. Dancers
gyrated about the fire. The dead head that looked down joined
the ashy disintegration of the body. The bearded chorus of
ancients ceased to sing of Ebarse. *Roas, Roas, Roas* was their
chant. Attila nodded and went to the princely hut allotted to
him. There Su-Jin awaited him with the latest lesson in the
spoken tongue of the Middle Kingdom. Su-Jin was a wandering
scholar expelled from the imperial civil service for certain amorous
irregularities with which, boys, you need not be much concerned.
Stooping, wrinkled, bald dome sunskinned, he greeted Attila
with parodic obsequiousness, saying: *'At til a hsien shêng hao ya?'*

'Hao hao. Ch'ing tso, ch'ing tso.'

It was with a new wife, Hild, from the brief Goth confederacy,
that Attila rode east. Three growing sons rode in their own
chariot. There was a cart crammed with gifts, some of barbaric

gold. Hild's gold locks flowed in the windy sunlight. An older and tougher Attila, much the grown man, led his thundering horde towards the camp of the Huen-Lun. Speared Huen-Lun warriors, slant eyes in a glint of fear and suspicion, obstructed Attila's path to the chief's tent. The chief, his former muscle now all fat, was borne towards Attila on a litter. Attila spoke the chief's dialect clearly but without arrogance:

'I come altogether in friendship. And why not? We share common origins, even a common language. My uncle, Uncle Roas, has charged me to bring fine gifts in token of our amity.'

'What do you want of us?'

'Friendship only.'

'Meaning that we do not attack each other?'

'What would be the use of it? Attack us, and you will be hewn to pieces. You see the formidable force of the Hun army. It is but a hundredth part of what I may call upon in time of war. No, the time may come when there will be advantage in our cooperation. Some of the gifts I bring are of Roman manufacture. You see how fine they are. There is much wealth in that vast empire. Why should we not build an empire greater than theirs? Let us be of one heart, as, despite the surface differences, we are of one speech. The time will come when we shall march together and swallow the West as a dog swallows a piece of meat. One empire.'

'Led by the Huns?'

'Led by whoever is most fit to lead. I travel east to confirm the existence of that empire. The empire of the Middle Kingdom and the empire of the rest of us – so shall the world be divided.'

'You have spoken to the Hiong-Nu?'

'I have spent two weeks in feasting with their chief. He glows and flames with my vision.'

'And now,' the chief of the Huen-Lun sucked in breath, 'you will do the thing that is not to be done?'

'Cross the Great Wall? Yes, so I purpose.'

'They are a haughty and insolent people. For them the rest of the world does not exist. They will tear you to pieces for the great daring. Their soldiers are thick like fire ants on the battlements.'

'They will receive Attila.'

'They do not speak your language.'

167

'I have taught myself to speak theirs.'

The Great Wall, with its punctuation of massive bronze gates, spoke a sentence without beginning or end. Horsemen in clattering armour rode forth from their camp on the plain. They confronted Attila with a bristle of spears. Attila cried haughtily: '*Women kiang-lah. Hung ni dai ho.*' Two doubtful captains conferred, their eyes never leaving the tresses of the princess Hild, which flowed in the wind that blew from the gates of the sun. They chattered in singsong over the gifts of Roman make. They opened the gates to Attila, the golden woman, the three boys, the unarmed secretarial escort. Soon Attila sat with the provincial governor Hu-Li. Hu-Li said:

'We have glanced over your credentials. The characters are not well formed. But we appreciate that you have humbly tried to learn the tongue of the children of the sun.'

'It is fitting to learn the speech of a great empire. But it would be presumptuous to seek to speak that tongue too well. I beg your honour's permission to visit the Emperor. I have brought fine gifts for him.'

'The Emperor is not to be seen. No man sees him. Your gifts shall be duly conveyed to him. I am empowered to ask what these gifts signify. What do you seek of the Middle Kingdom?'

'I come as the leader of one empire to pay friendly homage to the leader of another.'

'We know nothing of the empire you speak of and so may affirm that it does not exist. But of courtesy I ask where it lies.'

'Beyond your Great Wall as far as the sinking sun. It is a young empire but soon it will encompass all the earth to the limits of your kingdom. Your kingdom remains inviolate.'

'It is, I think, insolent to tell us that. It is a matter of simple truth that our kingdom is inviolate.'

'And yet I crossed your Great Wall.'

'It was out of curiosity and courtesy that this was permitted. The Middle Kingdom must not remain in ignorance of the world that lies beyond. All knowledge is good.'

'So I too believe. And so I am here.'

'Your gifts have been examined. We have neither horses nor artefacts quite like yours. And there is a woman with you whose hair is spun gold.'

'She is my consort. She is not offered as a gift. But that she is a wonder to the eyes I accept. Doubtless your Emperor would wish to see her.'

'None sees the Emperor. But I will do what I can.'

It was a ride of many days to the city of the Emperor, and it was a time of long waiting before an audience could be granted. It was in the dark hours long before the dawn that Attila and his consort were summoned from the silk beds of their lodging to meet him who, the sun of his people, hid during the day from his rival in the sky. Attila and Hild waited in the susurrus of silk garments in the bare court, where courtiers and captains and a whole ladder of chamberlains whispered as they listened for the distant first of a relay of gongs. When a near gong struck they prostrated themselves. Attila and Hild did likewise. Then a eunuch voice said that they were bidden to raise their eyes and be granted the favour of looking on the Emperor. He was a very old man who laughed softly at the golden hair.

'You and your lady are bidden be closeted with the celestial one.'

In a bare and airy chamber rice wine was served in porcelain thimbles. 'There is nothing,' the Emperor squeaked, 'at all of this in our books. Outside our domains there is nothing except empty earth and water and a few wild savages.'

'I am no wild savage, as you see. Nor is my wife. It has been written that it is not good to build walls around oneself and deny the existence of what lies beyond.'

'You exist. Yes yes, I see that. And you speak of an empire which I do not see and shall not see. And so I may not believe that it exists.'

'There are thousands, nay millions, who know nothing of your celestial kingdom and would affirm that it does not exist. You know it exists and so do I. It would be a matter of celestial courtesy to accept my word that I rule, on behalf of my imperial uncle, a territory as vast as your own.'

'I will accept that – as a proposition of the mind. And what does your – empire require of us?'

'Assurances of peace and good will. Acceptance of a great vision. That soon there shall be but two empires in the world, and one of them yours.'

'So I am, to use a poetic figure, to embrace a brother emperor in friendship?'

'So I humbly ask.'

'Consider that the embrace has been given and received. Now you will dine with us.'

It was no imperial banquet, but there were a hundred courses, most of which the Emperor waved away with a pearled flash of his overgrown nails. Snake wine was served. Live snakes were butchered on a silver dish and their blood allowed to drip into ornate but tiny cups. Attila bravely sipped. The Emperor said:

'It promotes potency. But you are a young man and doubtless potent enough. We have not seen your sons. Are they as golden as the goddess your wife?'

'One is. The further you move from the sun the more likely are you to carry the sun in your hair. This is a great mystery. In the north it is not a rare phenomenon.'

'Ah, I am made to feel most ignorant.'

'And in your imperial presence I am made to feel boorish, coarse, primitive, a barbarian.'

'My son, my imperial younger brother, you are no barbarian. See how Hang-So smiles at what the gentle beasts in the heavens report of the nobility of your blood and the grandeur of your prospects. But wait – no, he smiles no longer – speak now, Hang-So, of what is foretold.'

Hang-So was the chief of the imperial astrologers. He bowed from his hanging charts, on which dogs and monkeys bayed and chattered through the stars, from his desk, held on bowed slaves' backs, on which he had been tracing Attila's horoscope. He said: 'Clearly he is born to empire. But his empire has already been divided.'

The Emperor smiled, nodding at the sudden pallor of his guest. He said: 'I am sorry. The agonies of rule can be excessive. Perhaps I was premature in speaking to you as a brother.'

And so, boys, the great Hun and his horde turned west and home. Tomorrow I shall tell you of a brother's murder.

Tomorrow has become today, as it always does. And now picture the great Attila standing next to his elder brother Bleda as the shamans intoned their threnody over the blazing corpse of Roas. 'A good leader,' Attila had cried across the flames. 'A great paramount chief of the Huns. I, Attila, son of Mundzuk, nephew of Roas, former joint ruler of the realm with him, now take on alone the glory and the danger.'

The drunken Bleda was furious. In an echoing wooden chamber of the palace he reeled and railed. 'It was announced by the council. Joint chief sovereigns. What you said was unwarranted. The council will revoke it.'

'The council,' Attila stormed, 'will do as I say.'

'The law – the tradition – you fly in the face of—'

'Bleda, you are my elder brother and I do not deny the unwholesome fact. By legal right you should claim sole rule. But you have no gift of rule and no talent as a soldier. I have drawn the Huns into one people and commenced the building of an empire that shall be greater than that of Rome and Constantinople together. What have you done? Fornicated, swilled, lain all night in your drunken vomit, brought nothing to the council except stupidity and the fine flower of ignorance. This kingdom shall not be divided between us. Contest my right as the superior, despite my juniority, and you will meet a swift and irrevocable response.'

'You threaten me?'

'Yes, Bleda, I threaten you. I will trump up a charge of treason. An assassination plot. There is no shortage of possible devices to have you put out of the way. But you are my brother, my drunken fornicating elder brother, and I will find a use for you.'

Bleda blustered, staggering, foam on his fat lips. 'Humiliation, I see. And if I defect to the Romans?'

'Oh, do that, Bleda.' Attila smiled very affably. 'There are plenty of Huns who have defected to the Romans, seeking gold and a quiet life. One of my first tasks as paramount chief is to bring those caitiffs back and crucify them. You could have a very special crucifixion, as befits my elder brother. Special wood caressed by the carpenter. But you will scream like the others when the nails go in and suffer the same asphyxiation. What do you say?'

Bleda said nothing for the moment, merely frothing and

staggering. Then he said faintly: 'What is this – crucifixion you talk of?'

'Something I learned from the Christians.' Then he turned his back and sought his new generals – Onegeses the Greek and Orestes the Pannonian. There was a plan to discuss, nothing, for the moment, that concerned the wretched Bleda.

It was some weeks later that Attila, Onegeses and Orestes reined their horses on a hilltop very near to the border of our Eastern Empire. They looked down on the city of Margus, from whose many rooftops smoke peacefully ascended. 'There,' Orestes said. 'A fine market town. Crammed with potential loot. Do we enter? There'll be no opposition.'

'You mistake my plan,' Attila said. 'We do not behave like Huns. We behave like Romans. Duplicity can be a fine weapon. We camp here and await the messengers from Constantinople. We have done them the courtesy of shortening their journey by hovering on the city limits of Margus. Theodosius has had time enought to get my letter by heart. We are merely nudging him for his reply.'

A day or two went by before a relay of look-outs reported the appearance on the southern horizon of a Roman troop preceded by the imperial flag. Attila at once gave orders for a show of magnificence. The Roman envoys, Greeks, Plinthas and Epigene, he did not deign to see until dinner time two days after their arrival. He greeted them in a richly bannered tent set for a banquet, with, at each place, a napkin of Chinese silk. He was affable, subtly perfumed, dressed in the fashion of the Empire. Little bells were struck at each change of dish. The guests were overwhelmed by the delicacy of the viands. 'Your cooks,' Plinthas said, 'are Greeks?'

'Greeks, others,' Attila airily replied. 'Some adept at the best Constantinople fare. Others skilled in the kitchen of Ravenna. And then I have very rough cooks who throw raw meat at my guests.' His Greek was suave and, if anything, over-grammatical. 'Everything depends on what is required. Yes, gentlemen, what is required. I think you at the imperial court have had ample time to digest what is required.'

'It would be good,' Epigene said, 'to have from your lips the confirmation of what is required.'

172

'It is time,' Attila said, feeding his mouth with tiny white grapes and chewing the pips with relish, 'that the salary of the Roman general who was once my uncle Roas and is now myself was augmented. Gold seems to be losing its value.'

'The Emperor,' Plinthas said, 'sees no difficulty there. He proposes a generous increment. From three hundred and fifty pounds of gold to four hundred.'

'Seven hundred.'

'That, regretfully, he cannot accept.'

'Seven hundred.'

'The imperial treasury is not bottomless.'

'Seven hundred.'

'We're not,' Plinthas said, 'empowered to make a decision on that. We must consult again with his imperial majesty. But we can tell you what his answer will be.'

'The amount,' Attila said carelessly, 'means little. A mere token. I seek the Emperor's respect as well as his friendship. To men of his kind gold is a fair index of respect. Let me now turn to the other matter. The restitution of the Huns of my kingdom who have been living too long in your realms. I do not like defections. The Huns should acknowledge their true lord.' He clapped his hands. 'More wine for our imperial guests.' He leaned towards them and said: 'Restitution, and quickly.'

'The Emperor,' Epigene boldly said, 'denies that there are any Huns living in the confines of the Eastern Empire.'

'He denies, for example, the existence of at least two – whose names I shall be happy to give you – in his own entourage?'

'He says there are none.'

Attila nodded, as with content. He then said with quiet ferocity: 'I don't wish to diminish your appetite, gentlemen, but I'm forced to give an ultimatum. Seven hundred pounds of gold annually. The restitution of all Hunnish citizens living in his domain. If not . . .'

'Yes?' Plinthas said.

'War,' Attila answered, yawning. Then he dinged his heavy wine cup on the table, gently splashing the two envoys.

'War?' Theodosius screamed, pacing the marble of his palace in Byzantine sunlight. The court stood dumb around. Plinthas and Epigene still bore the red dust of their journey back. 'The imbecile! He has the insolence to – he has the gall—' He squinted at both Plinthas and Epigene. 'Can he do it?'

'He has,' Plinthas said boldly, 'Aetius on his side.' He should not have said that. 'I think,' he then said, 'he is merely testing his own strength. I do not believe he wants war. He merely wants our respect. He is but newly created sovereign chief of the Huns. He is, as it were, flexing the muscles of one arm while he feels ours with the fingers of the other.' A clumsy image, but let it pass.

'I said four hundred,' Theodosius said.

'He insists on seven hundred. But the figure sounds merely arbitrary. Muscle again.'

'Let him have it,' Theodosius. 'It's unseemly to haggle like a huckster. As for the other thing, I'm inclined to say no. This great polity of ours is open to all nations who wish to enjoy its freedom. He has no right to insist on the repatriation of—'

'He considers,' Epigene said, 'that he has every right.'

Theodosius thought. 'There are those two,' he then said, 'who were recently arraigned on a charge of high simony. Fancying a monstrance and stealing it and proposing to sell it. They pleaded the usual pagan ignorance. They're under a kind of house arrest. I think that we would be well rid of them. I think too that it would be politic to quieten Attila down for a time by signing some kind of spurious non-aggression pact with him. You, Epigene, can spend the day drafting it.'

'In effect, then,' Epigene said, 'we give in to his demands.'

'We are big enough,' Theodosius said. 'We quieten the yapping of an importunate puppy by throwing it some gristle.'

Plinthas and Epigene rode back to Attila's encampment in more finery than before; unfortunately heavy rain overtook them on the last day of their journey and they arrived bedraggled under a moist sun. Plinthas said:

'The Emperor has graciously, against much opposition from his counsellors, decided to accede to your lordship's requests. We have brought gold. We have also brought a signed and sealed undertaking to pay your lordship's annual honorarium with the requested augmentation.'

'Demanded, not requested.'

'As your lordship pleases. May we also deliver to your joyful welcome the lords Burra and Canaf, late of the imperial court at Constantinople, now restored to the kingdom of Hunnia?'

Attila looked at the two doubtfully grinning and mowing shaven and barbered and fashionably dressed defectors and said: 'More than welcome, my friends.' Then, to four brutal-looking members of his entourage, 'Take them. Crucify them.'

'Can,' Plinthas gulped, 'that not be deferred until the end of our official business? It is not, if I may say this, seemly—'

'First things first. Watch, gentlemen.'

The punitive act, boys, was performed with Roman efficiency. The two envoys were properly sickened by what they saw. Crucifixion, to Christian Rome, had become merely an item in a holy book, haloed somewhat by its having been converted into the material of a spiritual triumph. Had the Saviour screamed in this manner at the hammering in of the nails, they wondered; had he vomited and stained his nakedness, making his matted chest a banquet table for flies buzzing at his upright agony; had he so leapt fishlike as asphyxiation overtook him; had he been so obscenely incontinent in his extremity?

The two were quite dead when at length the other two stood coldly at Attila's table in his tent. Attila had read through the imperial document. He said: 'Yes, yes, the Treaty of Margus. It has a fine sound, yes? Impressive. The Emperor hereby undertakes to remain in a state of perpetual amity with the paramount chief of Hunnia. He will grant no comfort to our enemies. The theme of the treaty is peaceful coexistence. Between two mighty empires. History will remember this, gentlemen.' And he placed his signature – alpha, tau, tau – above the Emperor's. Orestes stamped the document with a great wax seal which bore Attila's image, crude but fierce. Iota, lambda, alpha. 'You may now bear the joyful tidings back. Your copy, gentlemen. My regards to brother Theodosius.' Such insolence. To Orestes Attila said, watching the horses' cruppers wag to dots in the distance:

'He won't honour it.'

'You want him to break it?'

'Of course I want him to break it.'

'And now the letters to Aetius?'

'Yes, Aetius.'

Aetius was, in his tent, seeking relaxation with a Frankish

woman. This relaxation, boys, probably took the form of an elementary word-game over cups of goat's milk. Do not enquire further. A voice from without called: 'My lord Aetius, the dispatches.'

Aetius, naked for the heat, donned his robe and, with a friendly slap on the rump, sent his Frankish companion away by the rear flap of the tent. 'Bring them.' To the orderly who brought them he said: 'Any report from the Eastern flank?'

'Visigoths, my lord.'

With deep contempt but also anger Aetius repeated the name. 'Visigoths!'

Then he read Attila's letter. It said:

Aetius, my friend. I regret that I can send no reinforcements for your armies in Aquitaine. My own territories are in disorder. There are problems with the Hun tribes west of the Volga. The Germanic forces are active not only in your area but also in mine. The Alains and the Akatzirs are raiding our strongholds in the Caucasus and around the Caspian Sea. There are Slav incursions around the Vistula. I have evidence that the Emperor Theodosius, despite his undertaking according to the terms of the Treaty of Margus, is encouraging the Akatzir tribes to the east of the Elbe to attack Hun settlements. I dream sometimes of you and myself settling once for all this nuisance of an Eastern Empire. But it must, alas, remain only a dream . . .

Aetius's reading was interrupted by the messenger's returning to announce that a number of Visigoths had been taken. 'Good,' Aetius said distractedly. He brooded over Attila's letter. Soon he could hear the intoning of a Christian hymn. He went out to see a number of Visigoth prisoners bound to stakes with faggots around them. A priest, one of the headquarters chaplains, was delivering a judgement to the assembled headquarters staff:

'In as much as the Visigoths practise a travesty of the Christian faith condemned by our Holy Mother the Church, namely that Arian heresy which denies godhead to the person of our Lord Jesus Christ, they are condemned to purge their sins through the cleansing element of fire. Place your torches to the faggots.'

Obediently, three private soldiers shambled towards the great central fire which was a true focus of meeting on this chill Aquitanian day. They lighted their bundles of twigs at it. Aetius, appearing, shouted:

'Stop!' He pointed at the chaplain. 'This is not an ecclesiastical court. The writ of the army runs here. Untie those men.'

The chaplain did not bluster. He said with authority: 'The law of the Church takes precedence over military law, my lord. I act under the instructions of my diocesan head.'

'Is there not,' Aetius cried, 'enough torture and killing without your adding to it in the name of the Church? Those men are prisoners of war, not tried and condemned heretics. Release them. Send them back to their own camp. Listen, all of you. We are not here to wreak vengeance on the enemies of Rome. We are here to absorb our enemies into the imperial peace and order we daily proclaim. We are Christians and must behave as our Saviour would have us behave. We stand for the spread of the faith and the glory of the imperium. Let those men go.'

'Let those men go, eh?' the general officer Ophonius said when they had, having been let go, gone. 'The Huns will not like that. They will see it as Roman weakness. No good telling the Huns about Christian behaviour when they get here.'

'The Huns,' Aetius brooded, 'are not coming. Not ever again. Attila is no longer commander of a mercenary force. They will not serve us or anyone for pay. Things have changed. Rome defends herself. Alone.' And he strode back into his tent.

And it is true that Attila's work was, for the moment, entirely one of pacification and consolidation on his eastern flank. Pacification meant slaughtering a great number of Akatzirs and setting fire to their camps. Kuridak, their paramount chief, was brought before him, his face a web of initiation scars and his hair a wiry tuft in a desert of shaved scalp. Attila said: 'Kuridak. You expected this.'

'Sir, it was against my will. The lesser chiefs insisted. They denied Hun authority in our region. I knew no good would come of it.'

'So you have lost all control over your own people.'

'Sir, they received gifts from men all in gold and silk who came

177

from the city of Const— the great city of the Eastern Romans. They were told to attack.'

'I would put it another way. The gifts were intended for you but never got into your hands. Your lesser chiefs grabbed them when you snored in a sleep induced by fermented mare's milk. But you would have been willing enough—'

'No, sir, I swear—'

'I cannot,' Attila said mildly, 'prove treachery, but I can prove incompetence. From this day forward your territories form part of the empire of Hunnia. And my son Ellak shall rule over you. Boy though he is, he is more of a man than you. Release him,' he said to the rough warriors who had understood hardly one word of the colloquy. 'Let his own people deal with their failed leaders. Their claws are ready.' And he rode away.

Back in his headquarters he found his brother Bleda drinking steadily. He spat his disgust at him. 'Why don't I kill you? Why don't I take your scrawny neck between my ten fingers and squeeze out the foul juice that you call your life?'

'Brotherly love,' Bleda leered. 'There's no crime worse than frat — fratri— You wouldn't last five minutes, Attilula. You daren't.'

'No, I daren't. There are too many elders who worship the law. The law being ghostly voices of the dim past which flit through the caves of their brains like bats but which they think to be gods. But I give you one last chance to show if you've any competence at all for government. I'm placing you as nominal ruler of the new city. A tribal settlement to be called Buda. It faces another settlement across the Danube. Two cities linked by barges. A key point of Hun communications.'

'Clever little brother,' Bleda smirked. 'You've pacified the north and you've pacified the east and now you're going to pacify me. A mere town governor. I won't take it, you know.'

'You will. You can lie all day in a drunken stupor and leave the real work to Orestes and Onegeses.'

'Damned foreigners.'

'They're better Huns than you ever had a hope of being. Get yourself measured for new robes. Call yourself the brother of Attila and you'll gain some respect. But do your drinking in private.'

'Bully. Damned bully.' He growled this, with a break in his voice, only after Attila had left.

But in fine new robes, he swaggered about the muddy streets of the nascent town of Buda, his crapula exacerbated by the noise of hammers and, in his half-shut eyes, the sharp metal of the sunlit Danube. He had a palace of a sort, all sawn pine and oak. In this palace one day, while its incumbent tottered about a construction site, Attila sought a report from Onegeses.

'So?'

'As you said.'

'No improvement.'

'He hunts. Hunting makes him thirsty.'

'Wild boar?'

'Very fierce.'

'With very sharp tusks.'

It was on fine white horses of the plain of Hortobagy that Attila and Bleda rode into the thick Danubian forest. Attila suggested that they hunt together, saying, with an insincerity that struck like vinegar through Bleda's fat befuddled brain, 'You've done well here, brother. In token of renewed love let us relax together in the killing of boar.' The beaters beat through the scrub. A horn sounded. The brothers followed its bleat. Then Bleda, ahead, called back:

'This way.'

They were in a forest glen very loud with the song of thrushes, but they heard no honking of wild boar. Grinning, Bleda raised his whip. He struck his brother, twice, thrice, across the eyes. Blind Attila moaned, raised his hands from the reins to his stricken sight, fell, as his horse felt Bleda's lash and stumbled, on to rotten leaves and moss. His eyes opened in pain to see Bleda above him, grinning, panting, his dagger drawn and ready. 'Frat— fratri— whatever it is,' Bleda panted. Attila kicked high and caught his brother's unprotected groin. He rose and wrested the dagger, which fell without sound into brown moss. He fell on Bleda, his ten fingers tensed and splayed. He looked, breathing desperately hard, on the expiring blood of his blood. He heard the roaring of a boar pack. They were already smelling blood. He remounted and rode off, still half blind. Riding back, eyes hurting more from the intrusive silver of the sunlight river than from the whip, he rehearsed already hypocritical words. My brother, in the flower of his manhood, gored by beasts of the wild forest. The shamans howled their threnody. Howled.

'Now,' Theodosius cried in his palace, 'now we know. A man who will stoop to fratricide.'

'But, sir,' Epigene said, 'he had nothing to fear from Bleda.'

'Oh, there's no reason in it. Sheer Hunnishness. A barbarous assassin shown at last as he really is. He's tasted the blood of his own brother. Fear the worst. Watch out for madness.'

Not madness, boys, but, a brother dead, what were the deaths of the unknown and nameless? Attila moved east over the endless plains in late autumn, the smell of snow already in the air, killing, pacifying. It was on the plains between two mighty rivers that Onegeses fell from his horse. The horse galloped away and then ceased to gallop, merely pawing the earth, his head with blaring eyes turned to his dismounted master. Onegeses had been left behind by the horde: he heard its unearthly thudding in the east. He looked down and saw his torn bare ankle dripping blood. Why? What had struck him? He saw drops of this blood, already rusty, weighing down grassblades. He followed the thin trail and saw something that amazed him. A silver tongue protruding from the soil caught the sun. A tongue? A point of metal. He crouched, cleaning away the earth. It was a swordpoint. There was a sword there, stuck in the soil, but upside down. This, boys, is a moment in time more momentous than you can realise. Onegeses took his own sword as a spade and dug away the earth. Soon the hint of a hilt gleamed dully. A gold hilt, glass or jewels encrusting it, clamped in tiny golden claws. After many minutes of panting work he dug out the whole sword. He held it to the sky by the hilt. He thought he knew what it was.

'I am certain now what it is,' he said to Attila after the eastern pacification. The sword was clean now of earth and highly polished. Attila handled it with cautious reverence. 'The legend is a very old one, and now it proves a reality. At that very spot, between the Volga and the Don, the king of the Scythians buried it, point upwards.'

'Which king of the Scythians?'

'Marak. Many many years ago. His own sword with the golden pommel, a marvel of workmanship, as you can see. The Scythians were to march west and never turn back. That swordpoint marked the limit of their retreat. The sword was to be worshipped as a god. To retreat beyond it was a terrible blasphemy.'

'These superstitions.'

'Never despise the superstitions of other people. This sword is known throughout the world – even beyond the Great Wall. The Romans call it the sword of Mars.'

'So even they bring the gods into it.'

'It is the best of omens. The very best.'

Attila nodded in thought, passing his scarred thumb up and down the immaculate sharp edge. 'Let one of our smiths beat the blade gently with nail and hammer so that my name appears upon it. You know what I mean. The name indented on the blade.'

'Hammered in like tiny pockmarks?'

'The similitude is infelicitous, but yes. A pity it cannot be done in Hunnish, since we lack a mode of writing. So it must be Greek or Latin. Not the whole name, no. The first symbol will be enough. The same in both alphabets. Alpha or A. Let it be done, Onegeses.'

Done, and the sword set high in the outer hall of Attila's headquarters, there to be worshipped by the vulgar as an emblem of power both living and to come. And the word of its magic spread wide. Small gifts of tribute came in from the superstitious, including, from the eastern plains, a vat of what was called oil but seemed not to be oil, being neither fat nor good for cooking. Thrown on flames it shouted aloud and threw fire at the heavens. It was said to be a great preservative of metals: a locked stone coffin brimming with the oil could keep out the demons of rust from whatever metallic objects swam therein. And another kind of tribute came from Ravenna.

Honoria was the pretty dark-haired daughter of Galla Placidia. While her mother worked on documents of state, she was busy, tonguetip protruding, writing her own document.

'And what precisely is that, Honoria?'

'Oh – a little story, a romance.'

'You've read all the romances in the library. So now you have to write your own. Very childish. Why you can't read Seneca, Virgil, Ovid I don't know.'

'They're boring, mother.' She added: 'Like life.' Outside rain bounded off the marble. It was only noon, but lamps had been lighted.

'A very childish thing to say.'

'You're always telling me I'm a child. So I talk as a child. But I don't write like a child.'

'What can you mean?'

'A man, a great warrior, finds a magic sword which will secure him the conquest of the whole world. He looks for the most beautiful woman in the world to share his triumphs. Doesn't that sound like a good story?'

'It sounds like nonsense to me.' A magic sword? World conquest? She got up from her table and padded over on bare feet. 'Let me see what you're writing.' Honoria put beautiful little protective hands over her manuscript.

'It's private, mother.'

'Stories aren't private, my girl. Stories are meant for the whole world to read, starting with your nearest and dearest.' And she made a dart for the manuscript with her long fingers made longer by uncut nails lacquered in gold (like, incidentally, her toenails). Honoria at once viciously tore what she had written, crying:

'There, you shan't see it. You're always prying into what I do. You and Valentinian – just because he's Emperor and you call yourself regent and think you're the first two persons of the Holy Trinity.'

'Blasphemy as well as insolence,' Galla Placidia said, trying to slap a face well guarded by two beautiful little hands. 'It's time you were taught to behave. You find life boring, do you? Perhaps a spell in a convent would help. No romances there, my daughter. Discipline and prayer. Now go to your room.'

The girl's flushed face broke out of its window of fingers. 'No. I'm going out dancing. There's real life going on outside, and you keep me shut up here like a prisoner. Am I not a princess? Don't I have the rights of my rank? I'm going out, I tell you. I *won't* go to my room.' Placidia blazed and lashed out with her long sharp nails.

'You'll do as I say.'

Honoria was first astonished, then she howled with rage. She tried to hit back. Her mother, forgetting that she was unshod, kicked at the girl's hard shin and howled in her turn. She hit out, harder. Honoria howled her way to her bedchamber. There, sobbing, she wrote.

What she wrote got to Attila by imperial courier, bribed with one of Honoria's mother's less valuable rings duly stolen. Attila listened to Orestes read it aloud while he breakfasted on fermented mare's milk into which rusks had been crushed. 'Tears,' Orestes said, 'tears all over it. Listen. "I am so wretched here and my mother and brother hate me. Dear Attila, when I heard of your magic sword my heart overflowed with love for you. I have never seen you, but I am sure you must be strong and handsome. I hear of your conquests with admiration. I write to you to ask you to marry me. Let us consider ourselves betrothed. I enclose a ring—" '

'She does?'

'She does. Here.' Orestes picked up from his lap a plain metal band, perhaps of bronze. 'Shall I continue?'

'Do, please. This is fascinating.'

' "I am no ordinary young girl. I am very beautiful, as they all say. My brother is Emperor of the West, and my father was the great Constantius the Third. If you marry me, you have a right to take as dowry one half of the territory of the Western Empire. Take it and take me, your loving and desirous Honoria." There, the Latin is not good. The verb governs the proper name. It should be Honoriam.'

'It's nonsense, of course. Do we reply?'

'I think not. I think we file letter and ring away. You never know when this kind of nonsense will make sense.'

The wearisome business of putting down insurrections went on. It was all Constantinople gold. Storming camps, killing, looting: painful necessities; how else could Eastern Europe be pacified? Scarred and weary, Attila addressed the captive chieftain Bogan:

'You were bound by a solemn blood oath to hold allegiance to your paramount lord – myself. You know who I am?'

'I know.'

'And now your people rise against me. Why?'

'They wanted the old days back. They don't hold with empires and laws and police. They wanted to be left alone.'

'The old cry. But the Emperor Theodosius didn't leave you alone, did he? He incited you to revolt, *paid* you to revolt.' And he threw a fistful of imperial gold on to the baked earth of Danubian summer. A Hun guard, with the simple directness of his kind, stooped to grasp it, but Attila hit out at him wearily with the flat of his workaday sword, not that of Mars.

'We could not refuse. The man is the Emperor of Rome.'

'Not of Rome. Of another city. And I am the Emperor of the plains and rivers and the mountains, to whom you owe obedience. You will not live to see it, Bogan, but your great Emperor, and he of Rome too, will be brought to their knees. Gold or no gold. Take him away. Crucify him with the others.' The crucifixes were part of the Danubian landscape now, and the screams of Bogan and others were a kind of demented birdsong. Orestes said to Attila: 'Here is the man I told you about. Scotta.' Scotta was swarthy, no blue in the dead black of his straight hair, with a broken nose ill mended and a twisted torso not mended at all. He squinted up at Attila and touched his forelock. Attila said:

'Know the languages of diplomacy, do you?'

'A sweet tongue in a sour body, your godliness.'

'Hold yourself ready.'

And then he struck. A great fair was held annually in the fields outside the town of Margus. Vendors and buyers came to it from all over the world, from India even and the Middle Kingdom. There were fine horses and cattle on display, exquisite textiles and delicate pottery, intricate objects of beaten gold and silver. There was also merrymaking, with dancing to sweet pipe and thumped drum and the twanging of harps, and there was also savoury food simmered in iron pots or grilled above charcoal, wine too from all the vineyards of the unbroken landmass that is our Europe (though we are not in it, being in northern Africa) and their Asia, and there were imperial policemen to keep order. There were also Huns, this time I tell of, their daggers hidden under peaceable red cloaks. These Huns awaited a certain signal, which came at sundown on the third day of the fair, and this was the firing of a Persian tent in which superb embroideries were on display. When the flames rose amid shrieks and curses

184

in many languages, the Huns drew daggers and struck policemen in the back. They then looted, driving cattle lowing with fear on to the plain, whipping off superb horses, grabbing a dancing girl here, a pale soft boy there, stuffing their bearded mouths with Arabian sweetmeats. The Emperor Theodosius, when he heard of the outrage, was very angry. He dictated a letter to Attila:

'How to interpret this abomination I do not well know. I should wish to think it an act of brigandage among your men which you propose to punish severely. Remember, this is the greatest fair of the Eastern Empire, its peaceful maintenance guaranteed by the imperial police, its final sponsor myself. I demand an immediate explanation.'

But, while he was spluttering this indignation at his amanuensis, Scotta, leering in a most grotesque costume of his own design – black and white and geometrical – had already limped his way in to the presence of Epigene, announcing himself as the envoy Scotta, on special service with the Emperor of the Plains, desirous of a private interview with the Emperor Theodosius the Third.

'You cannot see him,' Epigene said.

'So you say, friend. There is no urgency. He will see me sooner or later. Meantime I take it you will not be unwilling to take a message to him?'

'What message?'

'This. The disruption of the fair of Margus was not, as the Emperor is probably thinking, an act of brigandage. The Huns are too disciplined a people to indulge in gratuitous violence. The Huns, by order of their esteemed leader, were merely expressing dissatisfaction with the conduct of one of the ecclesiastical dignitaries of the Eastern Empire. This Christian shaman, a bishop is what you call him, ordered the violation of certain noble Hun burial places in the vicinity of Margus – the said bishop's what is termed I believe diocese. Golden ornaments were removed and the headstones broken. This is intolerable. The universal lord Attila desires the immediate punishment of the dignitary in question. By beheading.'

'This,' Epigene gasped, 'is,' gasping, 'monstrous.'

'Precisely what my master said. Do I await a reply?'

'You will get your reply.' And he stalked off. Scotta grinned, examined with interest the furnishings of Epigene's office,

185

secreted within his geometrical robes an onyx figurine of the Virgin and Child, then limped out to his lodgings. They would find him, no problem.

Theodosius said to the bishop Andoche: 'Is this true?'

Andoche, in full stiff golden episcopal robes, his chaplain beside him, two tonsured deacons behind, said, without unease: 'I cannot speak for the looting. For the breaking of the headstones I can. These were pagan graves placed near to sanctified ground. We are directly commissioned by Our Lord himself to put down paganism.'

'There is such a matter as discretion, my lord bishop. You know the Huns?'

'A grossly pagan people. Indeed I know them.'

'By their lights they have a just claim. They demand reparations. They also demand your head.'

'Impossible,' Andoche fatly smiled. 'Isn't it?' he added, not smiling.

'By imperial Christian law, yes, impossible. But the paramount chief Attila affirms that there is such a thing as international law.'

'Where administered?' Andoche said. 'There is nothing outside the Empire where such law could run. It is all pagan territory. It cannot be dignified with the term *international*.' He then added: 'Can it?'

'This is a quibble. Let me clarify, my lord bishop. I am requested kindly to deliver your person to the Hun authorities, as they term themselves. The Huns themselves will administer what they call international law. Meaning probably your torture, crucifixion and dismemberment.'

Andoche asked permission to sit down. Sitting down, he seemed desirous of lying down. An ague came upon him. 'Because I did my Christian duty. I did not know whose graves they were. All I knew was that they were pagan.' Theodosius said:

'You're a fool, my lord bishop. By your pious act you force me to yield part of the Eastern Empire to the Huns. The city of Margus becomes Hun territory. This is the price we pay for your *physical* salvation. Perhaps you would prefer martyrdom.'

'There are,' Andoche panted, 'men cut out to be martyrs. I never felt that martyrdom was my vocation. The age of miracles.

The age of martyrdom. Alike past, past. Alike. My diocese – my city – in the hands of pagans. I cannot live with it.'

'You will have to live with it. Margus remains a Christian diocese – this is a condition the Huns will accept. Christianity to them is an amusing show. And so you continue to be bishop of Margus.'

'I will,' Andoche groaned, 'request translation. I will see the patriarch—'

'Your big opportunity, my lord bishop. The conversion of the Huns. In their own city.'

He rode in, the tremulous bishop, on a piebald horse finely caparisoned. A Hun guard of honour ironically presented arms outside the stone church he called his cathedral. His Christian congregation cowered under a sun which had become Hun property. The bishop entered, congregation huddling after, to find two large Huns fighting each other in play and to the applause of their fellows with great metal crucifixes. Clang, boys, and clash: you would do well to shudder at the blasphemy of it. 'You are desecrating the house of the Lord God,' Andoche cried feebly. 'Do you understand me? Do you realise the punishment for desecration?' The Huns courteously permitted him to say holy mass. They ate their dried horsemeat and local bread, watching. When the sacred host and the holy wine were administered to the faithful, these infidels pushed in there to grab and taste, fighting the Christians to drink the blessed blood of the Lord God. You do well to shiver in this hot sun at the horror of it all.

It was not long after this that in Ravenna the young Emperor Valentinian the Third received the count Aetius. The news had reached the seat of the Empire of the West, and Valentinian, young as he was, appreciated its significance. Did Aetius realise it too?

'None better.'

'My brother Emperor asks for the whole of the Western army.'

'Including my army in Gaul?'

'One sharp brisk assault, he says. To show the Huns where the power lies.'

'They know where the power lies,' Aetius said. 'His imperial majesty of Constantinople has let the Huns into his domains. If he had stood firm over this business of the city of Margus—'

'How could he stand firm? How could he?'

'What he asks for is an impossibility. I cannot release even one maniple of the army in Gaul. Attila must do his worst.'

'You say that with a certain satisfaction. Whose side are you on?'

'On the side of the Empire, of course. Both halves of it. But I can't help. Well, my old friend has gone far.'

'Come far, you mean. Will come further.'

Further, boys, ah yes. Attila sat on a fine throne in the palace of the city of Buda, the sword of Mars hung above him but, in his untutorable Hun brain, no capacity to compare it with the sword of Damocles. He was flanked by Orestes and Onegeses. Before him stood a white or Mongolian Hun named Edecon.

'You know why I sent for you?'

'I do not know. But I am glad to be here.' Yet the flat face and the slitted eyes showed no sign of gladness or, indeed, of any other emotion.

'Your skill in keeping order in the eastern regions of Hunnia merits a reward of some kind. I consider that the best reward is an opportunity to show true generalship. Here in the valley of the Danube and beyond. You have been told of my intention?'

'You tested the strength of the Emperor at Constantinople. He has yielded you a city. Now you are to take all his cities.'

Attila smiled and said: 'I would not put it quite so crudely.'

'Why not?' Onegeses said. 'That *is* your intention.'

'It is, friend, somewhat more complicated than that. A matter of fixing the bounds of an empire. And what are the bounds of an empire? As far as you can go.' He pointed a finger at a common soldier of the palace guard. 'You – why do we fight?'

'To live, sir.'

'Yes. Other people plant grain and watch it grow to a harvest. We steal the harvest. Other people make statues of gold and useful objects of fine wood. We steal them. Ignoble, would you not say? We make nothing. Our only trade is war.'

'A trade of skill and danger,' Edecon said. 'So you test a man. Not by growing corn and carving wood. I wait for your orders, sir.'

'You're right. He's right, friends. I spit out the word *ignoble*. We march south.'

'To Constantinople?' Orestes grinned.

'We don't ask questions like that. We march south. We see how far we can fix the bounds of our empire.' But, rising from his throne in resolution, he sighed.

So on the march, ever on the march. The horde uncountable, foot-soldiers and cavalry, engineers skilled in siege machinery learned from the Romans, the dust, the noise, the screaming and whinneying. It was Edecon who forced the gates of Singidunum and, with no expression of triumph, lust or kindred feelings on his flat countenance, ordered various kinds of gratuitous violence. Citizens of Singidunum were thrown screaming on bonfires, regardless of age or sex, or else, quartered, stewed in pots and hurled to the hounds, boys. This was Hunnishness at its most unpleasant. There was also much looting. The cartwrights of the city were whipped into constructing more and more wagons to haul the stuff away. And yet what was it all for? Cattle, horses, grain by the sackload – this was reasonable enough – but why was that Hun sergeant gloating over an exquisite gold figurine of the Blessed Virgin, as the Empire called her? 'What will you do with it?' Edecon asked.

'Melt it down. Have it beaten. Ornaments for my women.'

'So,' Edecon mused, 'we wage war to deck our women and make them more dissatisfied than before. Sometimes, sergeant, I have my doubts. Tomorrow let the men swill and gorge. Let the day after be a day of recovery. Then we march south. Always south.'

South, in Constantinople, Theodosius, deeply worried, consulted with his military staff. Aspar, a lined and pared general in charge of the defences of the imperial capital, read off the Hun conquests: 'Singidunum – which the natives call Beograd or something like it. Illyria, Dalmatia, Macedonia, Thrace. They swarm.'

'Who is this man Edecon?'

'A Hun from the East. I don't think he quite realises the significance of what he's done. I don't think he sees the picture.'

'Attila will teach him,' Theodosius gloomed. 'Gentlemen, he's taken the city of Nich in the Serbian province. You know what happened in Nich—'

'The great Constantine was born there,' Aspar said with a shiver of awe. 'Founder of our city. And now a slit-eyed barbarian holds it.'

Attila came to Nich and, in the company of Edecon, Orestes and Onegeses, took wine, roast meat, and the fine white bread of the conquered while he watched indulgently a firelit orgy, frank copulation varied with a little light torture. Edecon said: 'It seems to me we've come as far as we can. You've fixed the southern boundary of Hunnia. As for taking Constantinople – there are difficulties. Our siege engines are not good when they are not broken. There's a shortage of military equipment. Our engineers are ill-trained. Military engineering is a Roman province.'

'You assume,' Attila said, 'that I wish to take Constantinople.'

'Our final objective, surely,' Edecon said.

'But what do we do with Constantinople other than loot it? Hold down a restive population? Learn the tricks of Byzantine rule? We Huns are useless in cities. Townships. Villages. Markets. We lose heart when surrounded by stone. Besides – I received a warning I expected to receive.'

'From,' Orestes asked, 'your friend Aetius?'

'The armies of the Western empire have been putting down insurrections in Gaul. Now there seems to be peace between Aetius and the Visigoths. Even, I hear, cooperation. Aetius says he would regret having to intervene—'

'If we took Constantinople?'

'We cannot take Constantinople,' Edecon said. 'Another day, perhaps. But not now.'

'Who,' Attila asked, 'is the man in charge of their defences?'

'Aspar. A good hard name. A good hard man,' Onegeses admitted.

'Arrange a parley.'

The meeting was arranged on a breezy hilltop from which, though at a great distance, the imperial city sparkling in the sun tempted like the display of a Hebrew jeweller. Attila shook hands cordially with Aspar, saying: 'You've been expecting an attack?'

'Whatever you say, we still expect an attack. But we're ready.'

'Your Emperor knows all about humiliation. I've no wish to proceed to the final humiliation. Your city is safe.'

Aspar frowned. 'You take Illyria, Dalmatia, Macedonia, Thrace – you have practically the whole of the Eastern Empire in your hands. And yet you baulk at the final step. I cannot believe it.'

'We Huns are not devious – not like you Byzantines. It is not convenient for us to try to take Constantinople. Withdraw an army from Hunnia, and part of Hunnia becomes restive. You're a soldier, you know of these things. I have to be back to quieten a restive people. Especially since my son, a provincial governor, may be in danger. We attack Constantinople – you defend it. A long siege to no purpose. My campaign ends with your Emperor's suing for peace. We wait here in – what's the name of the place?'

'Arcadiopolis.'

'I will send the conditions of peace with my envoy Scotta. That's Scotta over there. Not very handsome but very resilient. He has very strong teeth.'

The Grand Eunuch Chrysaphius kept Scotta and his armed escort waiting long in an enmarbled anteroom fragrant with flowers of the season. Scotta sniffed at them with relish. He sniffed with equal relish at the delicate perfume in which the gross body of the Grand Eunuch, when he appeared belatedly, was as it were, secondarily swathed. The outer swathing was of cloth of gold, and there was an insolent jangle of holy figurines threaded on gold wire about the Grand Eunuch's fat neck. He squeaked: 'The Lord Scotta?'

'Delightful. So I'm a lord now. Yes. Lord Scotta is here to see the Lord Emperor.'

'His imperial greatness is indisposed. I have been deputed to receive you. I am—'

'I can see and hear what you are. It is a sad thing to happen to a man.'

'That is not to the purpose. Eunuch means keeper of the bed-chamber. *Eune* means couch. I am no longer keeper of the bed-chamber. Will you be good enough to come this way?'

He turned and waddled the carpeted path he had come. To the delight of his rough escort, Scotta waddled comically after. Then he put on dignity. Awe came naturally when he found himself seated at a copious dinner for two, amid gorgeous hangings, fanned and waited upon by boys and girls whose robes were cunningly slit, boys, and this is disgusting, to disclose their slim nakedness beneath. Chrysaphius crunched at a honeycoated partridge, saying: 'I take it that a noble lord like yourself has – had – similar perquisites to these?'

'We live rough. A different philosophy from yours, Grand Eunuch. A warrior people.'

'You do not look much like a warrior to me.'

'Never judge by appearances.' Scotta crunched roast pig crackling and spat out the unchewable integument on to a gold plate. 'I've led troops in my time. My unprepossessing physique has been no great handicap. I must confess, though, that . . . ah . . . in this . . . ah . . . sumptuous ambience I feel a certain regret. A regret that I've missed so much. Perhaps we should take Constantinople after all. The Lord Scotta in satin and silk, with a Grand Eunuch of his own.'

'Perhaps,' dabbling podgy fingers in syrup, 'you may have to take Constantinople. The Emperor certainly will not yield to your peace terms.'

'Reasonable, I would say,' squinting at a fistful of charred wrens. 'Six thousand pounds of gold and an annual tribute of two thousand one hundred. Or shall we make it the round two thousand? The Lord Attila is not a greedy man. And this campaign has, after all, all been the fault of the divine Theodosius.'

'You must not say divine. He is not a pagan Caesar. We are a Christian nation. How his fault?'

'He permitted the despoliation of Hunnish tombs by one of your Christian bishops. He permitted the great Attila to invest the imperial town of Margus. My territory is yours, he says in effect. It is as good as an invitation to take over the entire Eastern Empire.'

'This is very specious talk. And, if I may say so, somewhat insolent. Do try some of these stuffed dates.'

'Thank you. The victor is entitled to a little insolence, Grand Eunuch.'

'Three thousand pounds of gold, you said. I doubt if there is so much in the imperial treasury.'

'Six thousand. And an annual tribute of two thousand one hundred.'

'You changed that to two thousand.'

'Did I? So I change it back again. Just a drop. Oh, very well, fill it. What is a mere hundred between friends?'

'Try a little of this flan. I have a Sicilian pastrycook. Honey and bilberries and finely minced larks' tongues. And tell me – which of these girls – or boys, of course – would you wish to be delivered to your bedchamber?'

'You're trying to seduce me, Grand Eunuch.' But he licked his lips.

He licked his lips, like a child during baptism, to taste the salt of the spray of the Bosphorus as he and Chrysaphius were rowed in a gilded barge under a mild sun. It was a mere pleasure outing, an item in a programme of seduction to which Scotta, now in fine Byzantine robes, seemed in good humour to yield. Chrysaphius, lolling on cushions in the stern, invited him to say more of what Scotta had termed a 'special resentment'.

'I deserved better. Here you see me – a mere envoy. I was promised a governorship in Northern Pannonia. I try to cover my resentment. After all, he's a great man. Also he is my sovereign to whom I owe unblinking allegiance.'

'Fidelity, I believe, is a business of mutualities. A reciprocal matter. Where is his loyalty to you?'

'Exactly.'

'Still,' Chrysaphius munched something very sweet, 'betrayal – a harsh word for a harsh deed.'

'I never mentioned betrayal. I never would. All I ask is a little – well, call it appreciation, my dear Chrysanthemum.'

'I like that. Chrysanth— A great man, I always say, should have a great soul.'

'Exactly.'

'The succession. I take it the succession is already arranged?'

'All those squabbling sons? No. Attila keeps consulting astrologers – finding out how long he's likely to live. He knows the Hunnish empire will be in difficulties when – perish the thought, perish it – he meets his latter end.'

'A mortal man despite everything, yes yes.'

'Like all, like all. Tell me,' he spoke with a sudden sharpness, 'what exactly are you proposing?'

'Oh, nothing really. I was merely thinking of a way in which your large talents could best be employed. You're wasted, as you must realise. The Eastern Empire's open to foreign talent. Therein lies its strength.'

'You're suggesting an appointment of some kind? What kind? Military? Administrative? Diplomatic?'

'Something of that kind. No hurry, though. But, first, dear Scotta, certain things ought to be regularised.'

'You mean one big thing, don't you?'

'Perhaps. The treasury is well stocked.'

'That was not the impression you formerly gave me.'

'Oh, I spoke the language of all bargainers. Suppose we say three thousand?'

'On account. Payable tomorrow. The remaining seven thousand can be held in escrow. I accept that I meet all the necessary expenses out of it.'

'They should not be too heavy.' He took a powdered sweet-meat from the gold dish that, near empty, caught the sun and made him squint. 'We take it for granted that you yourself would not be involved – in the act, I mean, the act, the act. No hurry. Think about it.'

'And would the divine Emperor approve?'

'As I told you, he is not divine, far from it. At the moment he's going over your . . . ah . . . master's territorial demands. What your master calls the eternal confines of the Empire of Hunnia. He naturally thinks they're excessive. Preposterous is the word he used to me.'

The sun yearned towards sinking and prepared a preposterous bed of purple, green, gold, primrose samite. On the banks of the Danube, in his oaken pavilion, Attila looked with some sadness on that same sun in its sinking. Life was not many days, and all days were desperately short. Edecon sat by him and said: 'You remember when we besieged Sirmium?'

'So many towns, so many names. What happened at Sirmium?'

'It seems a small matter, but you always say you're looking for – what's the word?'

194

'Pretexts. Yes, never perform an act of aggression without a pretext, Edicon. Always have a pious reason for an impious act, so the Romans would say, hypocrites.'

'This is a matter of one of their bishops. There were sacred vessels, as they call them, in that great church in Sirmium. Well, this bishop gave them to one of our commanders – no matter who, he's dead now – and told him to sell them to pay for his ransom – the bishop's ransom, that is. But the bishop got himself slaughtered. And the vessels got in the hands of a moneylender, what they call a usurer. And this man, Sylvanus is his name, sold them to another of these Italian bishops.'

'So?'

'Well, you see, sir, some of our lawful plunder is on Italian soil. The Western Empire's holding what's rightly ours, yours. Isn't that a – what's the word again?'

'Pretext. It could, true, be inflated into something useful. But not yet, Edecon. One thing at a time. Meaning the Eastern Empire. Meaning Theodosius's response to our demands.'

Back, in the meantime, to keeping pacified the Empire of Hunnia. It was not easy, but Attila had reliable generals, including his eldest son Ellak – who chid him with filial deference for withdrawing some of his troops from the eastern plains to assist an assault on Pannonia. But Attila swore it would not happen again.

'It will, father, you know it will.'

'Next time – where will it be next time? This empire is already bigger than that of Rome. It's a hard task holding it together.'

'The thing to do,' Ellak said, 'is not to stand still. Something I've learned. Leave it to me to move east.'

'As far as the Great Wall?'

'Why not? And you move west.'

'How did you know that was in my mind?'

'Because you taught me never to stand still. An empire on horseback – isn't that what we are?'

Yes, boys, that was what they were. And you will have in your young minds an image of an enhorsed Attila like a centaur snorting over the carnage, and you will not be far wrong. Carnage, a word meaning no more than flesh as a stuff, though piled high as a mountain and spread wide as a plain, with blood as sluggish rivers lacing it. Women and children, born and unborn, added soft flesh to the hard brown gashed and dismembered bodies of fighting men overborne by other fighting men. The achievement of Attila, who tried to make a glory out of destruction. And Attila, temporarily at rest from the carnage, asked Edecon:

'Where is Scotta?'

'Still with this fat eunuch in Constanti – whatever it is. Being seduced.'

'But really seducing. And who is to be – the would-be assassin?'

'Theodosius is sending two ambassadors – Maximin and Vigilas. Vigilas is not really an ambassador. Scotta insists that he carry the gold. He pretends fear of you. He wants clean hands.'

'Gold to pay his accomplices. They think they'll find accomplices?'

'They think the Huns are easily seduced by gold.'

'Well,' Attila said, 'we'll be waiting for them.'

And in Constantinople Chrysaphius assured his Emperor that all was in order. They should expect news in less than a month.

'You realise,' Theodosius said for the tenth time, 'that my name must not be associated with this . . . plot? A Christian emperor – involved in an assassination—'

'Call it self-protection, sir. With Attila dead the whole Hun kingdom will collapse. But rest easy on that matter. If any name emerges it will be mine.'

'Yes, your name linked to mine. I think the time is coming, Chrysaphius, when I must relieve you of the office of chief minister.'

'Your imperial majesty has been dissatisfied with my work?'

'Not at all. But the people don't like you.'

'The people never appreciate discipline. Yet discipline is necessary.'

'Secret police? Torture chambers? No, Chrysaphius, the time has been made opportune for you to go into retirement. No doubt you're well cushioned against that eventuality.'

'No man likes to be deprived of power and authority.'

'Power? What greater power, what higher prestige can you ask for than what this last act confers? To go down in the history of the Empire as the man who contrived the death of its greatest scourge? The end of the scourge of God. Think of it. And it is you, Chrysaphius, who control the sticking in of the knife. You know what he says? He says: "Where I set foot the grass will never grow again." Well, the green will flood the world and the Empire be whole as it was before. Thank God we're going to be rid of him.'

That is enough until tomorrow, boys. Drink deep of this bright air. Tomorrow there will be enough foulness to oppress your spirits.

See now Maximin and Vigilas, with their escort clinking with arms, riding along the bank of the great river to the Hun city of Buda, all wood and smoke and no glory of carven stone. The young son of Vigilas, whose name was Prophyme, rode behind his father, a boy of a golden beauty to soften even the heart of a Hun. His presence was, in a manner, to emphasise the peacefulness of the mission – Vigilas a good family man with a loved son, a father confronting another father, however Hunnish. Both envoys ensured their faces in prolepsis at the thought of greasy stews of horsemeat and mare's milk warm from the udder.

'A new civilisation to be imposed upon the world. As he thinks.'

'Not for long, Vigilas, not for long.'

Yet nothing could have been more civilised in the style of the Eastern Empire than their welcome. The two men and a boy met a sleek Attila, his wife's long golden hair was pinnaced and encastled in the style of Constantinople's most up-to-date coiffeur, and the viands served were exquisite. Even the servants were sleekly Romanised, though their faces were sore from enforced close shaving. At dinner Attila suddenly said:

'*Sunt lachrimae rerum, et mentem mortalia tangunt*. A lovely line. And so true, gentlemen.'

Vigilas, with some skill, translated. 'There are tears at the heart of things, and things doomed to die clutch the heart of humanity.'

'You speak our Hunnish language well, Vigilas. You almost make me feel there's a latent literature in it. Ah, if only I had time for the arts. But we have to concentrate on staying alive. Which means protecting our poor empire. Which means . . .' He changed his tone without raising his voice: the near flute became a distant phalanx of trumpets. 'I am not at all content with your Emperor's response to my demands.'

Vigilas stuttered. 'My I ttttalk Latin?'

'I'd prefer Greek. It is the more mellifluous tongue of the two.'

'Well, then. He considers that the towns you pillaged – if I may use the term without offence – should be permitted reconstruction and reorganisation under the aegis of Constantinople.'

'Meaning that we sucked them dry. So be it. We're done with them, for the time being. I refer to quite different matters. We'll discuss the business of the gold tomorrow. Now I ask for a reply to my demand for the repatriation of the Hun deserters on his territory.'

'There are,' Maximin said, 'only seventeen of these, according to the imperial census. They have, if I may use the term, gone to ground. Impossible to dig up—'

'There are at least three hundred. You know there are at least three hundred. I don't like lies.'

Maximin looked down at his golden plate, on which delicate fowl flesh cooled in its robe of delicate sauce. This was Hunnia, they were in Hunnia. He said with a small voice: 'I am not lying, sir. I am not responsible for the imperial census—'

'I hate deceit,' Attila cried. 'If you were not protected by your diplomatic status I would have you crucified on the spot. You're a liar, sir.'

'I object to that, if I may say so. I am no liar.'

'Guards,' Attila called. Guards appeared, not sleek. Attila pointed a manicured forefinger at Vigilas. 'Arrest this servant of the Emperor Theodosius. And arrest his son while you're at it.' The boy Prophyme choked on a grape pip. Maximin cried:

'We come in good faith from the imperial court to deliver messages from his imperial greatness. We do not deserve this treatment.'

'You, sir, are being treated with all the respect due to your office. Your colleague's office is somewhat – ambiguous. But I shall resolve the ambiguity before daybreak. Take them away. Let us have some music.' And while the father and son, pale and wordless, were led off, he calmly resumed the eating of his

198

dinner. Greek musicians discoursed a Lydian melody on flute and harp, with descreet punctuation from a tiny bejewelled drum.

The cell where Vigilas and his son were thrown was small, damp and rat-ridden. Small Danubian insects crawled over the boy when he lay on the dank stones for sleep, waking him crying.

'There there, my son.'

'What wrong have we done, father? What wrong?'

'Be brave.'

'But he's mad, isn't he? He changes from one thing to another – and no warning. Like Caligula, Nero, father.'

'They were exceptions to the rule of a rational Rome. Now you have a whole race dedicated to destruction.'

'The Antichrist? Is the end of the world coming?'

'It may be, son, it may be.'

Then they were both dragged out. They were dragged to a room well lighted with torches where Attila sat, transformed to an ogre dressed in rough skins, his jowls unshaven, his finger-nails black. Behind him stood a burly fellow nursing an axe. Before him stood the cringing Maximin. There was a table rough as a butcher's block and on it knives and pincers. 'Say nothing yet,' Attila said to Vigilas, who had no intention of saying anything. 'Leave the talking to me. Vigilas, you come here on a feigned errand. You present yourself as an ambassador but you are nothing more than a paid assassin.' Vigilas opened his mouth, but Attila anticipated his objection. 'No lie, Vigilas. Your baggage has been examined. There is more gold there than is proper for a travelling state official. The money was intended to buy your way to my sleeping presence and then to thrust the dagger in.' Vigilas's framed a round vowel. 'No, no, sir. The dagger has been found. A fine piece of Byzantine workmanship. This.' He pulled the weapon from his breast and brandished it.

'No!'

'Swego,' Attila said to the axeman. 'Take that boy. Cut off his head.' He admired for a moment the screams and protests. 'Alternatively, tell me who put you up to this. Was it the Emperor himself?'

'I tell you,' Vigilas said with little breath, 'you are wholly mistaken. Let my son go. This is barbarous.'

'Yes. Hunnish. Listen, Vigilas, I know all about it. My man

Scotta has told me all. But we need exact documentation. Or, to put it simply, evidence of direct imperial implication. Here is a good stylus and an immaculate tablet. Write in Greek or Latin, just as you prefer.'

'And if I do,' Vigilas choked, 'what will happen to me?'

'Think rather of what will happen to your son if you do not.'

The Emperor Theodosius had other things in the zone of his immediate attention than the hot though distant breath of Attila. He attended in full or overfull regalia the marriage of his sister Augusta Pulcheria to Marcianus Elavius in the great basilica of Constantinople. But, while the bishop droned, the bride looked demure and the bridegroom consciously warlike (anticipating the taking of a hymen like a city), a messenger came and whispered. Theodosius looked pale. Attila had sent Orestes to Constantinople. When, putting off the audience for three days, Theodosius learned that Orestes had the boy Prophyme with him, he divined that the breath of Attila had grown softer, as if sweetened with comfits. He bade Orestes be summoned to the presence. The boy seemed to carry in his eyes the memory of dire horrors. Orestes spoke firmly, saying:

'I bring the gravest of charges. Your principal minister is revealed as an assassin.'

'He has not—?'

'No, he has not. But you seem fully aware of his intention. My master bids me deliver these words: "Send me his head. Otherwise I shall come and decapitate him myself." I await your reply.'

'I can give no reply. You bring no evidence, no proof. Where is my ambassador Vigilas?'

'Safely in prison. I deliver his son to your imperial charge. Vigilas has provided the evidence in writing. Signed. Sealed. The head of the Grand Eunuch Chrysaphius. At once.'

'I am not to be bullied.'

'And my master is not to be assassinated. He demands the immediate execution of the deballocked malefactor, as he terms him.'

'I accept his territorial demands, tell him. I accept the southern limits of his empire. I know what he is really after.'

'The head of Chrysaphius. Oh, and here is the money intended to buy the entry of Vigilas into the sleeping presence of my unsuspecting master.' He picked up the leathern bag that lay at his feet and emptied a molehill of gold in a dull bright sluice on the marble paving.

'Insolence,' Theodosius cried. 'I shall order your arrest.'

'Do. My master will still require the head of the Grand Eunuch. Oh, and he has kept back one pound of gold in exchange for this boy's freedom.'

'I shall give you your reply,' Theodosius said. Something gnawed his bowels. 'I am not well.'

'In one hour.'

'In one day.'

'In one hour.' And Orestes strode out, leaving the bewildered Prophyme unheeded by Emperor or court. The boy ran home to his mother.

Theodosius rendered no reply to Orestes. He was sick. The opiates prescribed gave him bad dreams, all of which featured Attila. When he woke in the night the third day after the audience he was enrobed in chill sweat. He took a draught of wine from a cool jug and at once yielded a flood of sour red to the floor. He tottered to the office of his secretary, who worked late, and learned that the Grand Eunuch could nowhere be found and that Orestes had departed. He gave orders that the lords Epigene and Plinthas be dispatched to the Hun court with the news that Attila's request or order could not be fulfilled and that the Eastern Emperor was ready to draw up a deed of formal submission to the Hun's territorial exactions in the province of Pannonia. Then he said: 'I am indisposed. Confined to my bechamber. Unable to see anyone. Anyone.' And he tottered off.

The sword of Mars, newly burnished, hung above the throne of Attila, who, in barbaric magnificence, received two delegations – one from the Empire of the East, one from the Empire of the West. On one side of his throne stood Epigene and Plinthas; on the other the Count Romulus with his secretary Constant. Their escorts had, without ceremony, been granted the roughest hospitality and most of them, their stomachs sick, had confined themselves to their quarters. Attila spoke good slow Greek to the assembly, saying:

'I can with difficulty conceal my satisfaction that the Empires of the West and East face each other in my presence. As the East and the West form the same imperial entity, there is no reason why the one should not know the business of the other. To the lords Epigene and Plinthas, emissaries from the court of Constantinople, I say this: since the severed head of the Grand Eunuch Chrysaphius has not been delivered to me, according to my demand, the annual tribute of gold is hereby doubled. I shall come to Constantinople to sever that head personally in my own good time. To the Count Romulus of Ravenna I say this: the sacred vessels purloined from Sirmium and now in the diocese of Aquileia in northern Italy are, being Hunnish property by the rules of war, to be returned at once. I speak in the name of international justice. Otherwise . . .'

'Your majesty imposes a time limit?' Romulus spoke cheerfully.

'A month should be sufficient to prepare my armies for an Italian invasion.'

'Thank you. The Emperor Valentinian bids me deliver to you, along with the other gifts, this young man Constant – to serve as your secretary.' Constant bowed.

'A spy from Ravenna in my court?' Attila spoke gently. 'Take him and have him whipped,' he said to Scotta, who wore his own strange court dress of black and white. 'After all, he is now my property. He must learn our barbarous Hunnish ways.' Scotta smiled and nodded, making no move. Time enough. Attila stood and affably said: 'Gentlemen.' Then he left. The sword of Mars, a fine ornamental A on its blade, beamed at them all.

Attila, no longer as slim as a sword, was approaching the bulky glory of his mature years. His first wife Enga, no older than he, lay sick and dying, attended by her hopeless handmaidens.

'Will he come? Is he coming?'

'Word has been sent.'

'I have seen little of him in my life. A thing to be used. To give him heirs to his throne. I have things to say.'

'Word has been sent.'

'A wasted life. He does not see how it has been a wasted life. War and plunder. What has he done? What has he made? He will come to a bad end. What is he doing now? Is he plotting some new war? Men are like children. Breaking their toys. Breaking and never making. My mother once said to me that I ought to marry a farmer. Watch things grow – the seed, the harvest. And Attila – no blade of grass to grow where he treads. A great thing. Will he come? Is he . . .' But her breathing was painful, and she could say no more without fatigue. Her husband did not come until the breathing had ceased to be painful and the eyes beneath their lids looked up at a vacancy more vacant than the sky over the Danube. But Attila was present for the committing of Enga's body to the flames, the pipes shrilling and the drums thudding and the ritual screams of the women. And he wore red, which was the Hunnish colour of mourning.

He wore it when he sat alone with his new secretary Constant, who efficiently went through a large pile of unanswered letters. Constant said:

'Sir. Condolences from the Count Aetius. Shall I reply?' He spoke the nasal Latin of Gaul.

'No reply.'

'Sir. Should we not congratulate him on the forthcoming marriage of his son?'

'Constant, that is why we do not reply. His son Gaudentius is to marry the daughter of the Emperor of the West. He is seeking power through a dynastic marriage. We do not approve of this Roman deviousness. You're a Gaul. You know the Romans.'

'We have had the Romans a long time. My grandfather used to speak of the time when our city of Lutetia was the property of the tribe we call the Parisii. But now it is altogether a Roman city.'

'And are the people of Gaul happy with their Roman masters?'

'The Celts accept it. It's a kind of cooperation, not a matter of master and servant. The others – the Goths, the Vandals – they would like to rule Gaul themselves, but they would ruin it. The Franks already call it their country, the land of the Franks, Frankia or Francia. It is better that it be Roman.'

'Well,' and Attila sighed, 'it is land I shall never see. Too far. The wearisome crossing of the river Rhine. The towns and cities – are they wealthy?'

'Very wealthy, sir.'

'A pity I shall never see any of them.'

That was a message for Constant to send to his true masters.

It was the sky over Gaul and the earth on which Gaul was built that seemed to speak a different message. For one day the sky grew black and the hail pelted and lightning wrote Hunnish threats. Men spoke of the passage of comets. A thunderstone fell and the ground heaved. Aetius, in his headquarters in Gaul, had difficulty in quelling panic among his troops. It was a panic that convulsed the Vandals and drove their king Genseric to seek audience of Count Aetius. Aetius spoke wretched Vandalic and Genseric had made a Vandalic dialect of Latin, but they understood each other. Genseric cried:

'The signs in the heavens and on earth all cry aloud one thing. The Huns are coming!'

'The Huns are not coming,' Aetius answered with calm. 'At least not to Gaul. They may raid northern Italy or frighten Constantinople with their threats, but they are not coming to Gaul.'

'I say they are. And I say, Count Aetius, that the Vandalic forces are at your disposal to help clear them out.'

'King Genseric, what you really mean is that the Roman forces are to protect the Vandals if they ever come. Which they will not.'

'The same thing – mutual protection.'

'King Genseric, I have efficient intelligence services. I hear a report that you offered your assistance to the Huns should they ever decide to invade Gaul.'

'That is a lie!' Genseric shouted through broken teeth. 'Attila, assist Attila? He would swallow the Vandals like a breakfast. No, our hope lies with Rome or Ravenna or wherever your Emperor is. We Vandals are not fools, Count Aetius.'

'And the gifts you sent to Attila? What did those signify?'

'Gifts? Gifts? Yes, I suppose there were some small gifts. But a mere formality, from one king to another. Birthday presents or some such thing. But he did not send one word of thanks, Count Aetius. He sits brooding in the robes of a widower, but he is not brooding on his dead wife. You have there a true barbarian. Not one bit like the Goths and the Vandals, gentle peoples both that ask nothing but to be left alone. And I tell you he is coming to Gaul. I had a dream about it.'

'I see, a dream. All my dreams tell me that the fair fields of Gaul will rest unsullied by Hun hooves. But your offer of assistance is accepted. With thanks.'

What the disturbances in the heavens and the shaking of the earth were proved to signify was the coming death of a great prince. The Emperor Theodosius was weak after a painful illness that devastated his stomach, but he insisted on showing himself to his people to allay the usual rumours that he was moribund. He insisted even on taking part in a great military parade on the Field of Mars in Constantinople. The banners of the Empire were proud in the autumn wind, and the silver trumpets shrilled and echoed. At the thundering of the drums the white horse of the Emperor grew restive. The faintness of Theodosius did not permit his proper control of the beast. The horse reared and snorted and Theodosius fell to the paving of the saluting area. A horrified court looked down on a cracked skull and the start of the spilling of imperial brains, which were like those of any other man. The body was borne away, the cracked skull swathed, the swathing hidden by a crown of golden laurel, the body made to lie in state on a catafalque. The patriarch spoke noble words:

'He is gone from us, the Emperor Theodosius the Third, puissant ruler, skilled in the arts of peace, a terror to his enemies. His soul now reposes in the bosom of the Lord. The grace goes back whence it came, but the wisdom remains with us. For out of that wisdom he appointed his successor the high and mighty lord Marcianus Flavius, general in chief of his armies, to take from his hand the torch of empire, and to assist him in the feeding of its flame her of the blood, the high and mighty Empress Augusta Pulcheria.' And then came a funeral procession, magnificent in its solemnity, solemn in its magnificence, and in that procession waddled, well protected, the Grand Eunuch Chrysaphius. But he was not well protected enough. The anger of the commonalty got the better of its sense of decorum. Chrysaphius had been for too long the visible power of the state, fat, vindictive, fundamentally infertile. He had been the flabby charioteer clutching in pudgy fingers the reins of the stallions of petty oppression – taxgatherer and functionary of so termed state security, sniffer out of heresy as a pretext for summary confiscation of property. When the mob groaned as it abandoned the decency of distance from the funeral procession and closed in on its tail, the armed guards of the Grand Eunuch prudently withdrew and let rough justice do its work. Chrysaphius squealed as he was seized and hit out with arms wholly lacking muscle. The squealing was drowned by the death music. When his corpse lay at length unattended in the quietened street, a nameless patrician said something about its now being possible to hack that head off and send it to Attila. But, he added, Attila seemed to have forgotten all about it.

The new Emperor, Marcianus, had Attila's name high on the agenda of state business. Epigene, who had been appointed the new chief minister, raised the question of the Hun demand for an increased annual tribute. The demand, he said, had been expressed with insolent urgency.

'So the Scourge of God is raising his toy whip at us?'

'With respect, it would be inadvisable to underestimate—'

'Yes yes, but why there should be an annual tribute at all passes my admittedly weak comprehension.'

'Your lamented predecessor—'

'The treaty of Margus, yes, and the looting of the imperial provinces. We shall have time later for settling once for all with the Huns. In the meantime, send this message: "I have gold for my friends. For my enemies I have only steel." Send him that.'

'As your adviser I would say respectfully that it is inadvisable—'

'Send him that.'

When Attila received the curt message he was faintly amused. 'Read it out again, Constant.' Orestes was appalled.

'You stand for that insult?'

'I like to see a show of strength. When the time comes for striking again at the East we shall know we are dealing with a man. And this insult, as you rightly term it, makes up my mind for me. For the moment we leave Constantinople alone. We strike west.'

'Italy?'

'No, not Italy. There has been a small matter on my mind – the envoy Vigilas. What do we do with him? In what manner do we use him as a reply to the insolent message? Send him back whole, sleek, well-fed? Or his crucified corpse?'

'His head, I would say.'

'Crude, crude, Orestes. Let the man go. And now – how are the pretexts coming along?'

'The sacred vessels have not been returned. Valentinian refuses permission for you to enter Gaul and punish the defecting king of the Vandals.'

'There is another matter,' Attila said somewhat dreamily. 'It goes back all of fifteen years.'

Honoria, sister of Valentinian the Third, was now a handsome woman of thirty. She flushed with the memory of that old indiscretion when the Emperor said: 'Sister, I've received a very curious letter from this Hun man Attila. It's utterly demented, of course, but he claims your hand in marriage – along with a promised dowry of half the Empire. He says that the initial proposal was yours. What do you know of this?'

'I was only a girl. I was foolish. He must have seen how foolish, for he never replied.'

'Well, he's replied now. He says it has taken him fifteen years to make up his mind. Apparently you sent him a ring. He says that he is wearing that ring on the appropriate finger. He says that you and he are engaged to be married and the engagement has gone on too long.'

'I can't be held responsible for that now,' Honoria cried in some fear. 'It was a long time ago. Besides, I'm engaged to be married to Livius.'

'You'd better be married quickly. Not that that will make much difference to Attila. These Huns cannot understand our Christian monogamy. I wish mother were better. We need her advice. I say no to the Hun and the Hun will shriek of treachery—'

'And then he'll invade? He'll take Ravenna?' Her eyes, very wide, drank the Ravennan sky, rainwashed. She, a mature woman, lifted with a single strong hairy hand on to the saddle of the invader. Hun cheers, fires started, rape. But, she knew, she loved Livius, who was ten years younger than she.

Galla Placidia was beyond the giving of advice. She lay rambling on a bed ornate as a catafalque. 'So – I leave the Western Empire in hands – that have never learned the – skills of government. I fear for it. Aetius will take it – Aetius will rule.'

'Try to sleep, madam.'

'Soon enough I will. And then the Huns will come and share the Empire with Aetius. I can hear them now – the thudding of their hooves—'

'The rain on the roof, madam. Do sleep.'

'My son is in the council chamber now. Aetius has come from Gaul. And my son is giving him the Empire. He must not. Quick, my gown, my slippers.'

'The Count Aetius is not here, madam. The Count Aetius is in Gaul.'

In Gaul, in Gaul. Attila was ready. The sword of Mars would not go with him, but with reverence he kissed the pommel and the blade. He spoke to a posterity he reverenced only out of a superstition learned from the Romans. Soon, with other things, this superstition would be altogether liquidated. He said: 'The Emperor at Ravenna has been more than uncooperative. He has robbed me of my rightful bride. He has denied me access to my enemies. He refuses to yield the just spoils of Hunnia. All this is on record. Our cause is just. We march.'

And boys, boys, he marched. How terrible is this story. Remember the date – the twenty-fifth day of February in the year of our blessed Lord 451. Let it be engraved on your tender skulls as the day on which all the terror of Hunnia was unleashed. For the Huns, with Attila at their head, galloped west to the great river Rhine, then forded it into Helvetia. Over the Rhine, sacking the city of Trèves. The general Edecon with the Ostrogoth Theodemir smashed their way into Bâle, into Colmar, crashing open the gates of Besançon, burning, pillaging, ravishing. Orestes and the Gepidan Ardaric led their forces to Strasburg, Spires, Worms. Onegeses and Scotta and Vaast of the Frankish people thundered through Gaul. Four lines, four knives scored the great province as one scores the skin of a pig for roasting. Ah, roasting is the word.

Any pillaged city will serve as an example of all. A bishop down on his knees pleads for the women, the children, the holy priests and holy sisters of charity, the church itself. 'Spare us, spare them. Are you not men like other men, with hearts of flesh and not of stone?' The answer to which was no, for at a nod from a section leader a Hun soldier struck off the bishop's head and, dodging the red fountain, kicked it, still mouthing, into a huddle of whimpering children and their mothers. As for the church, this was fired, but not before the Huns had defiled the holy vessels and pulled Christ down from his cross to trample on his body. A priest suffered the cutting of his feet and was then told to dance. Living children were thrown, though mostly unconscious from brutal carnal abuse, on to the flames of a bonfire kept flaring in the main square. The desperate parents were held back by a cordon of Huns who mocked their screaming and beat at them with clubs.

The town of Metz sought to defend itself with a hail of arrows from the city's ramparts, but the Huns were merely irritated, as at the sting of the mosquito fly, and with a crude battering ram, splintered the eastern door. Here there was little more than a token butchering of the citizens, many of whom were spared to run off naked. The main preoccupations of the Huns were the loading of carts with loot and the castigation of the leaders of the Goths, to whom Attila in person spoke, saying: 'I expected better of a people once famed for their warlike propensities. Living under the domination of Rome, slaves to foreigners, you deliberately sought to frustrate the liberating mission of the Huns. All right,' he called to his officers, 'deal with them.' They were dealt with very barbarously, being transfixed with arrows from their own bows: their desperate prayers to the God of the Arian heresy did them no good.

As the Huns approached Saint-Quentin, they were met by the armed garrison prepared to encounter them in the field. This was an opportunity for the Hun infantry to show their proficiency in the use of nets for the entrapping of their opponents. Entrapped, fighting against the meshes, they were easily slaughtered. The town itself, quickly taken, was fired, the citizens first having been securely locked into the public buildings. Wheelwrights and cartwrights were temporarily spared from the holocaust, for there was now a troublesome shortage of carts for the loading of the booty. In Rheims, against a background of desperate screaming, Scotta charcoaled, for there was no shortage of charcoal, the line of the Hun advance on a whitewashed wall. Attila took a calm goblet of wine, asking:

'And if we follow the setting sun to the point of its setting?'

'We reach the sea. The western limit of our empire. We are a land-locked people.'

'And if we learned to sail the sea what would we find?'

'Misty islands. Britons, once savages in skins, now tamed by the Romans. A harmless race.'

'We forget them for the moment. For the moment we consider a grave problem. We have too many spoils. We need at least a quarter of our entire forces to transport them back to the Danube.'

'May I ask a question?' the secretary Constant said. 'Why are you doing this to my country?'

The Hun leaders laughed. Attila kept a face of gravity. 'Very simple. Very very simple. And it's so simple that I've forgotten what it is.' There was more laughter. 'Let us say that it's to remind the Romans that life isn't easy. To show how precarious their civilisation is.'

'So much waste. So much cruelty.'

'Like nature herself,' Attila said, temporarily inspired. 'We're a force of nature, we're storm and wind and thunder. We're earthquakes and comets and falling stars. Give me more of that wine.'

And so they moved ever westward, and the looting and the slaughter became a matter for Hun yawns. Some of them, laden with gold ornaments, leading strings of horses or herds of goats, wished to go home. They had also heard that they were approaching the edge of the flat earth and, like the sun, would fall into a great emptiness, though, unlike the sun, which was a sort of god, with no hope of climbing up again on the other side. There, to the west, flowed a great river. On it was a walled city. Attila said to Constant:

'Tell us about this city of yours.'

'Lutetia of the tribe of the Parisii. An island on that river which the Celts call the Seine. I know it is useless to ask, but I would beg you to spare the city of my birth. You have taken enough. You have killed, ravished and burned enough.'

'Who is to say what is and what is not enough?' And, with a mockery of courtesy, 'Let us at least pay your city a visit.'

In a market place of Lutetia, boys, a young and lovely girl, her golden hair concealed in a coif, talked to a number of the citizens: 'Parisii, people of a noble city. We know the Huns are coming.

210

We know how the Hun invader has treated the other cities of Gaul. There the citizens resisted and were cruelly slaughtered for their courage. But theirs is another kind of courage – not of the body but of the spirit. It is the courage shown by our Saviour once on Golgotha. We do not resist. We return good for evil. We pray. We are Christians, and as Christians we greet the forces of darkness.' She was the mouthpiece of the bishop and of all the holy men of the city. It was right, it was felt, that the beauty and innocence of the passive resistance of the spirit should find its voice in one whose beauty and innocence were as a Christian flame.

When the Huns galloped to the western gates, they were surprised to find them open. There were no defences. A trap? The troops were bidden make camp in the fields outside the city. Attila and his generals rode in. They met a large group of citizens ranged in order, their bishop before them raising a cross high. They were singing in what seemed a dirge in Latin. The headquarters company raised swords in preparation for striking them down, but they found it hard to get their blood up. Attila gestured that their swords be lowered. He rode on through streets mostly empty and came to a church greater and more magnificent than any he had yet seen outside of Rome and Constantinople. From within came the noise of chanting. 'Now,' he ordered, and his forward troops ran in brandishing and whooping. They met only the calm of chanted Latin. They cut down a citizen or two without opposition, but the chanting did not cease. A superstitious folk, the Huns were frightened as though already on the edge of the earth. Attila raged at Constant.

'What is the word these Christians use? For those who want to die?'

'To die to show their faith?'

'What are they called?'

'Martyrs.'

'Well, let them be martyrs. We'll nail them to crosses.'

'Why?'

'Why? Isn't that our right as conquerors?'

'I see. A right. Really a duty, I suppose, to the image of the conqueror. And you will get pleasure out of it? Strip that fair-haired girl naked and make her yield to her ravishers. She'll

211

accept it. It won't last long. Then she receives her crown of eternal glory.'

'What fair-haired girl is this?'

'Her name is Genevieve.'

'We'll see. Bring her to me.' Attila sat in the requisitioned mansion of a Lutetian merchant who had fled. It did not take long to find the girl. She was a flame in white among the praying citizens in the church dedicated to Mary – whether the mother of Christ or the whore of Magdala has never been established. When she stood before Attila and his leering bodyguard, the Hun emperor allowed his barbarous tongue to deform the name.

'Genvev.'

'Something like that.'

'My Huns are in control of this city. You know what we can do to you?'

'We have met refugees from other cities. Yes. You can steal, rape, pillage, burn. We expected you to do it here. You may still do it, of course.'

'You would stay calm in the prospect of your ravishing, dismemberment, having the teeth pulled from your jaws and your golden hair torn out by its roots?'

'The weak have to find their own kind of strength.'

'Which you have found?'

'Which some of us have found. If these things could be done to the saints and martyrs and to the Son of God himself, who are we to complain?'

'There is no God.'

'Of course. This you know. You have no theologians, no philosophers, no poets, not even an alphabet, but this you know. You interrupted me at my prayers. May I return to them?'

'You pray to somebody who doesn't hear your prayers. You waste your time. You also waste your beauty. If I were to take you now as my wife or concubine, at least you would be forced to look at reality – the reality of the flesh, of power, of conquest.'

'I already wear a wedding ring. Look. I consider myself to be the bride of Christ.'

'Married to a ghost, to a nothing.'

'If you say so.' She prepared to leave. None seemed willing to prevent her. Then she turned and spoke again. 'Tell me, great

Attila. There are three apples on a dish. I put another three apples to join them. How many apples will there be?'

'Don't play with me, girl. I am not a child at school.'

'Six apples. Six. And not all your power can make three and three into five or two or nothing. There are certain truths that power and cruelty cannot change. God is one of them.'

'You speak foolishness.'

'If you say so.' She closed her eyes and raised her arms. 'You are in God's hand, Attila. One of his children, just like myself. May you be blessed.' Then she left. Attila kicked at a statue of the suffering Christ. It kicked back.

Lutetia was not worth taking. So Attila said. They were to march south to the city we now call Orleans. Orleans was not soft. The reports said that the defences were impregnable. Orestes said:

'Our engines are insufficient for battering the gates. We lack skilled workmen to repair our battering rams. If we scale the walls they will pour boiling oil on to us. Orleans is a strong city. We'll have to starve them out.'

'A siege. How long a siege? I hear rumours about Aetius moving up from the south.'

'With his Visigoths. He doesn't know our strength. Don't worry about Aetius.'

The Huns were leisurely in their settling in to consider the problem of Orleans. They set up their tents and lighted their cooking fires in the meadows without the city. Attila and Orestes surveyed, from a decent distance, the sturdy ramparts, observing the sunset changing of the guard of ready archers. When a trumpet sounded from the walls and a tonsured priest appeared on the battlements, the maniple with Attila prepared to fire their arrows, but his hand signalled that they desist. He listened with care to the singsong Latin:

'It is my Christian duty to give you warning. We have sufficient garrison and ample supplies. We are prepared for a long siege. Our friends the Goths are coming to protect the environs of the city. Stay if you wish. But expect nothing to your advantage. I have done.' As the priest began to descend and disappear Hun archers fired. The city archers fired back with skill and pierced several. Attila ordered retreat.

In the night three battered siege engines were brought up to ram the outer fortifications. Within the city the bishop Ananius saw fiery pitchballs catapulted in from the outer darkness: there was no moon and clouds were gathering: they could expect rain. Meanwhile the city firemen quenched the missiles with ease. At dawn, with a dim sun proclaiming wetness, Ananius was surprised to receive a letter.

'How did this get here?'

'We let down a ladder on the south wall. One of the couriers of the lord Aetius.'

'Aetius?' He read. 'Aetius with reinforcements from the Visigoths. One week, he says. Too long, too long.'

Rain began to fall on the Huns placing their scaling ladders. On to those who mounted boiling oil was tipped. They screamed as they toppled. They had not met this treatment before. The Hun army encircled the city with caution: Orleans, boys, was a tough nut for the cracking. But the kernel was worm-gnawed. The rainbutts filled, but the grain stores would not last. Ananius thought it best to seek, in his innocence, a parley. A trumpet shrilled and a herald bawled. A white banner from the Hun camp waved acceptance. The bishop rode out through a well-guarded postern. He did not have far to ride. Attila greeted him without truculence. *Salve.*

'I am Ananius, bishop of Orleans.'

'The high shaman, yes. What do you want?'

'That is rather *my* question.'

'Easily answered, episcopos. Surrender of the city. Unconditional, of course.'

'A bishop can hardly consent to that. I bear responsibility for my diocese, my cathedral, for the unarmed and defenceless.'

'You've no choice.'

'Very well. I shall return and order our resistance to continue.'

'If you could do that, you would not be here. Besides, what leads you to believe I will let you go back?'

'For that I was prepared. My successor has already been appointed. I have made my peace with God.'

'With the big ghost.'

'As for my people, they can wait for the arrival of the help that is promised.'

214

'What help? The promise is not likely to be fulfilled. This you know. That is why you come to me.'

'Very well. May I make an appeal to your humanity?'

'You may do that. With what effect I shall not for the moment say.'

'I shall order the gates to be opened. There will be no resistance. You will find little enough to take. Our wealth is in our work and not in idle possessions. I have already melted down the sacred vessels and given the metal back to the earth. Our arms and engines you may take. I beg that you wreak no vengeance on the innocent. That is all.'

'We shall be there within the hour. No treachery.'

'We shall be ready within the hour.' The bishop smiled with rue. 'I take it that *you* will show no treachery. To talk of the innocent being treacherous to the Hun is, you must admit, bizarre. Rather like fire extinguishing water.' He blessed Attila conventionally and rode away. The sun rode an hour's worth of sky. Then two thousand Huns got ready for unopposed invasion. If there were a golden-haired girl in there burbling about the great nothing in the air they would have her down and rape her to martyrdom. But when they marched through the open gateway they saw nothing except a neatly piled mass of booty in the cathedral square – spears, swords, arrows in quivers, bows unstrung, sacks of grain, amphorae of wine. The troops began wearily to load, a burden now, a task like a duty to someone, faintly and horribly Christian. A choir of Christian voices sang to the big emptiness behind the locked cathedral doors. An effigy of a woman with a round thing round her head, nursing an infant with a like ring, though much smaller, looked down kindly on the loading Huns. Then the quick ears of Orestes caught a distant thundering. Hooves? The bray of a bucina? Attila nodded at him.

'Out. Leave the loot. We don't need it anyway. Those hills there to the north. Give the order.'

From green hills they looked down on the approaching standards of Christian Rome. Orleans had won. To rush down now on Aetius and Thorismond of the Visigoths? The Romans were already forming squares on the wide plain, ready if need be for the testudo. Wait. Sure enough, a squadron with the banners of the cross was confidently essaying the foothills. 'He believes he has the advantage of us,' Orestes said. Attila said nothing. When Aetius arrived the two leaders looked long at each other, saying nothing. Aetius ordered a soldier to unload wine and goblets. Aetius and Attila sat together on a fallen oak-trunk. It was a long time before either spoke. Aetius spoke first.

'Well, old friend. You thought you could take the whole of a great Roman province.'

'I've taken it, old friend.'

'No. You've looted. There's too much loot for you to carry back. Now your allies are quarrelling about the loot. All very sordid. This is not the way to build an empire.'

'I'm destroying an empire,' Attila said, 'old friend.'

'Oh, yes, I've seen that. First the creators, later the scavengers. Greedy little boys waiting for the plums to fall. Don't worry, you'll get into the history books, Attila. A few dull pages to yawn over. Destruction is hard to make interesting.'

'You didn't call this parley to rebuke me for my lack of a Roman Christian philosophy.'

'No, Attila. I climbed this hill to recall an old friendship. I don't want to fight you.'

'You're wise.'

'Yes? I don't think you quite realise the comparative strengths of our forces. Your secretary Constant has been a good intelligence agent.'

'Purveying false information. I knew he was a spy from the start. I don't propose punishing him.'

'Most humane of you. Attila, I give you orders unratified by the man in Ravenna. I was sent out to destroy you. On my own authority I tell you to make your way peacefully out of Gaul. March east, loaded with your booty. Cross the Rhine. Return to the Danube. Gloat over your thefts and massacres and occasionally wake in the night and wonder what exactly you've done with your life.'

'And if I prefer to stay and complete my conquest of Gaul?'

'You have an undisciplined army. Too many orgies, too many quarrels about loot. Your barbarous allies are already on their way home, gloating. There's dysentery in your forces. I command an army fresh and ready to fight. The Visigoths are with me.

216

Take your chance while you may. I speak as an old friend, despite your mockery. The Emperor will have my head for this.'

'But you yourself will soon be Emperor. I too have my spies.'

'Emperor of the West? No, I'm too old for that kind of torpid responsibility.' He did not, Attila thought, look too old: he was grey, his bronzed legs were thinning, but skin and eyes were clear, he did not carry a general officer's paunch, his motions were quick. Attila knew that he himself had worn less well. 'My son, perhaps. We're soldiers, you and I, Attila. I want to be killed on the battlefield, not poisoned in bed or at the banquet.'

'And how soon,' with a sudden viciousness, 'would you like your death on the battlefield?'

'An unworthy thing to say,' Aetius sadly smiled; Attila reluctantly grimaced in agreement: true, unworthy. 'I should like to delay it as long as possible. I don't wish to fight at the moment. Nor, I think, do you. Go home, Attila. Point at the rising sun and march. The parley is over.'

'That, Aetius, sounds as though you're dismissing me. Remember, it was you who sought me out.'

'Oh, stay, dine with me tonight if you wish. But you have much to do. Booty to be securely roped and reloaded. Orders to be relayed. Remember, though, you're not retreating. You're just going home.'

Not quite home, not yet. The road to the city of Troyes. The Huns, the Gepids, the Akatzirs, and those of the Goths who had not gone their own way, forded the river Aube. Attila dismounted his horse and let it shake itself while he went to a clump of elms to make his own water. An old man sat there, a priest by his dirty robe and tonsure, gnawing dry bread. He laughed without fear, seeing Attila. 'I know you,' he quavered, 'the scourge of God. I'm a prophet, did you know that? I prophesy. Scourge of God, you're going to fight the Romans. And you're going to be beaten.' He repeated that *beaten*, beating the grass. Three of Attila's bodyguard were ready, swords drawn. *Ignore him* went Attila's gesture. They rode on. When at nightfall they made camp Attila was thoughtful. He said to Onegeses:

'Astrologers. Magicians. From all the tribes. I want them. I want to know the future.'

'No man can know the future.'

217

'Astrologers. Magicians. Summon them.'

Fires burned everywhere under a lowering heaven. Images of the future were squinnied at in the flames. Goats were slit open live that the entrails might be examined. Two magicians made themselves drunk on fermented mare's milk that the god might descend into brains fuddled or in a fury and speak truth. There was a monotony of strange chants, of drums beaten, of flutes playing over and over the one theme of three notes. Meanwhile Attila sat upright and grave on a stolen bishop's throne and waited. When a watery dawn greeted the dank plain a shaman of the Gepids approached, bowed, and spoke bad Hunnish.

'Well?'

'The auguries of the tribe speak of a battle. This is confirmed by other scryings and induced visions.'

'It needed no night-long mumbojumbo to arrive at that conclusion. What will be the outcome of the battle?'

'In that battle your worst enemy will be slain.'

'His name?'

'His name was not given.'

It was from a beech-crowned hill further east that Attila and his staff saw the distant westward dust of an approaching army. Attila nodded and nodded. 'As I thought. I said: give him three days. He knew—'

'Knew what?'

'That we would not go home.'

'Look,' Scotta said. 'There is another formation. To the southwest. That will be the Visigoths. Under their king Theodoric.'

Of the battle that ensued, boys, I need say little. Visigoth horns and drums made their clamour as Theodoric surveyed the terrain. The Roman bucinae brayed nearer. Dust, dust and dust, the blaring eyeballs of the horses, the growls of the men, the rough formation of the phalanges of archers. The Huns on their hill responded to the brazen Visigoth challenge and thundered down. Frightened birds wheeled under the low clouds. Horses fell and whinnied in panic. The Huns hurled their nets to entrap the Visigoth infantry. Hun arrows soared and completed their piercing parabolas. The Romans forded the Aube where it was shallowest but constructed rapid pontoons where the river ran deepest and widest. It was the Gepids they slaughtered first.

218

The Akatzirs, who interpreted divination by opposites, did not believe that there would be a battle. Camped in a hollow, snarling over the division of spoils, they were surprised by the forces of Aetius, none of them spared, camp-following women and their brats struck down with great efficiency and small mercy. Now was the time to order the Roman cavalry to thunder to the support of the Visigoths. King Theodoric had plunged to the heart of the Huns, where Attila, dismounted, slashed and slashed. The king knew it was Attila. There was a sudden quiet and cessation of fighting as the two leaders looked at each other.

'So. We meet, Attila.' Theodoric spoke debased Latin. 'You are not so big as I thought. Not so formidable. But still hateful. You know me?'

'A vassal of the Romans.'

'No, not vassal. A free Christian people that does not care for unwashed barbarians. Attila, you have many enemies. But you have no worse enemy than Theodoric of the Visigoths. Fight.'

Attila would not. There was a far worse enemy to be slain. Theodoric swished his blade. Five Huns slashed at him and brought him down roaring. Then they stuck him like a pig. Scared, the royal guard retreated. It was struck down brutally and without difficulty. *Worst enemy*, Attila was thinking, looking with eyes slitted for the approach of Aetius. All he saw was the steady march forward of Roman infantry from afar in good order and heart. His own troops, blindly swiping as in a street brawl, were deaf to orders. He nodded towards the sounder of the horn.

Aetius sat at day's end at the heart of an orderly camp. He took wine. The general officer Lepidus reported that the enemy slain were incomputable. The plain was paved with corpses, some of which surged briefly and finally into life for a vomiting of blood. The barrier between life and death was on the battlefield sometimes a vague one. The enemy had set up ragged camp three miles distant. 'We finish them off at dawn,' he assumed.

'At dawn they will start their long march to the Danube.'

Lepidus did not believe his ears. 'We,' he said, 'let them get away.'

'Call it Christian chivalry. They know they're beaten. That's all that matters.'

Attila sat at dinner with his staff. Ill-roasted horseflesh, stale river water. The slain were incomputable. 'Still alive,' he kept on saying. 'Still alive.'

'According to all the reports,' Scotta said. 'A very hard man to kill. Rather like you. Still, tomorrow—'

'Tomorrow we march towards the Rhine. Limp, rather.'

The members of his staff could not believe their ears.

'Why not? Have we not all we want from this country? Gold and silver and horses and fine cattle and grain? And we are not retreating. We have merely been rehearsing the real campaign – the campaign yet to come. I will have a whole army ready for it. I will not have my men slaughtered needlessly. This battle has been useless – meaningless—'

'The Romans,' Orestes said, 'will call it their victory.'

'No. There's no victory without the severed head of Attila. That head remains on my shoulders. And will. And will remain.'

So, boys, we come to the last phase of the terrible story. And we begin with the reception of Aetius at the court of his Emperor. The Emperor Valentinian, in whose face, though now lined with care beyond its owner's years, Aetius still saw the unchecked petulance of a mere boy, left much of the talking to his new chief minister Maximus Petronius. This functionary Aetius remembered as a mere noble of the court, a sycophant, untalented in any serious business though skilled in the dance and the flattery of the great. He spoke with the insolence of his new office, saying:

'At least you don't enter the imperial presence with the assured gait of the conqueror.'

'Minimus, no, Maximus Petronius, isn't it? You're up in the world. A lot of things happen behind the backs of military leaders.'

'And a lot of things happen in their line of sight.'

'*You let Attila get away.* Why don't you say it?'

'I will say it instead,' Valentinian croaked. He had a slight throat ailment. 'You let him get away – twice. Why?'

'Do you mean Attila personally – or the heterogeneous horde known as the Huns?'

'Can the two be separated?' Petronius asked.

220

'Yes. It's the duty of a general officer to shatter the enemy's forces but to observe a traditional courtesy as regards the enemy leader.'

'That,' Valentinian said, 'was never the traditional Roman way.'

'It was never the traditional Roman pagan way. We happen to be Roman Christians.'

'And Attila happens to be the sworn enemy of Roman Christianity. But Attila was never the sworn enemy of Aetius, was he?'

'If,' Aetius said, 'you're imputing to me the memory of an ancient friendship – yes, I admit it. And if Attila is my enemy now, he's an enemy I admire too much to bring to Ravenna in chains.'

'At least,' Petronius said, 'you're honest. But it's a rather dangerous honesty, wouldn't you agree? You realise you stand accused of treason?'

'I followed my orders.'

'Not exactly,' Petronius said. 'You were ordered to remove from the Empire the fact of an enemy invasion and the threat of an enemy invasion. You drove Attila, loaded with loot, from the province of Gaul. And now it seems certain that Attila will drive at the heart of the Empire itself.'

'The Empire,' Aetius said, 'has two hearts. Which one do you mean?'

'He means both,' Valentinian crawked. 'He means both Rome and Constantinople. Look, I need something to allay the scratching of this beast in my throat. Call in that damned physician, Petronius.' Petronius struck a gong. It resounded through an enmarbled emptiness. Aetius said:

'I do not think, with all respect, you can be right. What did Attila want? Two things. One thing highly material – plunder, pillage. One thing which may be termed moral. I mean, to demonstrate the vulnerability of the twoheaded Empire. He has his gold and his jewels and his grain and his slaves and his horses. He has not proved the Empire vulnerable – that is the important thing.' The imperial physician entered, bowing, bowing, bearing a bowl of something steaming and nauseous. The Emperor grimaced and drank. He mouthed, his voice had completely disappeared. The physician, bald, swarthy, a product of God knew what racial mixing, performed a hand-dance indicative that the voice would return. He bowed and bowed out backwards. Petronius leaned on the embrasure of a casement and said:

'Your armies are at rest now, Aetius. Including your intelligence service. My intelligence service never rests.'

'And what have your spies discovered?'

'That the plunder taken in Gaul is buying new alliances for Attila. That he proposes a double strike south – to Constantinople and to Rome.'

'I do not believe it.'

'There are heretics,' Valentinian announced in a recovered voice which did not seem to be his, 'who do not believe in the Holy Trinity. But that does not render it an empty doctrine.'

'A strike towards Constantinople,' Aetius said. 'That has always been a possibility. A possibility, no more. He knows the impregnability of the defences of Constantinople. He has not responded to the Eastern Emperor's insult.'

'What insult?' Petronius asked, frowning.

'Of course, you don't know everything, do you, Petronius? Very high up, but somewhat new to the game. You have a lot of documents to read. Including the one which records the refusal of the Emperor Marcianus to pay the annual tribute to the Huns.'

'I don't think,' Petronius said, 'Attila is much intimidated by anything that is barked from the East. His pillagings in Gaul enable him to buy alliances for the ultimate bifurcated attack. All the hordes of the East and all the Germanic cannibals who still infest Europe.'

'I do not believe it will happen,' Aetius said.

'My lord Aetius,' Valentinian said, with the croak returning though still some way off, 'high general of my forces, your beliefs and disbeliefs hardly constitute either an offensive strategy or a system of defence. Your attitude to the present threat makes you an unsatisfactory commander.'

'I see.' Anger reddened his tones. 'I save Gaul while my lord Maximus Petronius sits on his arse in Ravenna cogitating my downfall. I take it you require honest speaking.'

'Honest speaking,' Petronius agreed, 'combined with a measure of respect.'

'You want me removed from the leadership of the armies. You have been feeding his imperial majesty here with calumnies to that end. Am I right?'

Valentinian spoke through moist throat clearings. 'This is a hot day and we do not require further heat. I suggest, nay, I order that the count Aetius send himself on a well-deserved leave. I have no intention of dismissing you – I am well aware of your services to the Western Empire, past and in prospect – but I think you require a little course of re-education in imperial policy.'

'Policy in the face of a grave threat,' Petronius added. 'From your friend Attila.'

'I do not much care,' Aetius growled, 'for the implications of that statement, my lord Petronius.'

'We have had enough of this,' newly croaked the Emperor. 'You may leave the presence.'

'I – ? May – ?'

'You heard me. When you are required you will be sent for. Enjoy your indefinite leave.' Then he left, trying to dislodge the beast in his throat. Petronius followed him, having first given Aetius a final malevolent smirk. Bare marble looked at Aetius and the honey of summer light poured in. Aetius decided he would now get drunk.

Hunnishly drunk, stupidly ringed and braceleted and bejewelled, the warriors of Attila watched their women dance clumsily to the ragged tunes of stolen pipes and drums and trumpets. It was the tenth or eleventh night of a continuous feast of victory. Attila was not present. Attila lay, not well, on a fine couch of Troyes workmanship while Scotta charcoaled an inaccurate map of the Eastern Empire on parchment purloined in Metz. 'The great cities, you see, still untaken – Ravenna, Aquileia, Rome itself.' Orestes was there. He said:

'But what do you mean by *take*?'

'Take such of the contents as we need – not only grain and livestock but slaves – craftsmen to grind grain, bakers to bake bread—'

'That is not what I would call *taking* a city.'

'And what, dear Orestes, would *you* call *taking* a city?'

'Colonising it. Establishing a Hunnish settlement.'

Attila spoke in pain. 'With Hunnish laws? Hunnish schools?

223

Hunnish architecture? Hunnish what they call music?' The scriking and thumping went on outside the palace, if you could call it a palace. 'These do not exist. *We* do not exist.'

'The pain is talking,' Scotta nodded. 'The pain is still bad.'

'I must look after my stomach. Some of these looted luxuries don't agree with it. Very well, the pain talks. Let it talk. We filch their grain, but they replant and have new harvests. We kill, but they go on begetting. Our destruction stimulates them to new construction.' And then: 'Who will remember us when we are dead?'

'Fear not,' Scotta grinned. 'We won't be quickly forgotten.'

'Bogeymen to scare children. The Huns are coming. We break. We take. A very dull history, the history of the Huns.'

'Those do not sound like your words,' Orestes said.

'No, those are the words of the enemy Aetius, whom we have neither broken nor taken.'

'You'll get him yet,' Scotta said. 'Meanwhile, your subjects are happy. The simple happiness of warriors. They adore their ring-giver, the lord who leads them to the happiness of breaking and taking.'

'Bearded children,' Attila said. 'Growing fat and lazy.'

'The time for being so must soon be over,' Orestes said. 'Our allies crave new conquests. We must be ready soon.'

'I would prefer to lie on my bed and read Homer,' Attila said. 'You have read Homer?'

'There's nothing in books,' Scotta pronounced.

'Achilles, Hector, Odysseus. They are not bogeymen to scare children. The Greeks called them heroes.'

'What did they do?' Orestes asked without interest.

'They fought.'

'As we do. Have done. Will do.'

'Odysseus,' Attila said, 'was a reluctant warrior. He preferred to rule his little island, to feed and cherish his wife and son. He was a farmer. He had skills. He learned the warrior's skills easily enough. Then he easily unlearned them. I'm dissatisfied, gentlemen.'

'Which means,' Orestes said, 'that you're ready for the – must we call it the great and definitive strike?'

'I feel old enough for it to be the final one. The last strike of the great bully who treads on a child's toys.'

'We take Constantinople?' Scotta was eager. 'We take Rome?'

'I must take some warm barley water. Julius Caesar used to drink it. He too suffered within. Get me some.' Orestes struck at a lolling servant whose face he did not remember having seen before. The servant ran out. *Aqua hordei. Callida.* 'Constantinople. We have news of the new fortifications. The Emperor sounds too confident to me to offer hope of an early conquest. Meaning the ripping off of the fine robes of the ladies and the strangling of them with their strings of British pearls. And shitting on the holy altars and pissing in the sacred vessels.'

'You sound low,' Orestes said.

'Oh, I *am* low. The Scourge of God has to be in the hand of somebody or something. The collective hand of the Huns. The Huns have no existence unless they fight. The leader is led. We strike at Italy.'

'Over the Alps?' Orestes asked, very eager.

'Mountain passes. There is a way through.' Barley water was brought. The servant was slow in setting it down. He spilt some on the bedside table from Troyes. He wiped the spot dry with the edge of his tunic. Attila took his drink without looking at him. 'What do we know of the fortifications about Ravenna?'

'The situation,' Orestes said, 'has hardly changed since you were there as a boy. They rely on their marshes.'

'The spring will soon be here,' Scotta said. In his eyes the spring delicately shone: the return of the swallows, the budding of the Roman crocuses.

'The spring,' Attila said. He sipped. 'And then the heat and the drought. I seem to remember that Italy was all fountains. How do they make them? Why do we have no hydraulic engineers who can build fountains? What is the matter with us?'

'Drink your barley water,' Scotta soothed. 'All up. Right to the bottom.'

Valentinian and Aetius walked to the bottom of the path of the winter garden and then turned to walk up again. Yes, he had enjoyed his leave. Though it could hardly be called a leave. He had schooled himself in imperial strategy. His intelligence service had taken no leave. A Greek who spoke Hunnish planted in Attila's entourage. He reported that there was no doubt—

'When? Where?'

'There was talk of a final assault on the Empire. Two forces. Attila has been consulting his astrologers. He is not well. They tell him to think of death.'

'They could tell him that any time,' Valentinian said. 'Final assault, the destructive crown of his career. So you must now admit you were wrong.'

'Petronius will now be pleased that I was. I would say that it is now Petronius's ministerial duty to advise your imperial majesty on the setting up of a new centre of government.'

'What can you mean?'

'Ravenna is within the range of an early attack. Even Rome. I would suggest you leave Italy and establish your court in Gaul.'

'Where? The Loire valley? Orleans? Lutetia of the Parisians? The Visigoths are everywhere, man.'

'The Visigoths have been pacified. This, with respect, you should know.'

'I stay in Ravenna.'

'Which is insufficiently protected and too far north. If not Gaul, why not at least Rome?'

Valentinian looked into the autumn sky as if conjuring a vision of the eternal or infernal city. 'See to the defences of Rome and it could be considered. Meanwhile, I stay where I am. If your friend Attila comes he will meet more than adequate resistance.'

'You still say *friend*.'

'Yes, Aetius. I still have nightmares about two old friends concerting for the division of an empire.'

'You can still,' he said loudly, 'think me so treacherous?'

'I eat and drink treachery,' Valentinian said, rather quietly. 'The air I inhale is treachery. One of the privileges of imperial power is the gift to revert to a creature of instinct. I smell treachery everywhere. I would like to think of you as loyal, Aetius, but I do not find it easy.'

'Perhaps you would rather I resigned.'

'Resign and find hospitality among the Huns? No, Aetius, you stay. You are watched. Even when you go to Constantinople you will be watched.

'I have no intention of going to Constantinople.'

'Oh yes, you have, or, rather it is my intention that you go. To consult our brother Emperor. He is sure of his defences. We may need his help in Italy. Your present task is to put in train the refortification of Rome. Then take ship. That is all, my lord Aetius.' They stood in leaf mould. Aetius awkwardly bowed and left. The next morning he rode, with a sufficient escort of men he knew and two or three he did not, towards Rome. His heart sank as he approached the ancient city and its still more ancient hills. It was a used-up city. Its day was over. It had known too much treachery and cruelty and imperial bombast. It could not, despite its bells and priests, be converted into the city of God. Moreover, a city of God should not properly need defence from battlements and casemates. He sighed as he rode to lodgings on the Palatine.

The din and dust of the work were not congenial: he was a man of the battlefield, not the garrison. He was no engineer: the engineer Calvus was all too competent among the cranes and hoists, the whipped slaves dragging in huge carts of stones and rubble. Pagan imperial Rome was carelessly demolished to provide rough reinforcement for the northern walls: voluted pillars, noseless statues, arches to the glory of the Senate and the Populus were pounded into the cemented mash of outer defence works. The work stopped but the flying of the dust did not when the Holy Father himself, in the simple habit of Rome's bishop, was borne on a litter to the blessing of these secular labours. He alighted. Minor officers kissed his ring. Aetius too kissed it and knelt for a blessing. 'Bless you, my son,' Pope Leo said, snowy of beard, vague of eye. 'So the Goths are coming again?'

'Not the Goths, your holiness. We fear the Huns.'

'Yes, the Huns. The unconvertable gentlemen from the Danube. They live very empty lives, my lord Aetius. It must be a very empty life without God.'

'Their lives are full enough, your holiness.'

'Negatively full. You have read Augustine?'

'I have, alas, little time for reading. As you see.'

'It is time, he says, to stop thinking of earthly cities. Sooner or later they are all pounded to dust, and we must learn to shrug our shoulders. The City of God is a different matter. No Hun horde can destroy that city.'

'Its priests,' Aetius said, 'can be tortured and burnt. Even its chief priest.'

'Meaning myself? Oh, the succession is assured for ever. We have the promise of him who chose the rock to build on rock. We have had all this before in the history of the Church. We are past being frightened. What would be interesting to me would be the probing of Attila's soul. He seems from what I hear and read to be a typical demoniac – one possessed by a single huge devil.'

'I doubt,' Aetius smiled sadly, 'if he'd admit to the ownership of a soul.'

'Oh, he has one. And one quite as vulnerable to the influences of evil and pervious to the power of good as the souls of the rest of us. I must pray for Attila.'

'Pray?' Had he heard aright?

'Pray for him. And then some day, not that I have many days left, hope to baptise him in the water of life.' A gleam that might be termed professional animated his eye. 'I would love to hear his first confession.'

'Your holiness will forgive me if I suggest that this is – well, a very idle supposition.'

'I will always forgive your minor trespasses, Aetius. But it is not easy to forgive your lack of faith. Attila is very dear to God.' And the old man went off to talk kindly to others. Meanwhile Aetius's secretary Theodorus, who had in his eye something of the look of one who watches – does not, the nobler office, watch over – he was in the direct pay of Maximus Petronius, no doubt about it, came to say that Aetius was to take ship from Bari in seven days, if the repairs to the *Paraclete* had by then been completed. So. Constantinople, a useless trip. Perhaps on his voyage he ought to read this work of Augustine. But what had Aetius to do with the City of God? It was Rome, Christian or pagan, mother of order, he had spent his life protecting. Somebody who had meant to praise had once called him *ultimus Romanus*, the last of the Romans, desperate but out of date believer in the erection of order and the cultivation of *virtus* in the brief time of light allotted between two horrors of eternal dark. He could not in his nerves and sinews accept that this light of life was a mere foretaste of a greater and endless light. Men did not deserve it. Men deserved nothing. Men had duties to perform and a little off-duty time to savour the small and impertinent pangs of fleshy pleasure. The city of human order survived them. But of this he could no longer be quite sure. Rome smelt of dust. The broken arms of statues pointed vaguely at something. Stone eyes saw nothing, except possibly the *Civitas Dei*. Constantinople sprang out of the dawn sea to announce itself as the future.

'He is well?' the Emperor Marcianus asked at dinner.

'A little tired. A little anxious.'

'A little irritable?'

'That too. With me certainly. I committed the great sin of sparing the life of the enemy of Rome. And, I suppose, of Constantinople.'

'Attila,' Marcianus said with finality and a smile of unworthy complacency, 'will not come here.'

'I believe,' Aetius said, 'that Attila approaches his final climacteric. I think he wants to end in a huge noise of destruction. The Emperor Valentinian, as you will have divined, sent me to discuss a joint defence plan.'

'He will not come here,' Marcianus said yet again.

'Well, then, you have forces free for the defence of the Western Empire.'

'Do you think,' the Empress Pulcheria asked, 'he will make for Rome?'

'I think he will make first for Aquileia. For the control of the Po valley. And then, yes, Rome. You see, the very name rings with a terrible magic. He has to destroy Rome. That is his final mission. He cannot forgive the Goths for getting there before him. So I am here to beg, on my Emperor's behalf, for the means of saving Rome.'

'Your view of the matter, my love?' Marcianus smiled on his consort with uxorious eyes. She was of great beauty. It would have been a pity, considering her name, if she had not been. There was a ravishing contrast of midnight hair and snowy skin, which the looseness of her robe did nothing to hide. The symmetry of her features was flawless, the nose straight but unassertive and the eyes set wide apart. But, boys, you are too young to wish to ponder on the divine mystery of woman's beauty and I am too old. She answered her husband's question:

'I doubt if Rome would protect *us*.'

Marcianus nodded. 'But we don't need Rome's protection. The true strength lies here in the East. The West is already doomed. A ripe fruit, as they say. Her day is over.'

Without much conviction; God help him, Aetius said: 'Rome is the centre of the faith.'

'You speak of a different kind of Rome,' Marcianus said.'As for the *old* Rome of the senate and the bloody games and the emperors cruel or inefficient or both – the Goths or the Vandals or the Huns can have it for all I care.'

'You mean that, sir?'

'Yes and no.' The Emperor shrugged. 'I say again, the future lies here. I can no longer think in terms of an Italian empire.'

'Whose Emperor demands that I bring back a reply from you. To that question. Will you, should the worst happen, help?'

'Is it going to happen?' Pulcheria said.

'I think so.'

Marcianus motioned to his butler that the cups be refilled. It was as if he were to toast something. But he said: 'I do not feel called upon to protect Rome. Blunt speaking, Aetius. I'm sorry. But you can tell our imperial brother Valentinian that if matters grow really, well, sombre I'll try to help him to protect the Po valley. But if Attila breaks through and takes the road to Rome – no. I have my own Empire to govern. Rome, to speak cruelly but truly, is a shell, a shard, a dead thing—'

'But still the centre of Christianity.'

'Really?' Marcianus said with feigned surprise. 'I thought that honour had passed over to New Rome, to Constantinople.'

'I see. We have a divided faith.'

'The truth is where the power is, Aetius. The truth and hence the holiness. The patriarch of Constantinople is the true leader of the faithful. The Pope – what can one say of a priest trapped in a city doomed either by decadence or its next invader?' It was Pulcheria who spoke these words.

'The successor of Peter, my dear lady Augusta,' Aetius said. ' "Thou art Peter and upon this rock—" '

'Christ,' Pulcheria said, 'made no mention of Rome. There was only one city he knew. Jerusalem. Some day that may again be what it was – the cradle and crown of the faith. But that day will be a long time coming. And when it comes Constantinople will contain Jerusalem. The faith speaks nothing to the lands of the sunset.'

Aetius felt a deep depression. He poured himself another full cup without waiting for the ministration of the butler. 'If Attila could learn – that a double empire was united – waiting with the most massive army the world has yet seen – he'd think twice.'

'Attila,' Marcianus soothed, 'is not thinking at all. You will hear no more from Attila.'

But neither imperial intelligence service had spies in the court of Attila when, on a freezing January day, the Hun chief spoke to his court, his family, his retainers, his generals. The great bare hall, unvulgarised by any display of loot, was heated by flares and braziers. Attila did not look well, but he spoke with vigour and decision, saying:

'We are on the eve of our final conquests and final consolidations. I say again what I have said before – perhaps too often. We are an empire still awaiting imperial fulfilment. In this empire there are or will be many kingdoms. Ernak, my youngest son, will reign over Gaul, when it is reconquered, and Italy, when it is taken. Ellak, my eldest, will be Emperor when I am too old to climb into the saddle – or when I fall from it. Uzindur, my son, your portion of the empire will comprise the territories between the river Oder and the river Dnieper. Denghizikh, helped by the lord Scotta, will rule over the whole of the Asiatic north. Gheisma – you will take the territory from the west of Pannonia to the Black Sea. Emnedzar – to you goes the Caucasian and Caspian province running to the eastern limit. Should Ellak die, the crown goes to Ernak. But I speak of the future. There is much work still to do. When the ice is loosened on the Danube, when the snow leaves the Alps – we march on Italy.' All noted that he said nothing of the Eastern Empire of the Romans. The general officers started to implement their training programmes. The thundering of cavalry would help to loosen the ice on the Danube.

And, in Ravenna, Valentinian looked sternly on Aetius. Aetius noticed that there had been an addition made in his absence to the imperial staff. He knew this plump little eunuch Heraclius, once destined to be a soaring voice of the basilica choir, later an assistant to the imperial treasurer. A eunuch in a position of power: it was more of an eastern than an occidental concept: the West was becoming easternised: it was the beginning of the end. Valentinian said: 'You've failed then.'

'Your embassy has failed,' Aetius said wearily. 'I was the voice of the Western Empire, no more.'

'A rather ineffectual voice,' Heraclius dared to say.

'Your eunuch's squeak,' Aetius said irritably, 'would not have been more effectual.'

'I don't like this insolence, Aetius.' It was Maximus Petronius who now spoke. 'Do not cover your own ineptitude with sneers at imperial ministers.'

'Is that what he is? I didn't realise. The plenitude of ministers at this court has become rather bewildering.'

'I repeat,' Valentinian repeated, 'you failed. You permitted our imperial brother Marcianus to insult us with his refusal. I can only conclude that the situation was inadequately presented to him.'

'There was a whole week of such presentation.' Aetius was weary. 'Not inadequate. Help will come when help is clearly needed – not before.'

'An immediate mustering of his troops on our soil would deter Attila,' Petronius said. 'This was the point you were to establish. Emphasise. Thump into him.'

'I have no power to thump. I wonder that you did not undertake the mission yourself.' Valentinian pronounced:

'You exhibited gross incompetence, Count Aetius. You evidently lack those qualities needful to the making of decisions of such weight. Imperial decisions. There was to be a marriage between my daughter and your son – at such time when my daughter should come of age. That marriage will not now take place. The affiancement is cancelled.'

'I see,' Aetius said with damped fury. 'This is the work of my lord Maximus Petronius, who has sons of his own. I take it that the grand eunuch Heraclius has no dynastic ambitions.'

'You may retire, Count Aetius,' the Emperor said.

'Retire from the imperial presence? Or retire from public life?

232

You will have to call on me yet, my lord, gentlemen. You will find me *in retirement* in Reggio-Emilia.' He left without bowing. Petronius said:

'Attila never had a better friend. I consider that his retirement should be permanent.'

'That,' Heraclius squeaked, 'could be contrived.'

'I will have no talk of assassination, do your hear me?' Valentinian was strangely agitated. 'You are in the presence of a Christian emperor. Thou shalt not kill.'

'Oh, my lord,' Petronius soothed, 'we had no thought of assassination. It was yourself used the term. Assassination is a terrible word.'

'Terrible,' squeaked Heraclius.

Terrible, boys, the raising of the sword of Mars in the sunlight of spring, as Attila gave the orders for the march towards the Julian Alps. For the sword was to accompany him as the outward sign of his inner resolve to rack, rend, trample into dust the great work of time. Already, as they approached the walls of Nauportus, the Huns had left behind them a trail of corpses and whipped off slaves back to the homeland drawing carts laden with spoils. To the general officer Edecon was entrusted the bloody task of battering the walls of Nauportus with newly furbished engines, making a breach in a tumult of rage and dust, lashing troops in under a storm of arrows and a searing rain of boiling oil. The news quickly reached Ravenna, and an incredulous Emperor tossed nightly on his bed and reluctantly admitted to himself that only one man – 'Only one man,' he cried in his sleep.

Claudinus had seen long service with Aetius. Scarred, hardbodied, with a smile of strangely childlike sweetness, he arrived at the villa of his old general on a warm day of late spring and found an unwarlike man, bronzed with the sun of his garden, tending a bank of roses. 'My lord Aetius—'

'Claudinus, old friend – I think I know why you're here.'

'We are to ride to Ravenna at once. Attila has already crossed the Julian Alps. You are to supervise the defence of the imperial capital.'

Aetius wiped earthy hands on his leather apron. 'Attila,' he said slowly, 'is not interested in taking Ravenna. Attila is interested in taking Rome. If I am wanted, it is in Rome that I am wanted. Tell the Emperor to meet me in Rome.'

Claudinus spluttered. 'I can't – I daren't – I mean, to return such a message. You're instructed to attend the Emperor at Ravenna. I'm sorry – I merely pass on an imperial command—'

'Rome, Claudinus, Rome.' And he went back to the tending of his roses.

The city of Tergestum, some of whose citizens had already begun to deform the name to Trieste, blazed, boys, like a multifoliate rose as Attila and his troops invested that great port of the Adriatic. Some of the horror of its sacking has been eternised in the lines of the Triestine poet Italus Fabricius which I now try to pluck out of a fading memory:

> Like fire ants swarming on a honey spill,
> Ants animated by a single will,
> A myriad of nightmare monsters screeched
> Until the tough protective walls were breached
> And gates of massy iron struck the dust
> That rose as mimic smoke from blazing lust.
> Ten thousand virgins fell upon their knees
> And raised their arms in disregarded pleas
> To spare the city, grasp the gold and go,
> But Attila was fire and they were snow,
> Snow to be stained by ruptured maidenheads.
> Bodies expiring served as downy beds
> For mass deflowerings. Then ten thousand blades
> Severed the heads of maids no longer maids;
> Ten thousand pikes then raised them to the air,
> Mute mouths beneath the banners of their hair.
> So ravish, kill and burn! the order ran,
> Exhibit the depravity of man
> As final virtue. Vomit in the cup
> Wherein the sacred blood was offered up,
> Upon the holy alter s – t and p – ss
> And up the moaning bishop's orifice
> Implant his bloody crozier. Give entire

The infant population to the fire
And let the screams excite an appetite
To scoff the scorched limbs in a single bite.
Let punctuate the savagery of drums
The descant of a million martyrdoms . . .

There is more, boys, much more, but perhaps it is a holy mercy that my memory fails.

The foreboding of the Emperor Valentinian was such that he kept hearing the thunder of the coming Huns even when closeted at closestool or hidden within the thick folds of his bed curtains. Raging at what amounted to a peremptory order from Aetius that he should meet him in Rome, he at first ordered his arrest. A solemn warrant was issued but Aetius told the issuing officers that this was no time for games. Rage cooling and fear heating, Valentinian rode with his family and inner court over the Appenines and confronted Aetius at his headquarters in the holy city.

'The Visigoths.'

'I will not have the Visigoths on Roman territory.' There was the hint of a muted scream behind the Emperor's words. Maximus Petronius nodded his agreement. Aetius said:

'They've been here before. We need a strong line of defence south of the Po. They'll best provide it. They've already crossed the Var.'

'No!'

'You wish me to resign my commission?' Aetius asked wearily.

'You may not,' Petronius said. 'Such an act would be treasonable. It is a question of the safety of the Empire.'

'Oh, yes, the safety of the Empire. The safety of the Empire depends on such peoples as regard the Huns as their enemy. The defence of Aquileia is our immediate concern. Aquileia controls all roads, including the road to Rome. I am calling on the Visigoths.'

'I forbid it,' Valentinian croaked.

'I am calling on the Visigoths.'

'You will hear more of this.'

'I hope we all survive to hear more of it.' And Aetius turned his back on the Emperor.

A great number of the more prominent citizens of Aquileia had turned their backs on their own city. They stood on the empty coast of the Adriatic under their bishop, who blessed in prospect what they planned to build. 'To build a city on water,' the bishop said. 'A city whose defences are the very forces of nature. No city built on land can be impregnable.'

'You mean a city built by the sea?'

'On the sea, on the sea. A city that shall control the commerce of the east and hold the faith inviolate from the barbarian.' The sea wind fingered his white beard as he watched the vision form. He was at first puzzled by the image of a roaring lion flying through the clouds, but he saw soon that it was not Attila but God's obscure blessing.

In mounting heat Attila looked down on Aquileia. 'Aquileia the impregnable,' he said.

'So they call it,' Scotta said. 'We will change that appellation for them. Look – how strange.' Flocks of birds were winging out of the city – heavy storks flapping, swallows in a more disciplined flight, a ragged army of swifts. Attila saw and said:

'The birds know. They know there is nothing to stay for. More than a good omen. Nature herself speaks. Nature knows.'

No poet of Aquileia has left hexameters on the horrors that followed the battering at the gates, the catapulted rocks, the seething oil and the hissing rain of arrows. Rams butted the northern wall while flies fed on the blood of fallen Huns. When the breach was made at sundown the Huns poured in, angry at the long resistance, and at once fell to hacking live flesh, firing wooden structures, crucifying priests, tearing apart the soft bodies of children. In a piazza mocked by a fountain they threw heads and limbs into bubbling cauldrons, fished out boiled flesh and gnawed it. They drowned the wild anguish with harsh songs of triumph and the unhandy beating of drums. The news spread south.

Worse news spread south as Aetius lay weary on his pallet bed in his headquarters. 'Mantua,' he was told. 'Verona. Cremona, Brescia, Bergamo, Lodi. Milan.'

'Where is he now?'

'South of Mantua.'

'The road to Rome.'

In a church of sturdy stone Attila presided over a warriors' feast. They took a brief holiday from butchery under the image of an uncomplaining blind Christ still to be wrenched from his cross and trampled. 'We cross the Appenines,' Attila said, 'tomorrow. And you know our target. Rome is more than a city. Rome is the memory of a whole race and the dying heart of a whole civilisation. From Rome expect no great booty. In Rome give ear to the voice of a certain responsibility. A responsibility to feel awe that at last we have forced open the inner organ of their empire. Enter the city quietly and with dignity. We shall install ourselves in the centre of our empire, not theirs. Do not waken the sleeping ghosts of a hundred emperors and a horde of Christian saints. Rome shall be our city. We shall give it a new name. What name I have not yet decided. First we take the city.' Few of those who listened over their gnawing and swilling understood his words. They understood only the order to march over the hills next day in a fury of summer heat, their banners terrible, their song loud and wild.

Valentinian was deeply agitated. 'I had never thought that we would have to beg. Go down on our knees to the barbarian—'

'Let us not make too much of a tragedy of it,' said the holy father Leo. 'Attila is a human being – hence a divine creation. He has the human gift of speech and the human faculty of reason. If speech fails, if reason fails – well, all will have been done that can be done. We are told not to resist evil. Evil burns itself out in time. Confront him boldly, my lord Emperor, but not defiantly. If he will not listen, then he will not listen. But he may listen.' The cool cloisters of the Vatican, the full-leafed plane trees, the chanting of the priests at a distance seemed to exorcise the approaching terror. Valentinian was rational enough when he said:

'I did not propose to confront him myself, holy father. I am merely the voice of secular government. What is needed is the voice of the Holy Spirit.'

'I see,' Pope Leo said. 'You propose that the bishop of Rome and father of the faithful goes into the lion's den. In some ways an amusing idea. Papa – father. Attila – little father. You know their language, Aetius. Is not that what the name means?'

'Our children cry papa. Theirs cry atta. Later, when they have learned love, they call him attila. An endearment. That too, I suppose is amusing.' Valentinian looked on his general with distaste. Pope Leo said:

'Well, we'd better start. Where is he now?'

'The last message received said something about his approaching Modena.'

'Let us pray together.' He slid easily to his knees; the others more creakingly followed. 'Our Father in heaven, may your name be blessed, may your kingdom come . . .'

Attila's kingdom did not seem to be coming. There were too many sick in his army. The heat was intense, there had been an unwise gorging of melons and a swilling of stagnant water. He did not know the name of the village where, himself sick in his stomach, he forced open the door of a poor hovel, seeking cool and dark. 'You can leave me, Scotta. Post a guard outside. I need sleep.'

'You need more than sleep.'

'Sleep is the best medicine.' The room he was in was bare, but it had a bare bed in it. It was also clean. He limped towards the bed, using the sword of Mars as a sort of crutch. He lay down, he closed his heavy eyes. What I tell you now may not have happened, but it is part of the Attila legend of the Appenines. It balances a little too neatly the earlier tale of the blessed Genevieve. Still, we will follow it. A golden-haired girl of great beauty entered the room. Her name was Flavia and she was blind. Attila opened his eyes and saw with wonder a smiling girl feel her way towards him. Then he felt the insect touch of her fingers on his face. He did not stir. He heard her say:

'Who are you, sir?'

'Who am I?' Then she saw that she was blind. 'A traveller. I came here to rest. I thought the house was empty. Is the house yours?'

'It is my house now. My father and mother are missing. They ran away, frightened of the coming of the Huns. I would not go. I'm not frightened of the Huns. Are you frightened of them, sir?'

238

'Sometimes,' Attila said grimly. 'But I think we're safe from them here. For a time.'

'I was in the kitchen, preparing soup. Are you hungry, sir?'

'I am not well in my stomach. But I think I could eat some soup.'

So you must see now this bizarre picture of Attila and a blithe blind girl seated together at a rough table with wooden bowls of a broth made with the tubers and greens of the girl's little vegetable garden. The girl chattered away. 'For, after all, I said, what harm could they do to a poor blind girl? I've nothing they can take. They must be reasonable people. All people are reasonable if you can talk to them. I sometimes pray for poor Attila.'

Attila nearly choked on his spoonful. 'Poor?'

'Well, he must be unhappy, or he wouldn't go around calling himself the Scourge of God. Little boys whip each other sometimes – in play, I mean, of course – calling themselves the Scourge of God. They play at being Attila, and Attila plays at being Attila.'

'Attila,' Attila said, 'would not be very happy to hear you say that. Is it hard for you – being blind, I mean?'

'Oh, I miss things. People's faces. Sometimes I ask people if I can feel their faces – with my hands – just to find out what they look like. Often they say no – as if they were frightened. May I touch your face?' Do not be revolted, boys, by the sickliness of this story: I tell you only what the old ignorant folk of the Appenines tell each other. Attila said she could, so she did. Flavia said: 'It seems a pleasant face. You're very old, aren't you? Your beard must be grey. Ah – that means that you're not from these parts. None of our men have beards. I thought you must be a foreigner – the way you speak Latin – some people call it Italian now. Where are you from?'

'A long way away. A great plain. A river. A lot of horses.'

'Pannonia?'

'Much further away. This is good soup. There's plenty of garlic in it. Garlic is a good medicine.'

Her quick ears caught the tread of men entering quietly but heavily. 'It's the Huns,' she said. 'The Huns are here.' Scotta looked with interest on a gentle Attila spooning in soup.

'Yes,' the gentle Attila said, 'the Huns are here. But don't be frightened.'

'Oh, I'm not frightened. I was thinking of you.'

Scotta had brought a message. His Holiness had arrived. His Holiness had travelled in intense heat under a ball of fire with no discernible sign of discomfort. He watched men of his escort and even officers fall to the road and he blessed them with cool compassion. To Aetius he said: 'This is bad campaigning weather. I have a feeling that Attila and his armies will not be too happy. Flies. Dysentery. They are not, I gather, a sanitary people. I foresee starvation, sickness, a difficult retreat. *They* did *not* foresee the difficulties of an Italian summer.' And at length, with a much diminished entourage, he came upon a place of many corpses stinking in the sun. These he blessed, Hun and Christian alike. Live Huns with spears, quartered among squawking chickens, rose to their feet in some doubt. The Pope blessed them smiling. He spoke two words of Hunnish. 'Atta,' he said, pointing to himself. 'Attila?' he then said. The question tone was understood. The brighter of the Huns came to a quite reasonable conclusion. This frail old man with the white beard was coming to hand over the keys of Rome.

The blind girl Flavia was amazed to hear from Attila, who translated Scotta's words into Latin, that His Holiness had come to her village. 'Take me to him,' she cried. 'He can work miracles. I may get my sight back. Why is he here? Why has he come to us?'

'To see me,' the gentle Attila said. 'You shall see him later. But now he and I have to talk.'

'You must be an important man,' the girl said. 'What are you – a bishop?' Scotta sniggered but Attila turned on him with a gesture appropriate to the Scourge of God.

'No, not a bishop. Thank you for the soup.' And he went out. He saw Aetius. The two nodded grimly at each other. Aetius saw what he had heard much about but had never really believed existed: the sword of Mars. Pope Leo was blessing everybody. Then Atta and Attila met. They sat together with no other company in the house of a farmer who had fled. It smelt powerfully of cowdung. Pope Leo said:

'Some might regard this as a historic meeting. But what is history? Errors scrawled on sheepskins. Fallible minds pretending to know the past. There are no historians here. I shall not write about this meeting. Nor, I think, will you. We are free from history. And yet we *are* history. Is my Latin too rapid for you? Good, I see it is not. I was asked to come and see you.'

'I,' Attila said, 'proposed coming to see *you*.'

'Yes, I knew that. Not exactly seeing me, though. Boiling me in oil or crucifying me or something even more barbaric. Barbarism is more boring than frightening.'

'So. You come to ask me not to march on Rome. Rome the holy city is not to be scourged by the Scourge of God.'

'If you would be so good.'

'You bring a bribe of some kind? Gold and silver?'

'No. You have more than enough of those commodities. I merely ask or request. If you wish, I will beg. I do not buy. Rome would like to be left in peace. I know you must consider peace as boring as I consider war, but you can get a lot of things done in a time of peace. War is a damnable distraction.'

'What sort of things?'

'I beg your pardon?'

'What sort of things can be done in a time of peace – other than preparing for war?'

'Oh, books can be written, music played, buildings built. God can be contemplated.'

'God is a tale for little children.'

'And yet you call yourself the Scourge of God.'

'Pardon me, it is you Christians who call me that. I'm presented as a divine punishment for Christian transgressions. But I admit that Scourge of God is a fine title.'

'A fine fairy tale title, I see. You must admit also that God is a rather splendid idea, even if you can't attach credence to it. The maker and sustainer of the universe. You must have looked at the stars on those wide Danubian plains of yours and wondered who made them.'

'Never. They're there. A badly strung set of diamonds. No more.'

'I see. You lack imagination. Perhaps there is little point in my asking you to leave Rome alone.'

'I will take Rome if I wish to.'

'I think not, you know. Your men are suffering from the heat. There is dysentery in your armies. The mosquitoes have bitten

241

them red raw. I think most of your men would be glad to crawl home – those that are able.'

'We do not crawl.'

'Oh, there are times when we all crawl. Bring in your scourge and lash my back with it and I'll crawl readily enough. We are all rather lowly creatures with a great need of God. Even if God happens to be a fairy tale he's a more interesting fairy tale than Attila the Hun. Creation is an immensely interesting concept. Destruction is boring. You see, it's all too easy. Your men are being destroyed now by the forces of nature, and you can't halt their destruction. Go home, Attila. We've had enough of you.'

'Had enough of me. We'll see if that's so. Your man Christ is said to have sacrificed his life for the sake of humanity. Would you be willing to sacrifice yours for the sake of Rome?'

'In principle, yes. You could crucify me now if I could believe that you'd keep your side of the bargain. But you were quite ready to crucify me in my own diocese without any bargain at all. Take my life if you wish. I'm an old man and ready to go. My successor is already named. I ask you to spare Rome in no spirit of humility. I ask you to consider the uselessness of exacting more suffering than you've caused already. The suffering of your own armies as well as of harmless men, women and children. Do you still wish to take Rome?'

'I am not bound to give you an answer.'

'Of course not. The privilege of the military conqueror. Attila, my son, have you heard of the devil?'

'Another of your fairy tales. But rather more appealing than the other one.'

'A fairy tale if you wish, but one that expresses the great mystery of evil. Lucifer the brightest of all the angels fell from heaven – so goes the fairy tale – because he refused to acknowledge that God was greater than he. As God was the creator, the fallen one had to concentrate on destruction. Sometimes he seems incarnate in certain human beings. When I see a lust for destruction, then I know that the devil exists. The devil is in you, Attila my son. If you are God's scourge in the sense that you are a whip in the hand of a being you do not believe to exist, then this might mean that God can use evil. But I think rather that you are the poor devil who would love to inflict suffering on God

242

and screams with rage because he cannot. You are a very little devil. You can't instil evil into Christian souls. You can't even make those souls suffer. All you can do is to take the work of their hands and the fruits of their fields and topple down what you are not clever enough to build. Take Rome if you wish, if you can. Rome will be remembered as a great work in which time and eternity meet and kiss. Attila will be remembered as a tiresome snotnosed urchin with a bit of the devil in him. Do what you wish. I am old and tired. I have a long journey ahead of me. I may not be alive when you get to my city. I may have cheated you. But there will be plenty of others to kill and rob and ravish. Enjoy yourself, Attila. You too will soon have to die. You have the grossness of death sitting in your face. Enjoy yourself while you can. Play in the dirt. Crack your little whip. History is already sick of you.'

So he got up, with an old man's creaking, and left Attila. He went into the sunlight of the piazza, where Attila's troops lay around chewing half-cooked meat, looking with curiosity on the ancient Christian shaman. About him settled a swarm of priests and citizens. The blind girl Flavia tried to break through this cordon for his blessing. When she succeeded Attila came out and sourly saw his blessing. But her soup of herbs and leaves and roots had settled comfortably in his stomach. That too was a Christian blessing. He was angry and confused and he stood saying nothing, doing nothing.

When the piazza cleared of its sacred visitor and his entourage it was already sunset. Attila rode with Scotta about the Hun camp, where men with the fever on them lay crying for water. They had been ready to defecate in the wells and hurl corpses in. They could not look beyond the day. They had not considered the march back. The flies had ceased their day's buzzing over the corpses, but the mosquitoes were alive, queens of the night. Attila looked bitterly at the falling sun, where Rome, queen of the sunset, lay. Scotta sought earnestly in his master's face some sign of a plan, of hope. He saw him take the sword of Mars from its scabbard, pocked with its capital alpha, which was also the Roman A. Attila said: 'Let him have it.'

'Who? Their shaman?'

'There's only one man who will break that empire. He will not break it on my behalf, but he will break it. Mars was never our god. I tried to be my own god of war but I am no god.'

'There are no gods. Who is to have it?'

'Aetius. Ride to Rome, Scotta. Take the sword. They will not harm you. Let Mars have back what is his.'

'With an escort?'

'Go alone. They will not harm you.'

And so the horde approached the Julian Alps. Carts laden with booty broke against stones, and there were no wheelwrights. Gold and silver and religious icons lay winking in the sun. They rode and marched in sullen silence through towns they had rendered unwelcoming, ravaged, inhabited with corpses and their own ordures. Stinking water. An empire of flies.

In Rome a mass, high and pontifical, was sung in a strong if wavering voice by Leo. The censers clanged and gave off their aromatic prayers. Burly monks intoned a *Te Deum*. And, in the squares, the common people burned out their night of secular rejoicing, dancing, clawing buttocks, swilling, spewing. There was a gross ballet. The blind head of a wooden Attila was carried swaying between the bonfires. The stuffed body of Attila was trounced with sticks and beaten with scourges before being given, with groans, to the fire.

In Ravenna Aetius was received by the Emperor. With Valentinian sat, not stood, Maximus Petronius. Aetius was not offered a seat. But he said cheerfully:

'We've seen the last of him – for the time being.'

'The last of him for ever.'

'Never be too sure, my lord.'

'No,' Valentinian said. 'Never be too sure, not so long as he has friends in the Empire.'

'The pattern repeats itself,' Aetius said. 'You're quick to call on me to drive him out, then you complain that I haven't brought him captive into Ravenna – to be gawped at by adulterous matrons and giggling epicenes. When I say *never be sure* I don't think I refer solely to Attila's powers of recovery. Your empire is very sick. Rome is a husk animated only by the vision of an eternal city. The future lies in the east. Meanwhile fear for your own crown, your own life. But not from me, Valentinian.' And

244

he stalked out with no obeisance. The enraged Emperor called him back.

'Do you hear me? I haven't finished with you.'

Maximus Petronius made a slow throat-cutting gesture.

For the time being? Attila, who felt freer without the sword of Mars and its blade of destiny, thrust from his brain certain images that had killed sleep: abandoned loot, abandoned corpses. It was with a fresh new army that he thundered into the territory of the Franks and railed at the ruler of the Franks, a terrified man bloated with good or bad living. 'Rank treachery, the treachery of a little coward unworthy to be chief even of a tribe of ruffians like the Franks. We made a solemn pact, you remember? We contracted an alliance, and you swore in blood to assist in the Italian campaign. But you skulked, held back, whined complaints about the impossibility of the venture.'

'I was right. It *was* impossible.'

'Next time, my little lord, you will be there. The alliance is renewed under fresh conditions. I demand the hand of your daughter. A blood alliance. I will make you part of the flesh and sinew of the Huns.'

The chief, Radonic, sat fearful. His daughter, the princess Ildico, showed no fear. She was a young woman of great beauty, hair like the sun on a wheatfield, clothes in silk of scarlet and laden with jewels of Italian workmanship. She said, without emphasis:

'If you mean an enforced marriage, I will not.'

'So the girl has a voice,' Attila said smiling grimly. 'She also has spirit. You, my girl, are to become Empress of the Huns. Does not the thought thrill you?'

'I am not a piece of property to be handed over at your bidding. I am a human creature with her own rights.'

'Women have no rights. Take her.' She shrugged as leering Huns strode forward on the shrinking boards of her father's throne-room. She did not resist. 'Instal her in one of the wagons. With a couple of her serving maids. You, sir,' he said to Radonic, 'are to be the father-in-law of Attila. You will behave as a father-in-law – you will show meek obedience to the will of the son-in-law who honours you. You will prepare your troops for the last of Attila's campaigns. The final assault on the Empire of the

Latins and the Greeks. Once for all, the bringing low of the
enemy. First – Constantinople.' The fire of his words, he knew,
was a fire reflected in glass. He knew that he needed treachery.
*If only Attila had not been betrayed at the crown of his skill and the
mountain summit of his power* . . . But he spoke fiercely until he
heard the breaking notes of panic. He said quietly: 'It is as well
to know the name of one's bride.' He saw a drop of sweat on
his hand that had dripped from his forehead. 'What is her name?'
  'Ildico.'
The Frankish princess was arrayed for the bridal. Her fine eyes
blazed and outdid her barbaric ornaments. Hildr, who was her
senior waiting maid, admired and said she was ready.
  'For the sacrifice,' she said. 'Don't the Huns cement their mar-
riages in blood? Hundreds of bleating goats and snorting pigs
put to the knife? And then the bride and groom roll in a tide of
beasts' blood—'
  'That is fantasy,' said Andegonde, the second maid. 'My lady
has been having bad dreams.'
  'Nothing can touch the Hun reality. Where is my dagger?'
  'You may not wear your dagger at the wedding, my lady. That
would bring bad luck.'
  'I may not even cut my own meat at the wedding feast? I must
take smoking hunks from the unwashed fingers of the groom?'
  'Keep it hidden, my lady.'
The dagger was sheathed in a scabbard of exquisite craft from
Florentia. Ildico tucked it with care into the waistband of her
silken trousers. And then she joined the procession that awaited
her outside the eastern door of the palace. It held torches and
hummed a song. The Danube was as noisy as a sea this night.
The chief shaman intoned over the drums: 'Hot as fire and
cool as water and solid as earth and eternal as the living air – so
be the unity of their coupling. Many may be the offspring of
these royal loins and may they all be warriors, frightful to the
gods of those who partake not of the rights of the kingdom.
Bless, bless and bless, such of the dead as be watching. Bless,
bless and bless, the yet unborn.'
Attila ate and drank with deliberate grossness. He called: 'Bard!
Sing of the beauty of the bride, according to the custom of the
Huns.' But it was only a recent custom. The Huns were no

musicians. The bard, a whiteheaded veteran of war conscripted to the new office, struck the strings of a purloined Gallic lute at random. Ildico winced. The song was hideous:

Ildico,
With skin like mountain snow,
Hair like the contents of the coffers of the slain,
Limbs long as the limbs of the steeds of the plain.
May her unnamable be fruitful, long may the seed flow
Into the loins out of the loins of Attila and Ildico.

The cups passed around, spilling freely in the carelessness of excess. Attila said, with conscious brutality:

'Rejoice, Ildico, that you are the last of the brides of the Hun. There are, have been, others. There should have been one other . . .' He drunkenly saw himself sober in Roman robes in the great basilica of Ravenna, placing a ring on the ring finger of a girl who giggled. She wrote, sent him that same ring, what was her name? He mumbled so that few could hear him. Ildico listened attentively. 'Married by the pope the unholy father of the stupid. Attila, Emperor of two empires conjoined as one. Ruled from Rome, Rome. And the Huns become farmers and growers of wine grapes. Peace under a blue Italian heaven. Who wants a blue Italian heaven? Stormclouds and the birds fleeting away from the smoke and flames. What we are we are and we will smash them yet. Not one blade of grass shall grow where the foot of Attila has passed. Drink, drink, this is a joyous occasion.' Loudly he said: 'Ildico, Empress of the Huns, sing for us. I know you can sing and sew and bake bread. We are yet to see whether you can bear princes for the ruling of the provinces of Attila. Sing.'

'Gladly, my lord,' she said. And pushing aside the untuned lute, she stood and sang in a hard clear voice, penetrating and resonant, saying first: 'This is a song sung in my father's kingdom on solemn occasions. This is, I gather, a solemn occasion.' And all grew silent and, soon, uneasily silent as she sang:

Cursed by they who forbid the grain to grow,
Who salt the earth with blood,

Who call a conquest peace and peace sleep,
Who batten off the makers and are themselves the unmakers.
Cursed be they who laugh at the deaths of others,
Who do not warm themselves with fire but kill by fire.
For where they make a desolation the desolation is for ever
And they have no future and no scribe shall perpetuate their
    name.
For the destroyers destroy all, even themselves.

The uneasy silence was prolonged until Scotta incontinently belched and then asked pardon. The homely noise dispelled unease and the cups went round again. Attila said:

'Not very appropriate to an occasion of rejoicing.'

'Rejoicing cannot be forced, my lord,' she said. 'Slaves have no cause to rejoice.'

'You're an empress, child.'

'A slave empress. And now, with your permission, I shall retire to my quarters.'

'You will be escorted to mine. There to await the bridegroom's coming.'

'Of course. Slaves have no choice.'

Ildico rose, but no others rose save her waiting women. She flashed sudden authority. 'My lord, your noblemen have no manners.'

'On your feet, swine,' Attila yelled, himself still seated. 'On your feet for the Empress of the Huns.' There was a clumsy upstanding, with belches and the uncouth breaking of wind. The Empress left with dignity, and the Hun nobles relaxed to a freer venting of noises. 'Pour,' Attila cried, 'the Roman wine and the Greek wine and the Gaulish wine. Wine of the conquered, blood of the slain.'

Ildico heard, dim in the distance, the noise of revelry. The flood of the Danube was louder. The bed was of deep flock and overlain with silk. She sat alone and primly on the edge of this bed, waiting. She had dismissed her servants and said she would do her own disrobing. She waited. She waited until, at the feast's height, Attila staggered in. He had drained a quart cup in one draught, and he had left the feast to cheers and the raising of ithyphallic fists. So a foolish smile was upon him as he toppled in, saying thickly:

'My love, my bride – let us see you in the white garment of your nakedness. A bridegroom's right – yes? Well – perhaps no rights. A little drunk. Entitled to it on my wedding night.' Through the mask of his drunkenness there appeared the reality of a man sad, tired and wholly sober. 'A little sleep,' he said soberly. 'And then . . .' He fell staggering on to the silk and loudly snored, a drunken Hun. She did not hesitate. From her waist she drew her dagger and raised it. No one heard a body thumping to the floor, a gurgling as of one drowning in his own fluids. No one found the dead Scourge of God until the morning, and the morning came late. Ildico was nowhere to be found.

Petronius and the eunuch Heraclius rode fast, with a small escort before and behind. They were seeking the villa of Aetius. They found Aetius tending his roses in mild sunlight. 'If you come to bring me news,' he said, 'I have heard the news already. Even from here I seem to hear the Huns howling over the plain of the Danube. Like dogs.'

'Ah yes,' Maximus Petronius said. 'The end of an epoch.'

'Time has no stop,' Aetius said. And then he sucked the finger where a thorn had struck. 'Epochs change into other epochs. Epochs and their ends – the artificial toys of historians. May I offer you some wine?'

'No wine,' Heraclius said. He said it insolently.

'You squeak still, Heraclius. You should try vocal exercises.'

'You,' Heraclius squeaked, 'are going to squeak, Count Aetius.' It was he who drew the assassin's dagger. Aetius's passivity belied the words he had just spoken. It was as though he was ready to be enfolded in a finished epoch. He fell gaping. A squeak from his dying lungs was not the squeak that the squeaking Heraclius had meant. Petronius said:

'The end of a great general. An army in great confusion. Now is the time if there will ever be a time. Back to Ravenna.' He turned to go. He turned back to look at the body among the rosebushes. 'Will they meet in hell, the two of them? Discuss old times? Perhaps we ought to dispatch this body as a gift . . .'

'A gift to whom?'

'True. Those little chiefs and princes are nothing. There was only one Hun. Come . . .'

The flies settled on the body of Aetius. The body of Attila was long consumed by fire, but the shamans wailed and the people howled. Like dogs left alone. Petronius and Heraclius continued their work of clearing up an epoch. The Emperor Valentinian was taking a breakfast of fruit, new bread, and very sweet wine when they entered.

'Really – you should have had yourselves announced – there are certain decencies. This is great insolence.'

'Appalling insolence,' Maximus Petronius said. 'Do you wish to say your prayers, Valentinian?'

'What is this? What stupid joke?'

The dagger of the eunuch Heraclius, wiped of the blood of Aetius, struck. It was not a good stroke. The Emperor flopped about the breakfast chamber, moaning, trying, as it were, to distance himself from the rent in his robe and the red tide that started to gallop. The task was completed with four stabs. He fell, trying to say 'My Lord and my God' as blood leapt fom his mouth. Heraclius, panting, said:

'Long live the Emperor Maximus Petronius.'

'Thank you, chief minister.'

So, boys, he wore the laurel crown, and it passed to another and then another, and they were all highly undistinguished men. They all permitted heresy and had too much power over the bishop of Rome.

'What happened to the sword, sir?' a boy asked. The sun was setting over Egypt and there was a shiver in the palms.

'The sword?' Nestorius was puzzled for an instant. 'Ah, the sword of Mars with its embossed capital alpha that is also our Roman A. It went to Rome with the effects of the murdered Aetius, whose own initial, by the chance of things, was already on it, and then it passed to the hands of another, a *dux* of the Saxon shore, whose name began with an A – what was it now? Yes, Ambrosianus or something. And some say he took it to the island of Britian, where it awaited another *dux Romanus* with an A crowning his name. It is a Christian sword now, and the metal blood of Mars has been expunged entirely from it. But that is nothing. The important thing to remember is that all empires die. They die from weaknesses within. And God sends a scourge to remind them that their decline and death is a punishment. Attila was no more than a great whip. Remember, boys, it's the City of God alone that survives, a city not made by human hands. But even that city is subject to the error of the human hands that direct it. Error, error, deadly error.' He beetled sternly at young Audax. 'You, boy, you have had your entertainment. Now let us be serious. Tell me what you know of the divine and human natures in the person of Our Lord Jesus Christ.'

'I don't know anything about them, sir.'

The boys had all seen this before: Nestorius looking for his stick in the long grass where he had lain it, ready to beat, crying, 'Young heretic!', while Audax got up and ran away. The Scourge of God, you could call old Nestorius. But he didn't take kindly to flattery.

·— MURDER TO MUSIC —·

Sir Edwin Etheridge, the eminent specialist in tropical diseases, had had the kindness to invite me to share with him the examination of a patient of his in the Marylebone area. It seemed to Sir Edwin that this patient, a young man who had never set foot outside England, was suffering from an ailment known as *latah* – common enough in the Malay archipelago but hitherto unknown, so far as the clinical records – admittedly not very reliable – could advise, in the temperate clime of northern Europe. I was able to confirm Sir Edwin's tentative diagnosis: the young man was morbidly suggestible, imitating any action he either saw or heard described, and was, on my entrance into his bedroom, exhausting himself with the conviction that he had been metamorphosed into a bicycle. The disease is incurable but intermittent: it is of psychical rather than nervous provenance, and can best be eased by repose, solitude, opiates, and tepid malt drinks. As I strolled down Marylebone Road after the consultation, it seemed to me the most natural thing in the world to turn into Baker Street to visit my old friend, lately returned, so *The Times* informed me, from some nameless assignment in Marrakesh. This, it later transpired, was the astonishing case of the Moroccan poisonous palmyra, of which the world is not yet ready to hear.

I found Holmes rather warmly clad for a London July day, in dressing gown, winter comforter, and a jewelled turban which, he was to inform me, was the gift of the mufti of Fez – donated in gratitude for some service my friend was not willing to specify. He was bronzed and clearly inured to a greater heat than our own, but not, except for the turban, noticeably exoticised by his sojourn in the land of the Mohammedan. He had been trying to breathe smoke through a hubble bubble but had given up the endeavour. 'The flavour of rose water is damnably sickly, Watson,' he remarked, 'and the tobacco itself of a desperate mildness diluted further by its long transit through these ingenious but ridiculous conduits.' With evident relief he drew some of his regular cut from the Turkish slipper by the fireless hearth, filled his curved pipe, lighted it with a vesta, and then looked at me amiably. 'You have been with Sir Edwin Etheridge,' he said, 'in, I should think, St John's Wood Road.'

'This is astonishing, Holmes,' I gasped. 'How can you possibly know?'

'Easy enough,' puffed my friend. 'St John's Wood Road is the only London thoroughfare where deciduous redwood has been planted, and a leaf of that tree, prematurely fallen, adheres to the sole of your left boot. As for the other matter, Sir Edwin Etheridge is in the habit of sucking Baltimore mint lozenges as a kind of token prophylactic. You have been sucking one yourself. They are not on the London market, and I know of no other man who has them specially imported.'

'You are quite remarkable, Holmes,' I said.

'Nothing, my dear Watson. I have been perusing *The Times*, as you may have observed from its crumpled state on the floor – a womanish habit, I suppose, God bless the sex – with a view to informing myself on events of national import in which, naturally enough, the enclosed world of Morocco takes little interest.'

'Are there not French newspapers there?'

'Indeed, but they contain no news of events in the rival empire. I see we are to have a state visit from the young king of Spain.'

'That would be his infant majesty Alfonso XIII,' I somewhat gratuitously amplified. 'I take it that his mother the regent, the fascinating Maria Christina, will be accompanying him.'

'There is much sympathy for the young monarch,' Holmes said, 'especially here. But he has his republican and anarchist enemies. Spain is in a state of great political turbulence. It is reflected even in contemporary Spanish music.' He regarded his violin, which lay waiting for its master in its open case, and resined the bow lovingly. 'The petulant little fiddle tunes I heard

253

in Morocco day and night, Watson, need to be excised from my head by something more complex and civilised. One string only, and usually one note on one string. Nothing like the excellent Sarasate.' He began to play an air which he assured me was Spanish, though I heard in it something of Spain's Moorish inheritance, wailing, desolate and remote. Then with a start Holmes looked at his turnip watch, a gift from the Duke of Northumberland. 'Good heavens, we'll be late. Sarasate is playing this very afternoon at St James's Hall.' And he doffed his turban and robe and strode to his dressing-room to habit himself more suitably for a London occasion. I kept my own counsel, as always, concerning my feelings on the subject of Sarasate and, indeed, on music in general. I lacked Holmes's artistic flair. As for Sarasate, I could not deny that he played wonderfully well for a foreign fiddler, but there was a smugness in the man's countenance as he played that I found singularly unattractive. Holmes knew nothing of my feelings and, striding in in his blue velvet jacket with trousers of a light-clothed Mediterranean cut, a white shirt of heavy silk and a black Bohemian tie carelessly knotted, he assumed in me his own anticipatory pleasure. 'Come, Watson,' he cried. 'I have been trying in my own damnably amateurish way to make sense of Sarasate's own latest composition. Now the master himself will hand me the key. The key of D major,' he added.

'Shall I leave my medical bag here?'

'No, Watson. I don't doubt that you have some gentle anaesthetic there to ease you through the more tedious phases of the recital.' He smiled as he said this, but I felt abashed at his all too accurate appraisal of my attitude to the sonic art.

The hot afternoon seemed, to my fancy, to have succumbed to the drowsiness of the Middle Sea, as if through Holmes's own inexplicable influence. It was difficult to find a cab and, when we arrived at St James's Hall, the recital had already begun. When we had been granted the exceptional privilege of taking our seats at the back of the hall while the performance of an item was already in progress, I was quick enough myself to prepare for a Mediterranean siesta. The great Sarasate, then at the height of his powers, was fiddling away at some abstruse mathematics of Bach to the accompaniment on the pianoforte of a pleasant-looking young man whose complexion proclaimed him to be as Iberian as the master. He seemed nervous, though not of his capabilities on the instrument. He glanced swiftly behind him towards the curtain which shut off the platform from the wings and passages of the administrative arcana of the hall but then, as if reassured, returned wholeheartedly to his music. Meanwhile Holmes, eyes half-shut, gently tapped on his right knee the rhythm of the intolerably lengthy equation which was engaging the intellects of the musically devout, among whom I remarked the pale red-bearded young Irishman who was making his name as a critic and a polemicist. I slept.

I slept, indeed, very soundly. I was awakened not by the music but by the applause to which Sarasate was bowing with Latin extravagance. I glanced covertly at my watch to find that a great deal of music had passed over my sleeping brain: there must have been earlier applause to which my drowsy grey cells had proved impervious. Holmes apparently had not noted my somnolence or, perhaps noting it, had been too discreet to arouse me or, now, to comment on my boorish indifference to that art he adored. 'The work in question, Watson,' he said, 'is about to begin.' And it began. It was a wild piece in which never fewer than three strings of the four were simultaneously in action, full of the rhythm of what I knew, from a brief visit to Granada, to be the *zapateado*. It ended with furious chords and a high single note that only a bat could have found euphonious. 'Bravo,' cried Holmes with the rest, vigorously clapping. And then the noise of what to me seemed excessive approbation was pierced by the crack of a single gunshot. There was smoke and the tang of a frying breakfast, and the young accompanist cried out. His head collapsed on to the keys of his instrument, producing a hideous jangle, and then the head, with its unseeing eyes and an open mouth from which blood relentlessly pumped in a galloping tide, raised itself and seemed to accuse the entire audience of a ghastly crime against nature. Then, astonishingly, the fingers of the right hand of the dying man picked at one note of the keyboard many times, following this with a seemingly delirious phrase of a few different notes which he repeated and would have continued to repeat if the rattle of death had not overtaken him. He slumped to the floor of the platform. The women in the audience screamed.

Meanwhile the master Sarasate clutched his valuable violin to his bosom, a Stradivarius Holmes was later to inform me, as though that had been the target of the gunshot.

Holmes was, as ever, quick to act. 'Clear the hall!' he shouted. The manager appeared, trembling and deathly pale, to add a feebler shout to the same effect. Attendants somewhat roughly assisted the horrified audience to leave. The red-bearded young Irishman nodded at Holmes as he left, saying something to the effect that it was as well that the delicate fingers of the amateur should anticipate the coarse questing paws of the Metropolitan professionals, adding that it was a bad business: that young Spanish pianist had promised well. 'Come, Watson,' said Holmes, striding towards the platform. 'He has lost much blood but he may not be quite dead.' But I saw swiftly enough that he was past any help that the contents of my medical bag could possibly provide. The rear of the skull was totally shattered.

Holmes addressed Sarasate in what I took to be impeccable Castilian, dealing every courtesy and much deference. Sarasate seemed to say that the young man, whose name was Gonzales, had served as his accompanist both in Spain and on foreign tour for a little over six months, that he knew nothing of his background though something of his ambitions as a solo artist and a composer, and that, to the master's knowledge, he had no personal enemies. Stay, though: there had been some rather unsavoury stories circulating in Barcelona about the adulterous activities of the young Gonzales, but it was doubtful if the enraged husband, or conceivably husbands, would have pursued him to London to effect so dire and spectacular a revenge. Holmes nodded distractedly, meanwhile loosening the collar of the dead man.

'A somewhat pointless procedure,' I commented. Holmes said nothing. He merely peered at the lowest segment of the nape of the corpse's neck, frowned, then wiped one hand against the other while rising from a crouch back to his feet. He asked the sweating manager if the act of assassination had, by any chance, been observed, either by himself or by one of his underlings, or, failing that, if any strange visitant had, to the knowledge of the management, insinuated himself into the rear area of the hall, reserved exclusively for artists and staff and protected from the rear door by a former sergeant of marines, now a member of the Corps of Commissionaires. A horrid thought struck the manager at once and, followed by Holmes and myself, he rushed down a corridor that led to a door which gave on to a side alley.

That door was unguarded for a very simple reason. An old man in the uniform trousers of the Corps, though not in – evidently because of the heat – the jacket, lay dead, the back of his grey head pierced with devilish neatness by a bullet. The assassin had then presumably effected an unimpeded transit to the curtains which separated the platform from the area of offices and dressing-rooms.

'It is very much to be regretted,' said the distraught manager, 'that no other of the staff was present at the rear, though, if one takes an excusably selfish view of the matter, it is perhaps not to be regretted. Evidently we had here a cold-blooded murderer who would stop at nothing.' Holmes nodded and said:

'Poor Simpson. I knew him, Watson. He spent a life successfully avoiding death from the guns and spears of Her Imperial Majesty's enemies only to meet it in a well-earned retirement while peacefully perusing his copy of *Sporting Life*. Perhaps,' he now said to the manager, 'you would be good enough to explain why the assassin had only poor Simpson to contend with. In a word, where were the other members of the staff?'

'The whole affair is very curious, Mr Holmes,' said the manager, wiping the back of his neck with a handkerchief. 'I received a message just after the start of the recital, indeed shortly after your good self and your friend here had taken your seats. The message informed me that the Prince of Wales and certain friends of his were coming to the concert, though belatedly. It is, of course, well known that His Royal Highness is an admirer of Sarasate. There is a small upper box at the back of the hall normally reserved for distinguished visitors, as I think you know.'

'Indeed,' said Holmes. 'The Maharajah of Johore was once kind enough to honour me as his guest in that exclusive retreat. But do please go on.'

'Naturally, myself and my staff,' the manager continued, 'assembled at the entrance and remained on duty throughout the recital, assuming that the distinguished visitor might arrive only for the final items.' He went on to say that, though considerably puzzled, they had remained in the vestibule until the final applause, hazarding the guess that His Royal Highness might, in the imperious but bonhomous manner that was his wont, command the Spanish fiddler to favour him with an encore in a hall filled only with the anticipatory majesty of our future King Emperor. Thus all was explained except for the essential problem of the crime itself.

'The message,' Holmes demanded of the manager. 'I take it that it was a written message. Might I see it?'

The manager drew from an inner pocket a sheet of notepaper headed with the princely insignia and signed with a name known to be that of His Royal Highness's private secretary. The message was clear and courteous. The date was the seventh of July. Holmes nodded indifferently at it and, when the police arrived, tucked the sheet unobtrusively into a side pocket. Inspector Stanley Hopkins had responded promptly to the summons delivered, with admirable efficiency, by one of the manager's underlings in a fast cab.

'A deplorable business, inspector,' Holmes said. 'Two murders, the motive for the first explained by the second, but the second as yet disclosing no motive at all. I wish you luck with your investigations.'

'You will not be assisting us with the case, Mr Holmes?' asked the intelligent young inspector. Holmes shook his head.

'I am,' he said to me in the cab that took us back to Baker Street, 'exhibiting my usual duplicity, Watson. This case interests me a great deal.' Then he said somewhat dreamily: 'Stanley Hopkins, Stanley Hopkins. The name recalls that of an old teacher of mine, Watson. It always takes me back to my youthful days at Stonyhurst College, where I was taught Greek by a young priest of exquisite delicacy of mind. Gerard Manley Hopkins was his name.' He chuckled a moment. 'I was given taps from a tolly by him when I was a callow atramontarius. He was the best of the younger crows, however, always ready to pin a shouting cake with us in the haggory. Never creeping up on us in the silent oilers worn by the crabbier jebbies.'

'Your vocabulary, Holmes,' I said. 'It is a foreign language to me.'

'The happiest days of our lives, Watson,' he then said somewhat gloomily.

Over an early dinner of cold lobster and a chicken salad, helped
down by an admirable white burgundy well-chilled, Holmes disclosed himself as vitally concerned with pursuing this matter of
the murder of a foreign national on British soil, or at least in a
London concert-room. He handed me the supposed royal message and asked what was my opinion of it. I examined the note
with some care. 'It seems perfectly in order to me,' I said. 'The
protocol is regular, the formula, or so I take it, is the usual
one. But, since the manager and his staff were duped, some
irregularity in obtaining the royal notepaper must be assumed.'

'Admirable, Watson. Now kindly examine the date.'

'It is today's date.'

'True, but the formation of the figure 7 is not what one might
expect.'

'Ah,' I said, 'I see your meaning. We British do not place a bar
across the number. This 7 is a continental one.'

'Exactly. The message has been written by a Frenchman or an
Italian or, as seems much more probable, a Spaniard with access
to the notepaper of His Royal Highness. The English and, as you
say, the formula are impeccable. But the signatory is not British.
He made a slight slip there. As for the notepaper, it would be
available only to a person distinguished enough to possess access
to His Royal Highness's premises and to a person unscrupulous
enough to rob him of a sheet of his notepaper. Something in the
configuration of the letter "e" in this message persuades me that
the signatory was Spanish. I may, naturally, be totally mistaken.
But I have very little doubt that the assassin was Spanish.'

'A Spanish husband, with the impetuousness of his race, exacting a very summary revenge,' I said.

'I think the motive of the murder was not at all domestic.
You observed my loosening the collar of the dead man and you
commented with professional brusqueness on the futility of my
act. You were unaware of the reason for it.' Holmes, who now
had his pipe alight, took a pencil and scrawled a curious symbol
on the table cloth. 'Have you ever seen anything like this before,
Watson?' he puffed. I frowned at the scrawl. It seemed to be a
crude representation of a bird with spread wings seated on a

number of upright strokes which could be taken as a nest. I shook my head. 'That, Watson, is a phoenix rising from the ashes of the flames that consumed it. It is the symbol of the Catalonian separatists. They are republicans and anarchists and they detest the centralising control of the Castilian monarchy. This symbol was tattooed on the back of the neck of the murdered man. He must have been an active member of a conspiratorial group.'

'What made you think of looking for it?' I asked.

'I met, quite by chance, a Spaniard in Tangiers who inveighed in strong terms against the monarchy which had exiled him and, wiping the upper part of his body for the heat, disclosed quite frankly that he had an identical tattoo on his chest.'

'You mean,' I said incredulously,' that he was in undress, or, as the French put it, *en déshabille*?'

'It was an opium den in the Kasbah, Watson,' Holmes said calmly. 'Little attention is paid in such places to the refinements of dress. He mentioned to me that the nape of the neck was the more usual site of the declaration of faith in the Catalonian republic, but he preferred the chest where, as he put it, he could keep an eye on the symbol and be reminded of what it signified. I had been wondering ever since the announcement of the visit to London of the young Spanish king whether there might be Catalonian assassins around. It seemed reasonable to me to look on the body of the murdered man for some indication of a political adherence.'

'So,' said I, 'it is conceivable that this young Spaniard, dedicated to art as he seemed to be, proposed killing the harmless and innocent Alfonso XIII. The intelligence services of the Spanish monarchy have, I take it, acted promptly though illegally. All the forces of European stability should be grateful that the would-be assassin has been himself assassinated.'

'And the poor old soldier who guarded the door?' Holmes riposted, his sharp eyes peering at me through the fog of his tobacco smoke. 'Come, Watson, murder is always a crime.' And then he began to hum, not distractedly, a snatch of tune which seemed vaguely familiar. His endless repetition of it was interrupted by the announcement that Inspector Stanley Hopkins had arrived. 'I expected him, Watson,' Holmes said, and, when the young police officer had entered the room, he bafflingly recited:

And I have asked to be
Where no storms come,
Where the green swell is in the havens dumb,
And out of the swing of the sea.

Stanley Hopkins gaped in some astonishment, as I might have myself had I not been long inured to Holmes's eccentricities of behaviour. Before Hopkins could stutter a word of bewilderment, Holmes said: 'Well, inspector, I trust you have come in triumph.' But there was no triumph in Hopkins's demeanour. He handed over to Holmes a sheet of paper on which there was handwriting in purple ink.

'This, Mr Holmes, was found on the dead man's person. It is in Spanish, I think, a language with which neither I nor my colleagues are at all acquainted. I gather you know it well. I should be glad if you would assist our investigation by translating it.'

Holmes read both sides of the paper keenly. 'Ah, Watson,' he said at length, 'this either complicates or simplifies the issue, I am not as yet sure which. This seems to be a letter from the young man's father, in which he implores the son to cease meddling with republican and anarchistic affairs and concentrate on the practice of his art. He also, in the well-worn phrase, wags a will at him. No son of his disloyal to the concept of a unified Spain with a secure monarchy need expect to inherit a *patrimonio*. The father appears to be mortally sick and threatens to deliver a dying curse on his intransigent offspring. Very Spanish, I suppose. Highly dramatic. Some passages have the lilt of operatic arias. We need the Frenchman Bizet to set them to music.'

'So,' I said, 'it is possible that the young man had announced his defection from the cause, possessed information which he proposed to make public or at least refer to a quarter which had a special interest in it, and then was brutally murdered before he could make the divulgation.'

'Quite brilliant, Watson,' said Holmes, and I flushed discreetly with pleasure. It was rarely that he gave voice to praise untempered by sarcasm. 'And a man who has killed so remorselessly twice is all too likely to do so again. What arrangements, inspector,' he asked young Hopkins, 'have the authorities made for the security of our royal Spanish visitors?'

'They arrive this evening, as you doubtless know, on the last of the packets from Boulogne. At Folkestone they will be transferred immediately to a special train. They will be accommodated at the Spanish Embassy. Tomorrow they travel to Windsor. The following day there will be luncheon with the Prime Minister. There will be a special performance of Messrs Gilbert and Sullivan's *Gondoliers* —'

'In which the Spanish nobility is mocked,' said Holmes, 'but no matter. You have given me the itinerary and the programme. You have not yet told me of the security arrangements.'

'I was coming to that. The entire Metropolitan force will be in evidence on all occasions, and armed men out of uniform will be distributed at all points of vantage. I do not think there is anything to fear.'

'I hope you are right, inspector.'

'The royal party will leave the country on the fourth day by the Dover-Calais packet at 1.25. Again, there will be ample forces of security both on the dockside and on the boat itself. The Home Secretary realises the extreme importance of the protection of a visiting monarch – especially since that regrettable incident when the Czar was viciously tripped over in the Crystal Palace.'

'My own belief,' Holmes said, relighting his pipe, 'is that the Czar of all the Russias was intoxicated. But again, no matter.' A policeman in uniform was admitted. He saluted Holmes first and then his superior. 'This is open house for the Metropolitan force,' Holmes remarked with good-humoured sarcasm. 'Come one, come all. You are heartily welcome, sergeant. I take it you have news.'

'Beg pardon, sir,' the sergeant said, and, to Hopkins, 'we got the blighter, sir, in a manner of speaking.'

'Explain yourself, sergeant. Come on, man,' snapped Hopkins.

'Well, sir, there's this kind of Spanish hotel, meaning a hotel where Spaniards go when they want to be with their own sort, in the Elephant and Castle it is.'

'Appropriate,' Holmes interjected rapidly. 'It used to be the Infanta of Castile. Goat and Compasses. God encompasses us. I apologise. Pray continue, sergeant.'

'We got there and he must have known what was coming, for he got on the roof by way of the skylight, three storeys up it is, and whether he slipped or hurled himself off, his – neck was broke, sir.' The printing conventions of our realm impose the employment of a dash to indicate the demotic epithet the sergeant employed. 'Begging your pardon, sir.'

'You're sure it's the assassin, sergeant?' asked Holmes.

'Well, sir, there was Spanish money on him and there was a knife, what they call a stiletto, and there was a revolver with two chambers let off, sir.'

'A matter, inspector, of checking the bullets extracted from the two bodies with those still in the gun. I think that was your man, sergeant. My congratulations. It seems that the state visit of his infant majesty can proceed without too much foreboding on the part of the Metropolitan force. And now, inspector, I expect you have some writing to do.' This was a courteous way of dismissing his two visitors. 'You must be tired, Watson,' he then said. 'Perhaps the sergeant would be good enough to whistle a cab for you. In the street, that is. We shall meet, I trust, at the Savoy Theatre on the tenth. Immediately before curtain time. Mr D'Oyley Carte always has two complimentary tickets waiting for me in the box office. It will be interesting to see how our Iberian visitors react to a British musical farce.' He said this without levity, with a certain gloom rather. So I too was dismissed.

Holmes and I, in our evening clothes with medals on display, assisted as planned at the performance of *The Gondoliers*. My medals were orthodox enough, those of an old campaigner, but Holmes had some very strange decorations, among the least recondite of which I recognised the triple star of Siam and the crooked cross of Bolivia. We had been given excellent seats in the orchestral stalls. Sir Arthur Sullivan conducted his own work. The infant king appeared to be more interested in the electric light installations than in the action or song proceeding on stage, but his mother responded with suitable appreciation to the jokes when they had been explained to her by the Spanish ambassador. This was a musical experience more after my heart than a recital by Sarasate. I laughed heartily, nudged Holmes in the ribs at the saltier sallies, and hummed the airs and choruses perhaps too boisterously, since Lady Esther Roscommon, one of my patients as it happened, poked me from the row behind and courteously complained that I was not only loud but also out of tune. But, as I told her in the intermission, I had never laid claim to any particular musical skill. As for Holmes, his eyes were on the audience, and with opera glasses too, more than on the stage proceedings.

During the intermission, the royal party very democratically showed itself in the general bar, the young king graciously accepting a glass of British lemonade over which, in the manner of a child unblessed by the blood, he smacked his lips. I was surprised to see that the great Sarasate, in immaculate evening garb with the orders of various foreign states, was taking a glass of champagne with none other than Sir Arthur Sullivan. I commented on the fact to Holmes, who bowed rather distantly to both, and expressed wonder that a man so eminent in the sphere of the more rarefied music should be hobnobbing with a mere entertainer, albeit one honoured by the Queen. 'Music is music,' Holmes explained, lighting what I took to be a Tangerine panatella. 'It has many mansions. Sir Arthur has sunk, Watson, to the level he finds most profitable, and not only in terms of monetary reward, but he is known also for works of dreary piety. They are speaking Italian together.' Holmes's ears were sharper than mine. 'How much more impressive their reminiscences of aristocratic favour sound than in our own blunt tongue. But the second bell has sounded. What a waste of an exceptionally fine leaf.' He referred to his panatella, which he doused with regret in one of the brass receptacles in the lobby. In the second half of the entertainment Holmes slept soundly. I felt I needed no more to experience the shame of an uncultivated boor when I succumbed to slumber at a more elevated musical event. As Holmes had said, somewhat blasphemously, music has many mansions.

The following morning, a hasty message from Sir Edwin Etheridge, delivered while I was at breakfast, summoned me to another consultation in the bedroom of his patient on St John's Wood Road. The young man was no longer exhibiting the symptoms of *latah*; he seemed now to be suffering from the rare Chinese disease, which I had encountered in Singapore and Hong Kong, known as *shook jong*. This is a distressing ailment, and embarrassing to describe outside of a medical journal, since

its cardinal feature is the patient's fear that the capacity of gener-
ation is being removed from him by malevolent forces conjured
by an overheated imagination. To combat these forces, which he
believes responsible for a progressive diminution of his tangible
generative asset, he attempts to obviate its shrinkage by transfix-
ation, usually with the sharpest knife he can find. The only
possible treatment was profound sedation and, in the intervals
of consciousness, a light diet.

I very naturally turned on to Baker Street after the consultation,
the fine weather continuing with a positively Hispanic effulgence.
The great world of London seemed wholly at peace. Holmes, in
dressing gown and Moorish turban, was rubbing resin on to his
bow as I entered his sitting-room. He was cheerful while I was
not. I had been somewhat unnerved by the sight of an ailment
I had thought to be confined to the Chinese, as I had been
disconcerted earlier in the week by the less harmful *latah*, a
property of hysterical Malays, both diseases now manifesting
themselves in a young person of undoubtedly Anglo-Saxon
blood. Having unburdened myself of my disquiet to Holmes, I
said, perhaps wisely, 'These are probably the sins visited by
subject races on our imperialistic ambitions.'

'They are the occluded side of progress,' Holmes said, somewhat vaguely and then, less so: 'Well, Watson, the royal visit
seems to have passed without mishap. The forces of Iberian
dissidence have not further raised their bloody hands on our soil.
And yet I am not altogether easy in my mind. Perhaps I must
attribute the condition to the irrational power of music. I cannot
get out of my head the spectacle of that unfortunate young man
struck lifeless at the instrument he had played with so fine a
touch, and then, in his death agony, striking a brief rhapsody of
farewell which had little melodic sense in it.' He moved his bow
across the strings of his violin. 'Those were the notes, Watson.
I wrote them down. To write a thing down is to control it and
sometimes to exorcise it.' He had been playing from a scrap of
paper which rested on his right knee. A sudden gust, a brief hot
breath of July, entered by the open window and blew the scrap
to the carpet. I picked it up and examined it. Holmes's bold hand
was discernible in the five lines and the notes that meant nothing
to me. I was thinking more of the *shook jong*. I saw again the

desperate pain of an old Chinese who had been struck down with it in Hong Kong. I had cured him by counter-suggestion and he had given me in gratitude all he had to give – a bamboo flute and a little sheaf of Chinese songs.

'A little sheaf of Chinese songs I once had,' I said musingly to Holmes. 'They were simple but charming. I found their notation endearingly simple. Instead of the clusters of black blobs which, I confess, make less sense to me than the shop-signs in Kowloon, they use merely a system of numbers. The first note of a scale is 1, the second 2, and so on up to, I think, 8.'

What had been intended as an inconsequent observation had an astonishing effect on Holmes. 'We must hurry,' he cried, rising and throwing off turban and dressing-gown. 'We may already be too late.' And he fumbled among the reference books which stood on a shelf behind his armchair. He leafed through a Bradshaw and said: 'As I remembered, at 11.15. A royal coach is being added to the regular boat train to Dover. Quick, Watson – into the street while I dress. Signal a cab as if your life depended on it. The lives of others may well do so.'

The great clock of the railway terminus already showed ten minutes after eleven as our cab clattered to a stop. The driver was clumsy in telling out change for my sovereign. 'Keep it, keep it,' I cried, following Holmes, who had not yet explained his purpose. The concourse was thronged. We were lucky enough to meet Inspector Stanley Hopkins, on duty and happy to be near the end of it, standing alertly at the barrier of Platform 12, whence the boat train was due to depart on time. The engine had already got up its head of steam. The royal party had boarded. Holmes cried with the maximum of urgency:

'They must be made to leave their carriage at once. I will explain later.'

'Impossible,' Hopkins said in some confusion. 'I cannot give such an order.'

'Then I will give it myself. Watson, wait here with the inspector. Allow no one to get through.' And he hurled himself on to the platform, crying in fluent and urgent Spanish to the Embassy officials and the Ambassador himself the desperate necessity of the young king's leaving his compartment with all speed, along with his mother and all their entourage. It was the young Alfonso

XIII, with a child's impetuousness, who responded most eagerly to the only exciting thing that had happened on his visit, jumping from the carriage gleefully, anticipating adventure but no great danger. It was only when the entire royal party had distanced itself, on Holmes's peremptory orders, sufficiently from the royal carriage that the nature of the danger in which they had stood or sat was made manifest. There was a considerable explosion, a shower of splintered wood and shattered glass, then only smoke and the echo of the noise in the confines of the great terminus. Holmes rushed to me, who stood obediently with Hopkins at the barrier.

'You let no one through, Watson, inspector?'

'None came through, Mr Holmes,' Hopkins replied, 'except—'

'Except,' and I completed the phrase for him, 'your revered maestro, I mean the great Sarasate.'

'Sarasate?' Holmes gaped in astonishment and then direly nodded. 'Sarasate. I see.'

'He was with the Spanish Ambassador's party,' Hopkins explained. 'He went in with them but left rather quickly because, as he explained to me, he had a rehearsal.'

'You fool, Watson! You should have apprehended him.' This was properly meant for Hopkins, to whom he now said: 'He came out carrying a violin case?'

'No.'

I said with heat: 'Holmes, I will not be called a fool. Not, at any rate, in the presence of others.'

'You fool, Watson, I say again and again you fool! But, inspector, I take it he was carrying his violin case when he entered here with the leavetaking party?'

'Yes, now you come to mention it, he was.'

'He came with it and left without it?'

'Exactly.'

'You fool, Watson! In that violin case was a bomb fitted with a timing device which he placed in the royal compartment, probably under the seat. And you let him get away.'

'Your idol, Holmes, your fiddling god. Now transformed suddenly into an assassin. And I will not be called a fool.'

'Where did he go?' Holmes asked Hopkins, ignoring my expostulation.

'Indeed, sir,' the inspector said, 'where *did* he go? I do not think it much matters. Sarasate should not be difficult to find.'

'For you he will be,' Holmes said. 'He had no rehearsal. He has no further recitals in this country. For my money he has taken a train for Harwich or Liverpool or some other port of egress to a land where your writ does not run. You can of course telegraph all the local police forces in the port areas, but, from your expression, I see that you have little intention of doing that.'

'Exactly, Mr Holmes. It will prove difficult to attach a charge of attempted massacre to him. A matter of supposition only.'

'I suppose you are right, inspector,' said Holmes after a long pause in which he looked balefully at a poster advertising Pear's Soap. 'Come, Watson. I am sorry I called you a fool.'

Back in Baker Street, Holmes attempted to mollify me further by opening a bottle of very old brandy, a farewell gift from another royal figure, though, as he was a Mohammedan, it may be conjectured that it was strictly against the tenets of his faith to have such a treasure in his possession, and it may be wondered why he was able to gain for his cellar a part of the Napoleonic trove claimed, on their prisoner's death, by the British authorities on St Helena. For this remarkable cognac was certainly, as the ciphers on the label made clear, out of a bin that must have given some comfort to the imperial captive. 'I must confess, Watson,' said Holmes, an appreciative eye on the golden fluid in his balloon glass, one of a set presented to him by a grateful Khedive, 'that I was making too many assumptions, assuming, for instance, that you shared my suspicions. You knew nothing of them and yet it was yourself, all unaware, who granted me the key to the solution of the mystery. I refer to the mystery of the fingered swan song of the poor murdered man. It was a message from a man who was choking in his own blood, Watson, and hence could not speak as others do. He spoke as a musician and as a musician, moreover, who had some knowledge of an exotic system of notation. The father who wagged his will, alas, as it proved, fruitlessly, had been in diplomatic service in Hong Kong. In the letter, as I recall, something was said about an education that had given the boy some knowledge of the sempiternality of monarchical systems, from China, Russia, and their own beloved Spain.'

'And what did the poor boy say?' After three glasses of the superb ichor, I was already sufficiently mollified.

'First, Watson, he hammered out the note D. I have not the gift of absolute pitch, and so was able to know it for what it was only because the piece with which Sarasate concluded his recital was in the key of D major. The final chord was in my ears when the young man made his dying attack on the keyboard. Now, Watson, what we call D – and also incidentally the Germans – is called by the French, Italians and Spaniards *re*. In Italian this is the word for a king, close enough to the Castillian *rey*, which has the same meaning. Fool as I was, I should have seen that we were being warned about some eventuality concerning the visiting monarch. The notes that followed contained a succinct message. I puzzled about their possible meaning, but your remark this morning about the Chinese system of note-naming, note-numbering rather, gave me the answer – only just in time, I may add. In whatever key they were played, the notes would yield the numerical figuration 1115 – CCCG, or DDDA: the pitch is of no importance. The total message was 1115117. It forms a melody of no great intrinsic interest – a kind of deformed bugle call – but the meaning is clear now that we know the code: the king is in danger at 11.15 on the morning of the eleventh day of July. It was I who was the fool, Watson, for not perceiving the import of what could have been dying delirium but, in truth, was a vital communication to whoever had the wit to decipher it.'

'What made you suspect Sarasate?' I asked, pouring another fingerful of the delicious liquor into my glass.

'Well, Watson, consider Sarasate's origins. His full name is Pablo Martin Melitòn Sarasate y Navascuez and he is a son of Barcelona. A Catalonian, then, and a member of a proud family with an anti-monarchist record. I ascertained so much from judicious enquiries at the Spanish Embassy. At the same time I discovered the Chinese background of the youthful Gonzales, which, at the time, meant nothing. The republicanism of the Sarasate family should have been sufficient to cast a shadow of suspicion over him, but one always considers a great artist as somehow above the sordid intrigues of the political. There was, as I see now, something atrociously cold-blooded in the arrangement whereby the murder of his accompanist was effected only at the conclusion of his recital. Kill the man when he has fulfilled his artistic purpose – this must have been the frigid order delivered by Sarasate to the assassin. I do not doubt that the young Gonzales had confided in Sarasate, whom, as a fellow-musician and a great master, he had every apparent reason to trust. He informed him of his intention to betray the plans of the organisation. We cannot be sure of the nature of his motivation – a sudden humane qualm, a shaken state of mind consequent on the receipt of his father's letter. The assassin obeyed Sarasate's order with metronomic exactitude. My head spins to think of the master's approbation of such a murderous afterpiece to what was, you must admit, a recital of exceptional brilliance.'

'The brilliance was, for me, confirmed more by the applause of others than by any judgement of my own. I take it that Sarasate was responsible for another performance less brilliant – the note from His Royal Highness's secretary and the exotic number 7.'

'Evidently, Watson. At the Savoy Theatre you saw him chatting amiably with Sir Arthur Sullivan, a crony of the Prince. *Grazie a Dio*, he said among things, that his long cycle of recitals had finished with his London performance and he could now take a well-earned rest. Any man unscrupulous enough to collaborate with that noted sneerer at the conventions, Mr William Schenk Gilbert, would be quite ready to pick up a sheet or so of the Prince's private notepaper and pass it on without enquiring into the purpose for which it was required.'

'Well, Holmes,' I now said, 'you do not, I take it, propose to pursue Sarasate to condign punishment, to cut off his fiddle-playing career and have him apprehended as the criminal he undoubtedly is?'

'Where is my proof, Watson? As that intelligent young inspector trenchantly remarked, it is all supposition.'

'And if it were not?'

Holmes sighed and picked up his violin and bow. 'He is a supreme artist whom the world could ill afford to lose. Do not quote my words, Watson, to any of your church-going friends, but I am forced to the belief that art is above morality. If Sarasate, before my eyes and in this very room, strangled you to death, Watson, for your musical insensitivity, while an accomplice of his obstructed my interference with a loaded pistol, and then wrote a detailed statement of the crime, signed with the name of Pablo Martin Melitòn Sarasate y Navascuez, I should be constrained to close my eyes to the act, destroy the statement, deposit your body in the gutter of Baker Street, and remain silent while the police pursued their investigations. So much is the great artist above the moral principles that oppress lesser men. And now, Watson, pour yourself more of that noble brandy and listen to my own rendering of that piece by Sarasate. I warrant you will find it less than masterly but surely the excellence of the intention will gleam through.' And so he stood, arranged his music stand, tucked his fiddle beneath his chin and began reverently to saw.